Alexander Terekhov

The Stone Bridge

Published with the support of
the Institute for Literary Translation (Russia)

AD VERBUM

Glagoslav Publications

The Stone Bridge

by Alexander Terekhov

First published in Russian as "Каменный мост"

Translated by Simon Patterson and Nina Chordas

Cover design by Andrei Bondarenko

© 2009, Alexander Terekhov
Represented by Galina Dursthoff Literary Agency

© 2014, Glagoslav Publications, United Kingdom

Glagoslav Publications Ltd
88-90 Hatton Garden
EC1N 8PN London
United Kingdom

www.glagoslav.com

ISBN: 978-1-909156-64-7

A catalogue record for this book is available from the British Library.

CONTENTS

THE FINNISH SKIER

I'VE NEVER WON ANYTHING IN MY LIFE.

On Sundays, there weren't many French, German or English tourists. The tour buses brought Poles, and uniformly faceless Chinese in baggy trenches came prowling. And what did they want? Gzhel ceramics, headscarves, matryoshka dolls… Serious customers came to Izmailovo market on Saturdays. One didn't expect much on a Sunday.

I nodded to my neighbor Rakhmatullin — he dealt in iron goods: samovars from the Batashov Company, old weights, padlocks, irons, bells and Melchior cup-holders from the old Kolchugino factory with the Kremlin depicted on them. Watch my things, the nod said, and I plodded to the steps leading down to the flea market.

There, on wind-blown, unlit wooden balconies, tramps, orphans rejected by school and proud old ladies laid out on blankets and wax cloths the refuse of humanity scavenged and stolen from abandoned and blighted buildings: bald dolls with rolled-up eyes, kerosene lamps, tin boxes that had contained sweets and tea from "Vysotsky and Co" with the famous tall ship on the logo, Christmas decorations made of colored cardboard, and scraps of wigs that looked like scalps. You could also find tin soldiers, but they were a rarity, there were mainly just plastic soldiers and toy monsters from Kinder Surprise eggs, but last June I had bought the vintage toy set "Soldiers of the Revolution" in excellent condition for a mere 300 rubles here, and sold them online on Molotok for 200 dollars. Locals repeated a story about an old lady who was once seen here taking "whatever I can get for them" for Red Cossacks from the 1940s, which sell for 1,500 dollars each on the Internet. Not many people have seen the Cossacks even in photographs, and no one knows for certain how many and which ones there are in a set, and she didn't even have 400 rubles to pay for a place. Why couldn't I ever run into an old lady like that?

Around Sunday lunchtime, the hot-shot souvenir sellers, connoisseurs of icons and porcelain, would shut up their goods under iron shutters and come down to the flea market with a lazy, lordly gait to look for an easy catch, to pick over the washed-up rubbish while the locals kept a nervous, hostile silence. There would never be anything left, almost never.

"Coffee, please!" I called out to the Vietnamese woman in a white apron who was pushing a cart loaded with thermoses, shrink-wrapped sandwiches and a crockpot of sausages. For 10 rubles I got a steaming plastic cup, and took two more steps, before I heard Rakhmatullin call out:

"The owner's coming… Vasilich, you've got a customer! Come back here!"

Just as there are borrowed days in spring that smell of autumn, this September Sunday was paying back its debts with sun and blue sky, as if the summer were taking a backward look.

A guy with a foreign-looking face enhanced by just the right amount of tan was looking at my soldiers. He grabbed one and held it up right in front of his nose, turning it to examine it closely. Which one did he grab there, this sunburnt guy with a black coat over a white shirt, his striped scarf tied in a gay-looking knot under his throat? I looked closer.

"*Hyello! Eett ees skyer solzher of Feenneesh vor. Eexcluzeev. Vahn hahndreed dollars,*" I said, in my best English.

The guy shook his head in amazement, making his black curls bounce around his face.

"Would you just look at this!" He called out, in Russian, to a friend who had the burly appearance of the guy's driver-cum-bodyguard. "A hundred!" and he placed the soldier on the shabby counter to have a better look.

The faceless tin skier in his camouflage coat, covered with flecks of green paint, had his right foot forward in an unhurried movement. He had gloves, ski poles, boots that had long lost their black color, and a machine gun slung over his stomach with the muzzle pointing upward… The helmet, buffed by a thousand touches, gave off a dull-lead gleam. One of my favorite soldiers. I don't like them all equally. I don't like the Bryansk Sailors on Parade for example, or the Battle of Kulikovo set, the Astretsovo Cavalry, or cavalry figures in general. But I collect all the soldiers of the Soviet Army, in 1:35 and 1:48 scales — that's the name of my enterprise, Soldiers of the USSR.

The driver tore himself away from Rakhmatullin's samovars, and looked from a respectful distance at his boss's whimsical behavior.

"A skier from the Finnish war. That soldier, as it happens, was manufactured in *nineteen thirty-nine,*" I said, switching back to Russian, and sipping my coffee. The guy studied the bait with a beatific smile on his face. He would be reminiscing now: as a child he probably pushed a tiny skier just like this across deserts of summer dust, amid grass forests, avoiding the dried shoelace forms of desiccated earthworms. "One of these comes along every year or so. I wouldn't sell my own, my friend asked me to — he needs money to buy medicine. A Canadian bought one like this on E-bay last year for two hundred. It's one hundred euros for foreigners, but I'll do a hundred bucks for you. Take it or leave it."

The guy put the soldier in his palm again and brought it up to his face — the way people stare at a medallion with a miniature portrait on it in good-hearted black-and-white films — then he tossed it up in the air and caught it, clenching it firmly with his fingers.

"Careful. You break it, you pay for it."

"And what about you?" the jerk smiled thoughtfully. He was a young man of around twenty-five, with a large-lipped mouth and dark empty eyes. Scum like that look older than their age when they're young, and then younger when they get old. "You dress like that… Like a soldier. Are you a soldier? Will you fight?"

There was something forced about his speech, as if he had to remember how to say things in Russian. I wondered if he was drunk.

Abruptly, he leaned across the counter and took the collar of my dirty coat in his free hand. He chuckled — he was very much amused by the stars on the coat's gold buttons.

"You have the stars," he muttered. "You're the Red Army! Then you must fight."

I looked sideways at the driver — get your moron away from me! — and chuckled along:

"You can buy everything. A coat. A cap with a badge. A holster with a pistol. And a document holder with a photo. As long as you've got dollars. Have you got dollars?"

He let go and immediately scooped up a bunch of yellowed books from the stall. One by one, they slipped out of his grip, fell back onto the counter: Stalin *On the Great Patriotic War of the Soviet Union, Stalin On the foundations of Leninism, Collective Farmer's Calendar for 1943...* He held on to one, opened at random and started reading: "There is no more so-called freedom of the individual — individual rights are now only recognized for those who have capital, and all other citizens are considered to be raw human material, suitable only for exploitation," — and then broke off. It was as if he suddenly remembered something. He stared at the text; his lips moved, opening and closing, making shapes around the sounds, and I could see the muscles of his neck twitch around his throat, articulating — he understood what was on the page, but he somehow couldn't speak it. He would've remained stuck in this loop if the driver hadn't touched him on the elbow. Then he came to life — he slammed the book shut and soberly pronounced the title on the cover:

"Stalin. *Speech at the Nineteenth Party Congress.*"

"Four hundred rubles."

"No doubt. Between the pages, you'll see, there's a tram ticket. From 1952. For one trip. Thirty kopecks. As a bonus," he said dryly. "The ticket is unused, you should hang on to it — one never knows. These books are in good condition," the guy eyed me unpleasantly. "Do you collect them on your trips *back there?*"

Enough smiling. I felt a stab of fear. I focused on sipping my coffee. Drunken smart-ass.

He broke off, having made a decision:

"Well, that's enough. Where's the Finnish skier?"

Five five-hundred ruble notes, and the man let the soldier slide from his palm into the pocket of his black coat. The pair walked off, swift and preoccupied, through the rows, toward the main stairs where sellers hawked ragged bear pelts, yellow-fanged boar heads and small armies of stuffed snarling stoats and sables. I pulled on my torn knitted gloves and started putting my soldiers away in biscuit and tea tins. I packed the containers into my newspaper-lined suitcase, tossed the books on top and clicked the locks shut.

"You sure conned them. Like a couple of kids," Rakhmatullin praised me. He was setting out backgammon pieces on a board. "You leaving already? Why so early? Stay a little longer — there's still money to be made!"

SHASHLYK

By the back way, through the painters' row, where there weren't so many customers, I carried the banging suitcase to the log cabin near the central stairs. Inside, in the dark, people sold mass-manufactured Dagestan daggers and stored suitcases for five dollars a week. I walked past the self-appointed veterans of the Chechen war (who had replaced the veterans of the Afghan war about five years ago) wailing their songs to keyboard accompaniment, and wound my way along the smoky chain of charcoal grills to the southern fence of the market.

"Shashlyk? Lamb! Pork!"

"No. Thank you."

"What do you mean, no? You've never had such shashlyk!" a red-cheeked guy with a shaved head, in a suit and tie, grabbed me by the shoulder and blocked the way. With a cop's pushy dexterity, he shoved me to the open door of the café Gorodets. It hurt, this shoving, the guy was good at it, I could feel myself getting bruised, and he wasn't going to let me get away. He almost knocked the breath out of me, and, scared and sweating, I looked hopelessly at the swarthy cooks manning the grills, who had stopped waving pieces of cardboard above their skewered meat, and at the familiar waitresses wearing white aprons over their knitted cardigans. What could I do? Scream? I stumbled into the café and checked my pockets. I knew it: the bastard had pulled out my passport and the rent receipts.

My sunburnt jerk with the scarf around his throat was sitting in the corner with a plate of food, dipping bits of meat in ketchup, picking up onion rings with his fork. The waitress poured him tea, and he motioned for her to bring another cup. With his mouth full, he blinked in welcome and pointed to the chair opposite.

The cop who had dragged me in sat down on a bench at the neighboring table with the jerk's driver and turned his attention to tea.

I sank onto the chair with a sigh, placed my elbows on the table and folded my hands under my chin. Then I unfolded my hands and let them drop onto my knees. I reclined back on the chair. I stretched my legs under the table. Then pulled them back. Everything seemed awkward. I ate here twice a week, I knew everything by heart, and yet I couldn't sit still.

The man finished chewing his piece of meat, wiped his lips with a napkin and put the soldier of the Finnish war on the table.

"I envy you. You're a free man! You don't sit in an office. You've remained a child. You play for your own amusement, well into a mature age. And you get paid for it! To control your own time — that's the right goal for a man's life." He raised his index finger. "And not to have a boss. What wouldn't I give for that. To collect old toys and sell them — how wonderful! Do you think that collecting pieces of the past can change anything? By the way, I have my own theory about grown men who play with toy soldiers."

The waitress, Auntie Masha, brought another cup of tea with lemon and took away the plate with the remains of onion and the shallow puddle of ketchup.

"Would that be all?" she asked.

"Drink your tea," the man nodded at me, while giving the waitress the money. He took something out from under the table — I didn't see if he had a bag there — and placed a printed-out photograph on my half of the tabletop, then looked around and whispered, bringing the cup of tea to his lips: "Look at her. She's dazzling. So many years have gone by, but still, she drives me wild."

The girl did not look remarkably beautiful. Thick, luxuriant hair framed a wide, adolescently puffy face. She had a dimple on her chin. Her nose, with a barely noticeable bump and a gentle downward tuck in the nostrils, was not Russian. Her upper lip was thrust forward, revealing a defect in the jaw structure, or perhaps indicating a moment of inner movement caught by the photographer — a smile forming, a word dying away.

If you covered the bottom half of the face with your hand and took in the wide, clear forehead, the distinctly traced eyebrows and most importantly the eyes, the girl looked uncommonly charming indeed. Her eyes looked with calm clarity over the right shoulder of the observer — there was living water splashing in them. But then when you took your hand away, all you saw was a healthy young girl, nothing more.

Her hair was of an awkward length — just reaching her shoulders— and curled at the ends. Her hairstyle was organized by a dark ribbon that revealed itself in a bow above her forehead; the bow's butterfly style dated the photo to at least half a century ago, and put the girl behind the desk of a high-school class. She was dressed in a sober jacket done up to the chin; you could see two large metal buttons with a simple design — grooves in a circle.

"She's dead," the man clarified dryly, as if this were of any importance. "She was killed by a bullet to the back of the head on the 3rd of June 1943. This fifteen-year-old *femme fatale* became an urn at the Novodevichy Cemetery. Nina Umanskaya, have you ever heard of her?"

For a time we kept silent, or rather he kept silent, and I looked out at the gates of the market — the stalls styled to look like fairytale huts and covered with fake tiling made of rubber — and at the newly built pavilion of Nizhny Novgorod folk crafts.

"Here's the summary of the case," the man said clearly, irritation creeping into his voice. "It's 1943, early summer. The Battle of Stalingrad is over, but Kursk is yet to come. The diplomat Konstantin Umansky has an incredibly beautiful daughter, Nina. The girl goes to an elite school along with the children of Kremlin bosses. Incidentally, Stalin's daughter goes to the same school. Lots of boys fall in love with Nina. One of these is Volodya Shakhurin. The boy is also from an important family — he is the son of the People's Commissar for

Aviation Industries. The children are finishing the seventh grade, and sitting for exams. Konstantin Umansky is appointed Ambassador to Mexico. On the 5th of June he is supposed to fly out with his family to the new post. On the 3rd, Volodya Shakhurin walks his sweetheart home. We can assume he's asking her, begging — he is 13 or 14 at the time! — don't go away, I love you very much. The girl probably tells him there isn't much she can do. Volodya takes a pistol out of his pocket and shoots Nina Umanskaya in the back of the head. Point-blank. And then he points the gun to his temple and fires again. For a while he keeps breathing. For about a day. And then he dies. The incident is reported to Stalin, and he exclaims, *These kids are real wolf cubs!* The case goes down in Russian history as The Case of the Wolf Cubs."

He pulled the photograph back, felt it carefully to make sure the sticky table hadn't smeared or soaked it, and put it away.

"Dull, isn't it? Schizophrenia, a teenage psychosis of unrequited feelings. It's all so plain and clear: our homegrown Romeo and Juliet!—that's all that's left. But no one," the man leaned over the table toward me, and everything that he said now seemed extremely important to him, his cheeks burned and his voice softened to a barely audible whisper, "no one, before me, thought of a very simple thing: why is everybody so certain that it was love? Why do we all think it was love that he wanted? The girl was killed. The boy is dead. And no one heard their conversation. So what or *who* is trying to make this seem so clear to us?" He suddenly smiled drunkenly. "I sense a professional touch. Someone worked very hard to make sure this one version survived for the future. And whoever it was had a reason. And someone is now sure that *it all worked out*. That everyone has been deceived, and no one will go back to dig around. They're wrong," and he finished with a playful, faggoty intonation, like something lifted from a British movie, "My dear chap, I want you to go back there. Everything must be changed."

He was giving me the chance to nod or at least move, but I concentrated on sitting more comfortably while I pictured myself getting up and leaving.

"I want to know who killed them."

Satisfied with my silence, the man (didn't his bodyguard realize that his boss had a screw loose?) started talking more freely, not expecting me to respond with anything that could blow up the rails he was laying down.

"Who killed them. And why. This is a job for a person who likes photography. The gaze of a photographer changes the object of the photo, if the photographer has, so to say, a special relationship with the object," he paused and gave me a suggestive wink.

"I've had a beast of a time trying to decide who to turn to," he went on. "The problem in Russia is that journeymen never grow up to be masters: everyone wants fast money. No one cares about the work." He broke off and changed the subject: "Do you visit the website 'The Last Frontier'? I do — it's totally wacky… All that New Age stuff, the fifth race… New cults. And there're so many young people there… They're into Kali, the Goddess of Death, I suppose."

He smiled at me in a friendly and sad way, like a hunter smiling at the carcass of an elk that has led him on a chase. Like a hunter with his muddy boot planted on the throat of his dead prey:

"On this website, I saw a transcript of a certain trial posted in considerable detail. But I won't bore you with the particulars. Basically, there was a young person, practically a child, who joined a cult — a real tragedy. Family abandoned, all possessions given to 'the teacher'. The young man's mind completely…" he pinched the fingers of his right hand together and rubbed them together, making a hole in an invisible fabric. "You know the story. Excessive fasting. Meditation. Drugs. There aren't any legal grounds on which this young person could be forced to return to the family. He — or she — is a free adult, they can choose what to believe in. The parents are in agony: all these years they spent nurturing their child, the apple of their eye, so to speak, and now this child serves some alcoholic with a bunch of criminal convictions like a loyal lap-dog and doesn't want to come back. Doesn't even recognize his Mom and Dad. You see what faith can do, eh?

"And what can the parents do, Alexander Vasiliyevich?" *My name, how did he know my name?!* "They can suffer. And wait. The used-up human material will be returned to them eventually. The problem is no psychiatrists could ever bring such an invalid back into a world where people fry shashlyk, fly to Egypt for seaside holidays, have children, or sell toy soldiers, for example. Instead: dark little rooms, the smell of medicine, mumbled mantras, uncontrollable drooling — forever.

"But the cults mainly target wealthy families. And the wealthy are not prepared to give up their children to the new Branch Davidians of the world. And thus, my dear Alexander Vasiliyevich, a paid service comes into being: forced deprogramming. Kidnapping, or recovery, if you prefer. Treatment. Return to the family. Haven't you heard about it? No? I believe you; the actions of these de-programmers are not, shall we say, particularly public. The cults certainly keep quiet about losing their cash cows. They wouldn't want their own corpses to come to light — every business has its waste. They'd keep quiet and have their own security services search for the missing people, the security and the guys who, let's put it delicately, provide protection for their business. So there you have it: a silent, shadow war with apartment raids, kidnappings, infiltrations, exchange of hostages, even shoot-outs, they say... No? With fatalities.

"Some of this came to light quite by accident. One of the young people who had been rescued threw himself out the window of a safe house apartment in Belyaevo during a therapeutic procedure. And broke his back, as it happened. Sychuzhnikov. Remember him? No? He happened to mention you personally... He was very much afraid that he would be finished off in the hospital. He's a nice enough guy, appears to be fairly sane. As long as you don't talk to him too long. But one doesn't need to talk to him too long to broadcast his story on television: a moving sound bite or two, and that's enough, next up are elections, corruption among officials, etc. But after Sychuzhnikov's story made the news, all these groups must have done the same math — and they all brought statements to the police: the Gaudiya Vaishnava, Money Tree, Blessed Virgin, Unification Church, the

Mormons, the Scientologists, Children of God and even a handful of the White Brotherhood followers. To this day, it is unclear what kind of psychological techniques the de-programmers relied on. In addition to kidnapping, the statements submitted to the police allege torture, beatings, food and sleep deprivation. Use of psychotropic substances. Forced manual labor. Is some of this lies? Yes, probably. It's politics, after all. But you and I, my dear, judging it all without sentimentality, may assume that the de-programmers, fighting fire with fire, probably used the same methods that the new cults did on the way *there*, in an attempt to bring their subjects *back here*.

"Incidentally, some of the young people who were returned to the world of police forces and market economies testified in court — I know, where's their gratitude, right? The exact number of kidnappings has not been established. Over sixty? The parents were charged one hundred thousand dollars and more in difficult cases. The children of poor citizens were of no interest to the de-programmers. Although poor people did also come to them — and begged to have their breadwinners returned to the family, fathers or mothers restored to their babies… I read into it — the stories are horrifying. Would move a stone to tears. But not you.

"Based on that testimony, some people got arrested — you must have heard this part, it was such a scandal! — among them retired and active-duty personnel of various security agencies. This triggered internal investigations in the Interior Ministry and the Federal Security, the FSB. Forty-two, in total, were arrested, sixteen were sentenced. The investigation is still going on. Not everyone has been found yet."

The man looked me in the eye and didn't blink. And I realized hopelessly that I would have to do it in front of him — to wipe the sweat from my forehead, my eyebrows and upper lip, to wipe my hand after that, and then undo, tear open the buttons of my coat, from the top to the bottom. And lick my burning lips.

"There's a person wanted by the FSB. The so-called information service of the Church of the End and the Beginning is also looking for him, with the help of the Izmailovo mafia. He didn't kidnap anyone.

He didn't take part in torture. He only worked on developing the clients. The circle, the connections of the victim... or the rescued person? And so, I thought, this is someone who can help me. This person. And his people."

He was handsome and well-groomed. One of those people who gets himself rubbed over with cream and has manicures. It was possible that his wet, tar-black curls were the results of someone's paid efforts. His youth was the one thing he did not buy. It was given to him. A triumphant, strong youth, which was now tossing someone else's life up and down in his hand, like a sea shell full of holes, collected on the Crimean shore.

"I'll tell you my train of thought. What does a sect do with a new member first of all?" He immediately answered: "A sect destroys the personal past. The past is not needed, it does not lead to salvation. To control a person, you must erase everything that has been experienced and fill the emptiness with the commands of the teacher. The man I'm talking about, on the contrary, returned the past to the victim, helped him to remember... But if you take into account that people came into his hands with a completely changed consciousness, empty, white paper boxes... They couldn't remember anything, and the past," the profiteer smiled with his eyes only, "this man, this agent wrote it over anew. At his discretion. You understand? And one important thing is that he did this for free. The investigation established that he was the only one who did not receive money — I found this particularly simpatico. What is money compared with this occupation? And I said to myself: OK. This is the guy I need."

"He's around forty, just over six feet tall. He has dark hair. He's going grey. A former historian? Although someone testified at the investigation that he saw him at the KGB institute while he was studying there. He's unlikely to have fled, I thought... He's in hiding," he looked at me again. "He's cut his hair short, wearing an army uniform... The only detail, I don't even know if it's true — he collects toy soldiers. All rather childish. But symbolic, you must agree."

He got up and slapped me on the shoulder with an unpleasant, lordly gesture. As if I were a dog.

I waited, as though I was supposed to be taken away somewhere for further tests, but nothing else happened.

Walking past the army backpacks and camouflage jackets, they — three of them — went towards the gates. They were being waited for by a riot squad officer in a black beret and an automatic pistol over his shoulder. He waved his hand, and a black BMW with a flashing light on it drove up, and a police Landover as an escort. The doors opened. The profiteer was seated in the first car, and the security ran to hop in… That was it. They had moved into the audience and would now watch me running around on my chain.

I took the photograph of the girl Nina out of my pocket.

The girl looked directly into my eyes with sad and questioning calm. Like a living person, as if her lips would open and she would say something to me. I tore her face in half and threw it into the bin for cigarette butts.

THE BRIDGE

IN AUGUST THE RUBLE COLLAPSED, AND LIFE SHATTERED. I DIDN'T believe in the end of Sberbank and a people's uprising, but everyone rushed to withdraw their money, and every morning at half-past nine I called the Sberbank office at Novopetrovskaya: are you allowing withdrawals? They gave out currency in portions.

The manager laid out the last three thousand, told me to sign in triplicate — and closed the account.

"Thank you."

At the next teller's window a gray-haired man refused to budge: "Give me my money!"

"Oleg Semyonovich, your pension isn't here yet!"

"I don't need the pension — give me my money!"

"Oleg Semyonovich, the money hasn't arrived yet!"

"Hasn't arrived? Everyone's getting money, but not me, where's my money?"

"At the Finance Ministry, with Yeltsin."

"So I'll go to Yeltsin then. I'm not just anyone, I'm," he goes on stabbing his red identity card with a crooked finger, "a war veteran. Are you saying there's no money for me?"

"There'd be money if you didn't drink it up. I don't know, ask your kids, ask your son, he'll give you some."

"I don't have a son!"

I stopped listening, and my thoughts turned to the women in my life, familiar and unfamiliar. Whom to go to in times like these?

The new or the tried and true? I had realized a long time ago that I ought to quit turning up in strange beds, but I seemed to need this truth brought home to me endlessly. Indeed, I seemed always to need undiscovered secrets, the heart-stopping instant of first nakedness, the thud, like a bell, in my chest; I needed new telephone numbers, whose seven digits promised the thrill of new parents, unmet neighbors, grandmas with phenomenal hearing, mischievous younger brothers, dogs that bit through telephone cords, and fathers who noiselessly picked up the receivers on parallel lines.

I thought of a few names, then called the one who lived closest:

"Yes," I said, "today, now, yes, I was just out of town, I called and you weren't there, I'll just come to your office, where are you now?"

"On Krzhizhanovsky, the oil and gas company, Sibur."

I met her there. She walked up to me, smiling, in red pointy-toed shoes, a black and white skirt on her wide hips. We crossed the street to an establishment that seemed halfway between bar and cafe; the waiter and the barman, dressed in white shirts, sat with their heads tossed back, faces up to the sun, on white plastic chairs they'd pulled out onto the porch.

She was seated across from me at a table in a small dining room, a large, vintage photo of Moscow on the wall, the yellow dome of the Cathedral of Christ the Savior still intact, and the waiter nodded confidently as she leafed through her menu, indicating that of course the restaurant would have each item on hand.

We ordered. I looked at her brown shoulders and asked, attempting to recall the details of her life: does your daughter still dance with that theater group? Did that friend of yours ever marry her Frenchman? Did your father find a job?

She asked about me. I answered: Me? I'm in retail now. No, nothing happened, why do you ask? She didn't know why. Perhaps she hadn't gotten enough sleep, she said.

At that point, absently and for no reason, we each turned to the window just in time to see the waiter making a furtive beeline for a store on the corner to buy everything we had just ordered.

We chatted further and she laughed, but I felt my throat catch, a flash of nausea at the hint of something alien in her manner, as if on the first visit to my dacha after winter I had found the place defiled by squatters, clothes scattered, drawers yanked out of dressers.

"The company's cutting staff," she went on. "No one knows anything for certain. Some say that everyone will be fired and Gazprom will bring its own team. Others say it's only the management that'll have to go, and everyone else will actually get a raise. Also I decided to go back to my husband."

In the empty room, under the air-conditioners, I understood immediately: there we were, still sitting opposite each other, still waiting for the waiter to come back from the shop, to put the pieces of bread with cheese and ham under the grill, to dice the strawberries and bananas for the fruit salad, to scoop out chocolate ice cream, so that we could eat and speak at leisure — but I wouldn't touch her. There was only an emptiness waiting for me there, a gaping maw, and snow was blowing in through it.

"I'm sick of going to bed by myself. And of waking up by myself. And my daughter really needs her father. He's changed a lot, you know. He says he understood everything while I was gone."

She wouldn't go anywhere with me. Though in six months I'd likely get a call. Still, maybe she'd give it to me right then and there, in parting? The waiter would still be away awhile, I could hike up her skirt and put her on my lap, this lover of stockings and crotchless panties.

"You'll move out of the city, of course?"

Her main message out, she then replied hesitantly and with effort:

"Yes, there's a place we can have in Lozhki village. Solnechnogorsk district."

"With a woman to help around the house. And a driver to deliver groceries. And three dogs, bull terriers."

"Two. A bull terrier and a Leonberger."

"The house must have three floors, though."

"Four. A sauna and a billiard room in the basement. But what about you? What do you sell?"

"Antiques."

"Antiques? Any other plans?"

I studied the picture behind her back, squinted and read the title. Apparently, it was the bridge that was the painter's main subject, not the cathedral that was blown up under Stalin, and later recreated to replace the swimming pool that had replaced the original.

"Me? Well, I'm thinking I'll work on — the Great Stone Bridge."

"Where is this bridge? What's so special about it?"

We talked like this for another hour. Then she left, and I crumpled up the piece of paper on which she'd written her new cell number and left it on the plate. I finished the last of my water. A blue-and-white label on the empty bottle said "Shishkin Forest. Pure drinking water. Still water from artesian well #1-99. Made in Russia. Moscow Oblast, Solnechnogorsk district, Lozhki village."

THE GREAT STONE BRIDGE.
THE HISTORY OF THE CASE.

THE GREAT STONE BRIDGE IS RECOGNIZED AS THE BEST LOCATION from which to view the Kremlin and study Russian life. The bridge has had the best view since the time of Cornelis de Bruijn, a Dutchman and painter, three hundred years ago; in more recent days, images of and from the bridge figured in the title sequences of the Vremya TV news broadcasts which replaced, for the Soviet people, the evening church service.

The view of the opposite side was sold as a secondary attraction: the Cathedral of Christ the Savior (absent for a time to accommodate the swimming pool) and the Second Building of the Council of People's Commissars (made famous by Yuri Trifonov as the House on the Embankment in the novella of the same name) — the dormitory of the builders of the Communist tower, a structure of politically-correct, unobjectionable luxury. A comfortable hive. The residents of five hundred apartments were later, to avoid a bloodthirsty expression, *changed* — as Emperor Stalin said to President de Gaulle, "In the end death is always the victor." The President, in his stupid cap that resembled an open tin can, of the kind that was ridiculed once and for all by comedies about idiotic French policemen, nodded, "Yes, yes…," he didn't understand what the emperor meant.

Of the Kremlin's towers, the closest to the bridge is the Water Pumping Tower (also called Sviblov Tower, after the prominent family who lived in a house next to it), and it is tall and gloomy. It used to pump water to the Tsar's chambers and gardens. Napoleon had it blown up as he left the city, and the hands of restorers made it less morose, but in my opinion the tower still has a cheerless look to it. In 1937 it was crowned with a ruby star, the crowners having noted the tower's prominence in the eyes of those viewers who went down onto the bridge to examine the goings-on of our land.

Moscow herself grew on hills, and between the hills flowed rivers, creeks and streams. Myriad *ad hoc* wooden bridges, sometimes just a few boards thrown over the mud— *mostoks* they were called — held Moscow life together. Some have even argued that the very name *Mos*cow contains an echo of the city's humble beginnings. The Great Stone Bridge was the first stone bridge in the city — and happened to be the last. When it was built, it was considered to be the fourth wonder of Russia after the Tsar's Bell, the Tsar's Cannon and Ivan the Great's Bell Tower.

Ivan the Third cleared Borovitsky Square, moving wooden houses away from the Kremlin thereby nullifying the fires that tended to burn them, and making Tatar sieges difficult. Moscow life, forced thusly outward from the verboten square, crossed the river and moved south, into the Strelets villages, along the road from Veliky Novgorod to Ryazan. Since these new arrangements required that supplies be transported across the river, Tsar Mikhail Fyodorovich summoned the craftsman Jagan Christler from Strasbourg, along with his uncle and his tools, which had names like magic spells: mattocks, bills, cant-dogs, parbuckles, trowels, salters. But just as the enormous cubes of white stone for the would-be bridge began to arrive in Moscow from Nastasin, everyone involved in the project unceremoniously died — both Germans and the Tsar.

The seventeenth century bore a striking resemblance to the twentieth. It began with troubles, and ended with troubles: civil war, an uprising of peasants and Cossacks, campaigns to the Crimea, Boyars "chopped to bits" by rebels, doctors who confessed under torture to poisoning Tsars, and Old Believers burnt at the stake during the month known to us now as Bloody April. It was a time when Russians suddenly and obsessively turned to their past, considered their own present, and then decided rather frantically to begin rewriting the books on every historical sore spot: the schism in the Church, the streltsy rebellions, the place of our land on the globe which had just been imported to Russia. Children and women argued about politics in the streets! Suddenly the common people realized: we also exist, we take part, we are witnesses. And how sweet it was to say *I*.

In the year when Boris Sheremetiev went to the Hapsburg court of Emperor Leopold and Prince Golitsyn led the charge to Perekop, returning from the Konka River with nothing because the Tatars had set fire to the steppe, a monk who was able to read the drafts left by the late German bridge builder finally completed the new wonder of the world — the Great Stone Bridge.

If one is to believe certain records, the monk's name may have been Filaret. "One of the common monks, by the name of Filaret" — that's how another monk, Siliverst Medvedev, recorded it in his truthful but far from comprehensive *Short Contemplations*. The year the bridge was finished, the *Contemplations*' author lost his head — he was too educated and eventually had to pay for being Tsarina Sofia's favorite counselor, for arguing with the Patriarch, and for consorting with the rebellious streltsy. "Beheaded on the Red Square and buried at the poor house with the queer of mind in one hole..." reports read.

The bridge had eight spans, and was made of white stone. It was four hundred and sixty feet — seventy *sazhens* — long.

The engravings by Pieter Picart (you can see small huts on the river — mills or bathhouses), the lithographs by Daziaro (poles under the spans, a few people dawdling and a predictable dinghy, its passenger being ferried across with one oar by a warmly dressed gondolier) and the lithographs by Martynov (the latter-day ones, with the two-tower entry gates that were demolished long before the lithographs themselves were actually published) all depicted the Kremlin and captured the bridge in the first 150 years of its life: flour mills with dams and drains, drinking establishments, the town-house of Prince Menshikov, crowds admiring the sight of river ice breaking up and beginning to flow in spring, the triumphal arch raised for Peter the Great's Azov victory, a pair of horses pulling a sled with two passengers — a priest and the quick-eyed Pugachev in shackles crying out right and left to the presumably silent crowd, "Forgive me, Christians!"

Sideshows brought wax figures, savages from Africa, and a siren fish recently caught by fishermen. Crowds at the shows gnawed on sunflower seeds and bought colorful balloons inflated with gas. Convicts knelt in the dust, with signs — *Arsonist, Robber* — around their necks. Constables with theatrical halberds, hirsute students smoking casually and short-haired girls in dark glasses, the Wolf Pack tavern in a dirty two-story building, the jetty of the Moscow Fishermen's Society (nothing more than a hut on a wooden raft with a bunch of boats tied to it) — and everyone seemingly with a sense that this life on and around the bridge couldn't last (especially when in the flood of 1783 three arches collapsed at once, crushing a fisherman and some washerwomen). Still, when Alexander the Second took the throne and had the great old bridge dismantled — the old masonry wouldn't yield to hammers and crowbars, it had to be blown up — people would not forgive him this deed and remembered it often and bitterly.

The new bridge was still called the Great *Stone* Bridge, despite the fact that when it was built again in 1859, cast-iron arches were anchored on the two stone abutments, laid with rails of the same material, and paved over half-timber boards — by engineer Nikolai Voskoboinikov. In photographs from the Gautier-Dufayer collection, you can see that the cast-iron bridge stood a little to the left of the old one, and now did not lead to Borovitsky Square, but ended at Lenivka, the shortest street in Moscow. Gradually deteriorating, the bridge nonetheless lasted the length of a human life — 75 years. There were plans to demolish it earlier, but wars and revolutions interfered, and then the bridge had a second life: a Soviet newspaper clipping informs that "the arches of the bridge were found to be in satisfactory condition and transported by barge to Zaozernaya village."

The best minds of Russian architecture (which had become Soviet architecture without evident effort) competed to build the Third Bridge: Peredery, Zholtosky, Shchuko, Shchusev. Vladimir Shchuko won with his powerful one-span steel arch. The losers had preferred the narrowness and multiple arches of Moscow's antiquity. Shchuko was the only one to experience a genuine epiphany, to look out his window in the pre-dawn mist and see there: MOSCOW SEA PORT. Canals! Moscow — Volga and the White Sea! Caravans of ships under the bridge! Swiftness, force and resilience, and all of it expressed in that single, surpassing insight, that one individual arch.

Vladimir Shchuko was the son of a military man, graduated from an academy in Tambov, tried his hand as an actor at the Moscow Art Theater, was noticed by Stanislavsky, and later took part in a polar expedition to Spitsbergen.

He started his architectural career working on the palace of a governor in the Far East, and was inspired by Rome, Istanbul, Athens, Florence, Milan, Art Nouveau and Russian Empire style, the traditions of Cameron and Voronikhin. He ended with countless plans for statues of Lenin (one was made — Lenin on the armored car, Finland Station), with the Lenin Library and with a fruitless seven-years of planning for that impossible colossus, the Palace of Soviets. And the Third Bridge, 478 meters long. He built it and died a year later.

On 5 March 1938, the bridge was tested: one hundred and forty ten-ton trucks and twenty fully-loaded trams rolled over it. Meanwhile, four Bolshevik polar explorers drifted over the North Pole on an ice floe, Japan was fighting in China, girls on advertising posters advised the public to drink coffee with liqueur manufactured by the vodka and liqueur department of the People's Committee for Food Manufacturing, and engineers were testing a new invention — a telephone answering machine. But these and many other first fruits of the general plan for the reconstruction of Moscow — metro stations, parks, streets, bridges — felt remote and overshadowed in the spring of 1938. Completion of construction projects coincided with the surfacing of right-wing Trotskyist vipers from the swampy depths. Technological advances were lost amid news of the so-called Trial of the Twenty-One with Bukharin among the convicted. The trial was concluded with the customary Russian executions of "beasts in human guise," the customary Russian accusations against rivals and a completely non-Russian submissiveness on the part of the victims.

Were there cases when members of your organization who had access to butter manufacturing put ground glass into butter meant for public consumption?

Yes.

Were there cases when your allies, accomplices of criminal organizations, put nails in the butter?

Yes, I confess.

And did you intentionally spread epizootic disease, which caused the deaths of twenty-five thousand horses in Eastern Siberia.

Yes.

It has remained forever unclear why in these cases, when hundreds of thousands of people could've maintained a dignified and customarily Russian silence, instead chose the shame of false confession? What happened then? Who promised them resurrection?

A pedestrian on the Third Bridge would very soon have stopped admiring the eternal Kremlin: the foundation had already been laid for the Palace of Soviets, and the pace of construction was such that you'd think something in Russia was about to end forever. In just ten months the frame of the Palace was supposed to rise as high as the Second Building of the Council of People's Commissars, and grow higher, to 320 meters at which point it would be topped with a statue of Vladimir Lenin (the index finger of which was itself five meters long). The sum of these two figures (320+100) was supposed to give a clear indication to the Statue of Liberty (33 m), and also the Cheops Pyramid, the Cathedrals of Cologne and Amiens, the Eiffel Tower, and finally the Empire State Building in New York, of exactly who was going to save world. Great ideas demanded stone edifices of a great size.

A shadow, though, a black shadow, was creeping, growing and thickening over Moscow, obscuring everything. It swallowed these weeks of executions (two thousand people were shot every day), and blotted out concerts, and the premieres of two films: *Volochaevsky Days* and *The Youth of the Marshall* (a biopic of young Semyon Budyonny, the cavalryman with the most famous whiskers in the Soviet Union). In its utter blackness, seething and shuddering, it conflated all events, as if saying: the only thing you'll ever see from the Great Stone Bridge is Russia, and nothing else; saying: now you may build only tanks and planes; saying: you can't kill that many of your own people anymore because there are already others coming to kill us. The steel of the Palace's frame had to be recast into anti-tank hedgehogs and railroad bridges when the Donbass was overrun by the German army and new rail construction was begun in the Russian North, where there was coal. In the end nothing could be annulled.

GOLTSMAN

Is a man always to remain alone?
Suddenly as hot as if I'd been wearing a tight-fitting suit, I staggered to a kiosk, bought an icy can of diet Coke, and listened to it hiss when I opened it. I crossed the boulevard, sipping from the can, climbed over a fence on the divider, went through some bushes, and sat down on a park bench. I drank, gasping for air, and listening to myself: still hot? Cooling down? My head burned, blood slammed into my left temple like it was a dam.

A man next to me on the bench looked at me, seeming aloof and free. He was old and exquisitely thin, with a disheveled and grey cloud of hair on his head. He had on soft casual pants and an ancient scholarly cardigan belted over his stomach, the kind you always see in pictures of dying Jewish physicists and immoral scoundrels who buy stolen violins and stamps. His cheeks, stubbly, looked like they was still getting used to the loss of their daily shave; he sat as easily as if he lived somewhere nearby and came here every evening to get some fresh air, on this bench, with the circus on Vernadsky Street behind him.

"Hello, Alexander Naumovich!" I cheerfully moved closer to him on the bench. "What are you reading these days?"

Goltsman smiled with pleasure, and we shook hands.

"Since Regina died, there's only one book I read. It's on my bedside table. It's the Bible. You know, it has *everything* in it."

"You know, I meant to tell you: the bed you and Regina Markovna gave me worked out great. I sleep in it all the time."

"And we had it for seventeen years before you. Until we needed a special one…" Goltsman paused in thought, smiling mournfully at something; his hand twitched at a memory and raised itself away from his lap, then swayed toward my shoulder, but collapsed instead onto the bench between us, exhausted. Everything was clear anyway. "You've got to go."

"There's nowhere for me to go," I looked up at the coldly trembling leaves, at the autumn, at my fleeting, meaningless life, and almost cried.

"But you know what's happening. Clearly someone has identified you. They've marked you as a target. We don't know who they are. I hope it's something commercial. If you don't agree to work for them, they will hand you over. You should leave. I don't see any other options." He spoke slowly, moving words like heavy furniture, making it clear that we were being followed even here, on this bench. We were guppies in a fishbowl. "You know our capabilities. They are quite limited. *If* we find enough money… *If* the right people at the prosecutor's office and court agree to help… You'll spend a year in prison just waiting for the trial. Or two. Why go through that? Look at all of this differently. Aren't you tired? You've lived some. You have experienced things that others often miss. Go somewhere warm, to the sea. You can have everything a man needs — a bit of a beach, honest work…" Goltsman wanted to add "a good woman", but blinked off the word with a tear in his eye. "Trust me, you don't need anything else. I need to know what you think."

I have so little life left, was all I could think. I've forgotten the meaning of childhood games, of moving toy soldiers in the grass, I've lost the joy of New Year's Eve, the sweet watermelons, enjoying the body of a beloved woman, the sweetness in the sound of my own name, the warm weight of a soaked shirt under a summer downpour— the world looks at me without interest. All I have left is to dream of a healthy old age, without soiling myself, and to hope to die in my sleep.

"I want to work on the Great Stone Bridge. You'll help me."

I had noticed Goltsman in reading room number six (scholarly research only) on the second floor of the historical library, I saw him in the archives of the Institute of Marxism-Leninism (it's called something else now, something about the socio-political history of the Russian state), I ran into him in the former Archive of the Central Committee of the Communist Party on Ilyinka. We would nod to each other. Exchange pleasantries. Then one day we started talking in the cafeteria, over apple tarts. He'd read me his works and ask why no one was interested in publishing them. With a slavish desperation, the old man carved out, as if with scissors through metal, sketches about heroes of the partisan movement in the winter of 1941. And then made the rounds of magazines and publishing houses, hopelessly, with his load of stories about these unwanted parachutists, lieutenants of state security, and sundry other incredible individuals who on a winter morning, with the hangman's noose around their neck, would say to the village residents gathered to watch the execution, "Our cause will triumph! I'm not afraid of death! I'll die as befits a patriot of the Motherland!" This while German motorcyclists were rolling from Khimki to Moscow, past the space where there now sits an IKEA.

Goltsman was only printed by Communist newspapers and the *Military-Historical Magazine*. I kept wondering: Why is he doing this? To keep himself busy? Does he need money? Does he pay rent on an apartment for his granddaughter? But Goltsman didn't have any grandchildren, and dragged his metaphorical pebbles to the graves of comrades with intentional stubbornness, as if he were taking part in some great construction project. His wife had cancer, and it took the disease three years to devour her; at some point it became awkward to call Goltsman at home and, if Regina Markovna answered, chat idly with a woman who was doomed to die slowly, consciously, while you stayed behind and watched it happen. Goltsman's son had given himself over to computers, and went to live in America.

No one still living had really known Goltsman in his earlier life, although there remained his pupils, and his beloved Motherland. In the prefaces to various KGB veterans' memoirs, Major General A. N. Goltsman was singled out for his achievement in collecting and recording the history of counter-espionage. In the archives, whenever a form required the retired researcher's "last workplace", Goltsman always wrote in his tidy, narrow hand, "Assistant to the Chairman of the Information Committee"; as a result, everyone thought he was a journalist. It was little known that the obscurely named Information Committee, in 1947, briefly attempted to unite the military (GRU) and political (First Department of the MGB) intelligence services — the Chairman of the Committee was the number two man in the empire, Vyacheslav Molotov.

For what Goltsman ultimately came to do for us, we didn't pay him. He helped us on an ideological basis, and he and I were not friends — I can't be friends with someone and pity them. Compassion only ever leads to unintentional cruelty, and anyway he didn't know how to be friends with anyone either. We served the Truth, and the rest was nothing, at the end of earthly roads there is nothing, and no one to call to. We simply met and said the things to each other that our work required. Until his wife died. Then Goltsman was taken by an invisible hand, crushed with a quiet crack, and put back on this bench.

"The idea is simple. To unpack the bridge. And get things across to these freaks, to bring them to their senses. They think that all the questions will be closed. That everyone will be buried. I want to show them."

Goltsman nodded — yes, he had been expecting this:

"That, my dear man, is hopeless. That is useless, dangerous work. It's not our business. It comes after all of us. There is only one way out for us. It is also open for you. The way out is — here."

I didn't turn. Instead, I looked straight ahead at the bikers racing towards the Sparrow Hills, carrying their blond girls in black leather — so I never did see what gesture he made to refer to the book that now ruled him — a cross? Three fingers pinched together?

"And we'll return."

"I don't see a way out. I'll do what I can."

We were quiet for a while, companionably. I finished my Coke and tossed the can into the trash-bin.

"What about this... young man? The one who contacted you? Do you think you'll have what it takes to, let's say, solve this problem?"

I licked my lips and considered Goltsman's question.

"He did scare me, at first. It all looked very real, more real than life, in fact. But then I went over it in my head — I spent all night thinking about this guy, replaying our conversation. And here's the thing: he wasn't sure how to get into his car. I mean, he didn't know where he was supposed to sit. At all. He went to the wrong car first, the security people had to nudge him to the BMW, and there, again, he didn't go to the right seat, they had to prompt him. If I'm lucky, I bet he came to the market alone, without the escort, and the rest of the show was timed, staged for my benefit. What if he just hired the security detail for an hour? Then, it's just him, acting alone — and he's wide open. He's just a clown with ideas. I wrote down the license plate number."

Goltsman considered this, his face impassive, and finally nodded: yes, that's possible.

He stood up. It was time for him to go. Now, in his retirement, when he was his own man and didn't use an alarm clock, he lived according to his own, very strict order.

"The Great Stone Bridge is by the House of Government. I've heard a lot about it, but nothing useful. We need to find a way in." He considered something for a moment and added, indifferently: "The result may be instructive."

Night is an unreliable time. At night, I become a boy. Everyone who knows me as a different person, and for whom I must be working, is asleep. I sit on the bed alone, and can't bring myself to turn on the light. As if there were someone else with me whom I might disturb. I can't turn on the light to read, I can't listen to music in the darkness. I can only feel that I am a boy — I can touch my face in the dark and smooth it with my hands; I can ignore anything uninteresting, I don't have to take an interest in pedestrian things. I can hold a ball in my hands, or quietly roll it to the wall.

A PROBLEM

IAM THIRTY EIGHT YEARS OLD. I HAVE TWO CHILDREN. I HAVE many grey hairs. I regard them with resignation, like snow lying on a roof — this will melt! — or like a scrape that is healing.

Five years ago I was reading a newspaper in the metro, on my way to work: several thousand years from now (or several tens of thousands of years), the Milky Way galaxy, where we live, will collide with the Andromeda nebula. We are barrelling towards each other at the speed of five hundred kilometers an hour. Or five thousand kilometers an hour. But by the time we collide, the Earth will have been a dead body for a long time. The Sun will run out of heat, and the Earth will turn into an icy crag.

For some reason, this did something to me, induced the sort of terror I had only ever felt as a child, and only on the metro, and only when I thought about the death of my parents. When I read the article, I immediately thought of my daughter. I felt death so strongly that it seemed this feeling would never go away. But ten minutes went by, and by the time I walked into my office, I felt better. But then later that summer there was a day when my daughter and I turned off into a ravine to look for mushrooms.

"Dad, is it true what they say, that someday the Earth won't exist?"

I played for time, pointlessly — "Who told you that?" I asked — but there, on the slope of that ravine I realized it fully and irretrievably: yes. There will no longer be anything. Everything will rot away like the grass. Yet this seemed impossible to reconcile with the fact of my daughter's existence, with the dear, sweaty smell of her head next to me. I turned out to be unprepared for eternal annihilation.

In the mornings and at night, I would think about it. Sometimes, the despair could be ameliorated by simple fatigue, or over-eating, by the catharsis of sex, by the sound of my son turning and breathing in his sleep. I moved carefully and tried to sleep more, but it was no good; the despair endured beyond consolation.

When I was young, I could rely on youth itself and the uncharted territories it still contained. When I was a child, life appeared a wilderness ahead, a dense forest, but now the forest had become thinner, and between the trunks I could glimpse what lay before me. It was as if I'd climbed a hill, and could suddenly see a black sea in the distance. There are other hills between here and there, smaller hills, and they would never again hide from me the sea into which I'm doomed to walk.

I took note: I still wasn't prepared to recognize that my son would someday die, that his elderly face would appear in an oval photograph worked into the cross on his grave, and then the cross would fall down and the grave would be plowed under. I wasn't ready to accept the appearance of other, new boys who would take their turn in living. I didn't want other boys, other old men, another spring, apart from mine, ours. I had to admit to myself: I wanted to take all of this and rush to my mother, to snuggle up against her, to run up to her and burrow into her. But I couldn't, Mama was dead.

I looked into people's faces, particularly old people, and saw how they smiled, sitting on the benches in bathhouses or on the soft seats of shuttle buses. They must know a secret that I don't know. The same death that I face awaits them, and earlier at that, as soon as tomorrow. So what were they smiling about, why weren't they hurrying, why weren't they devoured by fear? What did they hope for?

I saw death so clearly that nothing more remained before my eyes. My eyes were seared once and for all by the flame of my burning life, and I was irked by questions: Why should I think of it only now? How could I have lived without noticing this before?

Life for me will end when I die, and the consolations of succession, of children and grandchildren living on, will be mere anaesthesia, a palliative to keep me from causing a ruckus when I croak.

But it won't work, because I don't want *not to be* forever, I don't want the markers of my time to drift into oblivion, the blue school uniforms with metal buttons, coin-changing machines in the metro, parades on Red Square, cosmonauts, the invaluable newspaper *Football & Hockey*, tram #26, the voices of Levitan and Vysotsky… I don't want our time to petrify, abandoned to the elements by the young, who have learned to suppress the voices of the sick and the dying, and to ignore the hopes of the dead. These young people have bullied everyone into living by their rules, into living as if there were no death. There aren't that many old people, after all, and all they do is pat their dogs on park benches, rosy-cheeked and slightly foolish and ripe for mockery. And there aren't any dead people at all. They've been carried off and buried, they are neither shown to us nor contemplated. They're the majority, but they have nothing to speak with. No one wants to release the decaying from the earth. No one hears the subterranean groan of the great majority: bring us back!

What am I to do with this? I still have the gauzy curtain of time on my side the great *not yet*. And there's the thirst for powerful distractors: alcohol, skiing. Sky-diving. Or inspiration could be gleaned from various models of healthy longevity and excellent working capacities into old age.

There are also convenient forms of internalizing death, such as family, the nation (this one's a bit tougher), history. At least this last you can enter, albeit namelessly, as a mineral dissolved in water. Blood in the veins of your relatives. A hooked family nose.

Family, nation, history. Fine. But I don't consent to dying just so *all of this* can keep barrelling on while on a collision course with the Andromeda nebula! Nothing can bring back that old, sleepy vision of the future with its ordinary human limits: my son, my grandson, the apple trees that will grow without me, and the May beetles that will come back to the birches in the city park as they always have.

God is also a fine consolation, the idea that we'll die in our meted-out suffering, but then rise in physical form, with skin and hair (although our age will be uncertain), to enter eternity. Still, it's a labor-intensive business to get there: standing through services, repenting in your old age, mortifying the flesh, guessing at semi-familiar words in Old Church Slavonic, bequeathing a chandelier to a monastery...

But then there's such uncertainty about the proper place of cherries and girls in short skirts. Not to mention the territorial disagreements: billions believe in one thing, billions in another. Some sort of Islam, lamas, Catholics. Admittedly you don't see them fighting too much — they've divvied up the market.

I suppose I just have a bad feeling about it all for the simple reason that there is no practical evidence, not even the Pope can heal rectal cancer, and astrophysics does not confirm anything — it's quiet out there, God is silent for some reason, it's been a while since anyone had any *revelations*. And the shroud of Turin proved not to be old enough. No, I believe that there is consolation. There are saints, the Russian Orthodox Church, free meals for the poor. Orthodox nurses are kinder, as a rule, but also more expensive, and you do feel better when you place a candle for fifty kopecks, the fatter kind, and you light it for the repose of the soul of whomever. And it is true succor when the people flow around the church on Easter night... But I fear that there is no rising from the dead after all.

In the end, it seems, one thing remains, and it is a mighty beast of burden: the future. It carries everything that we pile on to it. In the future, science will develop and doctors will bring us all back to life! But that's hard to believe. What if they only grant eternity to themselves, their relatives and friends? How do we, the dead, keep track, stand up for ourselves and make sure they drag up *everyone*? We have no party, no constituency, and they, the people of the future, will be their own bosses. They'll probably skip the Neanderthals, and then crunch some numbers and tell the Middle Ages to stay dead, and then they'll decide only to preserve the ones who are alive, and not even all of them, just the lucky few. Although if I were lucky, and the administration made me an offer — *we'll leave you personally, but not your grandfathers and grandmothers* — I would agree, the bastard that I am. What choice would I have? At least I could remember them — forever! That'd be better than nothing at all.

There's nothing left but lies.

THE SEA

For the duration of my work on the great stone bridge I had to rent an apartment. I slammed the atlas of Moscow shut and chose the city of Feodosia, at the end of spring.

I flew there to bury my 37 years.

The plane descended: I could see the roofs of barns, garages and houses, cars, a sprinkle of graves, and another sprinkle of sheep. When I landed and walked down the endless Fedko Street, I was stunned by the undisturbed silence of the city: the rare passers-by did not wear heels, the air thickened, barbed wire slithered across the tops of fences, and at eight in the evening Feodosia was serenely asleep. The gutters had the smell of the nearby sea, and there was silence in the yards and gardens, an intoxicating silence broken once by the call of a seagull that swooped above me.

For some reason I went down to the sea instead of going straight to the hotel, and there the city opened up like a flower in springtime. Strings of lights were already blazing in empty cafés and bars, taxi drivers were waiting at their customary corners, music blared in empty discos, and waiters dressed as cowboys loitered before the evening rush of diners. The sea breathed, cold, calm and joyful. I walked like a traveler on another planet.

I shut myself in my room to read.
When I start a new job, I always read the lives of the fathers.
It is given to a particular class of righteous to record the acts of

all the righteous: "A difficult time began, characterized by distrust in people, especially those who had lived abroad for a lengthy period of time. Six months later, Muravkin was arrested by the NKVD. His subsequent fate is unknown." Of the first eight chiefs of Soviet foreign intelligence, seven were shot, and one died in a car accident — like the apostles!

Those who survived ("Ivan Andreevich Chichaev died on 15 November 1984 in his small apartment in a building on Serpukhovsky Val. At the funeral, his state awards were carried behind his coffin on scarlet cushions — the Order of Lenin, two Orders of the Red Banner, and the Order of the Red Star"), had to work their pens as payment, and paint, as it were, the metaphorical locomotive of the Revolution so it looked the way it should, so that it could barrel on, carrying the next generation whose turn it was to look into its hellish firebox.

I read these obligatory writings for the sake of their first lines. You see, the writers found it awkward to start with the dictated text right away; they couldn't quite open with such steely phrases as, "by order of the court," or "the decision was made to establish the facts, detain in secret and process for rendition," or "in the course of the interrogation Dagen categorically denied that he had spied for a foreign nation, and ten days later he died after falling from the tenth floor of the building where his office was located."

Instead, to gain some momentum, the writers had to add something of their own, and they permitted themselves a few idle phrases about nothing. And in these careful embellishments are contained the wind, the smell of lilacs, dry dandelion fluff flying through the air, carrying seeds. Such was all mere guileless invention, but it was in the invention itself that something survived which wasn't meant to: the unofficial and therefor superfluous parts of the lives being described:

It was a stuffy August evening in 1950. On the streets of Tel Aviv people moved slowly, like disoriented flies. Perhaps the only person in the entire city who did not notice the heat or the humidity was the resident agent of the Soviet foreign intelligence in Israel, Vladimir Ivanovich Vertiporokh…

Or:

A summer day in 1934 was drawing to a close. The head of the Foreign section of the Unified State Political Department A.G. Artuzov went to the windows, closed the curtains and turned on the table lamp with the green lampshade...

And again:

January is not the best time of year in Shanghai. Cold winds from the ocean blow through the enormous city, and the streets are often drenched in rain and snow. On a dreary day in January 1939, the Soviet intelligence agent Nikolai Tishchenko went outside, drawing his leather coat tight around himself...

I left my room and got the keys to the business center from the front desk. When I sat down and searched for "Great Stone Bridge," I got more than 2,000 results. I clicked on a random link. It was a long article published in the newspaper *Top Secret*, a story about a building on Romanov Lane (called Granovsky Street in the Soviet period), where Stalin's Marshals and People's Commissars lived, and after them their children and grandchildren. I read:

It is not out of the question that one of these children could have been carrying a pistol. The boy, Volodya, was the 15-year-old son of the head of the aviation industry, Shakhurin, a tall, blond man. The boy fell in love with the daughter of the diplomat Umansky, who was appointed Ambassador to Mexico. The girl's name was Nina, she was also fifteen. Her family lived in a different building, the so-called House on the Embankment, where the apartments were larger, guests were not accosted by overzealous door-men, and where the residents had inherited from the old Bolsheviks the habit of honest poverty and the reading of books.

Nina and Volodya had their fateful conversation on the Great Stone Bridge, halfway between these two buildings, on the stairs that lead down to the Variety Theater. He may have asked her not to leave. Or he was jealous. Or was simply showing off. In short, Shakhurin Jr. shot the girl, point-blank. Then he shot himself, and died a day later. This was in 1943.

The neighbors were scandalized — look what the bosses' spoiled brats did!

Stalin said, "Wolf cubs."

The boy had seemed all right, but everyone was immediately appalled by what he did. Nonetheless, Volodya was given a lavish funeral, with the building's entire courtyard covered in wreaths, although some said that his mother did not mourn him for very long: soon there were parties and Gypsy songs that could be heard in the entire building. The boy lies in Novodevichy cemetery, the girl's ashes are in an urn bricked into the wall there, with her father and mother next to her, having been killed in a plane crash in 1945.

I closed the browser window, went back to my room and looked out the window, into the night. The stars shone brightly as if freshly scrubbed. I lay down, turned off the light, and pulled the phone closer on the nightstand. I tried to think of happy, bright things, but I couldn't, it was all bleak. I had nothing: no home, no family, no woman, no parents, not even a job I loved. I might as well have been a limo driver for hire.

THE INVISIBLE MAN

Konstantin Umansky left a short, broken trail, fragile as footprints in the sand. Almost no one wanted to remember the dead father of the beautiful girl who was shot in 1943.

I met with Goltsman before breakfast, before the beach filled up with old women and children, and we sifted through Umansky's 43 years of life, until we saw it for what it was: a small, smooth thing, worked over by the waves until it was the size of the dash engraved in Umansky's concrete headstone between the numbers 1902 and 1945.

"He was Jewish. Born in Nikolayev, the son of an engineer. After the revolution he turned up at Moscow University, but studied for barely a year. He showed exceptional linguistic abilities. He knew English, German and French well, Italian and Spanish less so. As a very young man, he authored a book about new Communist art. A representative sample of the book: 'And although Kandinsky, as a consequence of spending long periods of time abroad, is often assessed in Moscow circles as a Western presence, I have no doubt whatsoever about his purely Slavic roots, about his eastern aspiration to break free of the fetters of the material, about his purely Russian and universal humanism'.

"The People's Commissar, Anatoly Lunacharsky, took note of Umansky and sent him, while he was still a seventeen-year-old upstart, to Germany "to foster the propaganda of new art forms." Once there, Umansky forgot the reason he had been sent, and became an employee of the Russian Telegraph Agency. He lived well, representing the agency in Europe for thirteen years — Vienna, Rome, Geneva, Paris.

Only occasionally did he visit to the site of the Socialist experiment back home in Moscow.

In 1931, however, he came back to Moscow, to head the press department of the People's Commissariat for Foreign Affairs. Accredited foreign correspondents remember him for his ferocious censorship: those who dared to write that there was famine in the USSR wouldn't get tickets to the sensational trials of the first "saboteurs." He accompanied western literary luminaries on their inspections — Feuchtwanger, Shaw, Barbusse and Wells. Stalin took note of him. It was reported that on several occasions he acted as an interpreter for Comrade Stalin. The People's Commissar for Foreign Affairs Maxim Litvinov called Umansky "Mr. Magic Touch" — the papers that he drafted were signed by the Emperor without corrections.

In April 1936, Umansky went to the USA, in the rank of counselor. Two years later, he was the Ambassador. He was disliked there. Some historians believe that in 1939-1940, the Soviet Ambassador functioned as a resident agent for the foreign department of the NKVD. Umansky was recalled at the start of the war, but no persecution followed. He spent two years in *de facto* honorable retirement as a member of the Board of the People's Commissariat for Foreign Affairs, and then finally was again appointed Ambassador, this time to Mexico, scheduled to arrive there on 4 June 1943. One legend has it that when he presented his letter of credence to Mexico's President, Umansky promised that in six months they would be able to speak to one another without an interpreter. Two months later, in October Umansky made his first speech in Spanish (the Mexicans didn't suspect that Umansky had studied the language for years). Ambassador Umansky became "a national hero of the working people."

On 25 January 1945 he boarded a plane to Costa Rica; it exploded in flight.

The historian Aleksandr Sizonenko provided seven hypotheses for the catastrophe:

1. Tragic coincidence. The pilot took off at the wrong time, flew into the wake turbulence from the plane that had taken off right before

them, and lost speed. Other evidence suggest that the pilot lost control of the plane, was unable to even out the roll of the aircraft, and during takeoff one of the chassis caught on the fence of the landing strip which caused the plane to crash and explode on the ground.

2. An act of sabotage by German agents.

3. An American operation, one of the many missions that were to curb the "Communist threat" in Latin America.

4. The Poles. Several hundred Poles fled to Mexico seeking refuge from the war. The uprising in Warsaw that was organized from London by the Polish government in exile there, was drowned in blood by the Germans, and the Polish capital was taken by the Red Army just before Umansky's flight, bringing in the so-called Moscow Poles. In retaliation, the London Poles blew up the Soviet Ambassador.

5. The Trotskyists, taking their revenge on Stalin for the murder of their leader. Umansky may have taken part in planning the assassination of the emperor's personal enemy; the operation was planned in the US, and it is unlikely that the Embassy was not involved. Further, during his time in Mexico Umansky tried to get Ramon Mercader, Trotsky's assassin, released from jail. Trotsky's widow Natalia stated directly that thanks to Umansky's efforts, Mercader was treated well in prison.

6. Umansky was killed by Mexican fascists — enemies of the USSR.

7. The NKVD. The emperor was preparing to destroy the Anti-fascist Jewish committee. Umansky's connections with actor and activist Solomon Mikhoels and poet Itzik Feffer, and his active work "in the Jewish sphere" in America and Mexico could not go unnoticed.

Goltsman put only two purple check-marks in his notebook, and after a long silence, said:

"That's all that exists in open sources."

He had shaved and had his hair cut, and was attired in a light white suit and summer shoes. When working, Alexander Naumovich always gave the impression of a slightly frightened person who had heard an unfamiliar rustle in the middle of the night.

"Don't you find it strange, Alexander Naumovich, that no one seems to remember Umansky personally? There hasn't been a single publication in the last sixty years. All the diaries, memoirs, letters, commentaries on letters that have come out? Nothing. Nothing from the foreigners — who was it he escorted around? Nothing by Gorky — and Umansky went to his banquets. Nothing from his friends, Mayakovski, or Yevgeny Petrov. Or Mikhail Koltsov — though they were supposedly close friends, like brothers. Not even the White émigrés… How come Bunin didn't take a poke at him — he made fun of everyone else. The subject of our inquiry is a charismatic man. A prominent diplomat. Died mysteriously in the prime of life. And the tragic story of his beautiful daughter… How is it no one remembers?"

"They say Gromyko didn't like our client. He served under Umansky in Washington; when he became the Minister of Foreign Affairs, he forbade any mention of Umansky."

"That's not very convincing."

"There's a one-page passage, a look at Umansky's life as a whole. Nothing significant. But the name of the author is noteworthy."

"One of the repressed?"

"If only! Ilya Ehrenburg," Goltsman handed me a photocopy.

Ilya Ehrenburg, deputy of the Supreme Council of the USSR of the third, fourth, fifth, sixth and seventh convocations, winner of two Stalin Prizes and the International Lenin Prize, vice-president of the World Peace Council, wrote several thick novels that no one wanted to read and seemed to be the freest person in the Union of Soviet Socialist Republics.

He served the country of victorious socialism and served the emperor, dooming some, when necessary, elevating others, when possible, and spending most of his life in the comfort of bourgeois capitals. He crossed the iron curtain with suspicious ease in search of "material" for work and, armed with approved talking points, defended the interests of the nation of workers and peasants in disputes with various giants, Cyclopes and monsters of world culture.

Ehrenburg became hugely famous, not to say notorious, for his vehement wartime goad: "If you have not killed at least one German today, you have wasted the day." The men on trial at Nuremberg all looked up as if on command when they were told that Ehrenburg *himself* had taken a seat in the viewers' gallery. Contemporaries (our witnesses) referred to Ehrenburg as a "communications officer" between West and East, "Stalin's court lackey", "an unsurpassed master of life" and a "screen." Even a tenth of the freedom that Ehrenburg received from the government would have landed any other man with a one hundred percent chance of being shot as early as 1934, regardless of the results of his work. And a ten thousand percent chance in 1937. And a labor camp in the early '50s, after the authorities adjusted the intensity of the Soviet Jewry's national self-esteem. Yet Ehrenburg lived out his seventy-six years without hindrance, outlived the emperor, and left for posterity three volumes of memoirs which he titled *People, Years, Life....* He wrote about the bloodier times in passing, by hints and innuendo and mostly focused on his own purity and his numerous friendships with Nobel laureates and other geniuses, while admitting in passing that he didn't know the answer to the question of why Stalin didn't have him killed.

The lack of a sufficient explanation (excluding for the moment the possibility that he sold his soul) means that the true life of Ilya Ehrenburg, dubbed during his lifetime the "conscience of the world," leaves us with a fractured, jarring echo, hiding something that it would be better not to know. The fact that only Ehrenburg had examined Umansky's life had to mean something.

Ehrenburg befriended Umansky, eleven years his junior, in 1942, and they met after work every night, at two or three o'clock in the morning.

Kostya was different from most people in Ehrenburg's circle. He was too young to have been one of the brilliant protégés of the disgraced People's Commissar Maxim Litvinov. Neither was he one of Molotov's people who might become the next People's Commissar and did not talk much about the past (*why?*). Umansky's book, *New Russian Art*, was published in Berlin and concerned itself with Lentulov, Mashkov, Konchalovsky, Sarian, Rozanova, Chagall and Malevich. Umansky was curious; he liked poetry, music, painting, everything interested him: Shostakovich's symphonies, Rachmaninoff's concertos, the frescoes of Pompeii, the first garbled output of the so-called "thinking machines." In his room on the fifth floor of the Hotel Moscow he hosted Admiral Isakov, the writer Yevgeny Petrov, the diplomat Boris Shtein, the actor and director Mikhoels, and the pilot Chukhnovsky *(high-society figures of the Empire, the founding fathers of the Jewish Anti-Fascist Committee. But where are his wife and daughter? When did he move to the apartment in the Government House?)*

Ehrenburg mentioned Umansky's extraordinary memory and hatred of the bureaucratic spirit. In his memoirs, he captured Umansky's informal voice, and this was now our only chance to hear it, albeit in Ehrenburg's retelling, twenty years after the fact of their meeting. Like listening to a soft tapping through thick ice. But better than nothing.

"We do not understand the things that we have the right to take pride in. We prefer to hide the best, arrogant as clumsy teenagers, but at the same time we are afraid that some nimble foreigner will get wind of the fact that there are no washing machines in Mirgorod."

Foreign correspondents, hated Umansky for his sadistic censorship. One of them wrote, "Kostya Umansky, the new censor, smiled at me with all his gold teeth and flashed his thick glasses. That brassy smile. It spoke volumes. 'I don't like you,' it said, 'because I am an egocentric Soviet fixer, but you'll see, I'll be promoted to Commissar.' He must have read my smile just as well. 'You pompous careerist,' it said, 'you're just exploiting the benefits of the revolution. You hate me because I can see who you really are — a little shopkeeper in the alleyways of the revolution.'"

Umansky on Americans: "They are gifted children. Sometimes charming, sometimes intolerable. Europe is in ruins, the Americans will be in command after the victory. After all, he who pays the piper orders the tune… Don't judge all of America by Roosevelt, he is far superior to the rest of his party." *(If he really wrote that, he only made up half of it.)*

Umansky on Picasso: "I once mentioned his name, and I was shouted at, told that he was a charlatan who mocked capitalism and lived off scandal. If you read Shakespeare's poetry to the secretary of some regional party committee" — *but had Umansky ever even seen such a creature?* — "who doesn't speak English, he'll say it's a mess and miss the poetry! Anything they don't understand is arcane for them. And their tastes are compelled, in any case, by Moscow."

Ehrenburg wrote: "I think Umansky was born under a lucky star."

But suddenly, the lucky star fell, according to Ehrenburg, "because of a tragic and stupid coincidence." "A teenager, a classmate," Ehrenburg reports, killed Umansky's daughter, "shot her after a heated exchange, he shot her and killed himself." Umansky adored his daughter. She was the only thing that held his family together. "I knew that there was great emotion in his life, that in 1943 he experienced such torments as those described by Chekhov in his story *The Lady with the Lapdog.*"

And then came the unexpected outcome of the drama.

"I'll never forget the night when Konstantin Alexandrovich came to see me. He could barely speak, he sat there with his head in his hands. A few days later he left for Mexico. His wife (*Raisa Mikhailovna*) was put on the flight to Mexico City all but comatose with grief. A year later he wrote to me: 'The sorrow I have suffered destroyed me. Raisa Mikhailovna is an invalid, and our condition is much worse than it was on the day that we said goodbye. As always, you were right, and you gave me some good advice which I, alas, ignored'."

In concluding this section, before getting back to the business of narrating his own life, Ehrenburg gives a final rhetorical shrug: what advice did I give him? I don't remember giving any advice.

The water was clear and undisturbed. The siren at the railway crossing trilled like a living thing. Trains came to Feodosia from the north, and the local residents, with the satisfied look of hunters on their faces, took the disembarking vacationers, like slaves in a marketplace, bent under the weight of their suitcases, to the apartments the locals had rented to them. These holidaymakers, despite the late May cool, stubbornly trooped down to the gray-pebbled beach. Seagulls dropped into the water when one least expected it. Girls stuck umbrellas into the pebbles and undressed.

We sat facing the sea, feeling its breath and the reach of its emptiness, and it blended with the sky far away in the distance, a warm eternity.

"What do you think, Alexander Naumovich?" I asked.

"He was a careful person. There are a lot of questions about him. No one seems to know the details of his daughter's death. What was the advice that Ehrenburg gave him? Could it have saved Nina's life? Some of the twists in his biography are difficult to explain. I think I probably will find out eventually whether Stalin really did know him. The plane crash, or explosion, is a separate topic altogether. But here's what I find most intriguing" — here Goltsman turned away from the sea and looked at me with his tense, heavy face, his blue eyes bright and almost transparent in his old age — "Litvinov, Molotov, Gromyko. Three Ministers. The top of the Soviet foreign affairs establishment. And they all knew our Kostya. Gromyko didn't like him and tried to make sure that he was forgotten. Litvinov and Molotov, as we know, couldn't stand each other. Umansky began his diplomatic career under Litvinov, and rose quickly. So why didn't Molotov touch Umansky when he had Litvinov placed under house arrest and all of his people purged? Then Litvinov was brought back and sent to the States — as Umansky's replacement. Kostya was recalled, but again, he wasn't touched. And two years later they gave him the ambassadorship to Mexico. Whose man was he? Why did you decide to start with him?"

"The parents of the boy, Shakhurin, lived to an old age, we'll find people who knew them and are still alive. Umansky's wife died with him in the plane crash in 1945; there can't be many left who knew the family. Something else caught my attention, too. The guy who came to recruit me at the market said that Nina was killed on the third of June. Umansky flew to Mexico on the fourth. For all we've heard about how he adored the girl, how come he didn't stay behind to bury her?"

We got up.

"This all needs to be checked," I said. "You don't like Kostya already. He's going to have a tough time with you, I can tell, but perhaps this will help. I got these from the foreign affairs archives, personnel file #1300. It cost two hundred dollars. I'm keeping track of the expenses."

I shook twenty-two photographs out of an envelope: a skinny Jew with a gap-toothed smile and a thick head of hair; the same man years later, after he matured and put on a lot of weight, in profile, with a high forehead; Umansky with the gray-haired Bernard Shaw next to an open car, with the Kremlin towers behind them; ancient Mexican women, big-boned and loaded with flowers, next to the extravagantly polished coffins of the plane-crash victims; Umansky's mother, a stout woman with a masculine face; a fuzzy-haired five-year-old girl standing in the grass on a riverbank, pulling up her white panties, her squinting, blissful father behind her. And so on.

Finally, two newspaper clippings with almost identical photos, both dated April 13, a Monday. One from a Washington newspaper and the other from the *Omaha World Herald*, with the caption, "Konstantin Umansky, the new Counselor at the Embassy of the USSR, with his young daughter Nina, on board the ocean-liner *Paris* after arriving in New York."

I held one of these newspaper photos a bit longer. A beautiful child in a good, warm coat, a tiny beret on her head, was hugging her young, handsome father, with her hand in the collar of his coat. Umansky was squatting down, and the girl seemed to be taller than him. Both of their faces glowed, and they had the same eyes.

"Their eyes are absolutely identical. So are their teeth."

"Here's another photograph. Look closely."

Umansky, wearing glasses, his face turned away from the camera,

CONSTANTINE OUMANSKY, new Counselor of the Soviet Embassy, with his small daughter, Nina, pictured aboard the liner Paris on which they arrived in New York. The Counselor, Mme. Oumansky and Nina reached Washington yesterday. Until recently he has been chief of the press section of the Soviet foreign service. *International News Photo*

works the tuning knobs of a radio with both hands. To the right there seems to be a balcony. Either curtains or patterned wallpaper. On top of the radio sits a portrait of the emperor and a coffee cup on a saucer.

"Look at Stalin's portrait," Goltsman said, and pointed. "See, there's something written on it, diagonally across the bottom. You can make out, 'To Comrade Umansky', but the signature and date are illegible. Can it be that Stalin signed a photograph for him?"

"We'll have to find out."

"Yes, that and another thing: did Gromyko write memoirs?" Goltsman asked. "Incidentally," he continued, "they say *The Lady with the Lapdog* was Stalin's favorite story."

LAPDOGS AND BLOODHOUNDS

I CALLED THE LOCAL PAPER AND PLACED AN AD: "REPUTABLE dealer will buy tin soldiers made in USSR. Paying $1 and up a piece."

I figured I had forty minutes until a rerun of last year's Manchester United-Bolton match came on, so I leafed through *The Lady with the Lapdog*, a story about (the preface informed me) the "everyday horror of life." I read and tried to make every line fit Umansky — like teenagers who, in my day, drew whiskers, glasses and Beatles-like mop tops on pictures of Politburo members in the newspaper.

Chekhov's main character had a twelve-year-old daughter. He was married early. His wife aged more quickly than he did, and became a dowdy, mean-spirited fool, to the point where he never wanted to go home. He was a philologist, but worked in a bank and began to have affairs on the side. At a resort, he picked up a little blond woman, her husband of German extraction and a "lackey". She went home to her husband after the holiday, but her lover couldn't forget her. So he found her. I am suffering so much, she said, I think about you all the time. They started meeting each other in hotel rooms. On the way to one such rendezvous, as he took his daughter to school, explaining to her why there is no thunder in winter, he suddenly realized that he was living a double life, that he was forced to hide the most important things, and that what was visible was nothing but lies. Outings with his wife to birthday parties, his work at the bank, arguments at the club — it was all a front, and it was probably the same for everyone, he guessed. For everyone.

The lovers lament that they have to hide like thieves. There was one passage that I read in full: "Anna Sergeyevna and he loved each other like people very close and akin, like husband and wife, like tender friends; it seemed to them that fate itself had meant them for one another, and they could not understand why he had a wife and she a husband; and it was as though they were a pair of birds of passage, caught and forced to live in different cages. They forgave each other for what they were ashamed of in their past, they forgave everything in the present, and felt that this love of theirs had changed them both."

I thought the story rather foolish. I couldn't fathom how it might have resonated with Stalin: who would he be thinking of, reading this? Surely, not the housekeeper Valentina from the closer dacha, a woman whom some of our idiots enshrined as a "life-long liaison." What was the "resonant drama" that Umansky said he experienced on the eve of his departure?

Umansky complained to Ehrenburg that he couldn't get divorced to be with the woman he loved. What would be the point, he asked, of his personal happiness, if Nina should be required to remain with the abandoned Raisa in the Soviet Union, in this impoverished, sweaty, bricked-in Soviet reality of ration cards and endless worries about firewood? If beloved Nina couldn't become the little mistress of the Soviet Ambassador's residence in Tacubaya, couldn't fly to the States to see her friends on holidays, couldn't learn horseback-riding under the gentle tutelage of the handsome officers of the Mexican General Staff; if it meant that Nina had to live without roller-skating, fishing on a yacht in the ocean, white dresses at balls, hikes into the desert at night, tennis and nylon stockings, turquoise swimming pools under orange trees, Chinese stores on 42nd Street and twenty-four-hour cinemas, a personal driver and masseuse — how then could he marry someone else?

Thus Umansky concluded, in a moment of self-delusion and self-congratulation, that he, a man who managed to prolong his own life so cleverly, needed once again to organize the future. He needed to trade his own happiness, his love of another woman, for his daughter's benefit and opportunity. He believed that the people who kept an eye on the world would vouchsafe him this fair trade, and that such people played by the rules and made shrewd deals like everyone else; they weren't madmen crazily swinging the scythe without looking at *what* they were cutting down. In the end, though, Umansky's plans were for naught. He stayed married, and yes, Nina packed to go to Mexico, but for this her head was shattered by a bullet.

Iraida Tsurko (*real surname Tsuryupa — the daughter of the People's Commissar for Food*): I used to visit Nina Umanskaya at home. I don't even remember her face. I only remember that one time she called the housemaid and told her to look at the clock and tell her what time it was, although the clock was right there in the room.

Tatyana Litvinova: Umansky returned to Moscow at the start of the war with his wife and his only daughter Nina (her parents called her Tita), a beautiful and charming sixteen-year-old girl. Her parents enrolled her in a government school, where initially, despite her foreign outfits, she felt like Cinderella. The uniform regulations were very strict, and girls competed with stockings, lace collars and bracelets. Nina, who had been educated in the democratic traditions of the USA, had a difficult time.

Artyom Khmelnitsky: Nina came into the classroom. Molotov's daughter Svetlana knew her, and they exchanged kisses. There were plenty of beauties in the class, but Umanskaya was different from our girls: she dressed differently, walked differently, her hairstyle was different, she wore shoes instead of boots, and nylon stockings — we didn't even understand what those stockings on her legs *were*.

Unidentified person, woman: Nina didn't come to us at the start of the school year. She was blond and dyed her hair, which at the time was almost something supernatural. And her legs were terribly crooked, like wheels. She was very beautiful otherwise. The photographs don't do her justice. When I remember my peers, I feel so bad for them: We were so poorly groomed. Our make-up was primitive. Many people had poor clothing. Nina, of course, really stood out.

Alexander Alliluyev: She looked like Deanna Durbin. She was rather stand-offish.

Yulia Baryshenkova: Nina was very approachable and humble; she quickly became everyone's favorite. She would share her breakfast, and break up a chocolate bar whenever she had one to give everyone a piece.

Tatyana Kuibysheva: Call me back in a week, I'm a bit ill… Oh, you did? Yes, but you know, I told you so much last time, I don't have anything to add. I didn't tell you anything? Well, I don't know anything! Did Nina come to see my sister on the day of her death? Yes, she did. And that's it. I don't know what they talked about, I was in another room, I had a small child. My sister tried to convince her: don't go, she kept saying, stay for a while, but Nina replied — no, I have to. It was in the morning. There is nothing more to talk about. That was sixty years ago. *How did you spend your free time?* I don't know anything. *What did the girls wear in your day?* I couldn't tell you. *Who were your friends?* I don't remember. I don't know anything! You've asked me so many questions, and the doctor is coming to see me now. Goodbye!

Tatyana Gnedina (*daughter of dissident Yevgeny Gnedin, who replaced Umansky in the press department of the People's Commissariat for Foreign Affairs under Litvinov, and who, after Litvinov's fall from grace, did time in prison. Gnedin's memoirs were published with a foreword by Professor Sakharov. Brief summary: I was badly beaten, and I signed everything*): I knew the story about the death from unrequited love. And I also remembered, vaguely, a remarkable girl named Agnes, who had incredibly artistic poise, so elegant. I remember her mother taking us to an expensive, incredibly elegant store on Leipzigstrasse, one early morning, sixty-five years ago. It was the store where the wives of diplomats bought silk underwear, the doorman opens the door, and I, an ordinary Soviet girl, was utterly lost, but Agnes (my God, you say that she was four years younger than me? She was six years old?) walked on ahead like a little princess, quite unruffled. She was genetically different from the people around here. She had exquisite long hair, while Soviet children had their hair cropped short. This memory was something I needed; I held on to it for so many years, but when you said the name the whole thing shattered in my hands — Nina, her age, death. Now I understand, this was the kind of girl someone could love in that way — to death. *Who else is alive, who remembers Umansky, his daughter and the circumstances of Nina's death?* Talk to Pavel Yevgeniyevich Rubinin, the son of our Ambassador to Belgium. He is a very worldly person. Litvinov's biographer Sheinis would've been helpful, but he is dead. He gave me a copy of his book with a touching inscription, but not long before he died I broke off relations with him. The Litvinov family? I broke off relations with them. Maxim Maximovich never made the slightest effort to help my father, but Ehrenburg, on the contrary, sent my father a pipe and a tie to his camp in Kazakhstan. There is also the daughter of Stein, the Ambassador to Italy, Inna. But I broke off relations with her. I always break off relations, yes. So not a word about me.

We found Pavel Rubinin eight months later, in October. The Ambassador's son spent the prime of his life as the personal secretary of the physicist Pyotr Kapitsa, and was now fading away as the keeper of a small museum in Kapitsa's house.

I walked around the Institute of Physical Problems, painted white and yellow, like all scientific establishments on Kosygina street and followed a foot-path that had been described to me by a scientifically-minded local as "leading away at a forty-five degree angle" past thick bushes to Kapitsa's villa. The house seemed to study me from under its cover of shaggy ivy like a sniper hidden in a haystack. I walked up the steps littered with maple leaves and listened: inside, things were quiet, so Rubinin would be alone.

I pretended to be curious, and went along with my guide for a personal tour. Here were Kapitsa's notes on his desk, and his glasses. A collection of bells. His Nobel medal. A bearskin — since he was young, Kapitsa liked to work lying on this skin. After contemplating all this, we sat in the living room and paid our respects to the organizational genius of Marshal Lavrentiy Beria. Kapitsa despised the marshal, but like all the fathers of the Russian A-bomb, he respected Beria's gift for putting together a great undertaking.

I faked more interest; I tried to look warm and attentive. Rubinin (a gray-haired and unexpectedly lanky creature) started talking about his father. The son of a Jewish merchant from Warsaw, and a graduate of the Sorbonne, the elder Rubinin had joined the Bolshevik party; then there were talks between the young Soviet Russia and the Emir of Bukhara, assignments to Kabul, Copenhagen, Ankara, Rome, more stops on the career ladder. When the emperor began to purge the ranks, Litvinov did not invite Rubinin to his home for four years, in order to save him. His wife, the younger Rubinin's mother, was the daughter of a resort manager and had been an actress in provincial theaters.

"When Father was recalled and fired after Litvinov's dismissal, Mama had to work a great deal. She embroidered hammers-and-sickles and various inscriptions on ceremonial velvet banners."

They still had a cheerful home: parties, frequent visits by Baturin, a bass singer at the Bolshoi Theater, and his wife, the harpist Dulova. I stopped listening for a while, until his last words:

"Mama died in the evacuation, in a fire..."

He had whispered this recollection, and it faded into silence. I understood — now that he fulfilled his duty to his mother's memory, there was nothing more to say. His father had married another woman, and therefore ceased to exist for him. I took a final look around, then started to say goodbye.

"By the way, in the '30s your family lived in the building of the People's Commissariat for Foreign Affairs on Khoromy Lane, number two, apartment six. You had a neighbor, Konstantin Umansky. Do you remember him?"

"I remember the name. But I can't say I can picture his face. When my father was dismissed, Umansky avoided him as if he were a leper, so, you know… My father kept silent until his death, but he understood what was going. Even before he went to prison, he called the Politburo members gangsters."

But not the emperor. I thought about the young Nina as I grabbed the door handle, preparing to leave, and to reduce Pavel Yevgeniyevich to two hundred words in my file. I stopped, though, and asked:

"What about you? What did you think? Your peers?"

He nodded with sudden bitterness, a gray shadow of a man:

"We… The children believed in the Soviet regime much more than their fathers. We were swept up and carried along with propaganda, playing Capture the Flag, and singing around pioneer campfires."

In twenty-four months, we only found two seventy-year-old women who were reliably identified as having been friends of Nina

Umanskaya. The first, the daughter of the Kremlin's medical director, quite happily worked filing paperwork in the admissions office of Moscow's city hospital number 67 on Salyam Adil Street. When we reached her, this former life of the party could only recall hearts she had broken: for instance, the sons of the State Defense Committee member Mikoyan, both pilots (they circled above her father's dacha, almost clipping the tops of the pine trees with their wings); or, Stalin's own adopted son, Artyom Sergeev (in winter they used to go skating at the indoors rink for aristocrats at Petrovka, 38; every year on November 8th, her birthday, General Sergeev sent her good wishes from wherever in the world he was fighting and serving).

"When I was late for school, the driver would turn on the siren… they sent a plane for me to go and visit Papa from Kuibyshev, where our school was evacuated." She admitted that Stalin did not make a "bloodthirsty impression" on her, and suddenly she said:

"We just lived well, that's all."

"Shall we have some coffee?"

Nina's second confirmed acquaintance was now a neatly dressed older woman with dyed black hair. Her speech was fast, with a noticeable delay whenever she was compelled to search for Russian equivalents to the precise English words she had in mind. She clearly felt thwarted when forced to settle for the eternal approximations of Russian — several times she threw up her hands, and on these occasions one got a sense of the childhood she'd spent in English-speaking countries. On the telephone, I promised Era Pavlovna to talk only about her classmate; I wanted to gauge how much she might remember.

I drained my coffee in one gulp; Era Pavlovna taught English, and was expecting a student in her apartment on the Frunzenskaya embankment. You'd never guess she was older than fifty-five, and I thought. That's what Nina would look like, if she hadn't been shot in the head.

"Umansky appeared to be a model diplomat — he was well-mannered, erudite, elegant, with such wavy, lovely hair. Raisa Mikhailovna Umanskaya was not pretty, but well-built. The most unattractive of the Soviet diplomats' wives was the English woman, Madame Litvinov — she was horse-faced, a real mastodon. Heavyset, tall, and she spoke Russian badly.

"The Umanskys lived at the Embassy; their Negro cook pronounced the Russian word *pirozhki* with the stress on the second syllable. I remember the future Minister Gromyko as a skinny, black-haired man, and I remember his wife, Lidia Dmitrievna, a petite woman, from somewhere like Ryazan. She was pretty enough, but utterly ignorant, our officers used to pull their hair out when she was scheduled to speak to the press. My mother had to sit with her and make her memorize the answers to the questions they expected. Once, someone asked her, on the record, how big her apartment was, and she said, 'We eat in one room and we sleep in another.'"

She met Nina and made friends with her at a pioneer camp for Soviet diplomats' children — they shared a room. She developed early, had a good figure, and put her hair into two dark blonde braids.

"Mama always told me: look and remember, memories are the greatest treasure. We didn't live on macaroni like some people. We didn't buy silver. The only item of luxury we brought back from the States was a Steinway piano. Nina and I liked the Broadway theaters, and tennis. We went roller-skating in Central park, and were big fans of Superman comics.

"We knew that in our Homeland there was hunger, ration cards, but we still missed it a lot and longed to go home.

"And then the Umanskys left, and Nina didn't write."

"How did you find out that Nina had died?"

"First I learned of Konstantin Alexandrovich's appointment to Mexico, and I was very happy — now we would see each other! And then came the terrible news about Nina. Her father had just been transferred to Mexico City, and Mama and I stopped there to visit him on our way back to Moscow. Raisa Mikhailovna arrived in a terrible state, she was flown there almost unconscious, on sleeping pills. She kept saying, 'I only came here because I am an Ambassador's wife and must do my duty. When I go back, I won't live!' Sorting through

Nina's things was a terrible torture for her. My parents decided not to let the poor woman see me, so she wouldn't be reminded of her loss — Nina and I looked somewhat alike. I only went out in public once, when the Embassy screened *The Great Dictator*, and I knew that Raisa Mikhailovna would not be in the audience. But it turned out that she came in after the lights were out, and took a seat right behind me. I had no idea she was there, and in the middle of the film I said out loud, 'Paulette Godard looks so much like Nina!' Raisa Mikhailovna silently got up and left the hall."

I asked the only thing I really wanted to know:

"They say that in Moscow Nina looked… a little… haughty."

Era Pavlovna responded immediately:

"That's probably just what it looked like to be surrounded by a large number of unfamiliar people. And unknown circumstances."

MATERIAL WITNESSES

I F MY WINTER BOOTS DIDN'T HOLD UP UNTIL THE SPRING, I WAS going to have a problem. I studied my footwear on the metro. They were a workman's boots, boots of construction sites and mud: they were covered in whitish streaks of salt, the shoelaces were threadbare, the leather was knobby and warped. These were not the boots I could take off in full view in a well-to-do hallway. A clod of mud stuck to the left one; no matter how much I tried to flick it off, how often I rubbed it off with snow — it came back, and always showed up on that left boot.

I counted days until spring. I let myself daydream about an office with a large reception area, and a secretary in there who would bring me jasmine tea ever morning, Bride's Choice from the tea boutique on Gogol Boulevard, and tear off sheets from the wall calendar to keep me informed... I got off the metro at October Station and ran to catch the trolleybus.

Judging by the fact that the Memorial House on the Embankment Museum only opened for visitors twice a week — on Saturdays and Wednesdays, and only for two hours at a time — the almost non-existent private life of the leaders of the Russian Revolution was no longer of interest to the general public. Only two chubby graduate students, sexless and English-looking, roamed the three large rooms in funereal silence, holding on to each other. The Museum was a converted apartment on the first floor. The students timidly looked at the everyday items of the Russian tribe's most important people, and samples of clothing and kitchen utensils from the times of the Stalinist tyranny, and seemed to be imagining blood everywhere, darkened, ineradicable spatters.

Ignoring the rugs, sabers and porcelain, I went straight into the former kitchen, where I found a card catalog of former residents that was being watched over by four old women who squawked and pecked each other like ill-tempered vultures.

"Excuse me, I would like to see everything that you have about the family of Konstantin Umansky."

They fell silent and regarded me with a tired hostility.

"Entry is free here. But it's customary to buy something."

I counted out enough small change for a black-and-white brochure *Konstantin Umansky, 1902-1945*, an installment in a series titled *They Lived In This House*. It was eight pages, about the size of a packet of cigarettes, and was held together by a single paperclip.

"What do you want Umansky for? Why not our fathers, for example?"

I lied succinctly about a newsletter of the Institute of Latin America, an anniversary issue, I had been sent there, and I had to ask, who but you...

The old women weren't used to speaking — it had been enough for them to show themselves, it seemed more than enough to *introduce themselves* with special emphases on the surname and the patronymic, and by their presence to confirm: yes, great things happened here. They came together twice a week to preserve their golden childhood, to keep alive the memory of old Bolsheviks, people in a group photograph with Lenin, whom they could call Mom and Dad, and they also kept the memories of the less-valued time of the Emperor, just as vigilantly, so I amused them with my treasure hunter's map, compass and shovel. They alone knew where the real treasures were buried, just as they knew that no one needed these treasures, at least for the moment, they told themselves. There was nothing to argue about, their cult did not need or welcome new members; my grandfather was a carpenter, not a People's Commissar, and I didn't live in this building — so I had no rights to anything.

"Thank you very much," I let them feel I was slightly shaken, after listening to one of them retell Ehrenburg's memoirs. "What a fate. And you tell his story incredibly well. Everything comes to life. It's amazing how you remember it all."

"There's nothing incredible about it," the old woman answered with a satisfied, sandpapery chuckle. "We lived here."

"Indeed. How did his daughter die?"

"I just told you! Weren't you listening? It was a case of unrequited love."

Ah, yes, yes. I closed the notebook and clicked the cap back onto my pen, which visibly relaxed some of the muscles in the old women's necks and faces:

"Oh, you know, it is so hard for our generation to appreciate the way things were. There are so many conjectures, and so much defamation. If it weren't for enthusiasts like you… They say all kinds of things, you know — that the boy killed her and survived himself, or someone killed them both… And so many years have passed."

"Did Khmelnitsky tell you that?" The one who seemed to be the leader of the pack gave a nasty laugh. "There's a photo that I remember seeing: Lenin with the Congress delegates, and next to him is a man with a bandaged head — that's Khmelnitsky father. He was an idiot, and his son was a bigger idiot still. Yelizaveta Petrovna, tell him."

"He must've also told you that a man came to the school, talked to the kids, and the NKVD looked for him later and didn't find him," Yelizaveta Petrovna muttered. "It's all lies. The residents of the building wrote down what happened," and she plopped a folder of local newspaper clippings onto the table.

All sounds dropped away from me for a moment. Here it was: only in paper can we find material witnesses in Russia, not among the living. I touched the newsprint, and blood pounded in my fingers.

SCENE ON THE BRIDGE #1 (building resident):
"On that (*in fact on the next*) spring (*summer*) day Nina was supposed to fly to the USA" (*to Mexico*).

"Nina laughed at this request *(to stay)*, waved goodbye to the boy, and began to walk down the stairs. And that's when Volodya took a pistol out of his pocket and fired at Nina. Then he shot himself in the temple... Volodya died in hospital the next day."

SCENE ON THE BRIDGE #2 (building resident):
"'You're staying with me.'
'You're being stupid!'
'I won't let you go!'"

SCENE ON THE BRIDGE #3 (building resident):
"In high school, a tremulous, shy, all-consuming love arose between them. When her father was appointed to Mexico, Nina told Volodya about it.

'And you'll go?' he barely managed to say, unable to imagine the separation.

For two days *(actually, there were at least six weeks between Umansky's appointment and the family's planned departure date)* the boy tried to persuade Nina to stay, but she was unyielding. On the eve of her departure, Volodya called her and asked to meet on the Great Stone Bridge — their usual spot *(this is a bit hard to believe, lovers tend to prefer city squares and deserted lanes)*, both families lived nearby, in the famous House on the Embankment *(not true, the Shakhurins lived on Granovskogo Street, now Romanov Lane)*.

'We have to run away,' Volodya said. 'I've thought everything through, we'll go to the Urals or Siberia, I'll work at a military factory...'

'I'm not going to any Siberia,' Nina cut him off. 'This is nonsense. Tomorrow I'm flying to Mexico with my parents,' and turned away *(the authors use their imagination to explain why Shakhurin shot her in the back of the head)*. He whipped out his trophy Walter revolver and pulled the trigger. The shot rang out, and Nina fell down. He put the next bullet into his own head."

SCENE ON THE BRIDGE #4 (a writer, resident of the building):

"Many people thought that something tragic might happen (*why?*). Volodya was known to be an impulsive boy, capable of extremes." *(This is invented forty years later to add psychological subtlety. What else could you come up with after a fourteen-year-old boy shoots his class-mate?)*

SCENE ON THE BRIDGE #5 (another writer, an anti-Stalinist):

"Without saying a word, Volodya shakily began to unbutton his corduroy jacket. He yanked at his collar, and the top button went flying to the ground. He jerked a pistol out of his inner pocket, clumsily, and the polished coal-black steel of the muzzle gleamed in the sun.

'Look, it's a Walter! It's loaded. There's a bullet in the barrel. Unless you agree to stay, I swear, I will hurt you… right now.'

'You're crazy! Stop being an idiot! You're breaking my heart.'

'If you talk like that, I'll kill you!'

'Let's see if you can.'

'Stop, I'm telling you!' the boy shouted harshly, seeing that the girl had turned her back to him and begun walking away. She turned for a second, and in that instant a shot rang out. A neat hole appeared in the fabric of her red *(the hack chose the color intentionally)* jacket, just below her already-formed left breast *(just the time to point this out)*, and instantly turned maroon, almost black. The girl managed to look in surprise at the smoke coming out of the barrel, before collapsing on the stairs.

The boy took several abrupt steps down the stairs, kneeled down before her and stared into her open, lifeless eyes.

'Nina! Ninochka!' he dropped the gun, bent over her, grabbed her by the shoulders and shook her."

He dropped the gun and shook her. Holes in red jackets, twists of smoke coming out of the shining coal-black steel of gun barrels.

I stared at the clippings and thought about it all.

"When they were found, was the boy holding the pistol in his hand?" I asked. Realizing, after a beat, that I wasn't getting a reply, I looked up — but it was too late: the old ladies had already exchanged glances, and I could tell that they found this question inappropriate, unacceptable, and that by extension my person had also become unwelcome, as if I had brought up death, an alcoholic granddaughter, or incontinence.

"Was there anyone who actually saw what happened?"

But I no longer existed for them. A kettle had begun to boil and cabinets were being searched for cookies.

I reached for my jacket:

"Where are the children buried?"

"Shakhurin is at Novodevichy. Nina... She is too, I think? Yelizaveta Petrovna?"

"Umansky took the urn with Nina's ashes with him, straight from the crematorium to the airport, and they all crashed on the way to Mexico... Over the Atlantic Ocean."

"No, he crashed two years later."

"Oh, well, then, I don't know. I can't tell what you're after, first you ask about one thing, then another..."

"Baryshenkova and Galka Lozovskaya said that Shakhurin's mother, Sofia Mironova, buried the urn in Volodya's grave."

I did one more circuit of the exhibit, from the Primus stove to the stuffed eagle; one of the women limped behind me with necessary explanations, pushing me towards the exit like a bulldozer.

"And what is that?" I pointed at a tall hamper-like contraption.

"A radio. Umansky brought it from America," the woman said before delivering a last bit of information and squeezing me out the door:

"Khmelnitsky tells everyone that Umansky brought forty radios and gave them out to our generals," she said. "But don't you believe him. I'm not afraid of anything. I went through the entire war.

Someone killed those kids. And then they got away with it," and she slammed the door.

I stood there for a second, paralyzed, and then suddenly felt chilled to the bone. Shuddering with cold, I trudged through the snow and the depressing February gloom, across the Great Stone Bridge to the Borovitskaya metro station. I glanced back, once, at the former House of Government, 2 Serafimovicha Street — it was now topped with a spinning advertisement for Mercedes, a three-spoke wheel — but I didn't look at the stairs where Shakhurin reportedly said goodbye to Umansky. The old lady may have gone mad, but an old lady is not a material witness.

The worst thing that could happen to us would be for them to have found this self-destructive Romeo without the gun in his hand.

The first prioress of Novodevichy monastery, Elena Devochkina, was buried next to her two attendants. When the bell in the bell-tower strikes midnight, their gravestone slips to the side and the women rise from their coffins. They cast a longing glance at their home, the warmth of their long-gone beds in the nunnery, no longer visible to the common eye, and then they bow to the four sides, climb the monastery wall and walk it, keeping silent watch. You can tell the prioress by the gold cross that gleams on her chest, and her mantle is longer than those of her attendants.

This is said to occur on full-moon nights, but not every month. I'm sure the nuns used to rise from their graves more often in the days before there were three million cars in Moscow and before the city's residents began to believe they'd run into tentacled aliens from red planets in their potato patches, or photographed glowing orbs flying at eight times the speed of sound on haphazard trajectories.

The soil, the clay of Novodevichy (we'll stick with this accepted toponym for convenience; strictly speaking, the new, Soviet-era sections of the cemetery were seeded in the place of the ponds abutting the southern wall *outside* the monastery), is a suitable place for the ashes of the beautiful Nina Umanskaya. What is the story of the

Novodevichy Monastery if not the story of maidens, or rather the end of their corporeal stories.

The history of the monastery bears some similarity to that of the Great Stone Bridge — both were founded at about the same time and both flourished under Princess Sofia. For two centuries, widowed tsarinas and other unlucky princesses were sent to live in Novodevichy; Sofia herself did not avoid this fate. Peter the Great, suspecting his sister of sending seditious letters, hung the rebellious streltsy on the prongs of the monastery wall opposite her windows by the Tower above the Pond.

During Lenin's rule and then the Emperor's, they turned the monastery into the Museum of Women's Emancipation, plowed under the graves of three thousand erstwhile citizens whose various meritorious deeds had earned them the distinction of being buried here; a hundred remained, those who were ideologically sound or harmless.

The monastery's frescoes, especially those adorning the walls of the Smolensk Cathedral, are described by guidebooks as "affirming the idea of Moscow as the Third Rome," a medieval theory whose meaning I don't know.

THE OVERSEER

B Y THE GATES OF THE CEMETERY, NEXT TO THE SOUTHERN WALL of Novodevichy, I found a person selling plastic flowers, a drunk, self-appointed guide offering tours "to figure skaters and hockey players," as well as two Ukrainians with straw-colored hair, who were too stingy to pay twenty rubles for a map.

"Brother, where's Khrushchev's grave?" One of them asked me hopefully.

And beyond the gates, there were twenty-seven thousand graves.

I bought a map; the names were printed in a font too small to read even with a magnifying glass. The people I was looking for did not feature among the two hundred graves the map's publishers deemed to be of interest to the paying public. I positioned myself between the cashier and her source of daylight, and smiled a smile that even I found revolting.

The woman opened a safe and took out a thick book with a protective newspaper cover.

"P... R... S...," she leafed, "Sha...Shakhurin, here you go. The first section. From the gates, you walk along the central alley. Keep going along the first party row, till you hit the military alley. From there, all the way to the wall and back to the Comintern section, that's the area you're after. You'll have to walk around to find the grave. It is the grave you want, isn't it? Or an urn?"

"Actually," I said, "I'd like to buy something else. Like this book, for example. I'm not so much after a grave, as looking for someone who could tell me things."

The woman scribbled on a piece of paper and tossed it in my direction. There was a phone number and a name, Kipnis.

"Talk to him," she said, and sighed, eyeing the drunken guide wearily. "He'll tell you things."

My transaction with Solomon Kipnis was conducted in silence, accompanied only by gestures and changes in the expression of the eyes. He was pleased that I had cash ready and did not ask why his registry of interments was so expensive. A quiet, balding, mournfully sedate researcher of the Novodevichy Cemetery, Kipnis nodded to me in satisfaction in the hallway of his Khrushchev-era apartment in Sokolniki. Then he realized that this would not be the end of our interaction.

"You... Can I help you with something else?"

"I need a consultation."

"Come on in, then."

He led me to a study — a tiny room with about as much air as a mine shaft or a cell, and I saw I had interrupted him at work: a copy of *Tomorrow* newspaper was laid out on the desk. I glanced at the front page — it featured an official photograph of the Emperor (the only light-colored coat in the dark young broad-chested mass, sprinkled with medals), taken after the Victory reception, with his victorious marshals, generals and admirals — rows of terrifying, bewitching power. It's hard to believe now that such power existed.

"Incredible! Incredible!" Kipnis repeated, looking at the newspaper from behind my shoulder.

I turned my eyes to Solomon Yefimovich's knitted socks, with leather soles sewn on to them, and didn't know what to say. *Tomorrow* was known to have escalated the so-called Jewish question, taking positions that ranged from arcane geopolitical analysis to the passions of a communal kitchen.

"This photo features an incredible number of people buried at Novodevichy. I'm preparing a new edition of my monograph about the cemetery. I've already thought of a title, but I don't know whether it's quite appropriate: *Seven hectares of the Soviet era.* I think it's a good title. That's my opinion. And I have to take it into consideration. What did you want to know? You told me on the telephone that you were a relative of Konstantin Alexandrovich Umansky, didn't you?"

"Yes."

"Umansky's last surviving relatives died forty years ago, I worked on this matter."

I stumbled, but did not change tactics:

"I'm a second cousin once removed." We smiled at each other like wolves, with our mouths only. "Dmitry Kamyshan's my name. I came here from Lviv, in Ukraine."

"Ah, yes. I've heard about you," Kipnis cheered up readily and shuffled some notes on the table. "Weren't you the one who handed over the photographs of your uncle to the Kharkiv Holocaust Museum? You are a teacher, aren't you?"

"Precisely."

"You are seventy-five, according to my notes. You look younger… But here's what I don't understand: why the Holocaust museum? Do you really believe that your uncle was liquidated by the NKVD in connection with the Jewish committee?"

I had learned that Kipnis could hardly wait to retire, so that he could do his research into the Novodevichy graves without distraction; nothing else interested him. Even the government stepped back and allowed him to work his way to the dead; he feared nothing. Seated at his desk, he looked at me with the indifference of a professional, or a person living on a conquered mountain peak.

"I'm interested in what happened in June of 1943. Shakhurin and Nina Umanskaya."

"I am generally familiar with this story. The Shakhurins and Umanskys are buried at Novodevichy. What would you like to know?"

"The girl was killed on the third of June, in the afternoon. Her father and mother flew to Mexico on the fourth. So they did not attend the funeral. Who did? Where? Why was Nina cremated so quickly? There can hardly have been enough time to perform an autopsy on the body according to the required procedure. Shakhurin had not died yet, the investigation had just begun, but Nina was already cremated. Why was the girl even taken to the crematorium in the first place? What was the need to cremate her, if, of course, Umansky did not take the urn to Mexico as some sources suggest."

"Unless someone needed to hide something," Kipnis wheezed. "I dare say you have a unique perspective on this story."

"Some people… don't believe that the events on the bridge happened exactly the way everyone assumes they did."

"Who are you?"

There's always a point in a visit to a doctor, when he already knows what's wrong with you, but puts you through the motions anyway: squat and stretch your arms out in front of you, bend over and spread your buttocks, going down his checklist from A to Z, and you obediently continue to show him everything and reply with the excessive detail because you've been taught since you were little: you have to explain everything, otherwise the doctor won't be able to help you, and there's no one else you can rely on. Turn yourself inside out, hang out your dirty laundry — the doctor will choose what he needs to save you.

"Every event in the past has its observer. You are an observer of Novodevichy, for example. And we are the new observers of what happened on the bridge."

"I'll call you," said Kipnis.

And he also said:

"There is nothing unusual about the fact that she was cremated. Time changes the methods of burial. Today, there are three classes of burial at Novodevichy: an internment of the body in the ground; a cremation with the subsequent burial of the ashes in an existing grave, for family members; or a cremation and installation of the urn in the memorial wall. In the 30s, there was a campaign for wider use of cremation. There was even a Society for Advancing the Practice of Cremation and Construction of Crematoria. The society sent its inaugural membership cards to Stalin, Molotov and Kalinin. Leninists, old Bolsheviks, actually believed in the revolutionary ideal, and when they died, they wanted to uphold the new order of life with their death, and be buried without liturgies or prayers, without taking up space in the fertile earth. Everyone was cremated back then. Children too."

He spoke of death as if it were a quotidian subject, the way old Bolsheviks must've spoken about it, those steel-hearted people who did not consider the prospect of their individual absence on the planet a tragedy, who made their peace and saw a certain kind of justice in a change of generations and the removal of the burden they would pose on the future.

I left then, waited for Kipnis to call me, which he did, a day later. Vladimir Shakhurin, fifteen years old, was cremated immediately, on the fifth of June, and the death certificate was issued the next day so as to enable burial. Someone responsible for interring the lower ranks of the empire wrote on it: "Give orders to the director of the Novodevichy Cemetery to allocate a plot for the burial of Shakhurin's son, and allocate according to Shakhurin's wishes." Someone of yet lower rank added: "Next to Dimitrov's grave, with an area of five meters." That size of the plot meant that Mr. and Mrs. Shakhurin intended to have themselves buried with their son, and chose a decent neighbor as well, the seven-year-old Mitya Dimitrov, son of G. Dimitrov, activist of the international Communist movement, and his second wife. The boy had died not long before, and a cheerless statue made of dirty rock was placed over him: a skinny boy, with white knee socks, his hands placed on his knees, holding a cap. He had thin lips, sandals, and a handkerchief sticking out of the breast pocket of his shirt — there is no more frightening statue in the whole of Novodevichy cemetery.

Another day went by before Kipnis contacted me again:

"In the archive, a letter from Umansky's brother Dmitry was found. On the twenty-ninth of May, 1945, he appealed to the deputy Chairman of the Moscow City Council: 'I request that the urn containing Nina Umanskaya's ashes be buried where her parents are buried. A niche could be made under K. A. Umansky's grave marker to accommodate the urn.' A resolution follows: 'Create a niche as suggested.' It is curious that Dmitry asked to bury the girl specifically in her father's grave.

There's another form in the file, the record of the actual burial: 'Nina Umanskaya, 14 years old. Novodevichy Cemetery. 3rd of June, 1945.' She was buried on the day of her death, but exactly two years later. And a stamp from the Moscow crematorium. So it turns out she was not buried until after her father's death."

"Where was the urn for those two years?"

Kipnis replied indifferently:

"It's not stated in the documents. One more thing... I thought you might find it interesting to spend a whole day at the cemetery on the sixteenth of August."

"What for?"

"The sixteenth of August is Nina Umanskaya's birthday. They say that on her birthday, someone brings flowers to her grave. After all, it's been sixty years..."

"So?"

"This must mean something. I thought about it, there are no relatives," Kipnis spoke with effort, overcoming the pain of being separated from his safe paperwork and archival files. "Who else would do such a thing other than someone who loved her? Perhaps it's the person you are looking for."

I looked up the Don Cemetery and Crematorium — the phone book advertised available niches there, practically in the center of Moscow, for only eighty dollars — and asked a lady in a leather jacket the way to the crematorium. She told me, then muttered something, and I turned around.

"What?"

"Do you have any spare change?"

Here, at Don Cemetery, death is more frightening than at Novodevichy: there are low walls like fences, and everything, absolutely everything you see is covered in grave tiles, each with a portrait of the person buried underneath, a picture etched in the porcelain, so no two tiles are alike. Everywhere you go there are dates and little oval photographs, like mirrors, and they flash in the daylight, catching your eyes. I instinctively wanted to hustle through the macabre and crowded grounds, but I made myself walk, directly to the office, where a dozing, sexless creature roused herself at the sight of me.

"Have you come to do the bricking-up?"

She sniffed impassively at the thousand rubles that I, with all possible circumspection and tact attempted to offer her, before retrieving from an iron cupboard a registration book of human ashes with "1943" written in ink on the spine; she opened it to a page marked, "June."

"I really shouldn't be showing you anything."

And so I looked upside down at the thin, crooked letters: Nina was cremated on the 4th of June, the sixth of twenty-two people, number 4282; the crematorium worked around the clock, you could assume that the girl went into the oven in the morning, 16 or 18 hours after her death. Not all the proper paperwork was submitted, and a note clang to the margin: "Dr. concl.?" Vladimir Shakhurin was cremated the next day, #4310, with a certificate from the Krasnopresnensky registration office. Shakhurin's urn was picked up by his family for burial. Umansky's urn was not. So she did not go to Mexico.

"Where do the urns go that are not buried immediately?"

"They are held for collection."

"Like in a room or something?"

"In a designated area, yes."

"How long are they kept there?"

"Six months. If no one collects them, the ashes are emptied into a common grave. Into a ravine."

"And during the war?"

"In the war they were kept for two to three years. We started putting them in the common grave in '46."

That would've been after all the living returned to their dead. Two years… Nina Umanskaya's ashes were held among several thousand urns for two years, waiting to be collected — why? What were her parents waiting for? Their own death? A cemetery plot? Marble for a tombstone? Or did it not matter to them, since she was dead anyway?

Three years later, I saw a new edition of *Notes of a Necropolis Researcher* by Solomon Kipnis in a shop window, and bought it. I turned it over in my hands, and flipped through it, but couldn't quite put my finger on what was wrong with the thing; although everything seemed to be the way it had been in the earlier edition I had read before — the author photograph, with Kipnis smiling broadly, in a white shirt; the dedication, which read, "To the bright memory of Allochka, my never-to-be-forgotten wife, I dedicate this book" — but something nagged at me. I looked at the cover again and saw something new.

The artist had designed the cover to look like a tombstone — with bolts in the corners. Under Kipnis' happy photograph someone had placed the dates 1919-2001, and this changed everything. The researcher in the photo smiled as if finally everything were in perfect order, and he was where he was supposed to be, among his own people; he had become part of the world he had inhabited, his studies *here* were finished, and submitting to his passions with pleasure, he would continue to research things from *over there*.

SHAKHURIN: RESULTS OF EXTERNAL OBSERVATION

ALL OF SHAKHURIN'S DEPUTIES HAD LONG SINCE ROTTED IN THE ground, except one who was still breathing: the colonel-general Alexander Nikolayevich Ponomarev. It took me two months, but then, on a Tuesday in April, I dialed a US number and I lied to the woman who answered about who I was. But I told her the truth about what I needed.

"Do you know a Shakhurin?" I could hear the woman shout at someone, while she covered the receiver with one hand. I could also hear the din of television in the background, and a dog barking; the woman laughed, then spoke to me: "He'll be ninety-one in two weeks. I'm younger by sixteen and a half years. His daughter comes into his room, and he asks, who's that? I'll let you try it yourself."

I heard a senile, sleepy voice say "Hello?" tentatively, as if its owner was peeking into the phone surprised at the machine's existence, and I said dully, over the Pacific or the Atlantic:

"Shakhurin."

There was a wheeze: "I remember him."

"What do you remember?"

"It was a long time ago."

Another woman jumped in:

"What… Do you… Remember about him?"

"About whom?"

"Papa! About Shakhurin!"

"I remember Shakhurin. There was such a person."

I could hear the woman take over in the background. She shouted some more, and then reported tiredly:

"He says Shakhurin was a Minister. He came under some kind of investigation and died."

I thought she was going to tell me more, but then I heard the colonel, in the background, saying very clearly:

"When are we going to eat?" and I hung up.

The Museum of Zhukovsky Air Force Engineering Academy: I found two articles about the People's Commissar for Aviation Shakhurin in the Academy's widely circulated newspaper, and inquired about the author. Indeed, he was someone who'd known Shakhurin for sixty years, and — what a coincidence — died two weeks before my phone call.

The Aviation and Cosmonautics Museum: nothing, except a model of Sputnik, which Aleksei Ivanovich gave to the museum as a gift.

The War Veterans' Committee: nothing, no one remembers him, "We searched for a week."

The Manometer Factory veterans' organization: the Secretary of the party organization who had worked with Shakhurin when both men were young, died six months ago.

"I'll need to see a proof of identity, please."

A decrepit old lady with two warts on her cheek examined my passport and went off to look for the keys to the repository. I stayed out on the stairwell, looking through the barred window at the wet, short-lived autumn snow, already broken by tracks: I watched crows jump around rooting for something inside the drift, and two dogs, a white one and a ginger one, run past. I noticed a long time ago that whenever you look through a barred window, the world on the other side becomes big, indifferent and wonderful. You don't so much long for it — because you know it's unattainable — as you simply enjoy it, without having anything to do with it, the way you enjoy a whiff of smoke from a distant autumn bonfire, a girls' laughter in the next compartment on the train, or the sight of some boys chasing a ball on the football field.

After much scraping and clanging, the old woman got the safe unlocked and brought me everything that was left from the People's Commissar Shakhurin.

A knife, place of manufacture — Zlatoust; gilt, engraving, blackening. Date of manufacture: 1944. A gasoline lighter, metal, plastic, place of manufacture — unknown.

Photograph of Shakhurin in a white jacket, Moscow Students' Pedagogical Division, 40 Arbat Street. 1932.

Photograph of a woman with inscription: "To Dear Mom and Daddy, warm greetings from Yevpatoria. Sonya." Shakhurin's wife's name was Sonya. Stamp on the photograph: Studio of Genrikh Letichevsky. Tel. D 1-74-5. The date — 19 6/v 37 — written in green ink.

Sonya, Sofia Mironovna. Here's her registration card of Communist Party member #00034516. She died in April of 1977. Party documents canceled by the Zhdanov Regional Committee of the Communist Party.

Year of birth: 1908; nationality: Jewish. Native language — Russian. Member of the Komsomol since the age of fourteen; card-carrying Communist at eighteen. Went to work a weaving factory as soon as she turned sixteen and worked as a finisher, measurer and machine setter. She and Shakhurin most likely met while she was a student at the Engineering and Technical Academy. Then, fancy that, she was the director of weaving production at a penitentiary, and continued to run various sewing and tailoring establishments until she retired. She stopped working during the war — until her son died.

Ah, yes, the various princelings of the 1930s acquired Jewish wives as part of the package of other entitlements, a dacha, a car with a driver and a special telephone for direct connection with the Kremlin — people called these "whirligigs." Jewish women stood out somehow in the cultured demographic that had been thinned out by emigration. In our times, professional anti-Semites have compiled long tables of the Emperor's servants' marital choices, in which they matched up Bukharin, Molotov, Kirov, Kalinin, Rykov, Andreev, Poskrebyshev, Budyonny, Yakov Stalin and many more with Polina-Abramovnas, Anna-Mironovnas and Raisa-Iosifovnas (nee Zundelevich) and then added a layer of crisscrossed arrows on top: there weren't enough Jewish women, and some of them had tried on more than one surname from the People's Commissars' rosters. This, according to the charts' compilers, unmasks the intrigues of a "global Cabal." But the purges and executions right before the war swept the slate clean of Jewish names, and when the war began the Emperor introduced a fashion for round-faced and stupid Russian housewives, former nurses and waitresses of garrison canteens.

Aleksei Ivanovich Shakhurin occupied a position in the fourth rung of the imperial regime, next to equally important People's Commissars of key industries. Above him was the Party leadership (five to seven people); the second rung comprised the so-called marshals of the national economy (not more than 10 people), and finally, right at the top was the narrow circle of leadership: the Emperor himself, Molotov, Malenkov (at the time) and Lavrentiy Beria. Shakhurin's number in the pecking order of the Empire would've been between 25 and 50.

Umansky, on the other hand, was lucky to make the top three hundred.

Was Volodya Shakhurin aware of his position? And even if he was, did his home-grown hammer-and-sickle credentials mean much to a beautiful girl who grew up in Washington and wore nylon stockings?

As classification limits expired and the "top secret" seals peeled off and crumbled from the dusty cardboard folders, Shakhurin's life remained a combination of absolute transparency and absolute impenetrability. He gave his soul to the cause of the Communist party, spent his life building Communism on earth, called the Emperor Father until the day he died (even after he spent six years in a solitary cell because of the "aviators' case"), and did his duty to the Empire, which in return promised him *something* comparable to immortality. He gave it everything and almost did not exist.

It was this "almost" I had to work with.

The People's Commissar died on 3 July 1975.

No one even heard him mention his son.

I slammed my hand into the photo on the desk before me, right into the Commissar's sepia-colored, well-fed face: What is wrong with you? You could've shed a tear, at least once. Could've missed your unborn grandchildren. Could've muttered: ah, if only Volodya were alive… Could've said: it's my fault.

But Shakhurin was silent, like everyone else. And this silence could conceal anything at all.

Aleksei Shakhurin's father was a copper-smith from the village of Mikhailovskoe. The man was wounded twice in the First World War, and spent the rest of his life soldering copper pipes (while his son, the People's Commissar dined with the Emperor in the Kremlin) for aircraft hydraulic steering systems.

Aleksei went to work at the age of twelve as an apprentice of an electrical engineer at Zabludovsky's office, then was a hammerer and mill operator for three years at the Manometer factory (he liked to sing while he worked); then came the regional committee of the Komsomol, the engineering-economics institute, the Zhukovsky Academy (back in the days when the Petrovsky Palace, in which the Academy was located, was at the edge of Moscow), jobs at aviation factories, and then suddenly the post of the First Secretary of the Yaroslavl regional committee, and a year later, the Gorky regional committee.

Shakhurin joked once: "Wherever I went, it was always to replace a Kaganovich." At the Gorky regional committee, he replaced Yuly Kaganovich, and at the People's Commission for Aviation he took over from his brother Mikhail Kaganovich. The latter was known for calling the cockpit of a plane a "snout" and knew nothing about aviation. It was said, the Emperor was indignant: "What sort of People's Commissar is he? What does he understand about aviation?" Shakhurin took over at the time when the enthusiasm generated by the record-setting flights over the North Pole and the minor aviation successes of the beginning of the Spanish War has already waned and the doomsday predictions of "we are not ready" were beginning to be taken seriously. Contemporaries claimed that Stalin summoned the youngest of the Kaganovich brothers, Lazar, who was at the time in the top 25 and had earned the nickname of Iron Lazar for bringing the stubborn Ukrainian peasants into the Communist fold, and told him: "Your brother got involved with right-wingers."

"In that case, let him be tried and sentenced according to the law," the iron lips uttered. Or, you can choose to believe what 100-year-old Lazar wrote in his memoirs, which was: "I fought for Mikhail! I demanded a face-to-face confrontation! My brother built all the factories, Shakhurin had the industry served to him on a silver platter!" After the first interrogation, Mikhail Kaganovich, who was remembered for being noisy and for his taste in decorating his office, went out into the corridor, got a pistol and shot himself in the heart. The imperial aviation industry got a new Commissar. It was January 1940.

Aleksei Ivanovich, like Umansky, like twenty-five thousand of the best Russians of that time, was made from the same mold as Stalin's Falcons. One can imagine the details: a phone rings somewhere, a messenger comes running, the watchman's son gallops to the telegraph office on the village council mare, the voice of the orderly breaks — a telegram unfurls, you are summoned by comrade Stalin, could you come immediately? The plane flies over trembling lights, gravel crunches and flies out from under the wheels of the car, "all my life flashes before my eyes" — and *then* the calm morning face of the guard by the Spassky Tower, vague but obligatory; an unusually red-faced old man in the reception area (Comrade Poskrebyshev, Shakhurin would learn later), and the muffled voice of the god (few were bold enough in their descriptions to go beyond the size of the office and higher than the cut of the boots, so we have "a man of medium height," "a grey coat," a "lightweight gray suit of a military cut," "a tightly buttoned jacket," "soft black boots without heels, of the kind commonly worn by highlanders in the Caucasus." But every time, "In his left hand was a smoking pipe.")

Comrade, how do you feel about taking on this task we want to entrust to you, a very important mission. You are new to it, but we think…We will soon summon you, goodbye. The touch of a hand.

"I left Stalin as if in a dream."

And the chosen ones rose into the heavens — from lieutenant-colonels to marshals of artillery in three years, for example. For Shakhurin there would be negotiations, aircraft motors, lubrication for barrels, conscientious fighters, heroic workers of the rear, the justice of party bodies, the complete non-existence of a man by the name of Lavrentiy Beria (without whom, in fact, nothing took place in defense or science). And even if, during this breath-taking ascent, there was a gaping seven-year prison sentence, the loss of one's front teeth to the interrogation of one's cousins and brothers to the firing squad, all the losses would be buried without a trace under the immeasurable mass of gratitude for having been given a chance to do what few dream of doing. To make a difference.

No love. No kids and card games, parent-teacher meetings, soccer, movies, banquets (just the standard toast "To victory!" Every one of Stalin's Falcons wrote about the toast); no telegrams from the front and old women in burnt-down villages, devastation and cannibalism, no orphans of the fallen and executed comrades. They would never again raise their eyes from the furrow, they dissolved into in quotes from the classics of Marxism-Leninism, they basically turned, by the end of their careers, into the Program of the Communist Party of the Soviet Union, and then they departed, and looked drastically different laid out in their coffins. They just had time to whisper, in a few short moments while the crematorium oven doors slid shut, the most important things, for posterity — a few legends about the emperor: yes, he wronged me, yes, he stopped calling and summoning me, but in March of '46, he suddenly put a chair in the first row of marshals at a festive photo shoot in the Georgievsky Hall — and on this chair he silently placed me, with his own hand! — and what could be a higher honor than this? Farewell, comrades!

Shakhurin's silence was published in two editions under the title of *Wings of Victory*, with a print-run of one million copies, and only contained three instances of minor memoir theft and elderly forgetfulness. For example, the former People's Commissar took special pride in reducing the personnel turnover at aircraft factories.

Perhaps he had simply forgotten that on the first day of missed work, the worker did not receive his bread ration cards, and the next morning he would be summoned to the enlistment office and sent to the front in the first echelon.

The remaining four hundred pages can be conveniently reduced to four words: *number of planes manufactured*. By July 1941, the Union produced fifty planes every twenty-four hours. A year later at the Kremlin, the Emperor was showing Churchill his men: "This is our People's Commissar of Aviation Industries. He is responsible for supplying the front with military airplanes. And if he doesn't do it, we'll hang him," and the Emperor indicated a noose being tightened around the neck, and then pointed: look, the People's Commissar is laughing at the joke with the rest of us.

The People's Commissar, however, was laughing at something else entirely. I can see him, in an instant, thirty years later: he takes off his glasses and puts them aside, rubs his neck where it had been chafed by the invisible noose, takes a deep breath that lifts his coat heavy with medals, and seeing me at a considerable distance, says indifferently: "I count on the reader's ability to perceive, behind the individual sentences, a greater whole." Once you boil off the murky *numbers of planes manufactured*, the deposit reveals a well-preserved love for the Emperor: daily reports, invitations to dinners, calls at weekends, a nearby dacha, another one further from Moscow, a mention of the Emperor saying to other People's Commissioners, "Meetings with the young Shakhurin benefit me personally." (He said that about many people, and it made many people's heads spin). A certain desire to pose also shows through. In the third month of the war, Shakhurin received the Star of Hero of Socialist Labor #14), and an hour later, purposefully leaving the gold star pinned to his chest (and even after thirty years he did not cross out in his book the word "purposefully"), he dropped in on the Emperor — even though he knew Stalin despised awards of any kinds, knew the man loved his shabby felt boots and probably guessed he would die under a worn-out coat — and trembled with adoration, delighting in the Father's reprimand: "You just can't wait to hang this on yourself, can you? Maybe you want nothing but celebrations? Parties! And who's going to work?"

I began to think that Umansky and Shakhurin had more in common than merely men of the same age. They both met some sort of ending in January of 1945, these men of average height, who acquired paunches in their desk jobs and were known as Emperor's pets, these lovers of beauty and luxury (Shakhurin wrote of wearing a purple suit to the XVIII Congress of the Communist Party, with a white shirt and a fashionable tie) who aimed high and each had a single child they adored. And lost on the same day, June 3, 1943.

I put the two editions of *Wings of Victory* next to each other and compared them line by line. The first was published during Brezhnev's rule, when praising the emperor was already being allowed, but only sparingly and in passing, while the second was published during Gorbachev's times, after a generation of editors had died out (including the internal ones), and things reverted to their original shape. To my surprise, only a few lines had been taken away from the People's Commissar.

In the first edition, there was only a passing mention that his "family lived out of town," but in the second, Shakhurin wrote about his wife three times.

He did not choose to bestow a similar gift of immortality upon his son Vladimir.

So then, his wife. Sonya. Sofia Mironovna. She's the one to ask.

FATHER AND SON

GOLTSMAN GLANCED AT THE NAME AND WAITED FOR ME TO SPEAK FIRST. "One source told me that Sofia Shakhurin's maiden name was Vovsi and that she was the daughter of Professor Miron Vovsi from the Kremlin hospital. Professor Vovsi was one of the doctors in the eponymous case."

"That is not true at all," Goltsman responded. "Her maiden name was Lurrier."

He was quiet for a bit, collecting his thoughts, then spoke again:

"I think I have succeeded in securing for you an appointment with one of our... our veterans. He will see you tomorrow," Goltsman took a sip of his coffee, swallowed, exhausted with effort: whatever he had to do to secure this appointment must've been akin to rolling a boulder away from a cave. And who was now waiting for me there, among woodlice and roots, under the cave paintings of hunting lions and deer?

"It's been several years since he went out. He is not well. Bed-ridden. But his head is clear. Although he may get confused about dates. You'll have fifteen minutes. He's a big person, you can talk to him directly. Just ask him a couple of questions. But carefully. Don't go in with all your hyper theories about the NKVD blowing up Umansky's plane." Goltsman gave a lifeless smile. "I don't know whether he will help. He will only say what he considers necessary."

"Do you mean that he will consciously deceive me?"

Goltsman squinted at me in stern warning. Alexander Naumovich was convinced that our office was bugged. That, generally speaking, everything was bugged, and someone was constantly listening. I agreed with that.

"He'll tell you what he'll tell you. Your job is to remember. Then we'll try to sort it out together."

Goltsman gave me two small books, and a third one, bristling with green bookmarks.

"These are books about the Minister of Foreign Affairs of the Soviet Union, Andrei Gromyko, written by his son. Memoirs and remembrances. We won't have anything else. I planned to find and question Gromyko's widow before she died. But our sources told us that Lidia Dmitrievna had progressive dementia, so it was no good anyway. Then I tried to track down their daughter, through the Moscow State Institute for International Relations, her husband used to teach there, but he died a long time ago. The daughter wouldn't talk to me directly, but she let me know, through someone else, that Gromyko had a good opinion of Umansky."

I checked the bookmarked pages. Andrei Gromyko, known to the enemies of the empire as the Great Mute and Mister No, was a PhD candidate in agricultural sciences by the age of thirty. In the spring of 1939, when the People's Commissar Maxim Litvinov was sent to relax at his dacha under house arrest while his team went off to their various early retirements, middling jobs and/or prison cells (with the single very significant exception of Konstantin Umansky), Gromyko made his breathtaking leap into the American section of the People's Committee of Foreign Affairs (without speaking any English and with only the experience of supervising a few teachers at a village school). Six months later he boarded the Italian flagship Rex to accompany Umansky to the Embassy in Washington — to do what? To help him? To keep an eye on him? To replace him?

All mentions of Umansky in the younger Gromyko's two-volume memoirs were cryptic, obscure; they could've confirmed almost any suspicion.

"The Ambassador of the USSR to the USA, Umansky, was

summoned to Moscow, evidently having failed to meet the expectations of the center." (*And what do you think, fifty years later, with access to all the archives? Why can't you just spit it out?*)

"As I understood later (*When? Under what circumstances? Why?*), there were complaints about him from Stalin and from Molotov both (*Why draw this distinction?*). And although Umansky went back to the US, from all appearances it was clear that his days there were numbered." (*Gromyko was the one who was supposed to replace Umansky, he was to be the Ambassador, but the war suddenly resurrected Litvinov — and Gromyko had to sit there and keep an eye on Litvinov for another two years, hating him the whole time, and when Litvinov was recalled and his turn finally came, President Roosevelt wrote to the Emperor: "Uncle Joe! Would you care to explain why you have replaced your Ambassador with a mailbox?" In blue pencil in the margin, the emperor wrote a satisfied "Ha!"*)

"The Washington establishment evinced a rather cautious attitude towards Umansky." (*Why? How did this manifest itself?*)

"The American press spread personal rumors about the Ambassador. Initially I thought that this was the consequence of a grudge borne by someone at the State Department." (*And later? What did you find out? It had to have been something big if you still won't talk about it!*)

Gromyko's son, Anatoly, reported hearing from someone that Umansky was smart, but lacked interpersonal skills. "In Washington," he wrote, "it was taken almost as a truism that the Ambassador was an NKVD general."

"Where is this son?" I asked Goltsman.

"He's the Director of the Institute of Africa," he answered. "Spends most of his time in Cyprus. He may visit Moscow in a couple of months. Only he was very young back then, just seven years old, younger than Nina Umanskaya — what can he remember?"

All people remember things, but only some have to answer for them.

I sighed in surprise and murmured to myself: *Palazzo.* The Institute of Africa had somehow come to occupy the Tarasov House on the corner of Bolshoi Patriarshy Lane and Spiridonovka Street. Built by Ivan Zholtovsky, the thing was a Renaissance revival masterpiece, *a la* Palladio's Palazzo Tiene in Vicenza.

I held the word, *palazzo*, lifeless and clicking, on my tongue as I looked at the building's the narrow windows, its heavy masonry. It was a gloomy, weather-beaten house. None of the southern sun that must've washed the original. Only the storms.

Anatoly Gromyko for a long time harbored the illusion that our meeting was impossible, but he overestimated his ability to avoid it.

The Institute's reception room featured stained-glass windows depicting the Virgin Mary with a dark-skinned baby, an Arab with a torch, and a half-naked black man with a Shpagin sub-machine gun. Glass cases around the room exhibited hats, slippers, rugs and a musical instrument that looked like a grenade launcher. I flipped through the books on the coffee table (*Economics of Developed Socialism, Algeria's National Liberation Front, Africa at War*), glanced into the inner courtyard where, in complete silence, snow was falling, burying the fountain and the dead strands of ivy. I finally came to stare at the cavernous fireplace. Who occupied this room in the Tarasov House originally, I wondered.

When I was finally ushered in to speak with Andrei Gromyko, son the former minister, he said, "I can give you fifteen minutes. I understand the fact of meeting with me is more important for you than what I might say."

He breathed the smell of old age at me from across his desk. He was jowly and boring, and talked as if he were blind, with his eyes closed, and with a dramatic flutter of fingers near his temple whenever he pretended to be retrieving a memory.

Behind him stood fringed drums and a pestle, black with age, in a mortar. He told me:

"We lived in the Ambassador's apartment on 16th Street, next to a school. Six rooms: three bedrooms, a reception hall, a large lobby… The Americans lived very well, and my father and I went to the movies every week. Have you read my book about the problems of the new mind-set? I'd give you a copy, but I don't have any. Go to the Institute of International Relations, it's at the kiosk there, go and buy it, and be sure to read it.

"My father came to the Commissariat at a time, you know yourself, when there were big changes going on. Umansky would come to visit us at the apartment on Chkalova Street, he'd put me on his lap, his wife followed him everywhere, like… like a duck following a drake. Father respected Umansky. And Umansky respected him. I can't remember if Umansky spoke English... But I do remember that my father couldn't stand Litvinov, and the feeling was mutual."

"And Nina?" I prompted him.

He remembered her, had a vivid recollection of her at an Embassy reception — they were having a lot of fun, they sat next to each other, she chatted. She generally liked to draw attention to herself.

"Years later, when we were teenagers, we found out that the son of some military man, a general, shot her out of jealousy. This was the first time I had experienced such a terrible thing, when someone I knew was killed.

"My parents always said some sort of dark fate hung over the Umansky family. Fate. That was their word — never mind that Father was a convinced materialist and believed in Marxism as a living, creative teaching."

"If I may, just one more question — you wrote that the Americans said Umansky was from the NKVD."

"I doubt there's any truth to that. I'd rather not talk about it. When we became diplomats, we swore an oath. Perhaps some people may find this amusing, but I still believe that I should not do any harm to my country."

I turned away in frustration, and made for the door, but Gromyko hurried after me, chattering incoherently, leaping from topic to topic: "The normalization of relations with China was spoiled by ideological aspirations, you know. And if only the Communist Party had permitted factions in the 1960s. In Sweden, for instance, there are no poor people, but in the USA there are such ghettos! Though, of course, the past shouldn't be judged by the standards of today; history isn't a railroad, after all…"

I backed out of the office, gulping for air, and sighed to the secretary:

"A complete waste of time."

She replied calmly:

"And what did you expect?"

Again everyone's asleep, and I cannot sleep. I've been lying here for a long time, just feeling my body, checking it, like a car, or a boat — touching the cool hull, listening to the water splash and mutter beneath… I'd like to see a doctor, if I could find the right one — not a specialist, but the kind who can explain everything, in general. A good doctor. I'd tell him things. For example, I confuse words. Yesterday, I meant to say "pelmeni" — you know, dumplings, — and instead I said "meatballs." My speech feels somehow — how to put it? — estranged from my mind, slippery: the tongue chooses the words by itself, as if I'm not there, as if I can't keep thinking about what I'm saying, it's too much. Sometimes, out of the corner of my eye I see little sparks on things, pinpricks of light — and then they disappear if I turn to look. I think my hearing is getting worse… My grandfather lost his hearing. My father too. I've had a trauma to the cervical spine and have a restricted range of motion. They suggested surgery, but I refused: it was too expensive, and they wanted to bolt two titanium plates into my neck. I don't trust chiropractors either. Someone told me I should swim, a backstroke could do wonders. But I can't find the time! I have nine crowns on my teeth — I try to have them checked regularly. I wear contact lenses. Last year, for the first time, I got seasonal allergies — nothing ever bothered me before. I have mitral valve prolapse. And a cyst in my right kidney. And, you know, I forget a lot of things — at the end of the day I couldn't tell you what I thought about.

Sometimes, I get a pain at the back of my head, on the left side. Especially during sex, it's the cervical spine trauma, there must be a problem with the blood flow. Even in winter. My great-grandfather died of pneumonia: they stopped at an inn, but there was no room, a whole wedding party took over the building, so he spent the night on the dirt floor. I won't take pills. I tried bath salts. I am athletic. Lots of aerobic exercise. A healthy sexual life. I never let myself be stressed, I don't work full-time, I'm focusing on taking care of myself. It's too late for me to have a family. Children need a normal family, and I can't provide that.

I only want to sleep, the way I slept when I was little, waking and dozing off again in the morning, while it rained outside, or snowed, or with the sun warming my bed... I want to remember what it was like not to jump up the second the light hit you. Not to know that I'm falling apart.

THE DACHA RESIDENT

A WOMAN WHO LOOKED LIKE A FOREIGNER LED ME THROUGH THE HOUSE: "As long as I'm coming in with you, I'll take him his medicine." She carried a tray with vials and cups, and reminded me with mild disapproval that I was not to talk for long — as few questions as possible! I followed her through the lived-in dacha without really noticing anything; I was distracted by the tension of lying to get in and by the relief that my lies, about who I was, how I found her, and so on, had been accepted.

"Sit here," she instructed as she bent over the great master. A monotonous susurration of bird voices wafted from the forest outside the window, while here, in the room, drops were being counted out, a particular yellow capsule was being searched for, hands covered with bruises moved feebly, and the spoon did its duty, eliciting a bubbling and clucking from the old man's throat, all of these ministrations completed by the dab of a napkin, and I kept thinking, *and now the woman will move aside and I'll say...*

In secret from Goltsman, I spent all night memorizing the photographs and the names that were supposed to stay dead and obscure, but came to light: Commissars of state security, department heads, office and section directors, residents. Sometime during the reign of Nikita Khrushchev, when their ten-year jail sentences "for assisting Beria" were about to run out, they all penned long supplications and pleas to be allowed, in light of their long records of service to the country (we did liquidate Trotsky... and what about the A-bomb we saw through to completion?), to meet their swiftly-approaching deaths at home. The pleas came with single-spaced histories of incurable, debilitating diseases, copies of blood work results and cardiograms, and they all got out. The men went on to live different lives for the next half century, and, avoiding writers and fuss, watched from their sunrooms and balconies as magpies and squirrels frolicked in their backyards.

"Fifteen minutes. Categorically!" And the woman disappeared, stationing herself behind my back.

The master, an armless heap of gray blankets, contemplated the April-crazed forest; his bluish lips seemed to crawl over each other like a pair of earthworms until I realized he was smiling.

I looked at the trees, along with him, just in case. The old man had meaty ears, squashed flat into a mass of mossy gray hair; his skin was bruised, chewed up, his nose covered in tiny blue veins. I had no hope of identifying him as one of the men in last night's set of photographs.

I chose to speak clearly, but not to raise my voice.

"Konstantin Umansky. Have you personally met him? "

"Once. I called on Beria, he was sitting there… He had just returned from America, right after Pearl Harbor."

He spoke with a dandified distinctness, not turning his head to look at me, enjoying the forgotten sense of his own power. I knew he was lying: Umansky returned from America long before the attack on Pearl Harbor.

"Umansky suggested we dissolve the Comintern and let up with the pressure on the Church. Then the Americans would help. We did as he advised."

"Did he work for the NKVD?"

The question wasn't nearly enough to get him off the track — I was listening to a record:

"Since the time he worked at the wire service. The Americans intercepted our cables. Operation Venona — have you heard about that? Umansky was the Editor."

This was not entirely accurate. Although the Americans did succeed in intercepting and decoding thousands of cables by the GRU

Intelligence, the naval intelligence, and the People's Commissariat for Foreign Affairs about operation Venona, they did not begin to accomplish this until after Umansky's ashes had been buried in Novodevichy for two years.

"He wasn't really a diplomat in the proper sense of the word. He was recalled to prevent him from irritating people... He was used in complex cases. Accomplished much. He established contact with Harry Hopkins." — *Who are you then?! Barkovsky? Pavlov? Mukasei? "Zefir"?* — "He worked on the Czechs... With Beneš. But the biggest operation of all — that was Mexico. After Teheran... we suddenly became a world power! And Mexico — it's the bridge to Latin America. All the money went through him... He had unprecedented success in recruiting agents. He often went to the States... Constantly humiliated Gromyko. He simply mocked him."

Suddenly he fell silent, as if realizing that he was talking too quickly, and would not fill up the allotted time. I also found myself at a loss, and had to think of something to break the dangerous silence:

"How did he die?"

"His plane exploded during take-off. An air"— he was having more difficulty speaking — "craft accident."

"The residency section in Mexico was headed by Lev Vasilevsky. I was told that he was an expert in sabotage. And after Umansky's death he was immediately recalled and promoted, to the position of the head of military and technical intelligence."

"Well, you certainly make it sound... No, it wasn't him. Lev requested permission to fly with Umansky on the same plane. He was refused..." The old man sounded surprised, but was determined to continue speaking deliberately; he went on: "Lev did not succeed in Mexico. The Americans detected him. He was responsible for the release of Mercader... the one who liquidated Trotsky... And he failed. He had a short window of opportunity to give a very large bribe to an official... who was responsible for pardons... And he missed it. And then there was a complaint about him from our Embassy in Washington, and from Mexico..." the master squinted disapprovingly and swallowed.

"He got used to living extravagantly back in Paris — cars, mansions… And in this, he and Umansky had a full understanding. They were friends. In personal reports to Merkulov they praised each other."

"Who is this Dashkevich?" I asked, casually, but the old man kept silent. I tried another tack:

"Did you meet Vasilevsky later? Did he talk about Umansky?"

"Well, he drank in public places. He wasn't hiding… He talked about Umansky's death."

"Why?"

"He liked to remember things. That's all."

The master strained his neck and tried to look somewhere above me. A small, tough hand jabbed into my back: my time was up.

"What do you know about the circumstances of the death of Umansky's daughter?" I said quickly and got up to leave, compelled by a snakelike hissing in my ear. The old man, falling asleep, whispered faintly:

"Yes, yes… The general prosecu… Bochkov was removed… He wanted to hush… Shakhurin's case… compromised… a huge number…"

And with this he fell asleep, his swollen eyelids slipped shut and stayed together.

"What's so *special* about it? Children, so what. Unrequited love!" I shouted, as I was pushed away from the sunroom and scolded, "What do you think you're doing? Look how you've upset him! We had an agreement!"

I was escorted out by another route, past the bronze bust in the hall, past the moose horns, I walked a damp black path back to the gates, got into the car and took out my squawking phone. It was Goltsman.

"Yes. I just left. I think I got something: he mentioned a man named Dashkevich. But I didn't understand anything, I didn't understand where he was lying!"

I was fuming; I was convinced the old man was covering up for Vasilevsky. Only when I got on to Rublyovka, driving away, cooling down, did I realize what he had tried to wheeze to me in reply to my last question:

"Love had nothing to do with it."

Lev Vasilevsky, Colonel, of age with Umansky, resident agent in Paris, commander of a special-ops group in Spain, he was in charge of illegal agents who followed the American atomic project. He did his job in the guise of the First Secretary of the Soviet Embassy, a Mr. Tarasov. Through a chain of happy coincidences, he avoided both execution and prison. For him, one of the best operatives of the Empire, "connections with Beria" meant a mere exclusion from the Communist Party. After rehabilitation, he became a writer, the author of fifty or so books. He also translated my favorite book as a child, *Captain Blood: His Odyssey* (together with Gorsky, former resident in London).

Why is it that after prisons and demotions for "serious violations of socialist law," after Khrushchev's insane lay-offs, despised by all government forces, the secret guards of the Emperor were able to slip themselves like noiseless underwater monsters into screenplay writing, editorships at the International Book Press, and jobs translating adventure novels? Were the grayish typewriter keys the only territory that could accommodate and reward their gifts of shape-shifting, their insight into human motivation, their ability to suggest? Suddenly, through the flickering of pines and birches at the side of the road, I saw a fleeing shadow — Dashkevich! Dashkevich was a stubborn beast with a vague position at *Foreign Literature*. Tomorrow Dashkevich would have to be intercepted. At midday, at his office, as soon as he dragged himself to his desk.

The phone rang again.

"Your suspicion has been confirmed," Goltsman said. "I've got a mention in *Harpers* from August 1944: 'Soviet overtures to Latin America'. I'm reading: 'The division of the USSR wire service in Mexico, with its enormous staff, is led by Yuri Dashkevich, who for fifteen years of his journalistic career has been in contact with the secret agents of the Unified State Political Directorate in different countries.' That's him."

In the morning I would have his address. I would have a man posted outside his door; I'd have Dashkevich followed to his editorial offices and meet him there.

There was one more thing I had to do. I dialed the number.

"I'm so happy you called," Alyona said when she answered.

"Alyona, I'll have some work for you tomorrow morning. Between ten and twelve. Bring your Welfare Center ID."

"Another old geezer? I'm so sick of it… They never remember anything."

"It's been fifty-six years since Nina Umanskaya's murder. What do you expect? I'm not even forty and I don't remember what people said when I was twenty. And they didn't pay attention. Never mind, if they want to lie, that's fine — we'll work with anything."

The trouble, I thought, was that we couldn't find anyone who was close when they found the bodies. How were they positioned, what did they look like?

"Would you like me to come over? I can fix something to eat," Alyona offered, interrupting my thoughts.

"No, really, I've already eaten. Just come."

She had probably gone out on the balcony, away from her sleeping husband and their child, and lit up a cigarette, to talk and watch the traffic on Frunzenskaya below. She wouldn't want to sleep now; this kind of thing was what she lived for. I heard her sigh, delighting in her power:

"I can't do it like that. I don't want to be just the next in line."

I found the TV remote and pressed the fifth button: CSKA vs Saturn, a rerun, in the middle of the second half, already 1:0.

"There isn't anyone else. You know that I don't love anyone but you," I sat down at the computer, clicking my way to some adult website or other: someone named Lidia was scarfing some sort of paté, showing her flabby flank. Scrawny, red-haired Yelena hugged a teddy bear to her non-existent breasts. Moronic looking Kristina had smeared her fat round breasts with thick foam that resembled shaving cream.

"Alyona, I can give you so little. But I want to tell you, when I think about you I'm not afraid of anything. It's so wonderful that you're on this Earth."

Alyona laughed, as if holding back tears:

"What are you saying, stupid… You gave me the whole world. You're the best thing I have, even if I don't have you. I don't need anything in return."

Angela: "I like to fuck. And you? Press here to find out." Sixteen photos.

"I really want you to be happy," I said into the phone.

"Sasha," Alyona exhaled and paused in her speech, sighed sadly. "I can see you're just looking for love. Someone hurt you, scared you a long time ago, and you decided that love does not exist. But it does. I live by it, I breathe it. Even if there is only one person on Earth who loves you like I do, to the end, this is already a great happiness. And I love you so… I lock myself in the bathroom, turn on the water and cry because I'm happy you exist. And because I can't stand not being with you. I will always love you, as long as I breathe. Even if you never call me and invite me to visit you again. And you forget my name. You'll dream of me. I'll protect you. Are you tired of me?"

Photo 9. Angela sitting up straight, with her legs spread to show off her black lace undies.

"What are you saying? You're the only woman I want to see next to me every day, always, and hear at every moment… But I'm afraid they've missed you at home… Go and sleep, baby…"

Photo 10. Angela on her side, holding her breasts in her hands. Six more photos. Is she ever taking off the undies?

"Good night, my love."

"Good night."

SONYA

Whenever I had a free moment to stare out the open window, to observe the cottonwood fluff ball up on my desk, I would feel a stab of anxiety and fear: for a while, at night, before I fell asleep I'd been sensing something beyond the surface of the investigation. There was something else hidden behind the teenage murder-suicide on the Great Stone Bridge, something dark, large, and rock-solid that sat in our path and forced us to dig around it. I told myself it was just the fact of a different time and different people's lives, but in the bright June nights, I couldn't shake off the sickening apprehension. There was a reason no one wanted to remember this very romantic story, not a single person agreed to help, no one spoke directly.

Best-case scenario, I thought, washing fresh cherries in a blue bowl, this "something" is a thread. We'll have to find it anyway; we have to know what connects the monk Filaret, builder of the Great Stone Bridge, to Ambassador Umansky's downed airplane. Without the connection, the Authority would not approve our trip back.

Solomon Sandler, the Deputy People's Commissar for Aviation Industries logistics, looking into the fifty-year distance, recalled: after prison, Shakhurin wrote a document about his descent into hell. Everyone who read it burst into tears. The document was taken by his five brothers.

Two of them were still alive, Viktor and Sergei.

Sergei Ivanovich, at least on paper, sounded like a perfect target: he was the youngest in the family (thus not yet senile), taught at the Moscow Aviation Institute (not a peon), and lived with the People's Commissar's family at the time of the tragedy (had to have witnessed everything). He picked up the phone when I called him at his apartment at the Patriarch Ponds and listened: I asked for a meeting, there was reason to believe that Volodya Shakhurin was not guilty of Nina's death, and we were prepared to help to assert historical justice.

I paused and braced for the blow of his long-hidden pain, for the burden of what had gone fifty years unsaid to tear open his soul. Instead, Sergei Shakhurin said merely:

"Have you read Aleksei Shakhurin's *Wings of Victory*? It's good that Aleksei Ivanovich is remembered. Could you leave me your telephone number? I'll talk to my brother and call you back."

And then he didn't call. I could not imagine what I'd done wrong, and after a month I dialed him again. He recognized me, remembered our conversation, and wrote down my number again.

"Have you read Aleksei Ivanovich's book?" he asked again. "Everything is written there. And go to the Museum of the Great Patriotic War on Poklonnaya Hill, everything is there, you'll see, you won't need me. I don't feel well."

What about Sofia Mironovna? Volodya? The manuscripts of the People's Commissar? Did Aleksei Ivanovich love his son? Did Nina ever come to the apartment?

The youngest brother was no longer listening, a dial-tone droned at me disdainfully, and I suddenly realized that I had done something, spooked something: my probing and poking has dislodged a glacier that was now sliding and crashing — the brothers, like gnomes, had hidden in their burrows, swallowed the key to the mountain, and hoped to die before we could pry them out. They would keep silent, and silence would save them, as it saved many in the years of the Emperor.

I waited almost two months, and then in mid-August arranged for Sergei Shakhurin to get a call from a young writer at *The Moscow*

Komsomol newspaper, a stammering, seventeen-year-old intern: *Everyone is muck-raking through our past, but our great history... heroes like your brother... I want to write about Aleksei Ivanovich... a whole page... when should I come by, we can select photographs together, and is it true that...*

The old man wrote down her work and home phone numbers and crawled off to consult with his brother. A couple of weeks later the girl followed up: well then? I've already read so much about the remarkable leader of the defense industry... She was advised to study *Wings of Victory* and visit the museum on Poklonnaya Hill — all the predictable directives. And a few weeks later: he wasn't feeling well, she was asked not to call again.

I let six months go by, one hundred and eighty days, enough to have everything be forgotten, lost in the routine of elderly worries and the management of benefits and rent receipts. The phone rang again and Sergei Ivanovich heard the nasal, unhurried voice of a PhD candidate from the scientific research center on the history of aviation in the city of Zhukovsky, who had just finished a draft of his dissertation about the unique logistical challenges of relocating industrial facilities to the Volga region and Siberia in 1941 — *And, as you understand, the central figure of the work is the People's Commissar... as an example of a highly effective... whose contribution to the victory is still insufficiently appreciated... and of course, to avoid any minor, stupid inaccuracies, you, Sergei Ivanovich, as a scientist yourself, must appreciate the effort... and if you could find just ten minutes to skim through the work, at least the key points... I know* Wings of Victory *practically by heart and had my photograph taken by the stand with Aleksei Ivanovich's medals at the museum on Poklonnaya Hill... So when could I see you?*

A month later Sergei Shakhurin responded: never, he said. His health was terrible.

I moped and sorted my soldiers, the latest acquisition: horsemen from the fifties, manufacturer unknown. I had a banner carrier and a horseman with a saber, but I was missing another horseman with a banner; I'd read that there were supposed to be three figures in the set.

When I first got them, I thought they were Bulgarians or something, their Cossack hats confused me, and I almost sold them. I smelled the metallic dust they left on my fingers.

They were a set, a caste… Perhaps one of his own should talk to Sergei Ivanovich — a test pilot, a non-fiction writer, a hero like Mark Gallai.

I sent Alyona, in her guise as *The Moscow Komsomol* reporter. She took a box of chocolates with her, but she wasn't even offered tea. Gallai was sympathetic, and called the Shakhurins, but could only shrug when they refused to see him.

"They've always been like that. Don't ask me why. I'm sorry I can't help you."

Alyona begged, desperate:

"Do you know if it's true what they said, that Shakhurin's wife was flown around on a strategic bomber?"

"Shakhurin's wife," Gallai said through his teeth, "was a common Jew."

A year later, we found an elderly nephew of the brothers, and he agreed to meet at a metro station, after asking a dozen times on the phone: "How will I recognize you?" I handed him a very nice letter and a list of flattering, trivial questions: What songs did Aleksei Ivanovich like? How did he celebrate his birthdays? How did he feel about soccer? What about hockey? Nothing threatening whatsoever, please tell your uncles there's nothing to be afraid of. I worked hard to make him like me, I had shaved for the meeting, I promised him undying gratitude, and said it was all for a sacred cause; if they didn't want to meet, then perhaps they could write. Three weeks later the nephew called back: No, they don't want to. Why? They didn't say. Just no.

The records of the Novodevichy Cemetery showed that the Sofia Mironovna Shakhurin's (nee Lurrier) parents were reunited there for all eternity when the remains of Yelena Abramovna Lurrier (nee Berezina) and six more people were moved from Dorogomilov Jewish

Cemetery to the grave of Miron Ionovich Lurrier (lumber trader, later a civil servant), who died at the age of ninety-two.

I went through the list of kin, and found a Nelly Iosifovna Abramovich, who informed me:

"Sofia Mironovna's father was from a family of Bryansk lumber traders. I'm Sofia Mironovna's cousin, our mothers were sisters.

"My mother wanted to learn so much that she managed to get taught by the rabbi, although Jews only teach boys. At the age of twelve she left home to study further; she got a job as a cleaning lady at a school, lived in a room with rats in it, but she studied. After the revolution, she was elected as the head of the local Komsomol organization, and at sixteen she married my father, the then twenty-five-year-old Iosif Abramovich, who had fought in the Civil War. Dad worked at the Merchant Navy Research and Innovation institute of the navy, until he was arrested. Mom stood up for him at the Party meeting. I can vouch for my husband, she insisted — and the next day she disappeared herself. They got ten years each.

"The two of us girls, seven and ten, were left with our grandfather and old nanny.

"No one would take us in, everyone was scared.

I had a wayward aunt — Rozalia, nicknamed Barefoot. She had gone through the Civil War as a nurse, married a telegraph operator, and given birth to twins, but the babies died. Everyone already thought of her as the woman with a ruined life, so she took us, adding our beds to her miniscule room, with her schizophrenic husband who sat all day by the window and repeated, 'Quiet... do you hear? They're coming for me!'

"In the prison camp, Mom rose to the position of the head of the planning department and increased the productivity of prison labor. Her success at this enterprise earned stunned praise from a government auditor, and she used the occasion to convey a clever petition to the top, thus becoming part of the meager wave of pre-war rehabilitations. Daddy came back first, though, at the end of '39, after two heart attacks. Mom, for the rest of her life, would dream of a sixteen-year-old boy in the camp who one day started to sing "The night is bright beyond the river" at work — the sentry killed him with one shot.

"Aleksei Ivanovich Shakhurin didn't like her recollections, and would laugh at her, saying, 'You just can't get past it, can you?'

"Our parents never mentioned the camp in our presence. When I hugged my father after his return, it was scary: inside him, when he breathed, something wheezed, gurgled and whistled, like the bellows of a ruined accordion.

"It was after my parents returned from the camps that cousin Sonya and Lesha Shakhurin appeared in our lives. They got the Kremlin medical genius Miron Vovsi to look at Dad, and I remember Dr. Vovsi said, 'He has nothing to keep him alive.' My father lived for another four years on the first floor in a building at Patriarch Ponds, he suffered terribly from seeing bars on his windows every day, and then he died — the fourth heart attack finished him.

"Sofia Mironovna worked in the sewing industry Bureau of the Supreme Soviet of the National Economy. She was thin, but after she gave birth, she put on weight, and couldn't keep it off after that."

"Nelli Iosifovna," I ventured, "I heard it said that Sofia Mironovna's appearance irked people. The way she dressed, and such... I haven't been told good things about her."

A mild-mannered woman, Nelli Iosifovna Abramovich gave me a suddenly stern look:

"People shouldn't judge her for standing out! That's the way she was. Why should a beautiful woman hide herself away? Why should she be afraid? She tried to live naturally and openly. And everyone dressed up back then. Marfa Peshkova wore luxurious gray lambskin. Did Ashken Mikoyan dress modestly? Women are just very envious...

"Her son, Volodya, was a special boy, I can't imagine him as an adult. He was good at languages, and in Kuibyshev, where they were evacuated from Moscow, he would just walk up to diplomats so he could practice his English. He visited the famous Ruben Ibarruri in hospital — Ibarruri was being treated for an arm wound — and heard him sing Spanish gypsy songs. He immediately got excited about learning Spanish. He bought a dictionary and wrote down a hundred words every day, and demanded that Nell (he called me Nell) test him, and so I quizzed him like a slave.

"He stuttered whenever he was excited.

"Nina Umanskaya was quite ordinary. And she wore glasses! She had ash-colored hair. But Volodya was thrilled by the fact that she spoke a foreign language very well.

"On *that* evening, the housekeeper Dusya called, saying: Volodya's in a bad way, he's at the First City Hospital. Mom and I ran out on to the Garden Ring Road, jumped into the middle of the street and stopped a trolley bus to take us to the hospital.

"We found Volodya in a very high bed in an empty ward. His head was wrapped in layers of bandages, a huge white cap. He was breathing. The doctors said that if he didn't regain conscious soon, that would be the end. Shakhurin, dark in the face, and grief-stricken Sofia Mironovna were right there. They were devastated, but, you know, families like theirs, at the time — people didn't open up. No one said, I love you.

"Then I saw Volodya in his coffin, and I kept thinking that any minute he would get up and say: Wasn't that a great prank I pulled on you?

"After Aleksei Ivanovich was arrested, Sofia Mironovna moved in to live with her childless brother Iona at the Clear Ponds. She put together care packages, and Aleksei Ivanovich's brother Sergei — the one you called, wasn't he? — took them.

"Aleksei Ivanovich came back gray-haired, but he looked quite healthy.

"The first chance she got, Mom asked him, pertly: 'Well, Lyosha, now it's your turn: will you ever be able to get over *that*?'

"There were two things he never mentioned: his son and prison. Only once, when he went to visit his niece in the infectious diseases section of the Kuntsevo hospital, and saw a square, jail-like window for food and medicine in the door of her ward, did he look away and moan softly to himself in anguish."

THE ONE WHO SAW EVERYTHING

I couldn't sleep. I thought about Dashkevich. I thought about Umansky. About what I should ask. Out of what Ehrenburg had written about Konstantin Umansky, two things remained unclear. According to Ehrenburg, Umansky sacrificed his personal happiness for the sake of Nina's peace of mind, and stayed with the family. But why, twenty years later, did Ehrenburg not name the object of Umansky's affection? Who was she? Is it possible she was a married woman? And a party member to boot? Still, Ehrenburg could have said *something*, he could have written, for instance, that Umansky 'fell insanely in love with an extraordinary green-eyed woman he met by chance at the summer terrace of the Vakhtangov Theater cafe where he used to meet his actor friends'... But there was nothing.

And the second thing. The broken-hearted Umansky reminded Ehrenburg from Mexico: you gave me good advice, and I didn't make use of it — now I wish I had. Does this mean that the advice, if followed, could have saved Nina from a bullet? But Ehrenburg exclaimed (if he wasn't lying): What did I advise him? I don't remember!

The man I posted outside Dashkevich's apartment, Boris, reported at noon that Dashkevich still hadn't left the building. At the editorial office of *Foreign Literature*, we found out that the old man had called and asked for the day off. He wasn't feeling well.

I couldn't wait any longer. I got ready and rushed off to prove the inevitability of fate.

Borya, wearing new glasses that looked cheap, as usual, walked along Verkhnaya Pervomaiskaya in the uniform of a police major, and, getting fully into the role of a district cop, unsettled the old women selling bunches of carrots and herbs on the sidewalk.

"The old man hasn't come out," Borya reported. "Our man is fixing the elevator on his floor. Alyona's here, but she's just sitting in her car. She told me to leave her the fuck alone. I think she may be crying in there."

I exhaled the smelly air, and quickly walked up to the building door, fully in view of Alyona's car.

Alyona opened the car door, shook her head in negation and shouted something unclear over the roar of traffic, something like: come here, I can't. We have to.

"What do we have to?" I shouted back.

"Talk!"

"We'll talk later!"

She climbed out of the car, closed the door, and remained there, glowering: hug me, please.

"What's with you, PMS?" I hissed, grabbing her and dragging her to the entrance by the arm, inside, the building, where the lobby floor was strewn with advertising pamphlets, past the flabbergasted owners of poodles and the young mothers with strollers. She grabbed at the mail boxes and wailed through a mucus-blocked throat:

"Why can't you talk to me? Don't you care *what's* wrong with me?"

"Alyona, stop it, all right? Sixth floor. Apartment sixty-nine. Yuri Dashkevich. You're from the social welfare center, did you remember the ID? Something about discounted medicine, coupons for free haircuts, it won't take long…"

"Why are we doing this?" She tripped, maybe on purpose, but it was stupid to try to walk in those heels anyway, I felt like hitting her made-up face! "You never explain anything directly! I'm *nobody* to you!"

"We'll talk later, not now! You'll drink some tea, fifteen minutes, and then Mirgorodsky will ring the doorbell. Your task is to make sure Dashkevich opens the door. Don't leave immediately, so he'll feel safer, I'll tell you when you can go."

"I can't do this anymore!"

I dragged her to the fire stairs, away from the elevators.

"Alright, what? What's this? What's happened?" I shook her a little. She whimpered and struggled in my grip. "OK, then. I'm sorry. I didn't sleep well, I know I can get intense on the job. That's it. Forgive me."

"I'm not going!"

"Alyona," I hugged her and brushed my lips on the back of her scented neck. "This is something very important for us. This person may know why Umansky's plane exploded. He may know about Nina. The Umanskys left the day after her death, and they could only have talked about who killed her in Mexico. Dashkevich is the only person we have left who served with them in Mexico, everyone else is dead."

"I don't want to do this anymore."

"And if he tried to avoid us, then that means he knows something. I beg you."

She tore herself away and neatly backed into a corner where tramps had made a home, dutifully baring her whitened teeth, the way women scowl in soap operas.

"Why are we doing this?"

"We want to know who killed Nina Umanskaya."

"Why?"

"Does it really make a difference, right this minute?"

"Yes, it does. Who do we work for?"

"The Kremlin," I said, cringing as I felt my heart sink. Now was not the time, everything was so wrong.

"You should know something. I'm only doing all of this for you and because I love you. It's very difficult for me. I wanted to go pick up photographs to make scans, from that old man from the Urals. His daughter opened the door screaming: after your talk he had a heart attack. He's in intensive care… And she cried so hard. She called me such names…"

"That's just a coincidence. The man's ninety-two years old. "

"I knew that. But you sent me there to ask him questions we knew he wouldn't like. So I asked. He felt worse right away, he asked me, let's leave it at that for today, come back another time. But I knew he wouldn't ever agree to see me again, so I kept asking. He was alone, his daughter went to the store. He was defenseless."

I glanced over her shoulder to where Borya stood waiting. Time was running out.

"I want you to know: love exists," she poked me in the right pectoral. "You are a very kind person, you love people, you're just hiding it."

She wiped her face and pulled out her make up to repair the damage.

"Shall I go now?" she asked.

I called Borya:

"She's on her way up. We're on."

I loitered by the elevators affecting a great interest in the drifts of home-made flyers on the noticeboard. An old lady entered and turned her back to me in fright, concluding on the spot that I was going to strangle her. Mirgorodsky lumbered in after that, blotting the sweaty forelock squished under his uniform cap:

"What she's doing, the idiot?!"

"She's just in a bad mood," I looked at my watch. "It's alright, I calmed her down."

"What the hell do you mean, you calmed her down?" Borya yelled. "I got a call: she's coming down!"

I had given her an order: fifteen minutes!

"They opened the door for her, and she went in," I could hear Borya sputtering into the phone. "And then she came back out. The idiot! She blew it! She's dressed like a prostitute, who would believe she's a social worker! They'll call the police any minute…"

I caught up with Alyona, her scrawny back. Would I grieve if tomorrow she was hit by a train? No. Would she cry if I bought it tomorrow? Yes, heavily and briefly.

"Don't worry, this is OK, it's all my fault. I should have thought of a signal, in case..." She slowed down and was turning around to see me. "Was he not at home?" I asked. And then shouted: "You should have found a way! Fifteen minutes! I told you how badly I needed this."

"Dashkevich died. An hour and a half ago. I've got to go, it's my turn to pick up Seryozhka from school. Call me in the evening."

I turned and looked again at the building on Verkhnaya Pervomaiskaya — the wind brought the smell of medicine and the sound of worn-out lamentations. We were too late. Someone else got here first. Dashkevich knew something. I turned to leave, but the building tugged at me, called out to me the way lost or misplaced things stay with you. What wouldn't I give to find a door with the plaque 'Collection of Abandoned Things' — one that would open into a room full of everything I had lost: the wrist-watch with the engraving "From the Chief of the military transportation command," the toy hammer found one year under the Christmas Tree, the twenty kopeks earned at the renovation of Grandfather Ukolov house, the little cross Mom wore around her neck... It got lost, the little cross, and that's when it all began — my life slipping away from me. *That* can't be helped, of course.

Borya and I sat at the bus stop on a rainy day with the serene detachment of vagabonds with no money for a fare. Finally Mirgorodsky said:

"As part of the death certification process, you know, we questioned Dashkevich's neighbors, and relatives. There is no archive. He didn't leave any memoirs. He didn't write anything."

"You didn't even have to ask."

"At the office someone overheard him talking to the scientist Sergo Mikoyan. The son of the famous Mikoyan. Mikoyan begged him: write down everything you know, don't carry it inside you. Abakumov and Merkulov have already been shot. They aren't here anymore. Dashkevich, of course, didn't write anything. But — I checked — Mikoyan is in charge of Latin America. In fact, he studied the career of our target, Konstantin."

We saw Goltsman hurrying towards us across the grass, almost tripping over himself, blushing youthfully, his gray hair disheveled in the wind.

"We found a witness. He saw them when they were dead."

A 1996 issue of the *Teachers' Newspaper* carried a tired retelling of the love between Shakhurin and Umansky with an unnecessary addition, so pointless that it was mysterious: the son of the People's Commissar for Social Welfare Lev Shaburov saw the dead Nina being carried away from the scene of the crime.

Within two days we had Shaburov's address and a telephone number. Shaburov hadn't had a chance to die yet, but informed the investigation weakly that he remembered nothing. Eventually, he gave in before the inevitability of fate. He hesitated for a long time about where to meet, not wishing to bring a stranger into his home. In the courtyard, he said finally.

I brushed my teeth before the hunt and thought: why should he remember that day? Weather? Her hair? The cop's face? It was fifty nine years ago. A lifetime ago. What do I remember, for example, about my first love? Well, I, if I tried, could remember everything. But this was not his first love.

He was waiting by the arch of a yellowish building, Leninsky Avenue 11, and looked at me fearfully. Neat shirt tucked into ironed pants. Clean brown shoes. Grey hair brushed back.

"Where's your car?" he asked.

I didn't have a car and told him so. We were stuck. He had tried to plan for this unknown moment, which is easier, makes you feel safer. But he'd probably spent the whole night on this one plan: first he would show me where to park in the courtyard, and then…

Now, though, I didn't have a car, and whatever he had intended next vanished from his mind. I gave him a gentle shove and led him by the archway past the smoking saleswomen from the Jeep shop, and the doors of a wedding fashion atelier; he shuffled before me in resignation, and I looked at the back of his head, at the putrid red spots, at his flabby, gnarled hands — mine would be the same one day.

People were walking their retrievers around the kiosks; the noise of Leninsky Avenue was left outside' three identically pot-bellied female municipal workers were watering the lawn.

"How did you find me?"

For some reason everyone finds this interesting. No one believes that one day it will happen to them.

"I couldn't sleep after our conversation," he said — I had called him a 9 pm — "and my whole life flashed before my eyes." I'm sure it did, I thought to myself. That's what we were there for.

To help him relax, I asked about his parents — who, from where? A shaking voice labored to sketch out a story of a blond woman, who in '38, a highly significant year, blazed an upward path through the central council of trade unions, and a lesser commission to become the deputy of the merciless Shkiryatov in the Party Control Committee. His father, on the other hand, managed the Vegetable Seed Trust; at the age of fifty-five he was drafted to be the commissar of an artillery division, and died of his wounds in Spas-Deminsk in the Kaluga Region. The man's hands started shaking, out of habit he squeezed them between his knees, he started to mix up names.

What did you see with your own eyes?

"I wasn't alone. I remember someone came running, shouting: Shakhurin and Umansky have been killed!" *He said: killed. So no one actually saw the moment of the shot, so the first people who came running up did not see a weapon in the hand of the suicidal boy.*

"Everyone started running. There were people standing on the bridge. And below, on the sidewalk as well. No one was allowed onto the landing on the stairs where the bodies were. Nina was lying face down" — *you looked from above, from the bridge?* — "right on the stairs" — *so she was shot when she was walking down the stairs or trying to run* — "and her dress was bunched up pretty far. I thought: what fat legs she has." *His hands were now shaking uncontrollably.* "There was a policeman standing on the landing. During the war there was always a policeman on duty under the bridge… I remember how fat Nina's legs were. But she was beautiful. Petrovsky's daughter was also beautiful. Tsurko was a beautiful girl, I once visited her at home. Smushkevich's daughter was the most fashionable, what was her name?"

"Roza," I prompted.

"Exactly! What was I talking about? Erka Kuznetsova, when she heard that Shakhurin didn't make it, said: bastard, he had it coming."

"So they didn't find the pistol in his hand, did they," I observed casually, as if this were something tedious and unimportant. I waited long enough for a silent confirmation, then decided just to go ahead and jump into the damned black hole, feet first. "Volodya and Nina weren't on the bridge alone, after all," I said. "There was also a third."

Shaburov tried to keep silent, then tired, and said, trying to grin at his own fear:

"So you know about that, too."

"Who was it?"

He swallowed, sniveled and blinked.

CLOUDS

I TRIED TO APPROACH THE CASE FROM ANOTHER DIRECTION. IT WAS clear that no one liked the charming Ambassador in the USA. There was a reason the Umansky family ended up in Moscow. And perhaps this, and not teenage love, was the reason Nina Umanskaya was killed.

I kept sketching clouds.

In the first cloud I wrote: "The third person on the bridge, people know about him, but are afraid to name him."

In another I wrote: "The third person: no one saw him on the bridge, but many know that he was there."

In the next: "What was he doing there? Was he with them? Or was this someone they meant to meet? " I crossed it all out. Why did he take away the weapon? If he was the one who pulled the trigger, why did he throw away the Walter, instead of putting it in Volodya's hand? If he was a witness, why did he not leave it where he must've found it — in Shakhurin's hand?

Boris Shtein, born in 1901, in Zaporozhye, graduated from the Petersburg Polytechnic Institute, spoke five languages, served the Empire in the People's Commissariat for Foreign Affairs, and was one of Litvinov's men, his Ambassador to Italy. When Litvinov fell out of favor, Shtein was recalled, but spared. We found his daughter living in the Profsoyuznaya district.

"Umansky was very handsome. He had those green eyes... He had two passions. One was women. I don't understand why he ever married Raisa. He had mistresses… The ballerina Lepeshinsksya, and many others. His daughter Nina was the apple of his eye, the *raison d'etre* of that family. A captivating girl. She resembled Kostya, but had something from Raisa as well. She had Raisa's large mouth, which looked out of place on the mother, but only added to Nina's charm. Kostya came to us after his daughter died: I was scared to look at him, he cried so terribly and cursed himself."

"He cursed himself?"

"Bitterly. And Raisa practically went mad after her daughter was killed."

"Inna Borisovna, why did he behave so provocatively in America?"

Stein's daughter, after some thought, replied with a truth that had not previously been revealed to me:

"Was that really his choice? Kostya knew only one way to be: he was the man the Party and Stalin wanted him to be. You know, my father, after he came back from Finland, was received by Stalin, and for the first and only time in his life, Stalin shook his hand. I wouldn't let him wash that hand for three days. Father wasn't naïve; he understood everything about our life, but he didn't explain it to me — he wanted to protect me. You should've seen the way he cried when Stalin died. Mom was incensed: how could he mourn a tyrant? Dad said: I'm mourning my ideals."

"You said that Umansky had two passions. What was the other one?"

"A passion for supreme power."

"Really?"

"Kostya was very particular. I studied at a lyceum in Italy, but in Moscow, Dad sent me to a regular school. But Umansky wanted useful contacts, and he knew he could get them through his daughter. He felt that he was on the rise, he wanted promotions, new posts… So he got Nina into *that school.* Although Ehrenburg told him, Kostya, don't do it. And Umansky later wept when he visited us: why didn't I listen?"

It was this advice that could have saved Nina Umanskaya, but Ehrenburg didn't remember it twenty years later.

"A passion for supreme power?" Goltsman asked, in the small gray room he occupied to the left of the reception in our office suite. His desk was covered with bound newspapers, clippings and folders with reports and photographs. "What kind of special school was this?"

"School #175 on Staropimenovsky Lane. It's still there today. Do you want to go there?"

"I'd like to look into a few things about Umansky first. Then America."

This is what it would look like:

Boots stomp on the floorboards. The escort knocks, sticks his head in — May I? — and brings in Umansky, steering him forcefully by the elbow. Umansky's head is thrown back, he can't see anything in the darkness that surrounds him. The guard steers him to a chair, prompting:

"More to the left, one step forward," and lowering him down onto a stool: "Let's sit down calmly. Sit calmly."

Umansky's brown eyes stare unblinking into the void. He sits hunched over, not finding a back on the chair; he is short, frail, with round glasses. He licks his lips now and then and bares his gold teeth in a tired grimace; he shifts to change his position and place his manacled hands more comfortably in his lap. He was allowed to keep a large cap on his head. The white corner of a handkerchief shows out of the breast pocket of his suit coat.

"I was born on the fourteenth of May, 1902, in Nikolayev, in the family of a machine-building engineer who worked for the Izoskov firm. Father: Alexander Alexandrovich Umansky. Mother: Teresa Abramovna Golshtern. The family moved to Moscow in 1907, and six years later my father died. After my father's death our family was very poor (he has to show he belongs to the proletariat somehow), *and I went to work as a tutor. I graduated from an eight-grade gymnasium and I studied for a year at the department of foreign relations at university.*

"My political views were formed when I was fifteen, when I joined peace agitators after the February revolution. My first job was as a dispatcher at the garage of the Peoples' Committee for Military and Naval Affairs (Trotsky's department, a good place to meet the right people). *Then*

I served as the secretary to the Head of the Press Center. At that time, as I had a sound command of foreign languages, I was detailed by the Central Committee to the Executive Bureau of the Comintern, and at the end of 1919 I was sent on a clandestine mission to Munich. (Immediately after the fall of the Bavarian Republic? Sounds unlikely. Was Kostya making this up, perhaps, to protect his CV from someone who couldn't forgive him his foreign suits?) *Following orders from the Austrian Central Committee, I opened the news agency ROSTA-Vienna to report on the Polish war* (Now, that's more like it)*, and in 1922 I replaced Comrade Mikhail Koltsov as the head of the Information Bureau of the People's Committee for Foreign Affairs.*

"*After I returned to Moscow, I wanted to study and was accepted into the History department of the Institute of Red Professorship, but I was seriously ill for a long time* (meaning, you took things easy). *I fell behind in my studies and ultimately went back to practical work, in the vain hope of pursuing my degree part-time.*

"*I was the interpreter and note-taker for Comrade Stalin's conversations with Emil Ludwig (1931), H.G. Wells and Roy Howard (1936).*"

"*Who recommended you for membership in the Communist Party?*"

"*Leonid Stark and Comrade Malkin.*"

He utters the second name casually, a toss-off. Stark is an old Bolshevik, Deputy People's Commissar for the Postal Service and Telegraph, Yesenin's protector. He served as a diplomat in Estonia, and then for twelve years in Afghanistan, and secretly represented the Comintern in the northern provinces of India; he was remembered for his difficult character and for pursuing personal goals in official service. Stark was shot in 1938, but who is this Malkin…Perhaps Boris Malkin, the head of the Central Press, another old Bolshevik, from Lenin's inner circle, and also a protector of Yesenin, but particularly of Mayakovski; did Kostya work as a secretary for Malkin?

"*Marital status: Married. Wife: Raisa Mikhailovna Sheinina, the daughter of Mikhail Aaronovich Sheinin, once the manager of Mondl's Dress and Haberdashery, and the peasant Alexandra Leontievna Lavrova, who died in childbirth.*

"*We met in Vienna; owing to her mother's death, Mikhail Aaronovich*

УМАНСКИЙ КОНСТАНТИН АЛЕКСАНДРОВИЧ.

Родился в 1902 году в г. Николаеве, еврей, из служащих, член ВКП/б/ с 1919 года, п/б № 0616451, образование имеет н/высшее, окончил 8-ми классную гимназию и учился один год в МГУ /отделение Внешних сношений/. Знает английский, немецкий, французский, слабее итальянский и испанский языки.

В 1925 году вынесено партвзыскание "выговор" за неуплату членских взносов втечение 4-х месяцев.

Работа в прошлом:

1918 г. П-IУ   - нарядчик в гараже Наркомата по Военным и Морским Делам, г. Москва.

1918 г. У-IХ   - инструктор в отделе распространения произведений печати Издательства ВЦИК"а, гор.Москва.

1918-1919 г.г.- секретарь заведующего "Центропечатью" ВЦИК"а, гор. Москва.

1919 год   - редактор газеты "Искусство" Наркомпроса, г. Москва.

1919-1921 г.г.- подпольная работа в Австрии и Германии /г.г. Вена, Мюнхен/.

1921-1922 г.г.- корреспондент РОСТА, г.Вена.

1922 год   - зав. информбюро НКИД, гор. Москва.

1922-1925 г.г.- зав. редакцией исходящей иностранной информации ТАСС, гор. Москва.

1925-1926 г.г.- корреспондент ТАСС в Риме.

1926-1928 г.г.- врио зав.иноТАСС, гор. Москва.

1928-1930 г.г.- зав. парижским отделением ТАСС и корреспондент ТАСС, г.Женева.

1931-1936 г.г.- заместитель заведующего, затем заведующий отделом печати НКИД, гор. Москва.

1936-1941 г.г.- советник Посольства, Поверенный в делах, затем Посол СССР в США.

1941-1943 г.г.- член коллегии НКИД, гор. Москва.

1943г.по н/вр.- Посол СССР в Мексике.

см. на об.

Был в следующих странах /кроме перечисленных в перечне рабо ты/:

В 1924 году - в Турции /сопровождал дипкурьера/

В 1928 году - в Кенигсберге /спец.корреспондент ТАСС на польско-литовской конференции/.

1932-1933 г. - в Турции, Швейцарии и США /сопровождал тов. Литвинова/.

Мать и родня по материнской линии находятся с 90-х годов в Австрии.

Жена тов.Уманского до 19.. года была австрийской подданной состояла в австрийском консуле и компартии до 1924 года. В настоящее время беспартийная.

Брат т.Уманского Леонид проживает в США и работает в фирме "Дженераль Электрик" инженером.

Справка составлена по материалам личного дела.

ОТВ.РЕФЕРЕНТ ОТДЕЛА
КАДРОВ

/Туманцев/

1/УI-43г.
ТЗ.

sent his daughter to be raised by her aunt, Maria Lenskaya in Austria. When she turned sixteen, Raisa went to work at the office of a chocolate factory; after we got married, she got a position at the Russian legation in Vienna."

"Do you have relatives abroad?"

"I have a half-brother from my father's first marriage, Leonid Umansky. He is about fifty years old, he left for America in 1915 to the city of (unclear). I am not in contact with him."

"Your wife told the investigation that your mother died in 1940."

"That is not exactly the case. I lost track of my mother. If she is alive, she would be about sixty-five now. My mother moved to Austria to live with her relatives who settled there before the Russo-Japanese war. I do not have any contact with her. I don't even know her address." (And her fate as a Jewish woman in the Third Reich doesn't worry you?).

"My residences in Moscow: the Hotel Lux (A visiting American remembered: "We sat on the floor in a stuffy room at the Hotel Lux, drank, played jazz and passed the time in other immoral ways"), *Tverskaya, 13 for six years; then Khoromny Lane, 2/6; then for two years Spiridonovka, 17, and then until 1942 I lived at the Moscow Hotel* (Why doesn't he mention the House of Government?).

"I have one daughter, Nina.

"I have been warned about the liability for giving false and incorrect information."

"You may go now. We will call you in when we need to."

Why wasn't Umansky allowed to stay in the US? Who blew him up in Mexico, him, such a harmless and by all accounts insubstantial character? In the Soviet intelligence reports, the United States was called The Country and Mexico, The Village. Maxim Litvinov was referred to as Grandpa. Umansky's code-name remains unknown.

Before the war, Moscow's hand touched the States only lightly, exploring but not seizing, not trying to clench the entire continent in its fist and hold on to it. Moscow had no need yet for nuclear secrets or targets for saboteurs in the planned third world war; intelligence officers disdained conspiracy, and the agents they recruited often saw no reason to hide their sympathies for the Empire. It was not until the mid-1940s that, as one Lubyanka chronicler neatly put it, "the era of permissiveness came to an end."

Kostya became an irritant to the Roosevelt administration. Why? Because of his childish meetings with labor leaders like Lee Pressman, the lawyer who joined the Communist Party at Harold Ware's invitation? ("Umansky," someone cabled, "took his usual precautions in 'shaking off the tail'; he persisted in his comical belief that his activities would warrant the attention of his host country's agencies.") His efforts to help defectors? Only two or three actually made it. Alexander Krivitsky, a military intelligence officer (aka Samuil Ginzburg, aka Walter, aka Groll), fled the purges of 1937 to the West and promptly gave up a hundred Soviet agents, including the cryptologist known as The Magus. Then he wrote a book called *I was Stalin's Agent*, from which everyone learned that Krivitsky and Umansky had known each other since they were boys; that Kostya had shirked the draft ("Why waste two years in the barracks?"), and that he tried to gain favors by eaves-dropping on his colleagues' conversation at the Hotel Lux for the benefit of the Joint State Political Directorate. According to Krivitsky, Umansky was "numbered among the few communists who have been able to get past the barbed wire that separates the former party of Bolsheviks from the new party. He has been very successful in this." Krivitsky himself was found dead on the 8th of February at the Belleview Hotel, and evidently this was supposed to be considered suicide brought on by a nervous breakdown.

A bit later, another colonel showed up State-side, with wife and daughter in tow — Aleksandr Orlov (also Feldbin, Nikolsky, or Swede), a genius at recruiting agents, author of the canonical textbook on the subject and the godfather of the Cambridge Five. As the Soviet resident in Spain, Orlov made sure the Spanish republic's gold was transferred to the Empire; girls shot themselves out of desperate love outside his windows. One July afternoon, a Soviet ship moored in a Spanish port, and Orlov was invited on board for a casual talk with the head of the foreign department of the NKVD. Orlov, whose son-in-law had already been arrested in the Empire, realized: it was death coming for him on that ship, so, like a fairy-tale character, he disappeared, with his daughter and wife, plus $60,000 of his operational funds. He, however, was alone among the Soviet defectors in managing not to end up with a nervous breakdown and a bullet to the head. Instead, after landing in the States, Orlov sent a personal note to the Emperor and the not-yet-executed People's Commissar Yezhov: if you don't look for me and if you leave my mother alone, I won't blow any agents' cover, and no documents about our Spanish dealings will ever see the light of day.

The emperor crumpled up Orlov's letter and said: Ah, don't touch that scum.

And the Cambridge Five did their work and shocked England by fleeing to Moscow.

Orlov lived quietly until 1973, changing names and residences in small Midwestern towns where every newcomer sticks out like a sore thumb. But with amazing regularity (and very often after the war), random American passers-by would suddenly address him in Russian: Well, how are you then? Living OK? Settled down? Well, God bless, keep on living for now… But remember what you promised. We remember everything. As should you.

Of course, Kostya had to play a part in the disposition of Lev Trotsky, that Soviet Judas. First, the imperial force pushed Trotsky out of Norway to the backwaters of Mexico, a country much given to left-wing upheavals. Then, almost immediately upon Trotsky's arrival, Mexico received from the Soviet government an offer to be part of a very lucrative joint oil business in exchange for sending the outcast further in the direction of the South Pole. When the Mexicans didn't take the bait, Lev Davidovich's journey through the crematorium of the Dolores Pantheon into the earth of his own vegetable garden became inescapable. One of the Emperor's best operatives, Nahum Eitingon, arrived in New York, where he headed an export-import establishment during the day and built a network of American and Mexican agents to carry out Operation Duck in the shadows. Five months later the duck quacked, Trotsky's room was riddled with bullets from machine guns through the door, but the man saved himself by hiding under the bed. Another five months later, Ramon Mercader killed Trotsky with an icepick and was thrown in a Mexican jail cell without windows, having identified himself as Frank Jackson, a Canadian businessman. He was beaten twice daily; photos in the newspapers showed him washing the floors in the cell. Mercader kept silent for twenty years; our people did everything to get him out, everything that Kostya could do.

The war and the A-bomb changed everything: the new resident agent in the USA received instructions from the Emperor personally. There were agents of influence, organized into four different networks, a base for Vasilevsky's infiltrators in Mexico, eight employees of Roosevelt's administration working for Soviet intelligence. But none of this any longer concerned Umansky, who was sailing and flying, by a long and circuitous route, avoiding German submarines in the Atlantic, to Moscow, wondering for how long he would be moored there and probably ruing his own coquettish request to Molotov: "I have been in the US for three years without leaving. If only I could have a chance to renew my contact with Soviet life again, for the shortest time, by a fast boat, without any delays in Europe, to receive your instructions, and arrange a number of practical matters…"

And then it was September '41, he was called back for *review*, and he was returning to renew his contact with Soviet life indeed, not knowing whether this would mean the barrel of a revolver coming into contact with the back of his head.

This was how I worked my way back, trying to read between the lines of what we turned up, turning things over in my mind. I realized I couldn't find a mention of Umansky's wife and daughter where it was supposed to be; when he was recalled in September of 1941, he returned alone. There was a note from October 2nd, about a conference at which Umansky was explaining to the leaders of our propaganda how important it was to raise the Jewish topic while the Germans were closing in on Moscow, and military drivers ran over people in the streets in the unfamiliar darkness of the black-out. In November he was received in Beria's office, and in December Ehrenburg visited Umansky at his bachelor pad at the Moscow hotel — but no one wrote anything about the wife and daughter. But if they didn't come back with him in September, does that mean that it wasn't Umansky who brought the girl under the barrel of the gun, and that someone else was to blame for her death? I had to check the enrollment records at the school; all these recollections of her being there "at the start of war" and "in the middle of the school year" may have been just old peoples' delusions and lies...

For an instant, a wave of joyful apprehension washed over me, and then retreated: somewhere ahead, I could almost see a silhouette, an outline of an as-yet unknown, but very real culprit, and I would find him very soon. It was he who sent Raisa and Nina to Moscow. Gromyko? Litvinov? Someone else entirely? I tried not to guess.

LIBRARY DAY

AT THE HISTORICAL LIBRARY, GRAY-HAIRED INTELLECTUALS WALKED about in baggy jeans that looked as if they had been stolen from their children, with sweaters sticking out from under their jackets; short-sighted catchers of obscure trivia bent close over rust-colored newspaper bindings; foreigners staring into flashing laptops got the materials they requested delivered obsequiously to their desks; female graduate students sipped from bottles of water, and with a rustle got apples out of plastic wrappers.

For observation, I selected a red-haired young woman in high heels, in a short checkered skirt, wide as a shepherd's hat. The skirt bounced as she walked, and she walked back and forth constantly, the buckles of her boots clicking. The girl moved a bit awkwardly, as if she did not wear heels very often and they changed her gait and made her slump to compensate for the considerable weight of her behind. Her hips swung like windscreen wipers — they were clearing her path, knocking aside invisible passers-by who might stand in her way, and they spread widely inside her skirt whenever she sat down next to a shapeless, large, bespectacled fellow with curly hair and a face you could never shave clean. She nuzzled him and kissed his ear, and hugged him tightly, squinting in response to my gaze. The poor guy. Even at the cafeteria he worked his food with one hand because he had to have the other arm draped around her waist… I couldn't wait to see what he'd do when he had to go to the bathroom.

Several days later he went to the library by himself, and the woman stayed with their daughter at the dacha by Sergiev Posad. I sent my driver off to look for mushrooms in the birch grove by the road, and the daughter was taken away by understanding neighbors to gather raspberries and look at rabbits. Some dacha! There was no hot water, and the cold water was in a barrel behind the summer kitchen. Covered in sweat, I climbed up into the attic, to a bed under the improvised gauze mosquito net, with an open children's book in the middle of the mattress.

"Darling! I love you so much."

She fussed on top of me, her salty sweating skin touched my lips, and all I could see was her face aged by the sun, and her sunburnt back, also at some point in the future, acneyed and scarred. I touched the hair under the horizontal scar from the cesarean, and began wiggling purposefully, to hurry things along. I felt myself sweat profusely.

She liked to be held, she licked her lips and put them out to be kissed… let me feed you, water you, rub you down, bring you a towel, why are you so sad, my darling; and she put out her lips again and laughed, making a question out of everything: When will the next time be? And I wanted to say, immediately, *Never*. But I knew it would be easier for her to hear it in three months, after she got over all of this. And I also knew that she would be useful, so I wrote down her phone number and relevant birthdays, and kissed her on her childishly puckered lips:

"I'll miss you," she cooed.

I fought through the thicket of her arms and lips to the porch, brushing hairy spider webs out of my eyes, turning away from the secret stroking and the jar of organic blackcurrant jam she wanted me to take home, and — God help me — saw on the road, next to my driver, on the dry ground sprinkled with gravel, Alyona in a white T-shirt. She smoked and waited, a smile forming on her face. She had parked her car in the shade of the birches.

Still on the porch, the woman asked:

"What's wrong? Your face suddenly changed."

"Nothing whatsoever. How can anything be wrong now?" I lied. "I'm so happy."

She walked me through the garden up to the gate, between the plums, cherries and dense raspberries that pressed through the fences: I asked her my questions and answered when she asked hers, and giggled when needed. Alyona suddenly turned away and went to hide in her car. By the gates, at the starting line of my next torment, I said:

"Well…"

The woman threw a conspiratorial look back and threw her arms around me:

"I'll wait for you. I truly will. Remember me from time to time."

She moaned, snivelled, rubbed her eyes and stayed behind by the iron gates of the gardeners' co-op Beryozka-4. I looked at my driver. He held up a plastic bag:

"Three brown caps and one boletus. And lots of morels. I was scared of going any deeper into the forest."

We should just get in the car and go, I thought. But I made myself go to the woman in the red car, to the open door, to the empty seat — hospitable as a dentist's chair— where I would say: Alyona, I never promised you anything, this should all end, death will come anyway and erase everything; all that is left to me is a little peace and a chance to finish my game of soldiers without any more exams and quizzes and being the good boy who jumps up to help grandma water the peppers. Alyona suddenly looked at me and nodded in welcome, dispelling tormented wrinkles:

"You didn't answer the phone, and then you turned it off. I couldn't stop thinking that something bad happened. I called the driver, but he couldn't explain anything: you'd turned off the highway, stopped, and you'd gone somewhere… At the office nobody knew where you went, and I thought: what if you needed help. And when I realized that everything was OK with you, do you know what I did? I started to remember our first days, only the good things. And we have so many good things, enough to last a lifetime… The way you smile. The way you hugged me for the first time. You do remember what you said? I need you very much, every day, if you were small I'd carry you in my pocket. The way we walked together and a white feather was flying in the air, and you said: remember this day… And I stood there and thought: everything will be good for us, everything will be good!" And then, angrily: "Sashka, I love you so much! Get in the car."

I shut the door and tried to fold myself into the space that was too small to accommodate my legs. Alyona reached over and grabbed me by the neck, pressed her dry tobacco lips to me, held me for a while and said:

"You must hurry. Shakhurin called. Sergei Ivanovich Shakhurin! And he said that he would talk only to you."

I was dumbstruck.

"Hello. Yes," He listened to my cautiously offered name and whispered, "I received your letter."

"Sergei Ivanovich, I wrote to you six years ago."

"It is yours. This telephone number was in it. I was going through my papers and found it. You wanted to meet."

Improbably, things were filtering to me, drip by drip.

"Can we meet?"

"Have you read Aleksei Ivanovich's book? That's good. Did you go to the museum on Poklonnaya Hill?"

"Many times. There's a window display with your brother's coat," I felt like a man standing over an anti-infantry mine barely seen in the grass.

"When did you go? I went there recently and the window is empty. I said: how is that? It turns out the medals were taken away for examination, to see if they are genuine."

"When can we meet and talk about Aleksei Ivanovich?"

"Let's say… I don't feel well, though… How about tomorrow?"

"Tomorrow…"

"At six o'clock. I go out in the evening to sit… on a bench. I am a part of citizen action, against the proposed reconstruction of the ponds... this mayor, you know... He said we taught him a lesson. Now I go to the bench."

"By the Patriarch ponds? I'll be there tomorrow. Where exactly?"

"Do you know the Krylov monument?"

That's it!

I hung up, sighed, licked my lips and kneaded my neck. The secretary flew past me and turned around in the door:

"How come everything works out for you? We waited so long!" And ran off on swift, cheerful heels.

KREMLIN WALLS

AND IT'S ALL USELESS. THEY WERE NOT DECEIVED, THERE WAS JUST silence in reply. The invalids, brought in in wheelchairs, — the final generation of the Empire — refused to speak their final word. Why?

If I had known for certain that with my incursions I would burn, crush and mutilate their final months and weeks, the silence of their pharmaceutically adjusted sleep, the predictable orchestration of their lives, would I have turned my horde back, called off my dogs? No, of course not. There's no pity. And there are many reasons. One of them is that the truth of the iron generation had long ago petrified into a polished, unassailable obelisk of calm and silence. And year after year, we lay siege to a city that no longer existed.

Perhaps this is no coincidence, and our patriarchs had planned it this way: for us to find the envelope marked "Last Will and Testament" empty, for us — the children — to run around pointlessly in the dacha garden looking for the last note with a clue about the location of the buried treasure. But how did they manage to do it? Or if they didn't, how did it happen?

The Germans were the first to be alarmed by the coming silence, when in April the seething red slush closed around Berlin, and Hitler shouted: "I should have done what Stalin did, and shot all my generals!" Goebbels spent nights poring over the personal files of People's Commissars and marshals of the Soviet Union, trying to glean something from biographic information and staring into their mute peasants' and workers' faces: What made them into who they were? It must have been that meteorite! And European citizens, pushing their panama hats back on their heads, observed a strange light in the East, and the hunters, who reached the epicenter of the explosion fifty years later, found only star-topped obelisks on mass graves and stone sculptures with outstretched arms that pointed to the bright future. The era of Ivan the Terrible — when the chronicles were broken off, and nothing was left of entire months and years except the occasional terror-stricken testimony of a foreigner, the mad shrieking of fleeing survivors and a commemoration book compiled before his death by the Tsar himself — repeated itself and was longer, deeper and more perfect in this new incarnation.

Writing down one's own thoughts was shirked, or overcome as temptation. The leaders stopped writing to each other in the middle of the 1930s, when telephones became reliable, and the frequent trips to dachas in the Caucasus stopped — they had built new dachas near Moscow. None of the leaders and their iron men — and these were hundreds and thousands of the same Russian souls that used to confuse literature and religion — dared to keep a diary after 1917, not a single one of them. The more cautious of them penned regulation memoirs, scrubbed clean like a first-grader's homework. Then the founding and essential documents began to disappear, then notes taken at substantive discussions and meetings at the dinner table, and finally the lead coffin, self-sealing from the inside — the Emperor forbid recording of his words. Maxim Gorky, with tears of an unclear origin, whispered about the Emperor, "A master. And the lord of time" (this seems to be an incorrect note, the period after "master" should be removed), and there ensued what historians call a complete written and verbal silence. We know what decisions were made, but have no indication of the motives behind them. Of course, we have reports of interrogations, in perfect order, and the blood will never dry on these. Their pages are like the magical soak-weed of fairy-tales — the longer you dry it, the more it drips, with the blood and suffering of individual human beings.

Whatever was spoken was powerless and meant nothing. The earthy, milk-scented individualized speech went feral and coarse to survive penned into newspaper columns and the leaden rows of standard typography. Any palpitations of emotion (as in the Tsarist days, when someone would write, "It is impossible for me, Your Imperial Highness, to persist with the knowledge that I am the cause of your worry. I never wished to displease you and it pains me to see the decision You made occasion such a disturbance in Your spirits. With Your permission, I have come to ask your leave and beg you, in accordance with the Russian custom, not to remember me ill. If I displeased you in any way, forgive me, and believe that I have served You to the best of my natural sensibilities and with all my limitless devotion") were liquidated along with the last Tsar, burnt, buried in lime, thrown into mines.

The people were afraid, they were silent, in the grip of the Stalinist terror, the tribe of slaves! They knew they could be killed. They knew of the camps, of the Lubyanka prison, of bullets to the back of the heads, their children in orphanages, branded for life. But the empire of fear could have collapsed at 22 minutes past four in the morning, on the 22nd of June 1941, even before Molotov, after a torturous pause and a sigh forced himself to start speaking into the radio microphone: "The Soviet government… and its leader, Comrade Stalin… have asked me to make the following statement…" Was it really just fear? The Germans were also afraid of the Gestapo, the concentration camps, no one wanted to be hung on meat hooks, or strung up on piano wire, or shoot themselves in their family estates under the supervision of an SS general. And yet, as soon as the command "Do not be afraid" sounded, they reached into their field bags and pulled out their diaries of the Eastern campaign, in which they had written, on various dates "the Fuehrer is committing one insanity after another" and "we are doomed." The Russian princes and men-at-arms stood mute, as they did in the days of Ivan the Terrible, even after the gallows went empty; they were all complicit in a great silence, hundreds of unwritten memoirs. Instead, they lived tormented by the oblivion that swallowed their fallen friends, hated Khrushchev for continuing Stalin's war around the globe, despised Brezhnev for his self-manufactured military glories that invalidated their own medals, and without a shred of belief in heaven or hell, went to their graves silently, in accordance with Lazar Kaganovich's dictate, "Nothing, to no one, ever." Both the disgraced and the victors were silent. Marshal Golovanov whispered to his wife, as he exhaled his last breaths, "Mama, what a terrifying life" — this to the woman, the girl who had suddenly kissed him first right there, by the main door of his building, and then fled in offence when he asked, "Have you had a lot of kisses like that?" And now she cried, "What's wrong with you? Why was it a terrifying life?" And he said, "You're lucky that you don't understand."

For clarity, to avoid any doubt that the erasure of all traces and the silence were not just accidental, it was not mere bed-warmers and grooms that waited for us to come, but senior leadership: Molotov, Malenkov, Voroshilov, Mikoyan, Kaganovich. Frost-bitten, crushed by the glacier, these nonagenarians roamed among us, wrote and thought something in their well-guarded retreats, did not see each other once in the thirty years of living in retirement side by side, and persisted without words, staring down plumbers and nephews who came to visit them. Much as people used to call for a priest on their deathbed, these men, when their time came, scratched with their monastic claws: restore me to the party! And nothing else! And said no more than the dead, keeping up their part in the conspiracy. You could almost see a greedy, drooling line of people waiting for Kaganovich's memoirs, and all they got was a bible-sized tome with the words "Long live the Communist party of the Soviet Union and its great leader Iosif Vissarionovich Stalin!" written 43,278,624 times. Only once, after the death of his wife, between his heart attack and death, did Malenkov open his eyes to the world and whisper: in October of 1941, the entire cabinet left Moscow, and I remained alone in charge. A fantastic trifle, not even worth checking because of its insignificance, and that was all. That — after the great sacrifice, the elimination of millions of people, after the leap from gathering ears of wheat to launching Sputnik?

All our maps and dossiers, the location of streets, communications hubs and blood supply centers, everything we know was reported to us by the children, Vladimir Shakhurin's peers, and is complete disinformation. The Absolute Power that ordered the fathers to be silent broke ancestral traditions, destroyed belief in God, erased family ties and even — not "even" but merely "and" — love. The Emperor, I am sure, was horrified himself when he read the letters: requests to be given any form (by order of the Central Committee) of rehabilitation. On his behalf, he offers to be permitted personally to shoot everyone who has been sentenced to execution, including his former wife. This is to be published in the press." The iron generation did not have children; they had offspring.

The offspring, the more honest of them, admitted: we didn't know anything, our parents were silent, father slept with a pistol under his pillow, I'm offended when Dad is called in the press a henchman. There's nothing to remember but French lessons at home, a cinema at the dacha and tennis at Silver Wood; our fathers were not friends with anyone (the habit of families being friends appeared after the world ended, on the 5th of March 1953), and if we ever visited each other, our fathers walked the paths of the Hills ahead of their wives with their women-talk, and we kids brought up the rear and plotted taking over the world. The fathers walked in silence — not afraid of the person they were talking to, but taking into account the essential weakness of the human being, the distorted memory, the ability to open one's mouth, to become distracted, to weaken from a coarse word and to begin to live by something insignificant. The fathers, wandering along the garden path, felt themselves to be links in a chain, the powerful hands of something incomprehensible — they did not belong to themselves; at any moment the person walking with you could prove to be an enemy, but there had been no instruction to report anything about him today, so what was there to talk about? Certainly not about the fact that spring was late and the children had grown.

Those of the offspring who were really irked by the "henchman" label, forgot their conscience and prattled: "If it hadn't been for father's resistance, both secret and open, to Stalin's lackeys, he wouldn't have survived as a human being with a soul and wouldn't have continued after the despot's death with the truly democratic reforms that he accomplished through much suffering in secret and that became the initial step toward the collapse of the totalitarian regime." And this about a man who had signed several thousand execution lists, and who wouldn't have thought twice about suffocating his own son with a pillow for words like "despot" and "lackey."

Since they never spoke about a thing, the fathers allowed the next generation to make them into anything at all with impunity. Lavrentiy Beria's son wrote a charming book about his father, in which he portrayed Beria as a kind person, a devoted family man (the one hundred and fifty or so mistresses whose names figured at the trial were just there to provide cover in various covert operations), a civil servant who always wanted there to be less blood, one whose plans and orders were repeatedly perverted — and all this was quite convincing, based on well-known documents and indisputable facts.

Even the Emperor's daughter, when she needed money — she had to eat, buy clothes, feed her children, and accommodate her own vision of herself as a young woman with certain needs — struck a book deal with a pitch to "write about my life in my father's home for twenty seven years." She squeezed and squeezed, but only managed to produce enough inanities for an emaciated little paperback: three dinners, two quarrels, a bit of gossip ("After my father's death I was told…"), detailed descriptions of her nanny and then her first love, feeble reminiscences prompted by photos ("Here's Kirov in a shirt, in slippers"), quotes from the Emperor's letters to Setanka, and the flimsy idea shared by all of the offspring: Beria was the one to blame for everything, he played however he wanted with poor old Dad. She lived, as did all of Volodya and Nina's peers, blindly, like a deep-water cave fish, immersed in her own well-fed life; she did not notice the war and ordinary people.

One American reader slammed the book shut with the disappointed conclusion: "Well, this isn't going to bring down the walls of the Kremlin." That's right. Nothing ever will. That's the way things have been arranged.

The librarian on duty softly cleared her throat and asked everyone in the reading room to check in their books, nodding at the clock on the wall. I got up and, stacking my heavy, dusty pile, had to admit: we couldn't even establish the basic police details of critical events. Even the last ten minutes of the Emperor's agony at the Kuntsevo dacha, with six (at the very least) adult witnesses frozen in terror are not subject to a reliable reproduction of the scene. Did he call people to him to say goodbye? Did he nod to Bulganin to step aside? Did he or did he not hold Malenkov's fingers in his hand? Did he mumble: "What did they do to me?" Was he kissed by that "monster", "hangman", "chameleon", "born sadist", "vampire", "one of the most famous villains" Beria? Is it true that he smiled like a wolf? Did Voroshilov give him a spoonful of broth? Did he turn away from Khrushchev? Did he accuse Molotov of poisoning him? Did he ask for the door to be opened — he couldn't breathe? Was he even conscious in the first place? And who exactly was present? And finally, what is the source of the very reliable information that the Emperor, in his last moments, crossed himself broadly in front of an icon? How could there be an icon at the Kuntsevo dacha?! None of this — not any of this — is what actually happened.

The rejection of personal truth, the abnegation of one's fleeting imprint in the sand produced a supernatural, addled complacency: hundreds of thousands of revolutionaries confirmed wretched, shameful accusations concocted by morons, without doubting that they were acquiescing to their own death; they signed everything and testified (some at an open court and in front of a foreign audience, who came for a look at the Russian bull fight), increasing the scope of the harrowing, reporting new names to the investigation. No one fled to the taiga with false documents, no one tried to hide in abandoned monasteries, to shoot at those who came after them, running from window to window, remembering the skills of the Civil

War. Everyone (apart from rare suicides) knew everything and they were not afraid; they sat and waited for the footsteps to come and get them, in order to carry out everything they were told, and thus to preserve their complicity with the Absolute Power which gave them an overwhelming sense… of what? I think it must have been a feeling of immortality. You have to be ignorant to say that they lived in fetters. They lived with meaning. A meaning that was determined for them. And falling out of this meaning was worse than death, it was absolute non-existence, and the empire had already given them a clear idea of the *Absolute*.

For the common folk, there's one explanation: torture, they were simply tortured, beaten down. The human is weak when it has a heel marching over its fingers and hasn't slept for a week… But there comes a moment after the three-minute trial is over and there's nothing left between the convicted man and the grave except a last shred of breath so as to speak words that no one would hear — and still they shouted "Long live Stalin!" The stone-hearted People's Commissar Nikolai Yezhov sang The Internationale on his way to the execution; the unbending Abakumov, after three months in chains in a freezing cell shouted to the flying bullets: "I'll write it all to the Politburo!" Nikolai Bukharin, who sent fifty love letters to the Emperor from his cell (no one was allowed to prepare for death so thoroughly, to think it through), threw up his hands, and what did he say? "…I am writing and crying, I don't need anything anymore… But I am preparing myself to depart from this worldly vale, and I feel nothing for you, or for the party, or for the entire undertaking but a great and unlimited love." Who could doubt his sincerity?

Only Zinoviev (according to legend), when he entered the basement where he was to be shot, suddenly raised his arms: *Sh'ma Yisrael Adonai Eloheinu Adonai Eḥad.* The Emperor was informed about this scene in front of an audience, and everyone laughed until they cried.

Superconductivity, this is what they were supposed to provide, and what they provided. Carry out the Emperor's will, do not obstruct its transit, but on the contrary, accelerate and propagate it through your existence. This was clear to the footsoldiers and Commissars alike.

Well, we'll leave it at that: people who stop speaking and writing their own thoughts evidently begin to think differently, and this is something, I believe, for neuro-psychiatrists and anthropologists to investigate. We were seriously concerned with a different peculiarity of their mental activity: Stalin's Falcons, the iron people, forgot how to *remember*. It's not that they didn't remember anything — they just didn't remember their own lives.

When someone tried to remind them, the old men and women frowned, as if something was flashing by before their eyes with the persistence of a summer gnat; they looked intently, wiping away the moisture oozing out of their eyes, they stared, but…no. They were not there. They couldn't see themselves.

What we were after, from their point of view, was a minute, worthless incident — someone killed someone, for some love, in the summer of nineteen forty three. At first, I sometimes thought: if only the Emperor were alive… Later I realized: he wouldn't have remembered either.

KUIBYSHEV, KUIBYSHEVA

WITNESS A: VOLODYA EASILY CAPTIVATED PEOPLE, ESPECIALLY people from a lower social group, who were supposed to be easily captivated.

WITNESS B: I used to be taken to spend time with Shakhurin like I was his toy. I knew that my job was to go to his dacha at the drop of a hat. We were in the same grade at school. My father served as a Commissar's deputy, but my math teacher Mr. Gurvits once looked at me in a certain way and said in Latin: "What is permitted to Jupiter is not permitted to a bull," and I understood my place. I went to apprentice at the aircraft factory, and didn't ever speak to my parents about having my own motorcycle. When Volodya and Vano Mikoyan got Harleys, my father could also have gotten me a motorcycle, but with a peasant's instinct he realized he should do things in moderation, and of all the privileges that were accorded him he only made use of one — two season tickets for the Moscow football team, Dinamo.

There was always a big difference, an abyss, between a rank-and-file member of the Politburo and the Secretary of the Central Committee. The same applied to the difference between a People's Commissar and a Deputy People's Commissar. And the same abyss, although it was not obvious, separated the children. It wasn't just the size of their apartments, but something more significant.

My father kept silent until his death, and tore up everything he ever put down on paper.

The most vivid memory of my life is the first fly-over of jet fighter planes. Fifteen MiGs and Yaks flew over Red Square. Black vans, of the sort that took people away, were parked within sight of the grandstands where the aircraft builders sat, just in case there was an accident.

Volodya was blond, with wavy hair and very blue eyes. He had a slight stutter.

WITNESS A: He dragged me to the attic and showed me a brick wall: there was a treasure trove behind it! We smashed it with crowbars, we broke the bricks, made a huge hole, and behind it — no treasure, of course, only the view of the street below. Just as we came down into the courtyard, Aleksei Ivanovich was coming home: he didn't know anything about the hole, just saw us there all covered in dust, and without saying a word, he slapped his son on the face with all his might! And I was sent home immediately.

Preliminary investigation of school #175 identified presumed classmates of Vladimir Shakhurin: G. Lozovskaya, Yulia Baryshenkova, Nina Umanskaya, Artyom Khmelnitsky, a Mr. Kuznetsov, a Ms. Streltsova, Leonid Redens, Svetlana Molotova, Bakulev, Barabanov,, Kirpichnikov, Kuibysheva, G. Romanov, Bolotovsky, Anatoly Borisov, Vlad Skryabin.

The school's principal at the time was Olga Fyorodovna Leonova, deputy of the Supreme Soviet of the USSR, awarded with the medal of the Labor Red Banner.

Deputy principal: Ms. Groza (only surname established).

Class head: Natalya Buchneva (5 Staropimenovsky Ln., Apt. 21). She was 40 at the time of the incident in question; we believe it would be unproductive to pursue information on her family members.

Math teacher: Yuly Gurvits (lives above the "Pedagogical Books" store), age 60 at the time of the incident in question; we believe it would be unproductive to pursue information on her family members.

"Have you ever seen a Walter revolver in Volodya's possession?"
"No."
"I didn't."

"No… when would I have?"

"I don't remember."

"I once saw him shoot a BB gun at the dacha… He blew up some insulators on a utility pole. He didn't have a pistol."

"Did you hear about Volodya hitting a classmate in the face at school?"

"No."

"I don't know."

"I only heard it from you."

"No, he didn't hit someone, he killed someone, he killed Nina Umanskaya."

"Yes, I remember that. But it was a girl he hit, her name was Galya."

"Yes, he once hit Galya Kuibysheva at a geography lesson. Volodya was called on to answer questions about cities of the Volga region, and he was giving a good answer. Galya said, 'Of course, it's easy for him to talk. He had a chance to study the outskirts of Kuibyshev really well.' Shakhurin walked up to her and slapped her."

"Actually I think he hit Galya during recess, not in class. But it all started with the discussion about Kuibyshev, that's for sure."

Why would Volodya know so much about the city of Kuibyshev?

"Everyone did. The school had been evacuated there after the war began."

August. The summer agony of 1941 was ending. Konstantin Umansky was wrapping up his last three weeks in Washington, and the city of Kuibyshev was being prepared to replace the capital. If you knew just the right crack in the fence, you could peek at the renovated mansion awaiting the Emperor; people took notice of a beautiful black-eyed housekeeper. The people's Committee of Foreign Affairs, the Soviet Information Bureau and aircraft factories had already been moved along with the Bolshoi Theater and school #175. It was common to refer to the different classes by the name of the Main Pupil: class of Svetlana Stalina, class of Vano Mikoyan, class of Svetlana Molotova, class of Sergo Mikoyan. Many wanted to study at the school, but no one wanted to teach there.

And Kuibyshev... The Emperor's daughter didn't like it: the city was old and dirty, with paupers, orphans, "a lot of lame, blind, lop-sided, crooked-legged, crooked-armed people and other cripples," as she later wrote. Wounded soldiers did not inspire sympathy, and neither did the enormous river, the remains of merchant estates, all those little steamboats and spring floods; the city seemed menacing, people muttered in the street, "Now that this fancy crowd's here, it won't take Hitler long to bomb us too!" Kuibyshev suffered: apartments were crowded with new arrivals, the tenants of several houses were evicted to make room for more important people; over-crowded schools worked in four shifts, the last shift started at eight in the evening, and kids fell asleep after the third class. Prices went up, food disappeared, people ate cutlets made of sawdust, pancakes of potato peelings, drank acorn coffee with dandelion roots, and donated blood for the injured. The pupils at school #175 did not notice any of this. Svetlana Molotova wrote to her parents on the 16th of August, 1941: "We've been given a wonderful townhouse, and out of town we have a wonderful little dacha.... I haven't written much because there's nothing to write. I live very well."

The Emperor was not interested in school #175, nor with other personal things that did not have any relation to the Future (even to Eternity), but he did hate it. Power and money in the Empire were not to be inherited, and the children of the leaders were meant to share a common ration and utter obscurity. The teenagers with terrifying last names were supposed to wear patched pants and darned stockings, and sit at desks with former street urchins and children of fallen revolutionaries who grew up in orphanages — they were supposed to be on common ground. But the common grounds could not hold against parental love and the fear of ordinary people, these kids' nannies and tutors, they too wanted to breathe and bring home groceries for their families, to die of old age, placing their shriveled paws on the heads of their great-grandchildren. The children of the iron men were brought up as if they were golden. They came together in school #175, which everyone looked upon in fear, and Maria Svanidze, the friend of the Emperor's second wife, wrote in despair, "They've been given an absolutely perfect environment. The horrible thing is that the children feel the privilege of their position, and this ruins them forever. They are doomed to irrelevance and obscurity because of the exclusivity of their position." This was one of the few second-tier thoughts that came to Ms. Svanidze's mind; usually (no matter how many of her relatives and friends disappeared) she focused on her love for the Emperor and on how hard things must be for "Iosif." In 1942 she herself was executed, and thus her thoughts came to an end. Another twenty-year veteran of education who was fired from the school "for the bad upbringing" of the Emperor's son wrote the truth to the emperor in torment, "The question will remain unresolved until a real connection between the school and the family is established." Another teacher admitted: educating the children that attended school #175 was "at best useless, and at worst dangerous."

Vladimir Shakhurin studied in the sixth grade (in Kuibyshev for the 1941-1942 academic year), in the class of Svetlana Molotova. The local teachers were utterly oppressed by the luxury of appearance and the freedom of manners of the entire school #175, but there was only one class where they refused to teach outright: Svetlana Molotova's 6th grade, where things were completely out of control as the children fought against the lives they suspected had been laid out for them.

"The kids aren't stupid, the discipline is all right," Svetlana Molotova wrote, "but among the boys there are some real desperados…"

They sat in the front — the squat Svetlana and the tall Sonya Streltsova — at a special desk: Molotova had troubles with her spine, she wore a corset, and the special desk went with her to Kuibyshev and back. Streltsova accompanied Sveta everywhere, she and the bodyguards who waited for the end of the school day in the Young Pioneers activity room; when the girls walked home down Gorky Street, two inconspicuously impressive comrades followed them along the pavement, and a car crawled after them, while the passers-by froze.

When the unpedigreed Sonya appeared at the school, people said that she was the daughter of Molotov's driver, Streltsov, who was killed in an accident (possibly while saving the People's Commissar's life), and Vyacheslav Mikhailovich and Polina Semyonovna took in the girl to raise her as their own. That was all lies of course. The driver did not die and outlived his daughter, who died relatively young of kidney cancer. Sonya was taken in like a puppy, she lived to provide company for Svetochka and to prevent her from hanging out with god knows who. Dressed in identical squirrel-fur coats and fluffy hats with pompoms, the girls both graduated from MGIMO, the Moscow State Institute of International Relations, and seemed to be joined at hip, until the son of the aircraft designer Ilyushin was brought up and chosen for Sveta, and Sonya was let free. Svetlana and Ilyushin eventually separated; Sonya, before she died, admitted: it was difficult for me, all of this… it was very difficult.

The children were taken to Moscow to see their parents on American war-aid Douglas bombers with eight seats. On the day German bombs found the Bolshoi Theater, the university building on Mokhovaya and the Central Committee on the Old Square, the Emperor's daughter was delivered down the stairs to the underground headquarters and left there to create family warmth. She saw her absent father. He looked at the map, at the Russian armies; he asked, without looking at the girl, addressing a non-existing daughter he had imagined, the one he should have had:

"Well. How are you then? Have you made friends with anyone from Kuibyshev?"

"No. You know, we're separate. We're in a special school."

"How's that?" The Emperor became angry (many recall what this looked like: he'd glance at the culprit quickly from under his furrowed brow), loath to waste his energy on this too. "A special school? Some government! The Muscovites have arrived! Give them a separate school" and he threatened: "Accursed caste!"

The caste. That's why Ehrenburg tried to keep Nina away from school #175, and the hot-headed, charming, greedy Kostya put his daughter as close as he could to Sveta Molotova.

WITNESS G: "Like all Jewish mothers, Sofia Mironovna wanted her son to study music. Volodya went to some music teacher for lessons, and then ran away from with this teacher's daughter, they crossed the Volga in a boat, and organized a family life for themselves until he was found. 'This upstart wants to marry my Vovochka!' Sofia Mironovna cried. You should try to find Yurka Korenblyum, if he is still alive, of course, he drank like a fish. If you find him, say hello. No, I won't see him, I want him to remember me as a young woman."

WITNESS KORENBLYUM: "My real last name is Kirshon (Kirshon Sr. wrote plays, and was shot on the 28th of July 1938 in connection with the case of People's Commissar Yagoda, after he stopped being useful as his cell's rat; 'Once I asked an aspen...' you know, that famous song? He wrote it), my mother changed her name and took the children away from the war to Omsk. There she received a letter from Kuibyshev, from the pregnant Dzhema Afinogenova. Dzhema wrote, 'I've been widowed, come and stay with me, it's easier to live together.' The playwright Afinogenov, my father's friend, was the only victim of the bomb that hit the Central Committee. He was being sent to the USA to step up our propaganda, stopped by the Central Committee to pick up his paperwork, and was killed when the bomb hit the building.

"We moved to Kuibyshev with nothing; the only valuable thing we had was an old coffee service. Sofia Shakhurin talked Mom into bartering it for food. I went to school with her son, Volodya."

"Did Sofia Mironovna know your real name?"

"It wasn't hard to work it out: she was very connected, especially in 'cultural' circles, but she allowed us to be friends. Volodya, I remember, was completely blond. He had phenomenal linguistic abilities: English, German, he read Hitler and recited something by Goebbels with great enthusiasm." *(Is he lying? A Soviet boy... in the terrible October of 1941... books by Hitler? Enthusiasm?)*

"Did you hear anything about him running away from home?"

"Did I! Why, I ran away with him *(is he lying?)* and with that... what was her name?.. Natasha! He decided to force his parents to take the girl to Moscow. We put together food for the journey, crossed the

Volga on a ferry and slept in the forest. The state security people came looking for us, they scrambled search planes overhead (*lying?*), they found us and took us back. Right in time for the exams. I remember the teacher came to our home to give us the exam. He was offered a glass of tea and a pastry on a saucer. And there was terrible hunger in the city at the time. I remembered for the rest of my life: the teacher drank the tea, but the pastry, as was appropriate… he left unfinished."

"What happened to the girl?"

"After the running away episode I only saw her once: on Smolenskaya Square, she was walking with the sculptor Nikogasyan, a well-known, shall we say, connoisseur of female beauty. She grew up to be a striking, beautiful woman."

"Do you think Shakhurin suffered from a mental disorder?"

"What makes you say that?"

"He ran away from home in sixth grade. The following year, he hit Galya Kuibyshev in the face, as it turns out, because she dared to mention his Kuibyshev adventures. He killed Nina Umanskaya, and shot himself. Early schizophrenia, perhaps?"

"I don't know… Anything's possible, but… There was, of course, this fixation on girls. He had a desire to possess everyone, and it was somehow combined in him with a fierce desire for loyalty. Did you notice that his running away, an amusing action, and the murder, a horrible action, have the same motive?"

"What motive is that?"

"He didn't want to part with the girl he loved."

WITNESS H: *I remember him: he was short, light-haired, with a buzz cut. He spoke slowly and clearly.*

Our fathers were put in their places, and we knew who was entitled to what. Volodya was just the son of a People's Commissar, so he was, sort of, third-rate. Still, he aspired to higher things, he was interested in the way things worked in the Kremlin. He had plotted out a path upward for himself and believed that his future depended on him successfully carrying out the intrigues he had planned.

"You're talking about a fourteen-year-old boy."

"Well, this is what he was like. Once, I was invited to the Shakhurins' dacha to go skiing. I thought we'd talk about films, girls and teachers, the usual stuff, but Volodya wasn't interested in those things. Instead, he had his own miniature Politburo going: who had offended whom at school, who had done what… And he was very neurotic."

"Do you think he was close with Nina Umanskaya?"

"Close? You mean, intimate? That's unlikely. Only a limited circle of people were allowed to be with Volodya — in this circle Sofia Mironovna controlled everything without exception."

"You said 'very neurotic'…"

"That's what I said. But I'll say something else: he was also growing up a very cold-blooded boy, he controlled his actions. He… I don't believe he was the kind of person who would kill himself."

"Not even in panic? After he saw what he'd done?"

"Not even in panic. He couldn't have. Oh, I remember: Volodya's favorite phrase was 'we'll get this organized.'"

"Thank you. Do you remember anything else, Sergei Vladimirovich?"

"No, nothing that would…"

"Any details? Everything is extremely important."

"You know, I've been talking to you and all this time I've been thinking to myself: it's amazing to what extent we've been influenced by American films. All that Roman history, romantic acts, heroics… Tragic love. Our fathers didn't keep diaries, but we did, in fact! We wrote letters, yes…"

"Did Volodya keep a diary?"

"I don't know it for a fact, but it's possible. He had these notebooks he used to hide from his mother. They say, he even… when… after the thing on the bridge happened, he had some papers in his pockets when they found him."

"What happened to these papers?"

"How should I know. The investigating bodies probably took them."

"Letters?"

"What?"

"Were there letters? A diary?"

"I said: *I don't know*. Perhaps there wasn't anything at all and someone made it all up. Or it might have been just a list…"

"A list?"

"How should I know? I didn't see Volodya when he was dead.

"You didn't, but still someone must have said something if you remember this. What did people say back then? A list… of names?"

"You're really interrogating me…"

"What could Volodya have written?"

"All I know I've already told you… let's wrap this up now."

"Books he's read?"

"Listen, I'm an old man, I already forget what I knew. And you want me to remember what I didn't know?"

"Perhaps a list of people who came to his home? To Sofia Mironovna?"

"I'm supposed to take medicine, and I can't remember *that* — only when my wife reminds me…"

"Girls? Someone from school? Who was friends with whom?"

"Oh, I don't know! That's it. My graduate students are waiting for me, so thank you for the chocolates and the coffee, although you shouldn't have, I doubt I've been of any help to you…"

"What's keeping you from telling me?"

"About what? I don't know about anything! You just picked on a word and now you won't give it up. There was no list! Here, by the way, look at this photo: my father is opening a session of the Moscow Soviet."

"Very nice. Well, thank you. And get well."

"That would be good, because I've got this noise in my head, here on the right, it's like a bee-hive, buzzing, humming… and on the other side, it's like trains, and they honk… They don't let me sleep… I can't sleep at all. And so many people have already suffered… because of that list."

THE MURDERER

A PACKING LIST, A LIST OF LOVE CONQUESTS, A LIST... A PERSON makes a list when he is about to do something, or when he wants to understand something. A list is a forward-looking document. A shopping list, a guest list (to work out a seating chart), a birthday list for May, a list of New Year's resolutions (mine is not to mess with minors and faithful wives). A check-out list of documents received, of facts not to be released to the public; a playlist, a most-visited list, a list of endangered species found in the Tula region.

Would there be a to-do list for the murder of Nina Umanskaya? As in, here are the steps I need to take, and here are my classmates who will help me and whose parents will be reprimanded for their poor upbringing to the extent that the prosecutor general will be sure to hush it all up — well, let's say that's a *theory*. Another theory would revolve around a list of parents who could help a polyglot seventh-grade dreamer conquer the Kremlin.

A list... of weapons? Homosexual friends? A list that was important enough for the boy to fold it into his pocket on that decisive day — was he planning to read it to the fatally beautiful, tender, curly-haired and bowlegged Ambassador's daughter on the bridge, was the list supposed to surprise her/shock her/make her fall in love with him and not go to Mexico? Although she wouldn't go anyway — he had a pistol as well.

A list.

I hate papers sticking out of dead people's pockets: it's perfectly possible that someone stuck a few sheets of paper into the boys pocket after the shooting, to explain everything more quickly and without consequences, to tie up all the loose ends so neatly that even sixty years later, we, too, would swallow the bait and be reeled in on an invisible line to our final destination in the frying pan.

Here he comes, not knobby-kneed and lanky as one always imagines university professors, but a little old man in a cap, creeping along the boards thrown over the mud on the construction site where the city has dug up the sidewalks around the ponds. He carries a rolled-up newspaper, Sergei Ivanovich Shakhurin, brother of the People's Commissar. He's not a man — he is a fortress: six years of my sleepless siege, catapults, mines, and a sea of exhausted hatred, and now he has crawled out of his burrow and walks without looking around, in feeble short-sightedness, seeing only the walls of his own world, small as a cardboard box for a hamster, where he is doomed to scrabble around until his last day…

He walked like a wind-up toy: left-right, left-right, his destination a vacant bench that he had picked out ahead of time, and inside him something crunched with a metallic noise. I knew instantly: he is empty, there's nothing there, it would have been better if we hadn't found him, if he had remained a telephone number, a hope, a keeper of family secrets.

"Ah? You? Let's sit down."

He unfolded his newspaper on the bench, and we sat facing the Patriarch Ponds. I put on a smile and talked about the weather and the surrounding landscape. The brother of the People's Commissar suddenly came to life at the mention of the landscape.

"I'm an activist in the protest movement against the reconstruction of the ponds," he wheezed. "Have you read Aleksei Ivanovich's book *Wings of Victory*? There is a separate display on him at the museum on Poklonnaya Hill… Have you seen his uniform? I," he lost the ability to produce sound for a second and swallowed a few times, remembering where he was and who he was, "I went in and the display case was empty!" He gave me a stupefied glance from teary, senseless eyes. "And they said: we've taken the medals away... to see if they're genuine or something..."

"For inspection."

He nodded in relief, and on a wave of gratitude he leaned toward my ear:

"Do you know that Aleksei Ivanovich was in Beria's so-called sanatorium?"

I nodded. His voice oozed, dripped meagerly from the noise of his breathing:

"We didn't know anything. All those seven years. I brought packages. Once, I was sitting in the waiting room, suddenly a man came up to me... He said: Aleksei Ivanovich will be out in a week. He turned out to be Seleznyov, Aleksei's deputy. He was the first to be released. He was the one who said that Aleksei Ivanovich was in the internal prison in Lubyanka, that he had been there all those seven years. But we didn't know anything."

"Did he tell you anything? About interrogations? About the prison?" I asked with urgent clarity.

"We didn't know anything. Aleksei Ivanovich said: We will never return to this issue. A great man! Stalin called him in almost every day. Did you know that? He carried out the evacuation in such record-short time. The constructors respected him. I stopped by to see the general constructor of the Saturn factory the other day, and he said: I'll give you money to reprint *Wings of Victory*. And it's already been reprinted three times... Have you read it?"

"Yes."

He didn't seem to see me.

"It would be nice if he were remembered well, Aleksei. I had five brothers, and now I'm the only one left."

So that's why he crawled out.

"And as for meeting... we refused because everyone was only interested in Volodya... Only about how he was killed..."

So he was *killed* after all.

"It was a great tragedy for the family. He was a good boy. He liked the opera. He used to go around humming arias," the old man suddenly chuckled. Something flitted before his mental eye, a sharp a clear picture, if only for a moment.

"Your brother Aleksei Ivanovich," I began mournfully, "Did anyone ever try to restore justice?"

"We didn't know anything. Umansky believed that it wasn't Volodya who did it, but what could we do? Aleksei Ivanovich involved Sheinin in the investigation. And they said to him: what is this investigation? What's there to investigate? Do you want to end up shoveling rock in the mines? And Aleksei Ivanovich got scared… he'd already been in prison. Did you know about that? Have you been in the museum on Poklonnaya Hill? There's a display… With Aleksei Ivanovich's parade uniform. Last time I went there, the case was empty!" he faltered in horror. "What's going on? And it turns out," he giggled in relief, "the medals were taken away, to make… for being genuine…"

"An inspection."

"Yes. I told them: it would be good to immortalize the memory of Aleksei Ivanovich. To name a street after him. A factory. The constructors respected him. The general constructor of the Saturn factory promised me to sponsor a reprint. Have you read *Wings of Victory*?"

It was all I could take. I got up from the spread-out newspaper and walked along the fence of the concrete hole that is now called the Patriarch Ponds, faster and faster, so as to outrun the call should the old man call out to me again. For two months after this, he called me every day, and then, I think, stopped doing so for a good reason.

My neck and the back of my head hurt all afternoon and I couldn't get comfortable at the office. I was watching a Molotok auction for a motorcyclist figurine listed as made in the 1940s or '50s — it wasn't, of course, from the '40s, but it really was an early one, finished in the blue-black nitrocellulose lacquer known as *Zaponlack* that was used before the simple silver paint became ubiquitous. A few of us, connoisseurs, were competing against the enemy of our community —

someone with the user name "all-searcher" who'd been everywhere and for the second year running was buying everything at three times what we could afford. We started at a thousand rubles, and raising by fifties, reached fifteen hundred when the lot was removed from the auction. Never mind, I had two motorcyclists like this, one even with a five-corner seat…

The surname was familiar, by the way — who was this Sheinin?

"An important figure. Lev Sheinin. The head of the investigative department of the Prosecutor's Office of the Soviet Union," Goltsman produced from his tedious index cards. "He was USSR's State Prosecutor at the Nuremberg Trials. Also carried out government missions in Turkey and Iran. A writer. His *Notes of an Investigator*, by the way, was a sensation. Young people signed up for jobs in law enforcement in droves after this book came out. Let me read you what one passionate liberal wrote about him: 'Sheinin is a man of letters and a playwright, but also one of Vishinski's most nimble assistants during the political trials of the 1930s, including Bukharin's trial. Energetic, alert, painfully paranoid (Sheinin was convinced, for some reason, that he would get colon cancer), both a cold-blooded player and a solicitous deal-maker, Sheinin is deep in sins, and the secrets of these sins are great.' And also: he was capable of eliciting from a suspect 'a strange apparent agreement with the most ridiculous propositions.'"

"But this means… Do you understand what this means?"

The story of teenagers killed by unrequited love on the Great Stone Bridge was packaged for posterity by the best bloodhound of the Empire, and if we didn't like something about the package, we were outmatched on the other side.

"Would you allow for the possibility that Sheinin may in this case have been acting in the interest of establishing the truth?" Goltsman asked, following the changing expression of my face.

"I think that besides the interest of the truth, a bunch of other interests were thrown in there. And the truth may have been trampled down in the process of reconciling all the conflicting interests. But so far we've got nothing, not a single confirmed fact. The third person on the bridge; the vanished pistol; statements that the kids were killed — all rumors, recollections about recollections. And everything that I hear about our clients oppresses me somehow… There's something nasty inside this story"

"I agree," Borya, dull and somewhat tipsy, nodded. "When asked, five residents of the House of Government said voluntarily and independently of each other: they had also heard that some terrifying papers were found on Shakhurin's body. No one actually saw these papers, of course. Only one senior citizen, of no political affiliation, said she knew for certain what exactly the papers were that the boy was carrying," Mirgorodsky suppressed a smile. "Documents protesting Stalin's regime. And Shakhurin shot the girl because she refused to carry them by diplomatic pouch when they moved to Mexico! It all comes together, don't you see?" Borya laughed hysterically, squealing and wiping his eyelids under his glasses, then fell silent. "We need to get out of this fairytale. Before it's too late."

After half an hour more of idle speculation and brewing tea, Goltsman suddenly asked:

"How about that individual, the young man. The entrepreneur who identified you at Izmailovo…"

"Chukharev."

"Chukharev. He had his own goal, didn't he? Before you shook him off? I assess the situation as follows: he planned to use us in a similar investigation. This investigation was prompted by some information he had obtained. We don't yet have this information. We can save time if we find him and convince him to share the information, given that we're now in a better negotiating position."

That made sense. But — we could have done this at the beginning, but we didn't because we did not want to deviate from our own procedures and lose our way. This guy, if we come clean, may want to follow us to the bridge, and the Authority will never approve of that.

"I'm not saying there's no risk in it," Goltsman inserted. "But it's time we sacrificed something."

Mirgorodsky got up and left. Some more time passed, darkness fell, and under the streetlights the cottonwood leaves sparkled after the rain.

I nodded to the secretary: "Go home. It can all wait until tomorrow."

I walked behind her offended back, turning off lamps, pulling out plugs from sockets, disconnecting workstations from the Internet. Monitors faded with a popping sound; the air-conditioner choked; a perplexed shiver crept over the fridge, and then there was only the muffled rhythmic whine and clank of the garbage-truck tipping the trash containers into its maw in the yard below. I locked the top and bottom locks and slid the bolt into its brackets.

I went into the room where the moonlight didn't reach and sank to the floor.

AMERICA

MAX WALLACH WAS BORN IN JULY 1876 AND DIED SEVENTY-five years later on December 31, having lived most of his life not as Meir Henoch Mojszewicz Wallach-Finkelstein, but Maxim Litvinov, called Papasha in the Party and "Stalin's standard-bearer for peace" in the newspapers. The son of a minor bank official, he began life in a Jewish family in Bialystok, went to cheder, and eventually rose to the position of cashier-accountant. All his life, he remembered the pogroms, considered himself Russian, and adored his mother, whom he, nonetheless, never mentioned because he had left her behind, together with the rest of his past, retaining only a bundle of family letters and his favorite dish — fried herring under a poached egg (which made his wife flee the room with her nose plugged whenever he made it).

At the age of forty (there was a dim recollection of an earlier common-law marriage) he married the English writer Ivy Lowe, a horse-faced daughter of a Jewish Hungarian colonel who corresponded with H. G. Wells and was a proponent of free love.

Tatyana Litvinova (Brighton, England): Everyone liked Umansky and everyone called him Kostya. He was smart, witty and charming. He was the youngest of the Litvinov Pleiades's which included Surits, Shtein, Rubinin, and Stomonyakov. All of them looked up to my father as a teacher, knowing his honesty and integrity.

Kostya was more a Bohemian than a civil servant, although the war changed him in many ways (except his propensity for tumultuous love affairs) and he became more bureaucratic.

His wife was a bore. She was fiercely jealous of Kostya, suspected that he cheated on her, and whined constantly — now she needed a fridge, then she couldn't live without these special vitamins... She would greet us in their sitting room and warn us: if he asks you for money, don't give him any. Kostya was the kind of person who'd invite you out for breakfast, then disappear at the last possible moment and leave you stuck with the bill.

The Emperor needed America, and Litvinov delivered it for him. For establishing diplomatic relations with the United States, the Emperor gave the People's Commissar the dacha in Firsanovka — Stalin himself outfitted it lovingly for his wife, but the wife shot herself, and the Emperor did not come to her funeral. Or so the story goes: in fact he did come, and sobbed so hard that the coffin shook.

Litvinov used to say: "Yermak, for conquering Siberia, got a fur robe off the Tsar's own shoulder. Stalin gave me Firsanovka."

And to his wife, he added: "This is my St. Helena."

Tatyana Litvinova, Brighton, England: Mama considered it to be the height of hospitality to greet guests with "Please, don't overstay your welcome." After receptions, she complained: my smile is tired. Mama very much wanted English to become our native language, so we sang English songs at night. We often boycotted her wishes, too. We wanted to be like everyone else. The fact that I didn't have a country grandmother in a headscarf and felt boots is something that I still regard as a deprivation. My parents asked me not to tell anyone that we had gone to Paris and seen the Eiffel Tower. But we wouldn't have told anyone anyway.

The silver-tongued Roosevelt convinced his own people that they should just accept the presence of the Russians, these drunk, crazy, narrow-headed, filthy burners of their own forests. But why did he do it? Why he divided up the earth on equal terms with the Emperor is something that English-speaking people don't understand to this day. Was he gullible, was he forced to do so because of the Nazis, did he just not care, was he naïve and looking for a simple solution, was he malleable? Did he believe that Stalin, once he overcame his suspicions, could be brought into the civilized fold? How could Roosevelt swallow the past that tore at everyone else's gullet? Churchill certainly couldn't — he whined, moaned and agonized aboard the bomber that carried him to Moscow: "I thought about my mission in this gloomy, sinister Bolshevik state, which I tried persistently to strangle immediately after its birth, and which I believed to be the mortal enemy of freedom," he wrote. Only the Emperor knew what to do with the past, but as always, he pointed in another direction through his interpreter. "Stalin says that this all belongs to the past, and the past belongs to God."

And what about the present? Back then, at the beginning, no one suffered more than the Americans from the Kremlin's facelessness. They spent years sitting in Moscow waiting rooms and studying the potted plants in search of at least one normal, simply *living* person, capable of listening and understanding a question, of explaining what was *actually* going on, but — trapped in a nightmare — they just wandered from bad to worse: the Emperor was an "unnatural person." Litvinov was "stubborn owing to his Jewish origin," and "completely devoid of a conscience, it would seem." Molotov was "just an idiot" and a "robot," Umansky was a "walking insult," and the "head gang" was sitting in the Kremlin. The Americans believed in *people*. The Americans literally went mad from the first breath of Russian air: from the soot-belching gas cookers, the disappearance forever of citizens with diplomatic passports and the endless waiting for permits and authorizations; from the parcels of food pierced with iron rods at customs; the plumbing that didn't work, the demands for cheap loans, the disregard for laws and thousand-year-old rules for getting along; the external surveillance, the support of the US Communist Party, the brutality, the arrogance and stockpiling of firewood. When twelve American diplomats (with three dogs) boarded the Moscow-

Vladivostok train to familiarize themselves with their new place of residence, the endless desiccation oppressed them, the unwashed plates and bowls, the queues, the envious glances at stations and the silence of the unrevealing land. The people of the truth, meanwhile, were dispassionately adding pages to their patient records: the Americans got bored, got drunk, threw themselves out of the windows of the train, one fell off the bunk along with his dog on to the pregnant wife of the first-rank military engineer Kaganov; someone "revealed his sexual organ and urinated, soiling the compartment in the presence of the elementary school teacher M. Belenkaya." The train rolled on and on, and this hopeless and incomprehensible reality did not seem to end; the interactions with Russians were humiliating in ways that were hard to understand. "It is not any lack of information that makes us rack our brains over the mystery of Russia. We are simply unable to understand the truth about Russia when we see it," Kennan would write much later.

This is what Roosevelt must have thought about a great deal. The President did not understand the Russians. The Emperor (who had thought little about America until then) took note of this deficiency, but did not hurry to provide any illumination, as this could be exploited, so Roosevelt continued to wander between boogeymen, shadows, and masks.

Roosevelt and Stalin made their opening moves. The President advanced William Bullitt, of the Paris Peace Conference fame. The Emperor sent Aleksandr Troyanovsky, an old Bolshevik.

Ambassador Bullitt was whisked from the Moscow airport straight to a banquet, to warmth and comfort, to soft couches, into the Kremlin apartment of Marshal Voroshilov; he was fed, given plenty to drink, everyone liked him, evening and night he was doted on and admired like a rose bud in the circle of the "head gang." For him, an American citizen, the killers of millions gathered around, and the tipsy Ambassador found that they were all to a man "smart, energetic, experienced people," "incredibly perceptive," "with a sense of humor." He observed the "handsome foreheads," "wonderful self-possession," and "kindness." The masters showed a charming "care for the well-being of the working class." The Ambassador was given more to drink, and toasted with heart-felt words, and he could feel, he could know: it was *he,* William Bullitt, who had won the Soviets over with his personal charm, and the charm of American prosperity, and from now on *he* would balance and determine the fate of the world with these new friends of his, these fine fellows, marshals and People's Commissars, the shareholders of one-sixth of the world's land surface… He breathed in and out, happily — it was an incredibly successful beginning! Suddenly the light around him grew brighter: the Emperor himself, in flesh and blood, in all his unbearable real-ness, was coming toward him — a flaming piece of flesh, ball lightning hovering above the living-room rug — others retreated, their faces awash in divine heat, and out came the words: "I would like you to understand: at *any* time, *day and night,* if you wish to meet with me, let me know — I *will receive you immediately,*" uttered the Highest Being — he for whom, until that very moment, no ambassadors and no powers of any countries had existed. Bullitt, the U.S. Ambassador, existed!

And he did not simply exist — as he saw the guest to the door (this not just for the sake of dead rules), the Emperor whispered into his ear: What do you want? What can I do for you? Yes, I'm asking seriously — he cut off the Ambassador's bleating of "I wouldn't dare… It's really not the time…" — Go on, ask! Do you have any wishes? A dream, perhaps? There's not a soul on earth (What's diplomacy got to do with it? We're friends!) as dear to me as you are, do *me* a favor: ask!

World history curled up on Bullitt's lap like a calico cat, and — although something quivered, something wintry and cold stirred at the back of his mind: *don't ask*; somebody's warnings, instructions — he took the plunge: Yes, there is one thing I would like to receive (that's exactly how he put it — "I would like to receive"). Give me land, fifteen acres on the Sparrow Hills (the site once plotted for the Cathedral of Christ), and we will build the American Embassy there (something he and the President dreamed up right before he left), and it will soar, a majestic vision of America, a mansion like Jefferson's, who wrote the Declaration of Independence, visible in any weather from everywhere, a new Monticello on a hill, above Moscow and the Soviet Union. Give me this land!

"It's yours," said the master and lord of time and earth.

And suddenly the Emperor drew back the hand extended for a farewell shake, grabbed Bullitt's head in both hands, and forcefully kissed the Ambassador, and didn't let him go until he got a kiss in return. Bullitt floated away like a balloon, dumbstruck, blissful, blubbering and dancing a bit, sweating from the warmth of human hearts. He walked through the streets, the hotel corridors, turned in his bed, flipping the pillow over to the cool side, and couldn't asleep: *all of this* has just happened to me, *it's me*, I will never be the same. He was bursting with power, he thought about the vast plains of Europe, he was concerned about the Balkans, the threat of Japan, the short friendship of Germany and Poland — the Pacific Ocean! The planet was overflowing with things that had yet to be done… Bullitt got up, woke the secretary, and dictated to him in the middle of the night, with interruptions for his own amazed pauses: My president! I have just come from the Kremlin, and achieved a great deal — and the earth trembled under his feet, the hair stirred on the top of his head, and the lamp did not go out until morning, a single light in the night.

William C. Bullitt, the first U.S. Ambassador to the Soviet Union, lived another three years in the Empire. Over one thousand days.

After that first night, he was never again invited to the Kremlin. He never talked to the emperor, not even on the telephone. He never saw him once, not even from a distance, not even at a reception. *Never.* Neither did he see Marshal Voroshilov again. Or "the President of the USSR" Mikhail Kalinin. Not a single one of his new friends at all. He was forgotten. His life in the Empire lost all meaning; the mirrors did not reflect him, people looked straight through him. He was ashamed of his first night's euphoria, his unfulfilled life, and, most certainly, wondered more than once whether it all really happened to him. There was no trace, no consequence. Once a year, for fifteen minutes, he was received by Molotov who would read to him a demarche from two years ago, submerging the Ambassador's mind into even-deeper darkness. The Ambassador would arrive to these meetings unshaven. He would suddenly wave his arm, moving objects that did not belong to him around on the table. Feeling stifled, he would undo his shirt collar, trying to break through the shroud of his own non-existence, and once finally exclaimed, close to tears, "Our cooperation is a small and weak plant, it should not be urinated on." Molotov finished reading, and without raising his domed head, said: "Goodbye."

Troyanovsky served in America during quiet years: the mutual excitement had passed, there would be no loans so there was nothing to talk about. The Soviet Ambassador did not demonstrate the quality of superconductivity that the Emperor's authority so desired: he imagined things constantly and without permission; he used words like "I think" at inappropriate times, and sent sincere letters, keeping a certain authenticity on his face. Roosevelt liked him, and he consulted with his black driver about how to unravel American-Soviet difficulties — unless this last fact is a lie and a borrowing from Roosevelt's own mythology which maintains that the President used to hone his speeches on an ordinary painter touching up the White House. Litvinov wanted to send one of his own people to America, so he and Troyanovsky fought, as everyone fought in the empire — under the eye of the Emperor.

Litvinov, in a letter to Stalin: "…this is not the first instance of Troyanovsky's lack of discipline and ignoring orders. Unless Troyanovsky is reprimanded, we are not protected from further serious difficulties with America."

Troyanovsky, in a boiling, poisonous letter of his own: "I know that this man is extremely angry with me because the Central Committee did not agree with his position on staffing the Legation. He is now taking his anger out on me. He is sufficiently petty to make personal accusations… I am forced to raise the issue of my being recalled for I realize that it is impossible to remove Litvinov." The Emperor underlined the words after "for," and ordered: "Don't show

Litvinov, but I want to hear out this Troyanovsky." On the basis of this, Troyanovsky was kept in Moscow for the next six months, and by the time they let him go, he lost his vision. He whispered to a confidant, his counselor Skvirsky: "I went, I was received, I've become blind, I don't see what will happen to me now…" Skvirsky didn't listen, and said confusedly: "I'm being recalled for a promotion — the Legat to Afghanistan." At this, Troyanovsky finally *saw* a small chink of light, something shining through. He stared into the emptiness, at the space left vacant by Skvirsky, and kept looking until the letter "K" appeared there: Konstantin Umansky.

Roosevelt also squinted painfully at the shuffling behind the wall and the turnabout of hazy figures in the Russian twilight, and, irritated by failure of rationality, ordered: "Find out more about him. We shouldn't stay passive." And the message came back: Umansky is the man responsible for the barbed-wire collars on the foreign press, the "golden fang," we hate him. This is who the Emperor had sent.

"My appointment was greeted surprisingly well," Umansky reported. "I didn't expect it. I was worried that those who wish me ill would invoke my sins along the censorship lines." What else could he have written?

Troyanovsky thought his replacement was a talented but vacuous man.

AMERICA II

EANWHILE, AT THE OTHER END OF THE WORLD, THE EMPEROR also got curious, picked up a personnel file, rolled the few facts around in his mind and ordered: find out more about this Umansky. The object of his interest had written and published anonymously and under a pen-name for ten years, he served faithfully and *shaped the thinking* of foreign visitors. Bernard Shaw, with his woolly, Father Christmas shock of gray hair, squinted happily in the warm sun under the watchful eye of Konstantin Umansky who supervised his

travel: "It's a great consolation to go to one's grave knowing that world civilization will be saved… In Russia I was convinced that the Communist system is capable of taking humanity out of its crisis and saving it from complete destruction."

But the famine? What about the famine? Someone bold and not local (or paid-off and instructed) asked: "What about the famine?" Cannibalism had become common in the Volga region.

"Come off it, when I arrived in the Soviet Union, I ate the richest meal of my life!" And the train whistle sounded, and white-cuffed hands rose in the air and waved.

Umansky's next achievement: H.G. Wells was allowed to see the Emperor. Was it on this day that the Emperor took his first closer look at the short, puny man, with round glasses and a gap between his gold teeth?

Wells, the hero of Russian high school students and collector of tin soldiers, could feel Death coming for him and in the time that remained he had decided to devise a plan of daily happiness for the population of the Earth, and to begin by making himself, as he reportedly put it, the "postman in the love affair of two giants." He imagined that the Emperor and Roosevelt would entrust to him, the writer, the secrets of their souls, and that he would carry them above the salty expanses of the Atlantic, correcting, enriching and digesting them — and the three of them would bring happiness to the population, finishing what Christ had begun… With an expression of serene boredom on his face, the Emperor listened and listened (as Umansky interpreted) to Wells' plans for re-organizing the world on the foundations of justice, and suddenly, without any connection, the English writer leapt to the point:

"Iosif Vissarionovich," Umansky said, "He asks: what would you like him to tell Roosevelt?"

"Nothing."

Nothing.

Umansky, this anonymous-pseudonymous shadow, the English and German language of the Emperor, the master of inspiring the necessary thoughts by means of soft couches, flowery meadows, caviar and vodka, appeared before Stalin for the first time on 13 December 1931, at the meeting with the writer Emil Ludwig (one hour and 50 minutes), and the last on 1 March 1936, for the talk with the theatrical newspaper magnate from the USA Roy Howard (three and a half hours). The Emperor gave the latest in the line of visiting American idiots a sensation by saying, "We will have alternative elections to the Supreme Soviet." Signing his photo for Howard, Stalin suddenly raised his eyes: "Shall I sign a photo for you as well, Comrade Umansky?"

"Yes. Yes. Of course!"

And a month later Ambassador Troyanovsky sensed him hovering behind his back, Litvinov's protégé who was pleasing to everyone and who thought correctly. Troyanovsky ignored him for weeks, stubbornly reporting what he did, while Umansky reported *what was needed* — the Ambassador had to be changed! — until he was told "enough," and beckoned across a terrifyingly expanding Germany to receive recognition for his labors.

Umansky dusted himself off and presented himself as the new Ambassador. Much later, after the war had started, the President's adviser Hopkins suddenly recalled Troyanovsky at the table as "a good ambassador": "He understood the Americans, and the Americans understood him, it was always possible to reach an agreement." Nothing like this could ever be said about Kostya. The new Ambassador put the photograph signed by the Emperor in a silver frame decorated with a birch twig design, and whenever the young diplomat was photographed at work, or at infrequent moments of restorative leisure, the photo somehow always made it into the shot.

The Americans could not grasp the individual non-existence of the Russians. They thought that they did not like Umansky, but what they did not like was the Empire, and Umansky, as was fitting for the Ambassador of the Muscovites, fine-tuned his irony on the "stupid" Deputy Assistant Secretaries at the State Department, where he would end negotiations with shrill tirades, and pretend that "firmness is equivalent to rudeness." He could afford it: the Soviet Union wasn't going to get the loans anyway.

What did they talk about at the State Department? The American ambassador complained in Moscow: *every day* your Umansky comes and asks! Comes and asks! He isn't asking for anything, was the unchanging answer, he is just *following up on things*. About welding machines, the convention on the protection of seals, the outrageous detention in broad daylight of the Soviet citizen Gaik Ovakimian on a fictional charge of espionage (what actually happened was that one of his agents, in a fit of panic, went to the FBI and identified Ovakimian as the chief of Soviet scientific intelligence gathering operations). They conducted a voluminous correspondence on trade issues: the Soviet

Union exported matches, squirrel pelts, hundreds of thousands of bundles of sheep intestines (regular Kalmyk ones and Transcaucasian), buckskin, bristles, badger hair ($10 a pound), caviar, sturgeon, beluga, fox pelts from Central Ural and Southern Ukraine, and especially rags (withstanding competition with Romania and Poland).

Even when he was telling necessary lies, Kostya liked to posture, he spent three years drunk on his own importance, and forget about the snows. He was not summoned to the Kremlin; his teacher Litvinov protected him for the time being, kept him far away from the mass graves and nocturnal shootings; but time ran out, and in early 1939 Maxim Maximovich sensed a change: the handshakes he received in the Kremlin had grown weaker. In the dead of night, with a suppressed laugh, he admitted to his Englishwoman: "Are they really trying to reach an agreement with Hitler behind my back? I can't believe this idiocy..." As if the Emperor had a choice in the game, when all the other participants wanted to be the first to feed the Reds to Germany.

It was Litvinov who still had a choice. Every evening, his pillow was placed on top of a loaded pistol, and the first and central law of his apartment in the House of Government was: *you don't knock on Daddy's door after Daddy has gone to bed.* A knock would mean they had come for him and he would shoot himself. One day his young daughter forgot about this and in the heat of some game ran up to the door and knocked.

Litvinov waited.

And opened the door.

But in spring, a day came when across the threshold of the former imperial dacha in Firsanovka came the riders of the Apocalypse — Molotov, Beria, Georgy Malenkov — while outside soldiers with NKVD badges took their positions. Litvinov could not get up, and looked at the guests as if they were his favorite movie rolling on a screen: so this is how it comes. He was not to disappear just yet, Litvinov was told, he was to be crucified publicly on May 1 and be seen alive; after the May holidays he was crushed at the Plenum — the new People's Commissar Molotov shouted: "Do you think we're idiots?!" (yes, Vyacheslav Mikhailovich, yes, he did think you were an idiot) — and according to imperial custom, the designated executioners were friends of the family: Marshals Semyon Budyonny and Kliment Voroshilov.

As the sacrificial drums beat on, Litvinov also suffered a private shame: he knew his office on Kuznetsky Avenue would be searched. It wasn't his letter to the emperor asking for retirement that he was ashamed of, however, but the unfinished chocolate bar in his desk drawer. He also liked chocolate truffles and kept them until they went moldy; prison had taught him discipline, and he did not eat the chocolate all at once, but rather piece by piece.

The wording for the press, on the other hand, gave him hope — he was said to have removed himself "in accordance with his own wishes," which meant life ("in connection with a transfer to another position" meant a somewhat delayed death; "unable to manage his duties," or "proved unworthy of the public trust" would've meant immediate death), but salvation was issued only individually, and he told his son: "You will definitely be taken in." The employees and friends of the "uber-spy" were arrested and tortured, and his envoys were recalled and dismissed.

Ivy Valterovna was meanwhile teaching English in Sverdlovsk (now Yekaterinburg). She loved to do so and taught everyone: officers of the General Staff, the physicist Leonovich, actress Ranevskaya, psychiatrists, even her housekeepers, while she herself dreamed of getting rid of her accent in Russian. Litvinov did not have it in him to talk to her, so instead it was his daughter who whispered the news to her mother over the phone, and the crazy English woman shouted in reply, over the noisy connection: I heard everything! He was dismissed! The newspapers, true, were silent, but she heard it from acquaintances — and then she added in a lively voice: we're putting up hay here, is that the right way to say it?

"You need to come," the daughter said in a dead voice.

"Do I? I was planning to, but only after the exams," the English-woman was somewhat surprised.

The daughter was tired; not knowing what to say next, she listened and asked in the end: don't you think that it would be better for us all to be together right now?

The English woman held a puzzled pause and started to pack her suitcase without special hurry.

On the other side of the world, Umansky (repeating Troyanovsky's fate) also opened his suitcase to pack and stared into it as if into his own coffin — the long hand of Moscow reached him too, a tap on the shoulder, the telegram that was still sudden even though he had always expected it. This would be the end of his career; he was invited to undertake a journey to the heart of the earth where he would either pass through the eye of a needle or leave through the crematorium's smokestack. Umansky searched his past, looking for a way out, but he had that shameful father-in-law, the haberdashery manager, unpaid party dues in 1925; a recommendation to the party by Stark, who was now the enemy of the people; the Austrian underground; the indelible "replaced comrade Mikhail Koltsov in his position." It had finally begun, he thought.

But it had begun earlier. His friend Koltsov (people sometimes confused them) did not disappear without consequences for Umansky. He was beaten for five months, until, like hundreds of thousands before him, Koltsov admitted everything, and like a beast of burden that had been whipped bloody, he pulled the wagon he was hitched to by the NKVD, and they piled a few bodies onto his load, just in case, people still carousing and drinking on the outside, Litvinov's protégés. And he drove them all, obediently increasing his pace.

"In 1932 I became close to Radek, Shtein, Umansky and Gnedin," read Koltsov's confession, "and this group of enthusiasts of Soviet-German friendship had established important connections with the Germans (here Koltsov had his fingers stomped on), and I was dragged into a criminal spy ring."

"An American was present during many conversations at Umansky's apartment, the journalist Louis Fisher. He was a close friend of Umansky's and had an enormous influence on him. Umansky internalized his opinions on all political issues and did not hide anything from him…"

"I (Koltsov was hit in the groin), speaking plainly, was recruited by Radek and from 1932 to 1934 I communicated spy reports with Umansky's participation and assistance."

It cannot be said of Koltsov (or of others) that he was caught completely unawares — the iron men knew what was expected from them. The illegal Political Committee of the Executive Committee of the Communist International published a secret code of conduct, titled "How a Communist Should Behave under Investigation and in Court." Page four contained potentially life-saving advice ("Some communists, when arrested, believe that it is better at the investigation to give testimony, and then deny it in court. This view is completely mistaken and very harmful…") which was supposed to be skipped by real Communists, who were expected to take their guidance from page eight: "…An arrested communist, in thinking through his plan of action, should always put the interests of the party first, and only then contemplate how to escape from charges made by the investigation."

When he was told whom to incriminate, Koltsov fabricated blame for each target, out of his own material, but custom-fit. He made things up, but he kept them truthful. This was about real people who were still alive, with a functioning circulatory system, and for verisimilitude, he tore meat out of them, raising his edifices on shifty grounds: such-and-such never said anything, but he may have thought things, and if he thought, he would have thought like this; if such-and-such ever thought this — he let it slip; if he let it slip — he might as well have said so; he talked about this — he really wanted it to happen; "he wanted" meant "he plotted against the Emperor." For each man, there was truth was behind one of the dashes in this sequence, but *which*? Koltsov was a writer, he must have found something to work with: a heart-to-heart in the kitchen late at night, a confession, simple observations of people he loved.

Did Koltsov imagine that when he showed his good friends in this unexpected light in his final document, he would condemn them? Did he prepare himself, during restless nights, for line-ups with friends, dazed and smelling of beds from which they had been dragged, sullied by him, while he sat opposite, an unrecognizable person with non-responsive pupils ("Not Koltsov, a completely different person, an old man," remembered one of these friends who saw him and survived to tell).

Two hundred meters from Koltsov's bunk in the internal jail of the NKVD, his friend Kostya, recalled from the USA, slept on a bed at The Moscow hotel. He spent his days in the Commissariat's offices, giving exhaustive replies to questions like, "Well, how are things going in America?" but in fact trying to say one thing: I'm not with Litvinov, I'm with you, I'll help, I wish to have the chance to prove my devotion to the Emperor and the new People's Commissar, Vyacheslav Molotov.

TATYANA LITVINOVA, BRIGHTON, ENGLAND: We were friends with Marshals Voroshilov and Budyonny from the time we became part of the golden cage, those two hundred families who were fully provided for by the state. Friendship consisted of getting together to eat. Voroshilov grumbled: no billiards. The artists I met with thought Voroshilov was a scum. Maxim Maximovich considered him to be a charming, kind-hearted village mechanic. And Budyonny was scared of my father.

I met him after my father's dismissal and wanted to hug him — it's uncle Budyonny! — but he pretended not to recognize me. He turned out to be a coward. When he happened to see father in the corridor of the Kremlin cafeteria, he glued himself to the nearest window sill, hesitated and finally fired off, "I'm afraid to catch cold," and ran away.

Voroshilov, after flaying Litvinov at the Plenum, extended his hand to him, "Of course you understand everything…"

And Litvinov shook this hand, he had prepared himself for all the betrayals. Why did they all do this, his daughter remembers him wondering, they won't save themselves by doing so… *There* they know who I was friends with anyway, this knowledge cannot be erased. That means they are trying to *show* that they are scared. They think the Emperor likes it when people are scared. Litvinov acquitted everyone. Apart from one person.

The Litvinovs were moved from their townhouse on Spiridonovka to the dacha, where they were kept under a magnanimous house arrest. The two trucks sent after their belongings, arrived at the dacha half-empty — their furniture was government-issued, so all they had to bring was books, children's clothes and two bicycles. One of the drivers talked to Tanya Litvinova the whole way, and seemed very sympathetic; nonetheless, he strongly suggested that the bicycles be taken away "for safe-keeping." The family was fed and serviced. When instead of three cars parked outside the dacha's solid muted-green fence Litvinov found eight, he picked up the phone and used his government line for what would be the last time.

"We're keeping you safe," Lavrentiy Beria told him. "You don't know how valuable you are, Maxim Maximovich!"

"I do, but others might think..."

Beria hung up. The next morning, six men in crisply ironed green overalls walked past the family seated at the breakfast table into Litvinov's office and soon returned with phone cords looped on their shoulders. The children laughed and ran to see what Daddy's office looked like without his important phone, and life took appropriate form: the retired *pater familias* took piano lessons, missed his newswires and took the kids for walks (two guards walking ten steps before them, and two more ten steps behind). Litvinov carried Esbit tablets with him on these walks: he made small fires in the fields and burned his books, culling his library just in case. Misha, his son, would sometimes catch a page and scan it before it went into the flame, but the little girl was bored — this was all about politics, some Trotsky or something, she couldn't care less. The children lived as they always did, nothing had changed for them — it's just that no one came to visit any more.

AMERICA III

PAINFULLY, THE FAMILY TOOK NOTE OF PERSISTING AND abandoned loyalties: Shtein was the first to visit — he had been recalled from Italy and was also uncertain about his prospects. Litvinov's stenographer also stopped by. Surits, left without a job, was scared, but came anyway, Rubinin was arrested — he couldn't be blamed. One night at the theater, an unnamed female friend was not afraid to approach the Litvinovs, and Maxim Maximovich exclaimed: "Oh, you're a brave woman!" Umansky did not appear once, as Litvinov's biographer, Sheinis, recorded, with an almost gloating triumph.

TATYANA LITVINOVA, BRIGHTON, ENGLAND: Many people abandoned him, but Umansky's distancing hurt Maxim Maximovich most of all. My father was not prepared for this betrayal. It was so out of keeping with the image that had formed in our minds — we thought him a bohemian, bold, open person. And suddenly — this treachery, he turned out to be mean and ambitious.

This was significant, and the Emperor certainly found out. Molotov also may have remembered the fact that Umansky's papers were cleared by the Emperor without corrections. This was important (like Koltsov's confessions and those of many others), but not to such an extent as to let Kostya go unchanged, and so on the 15th of October, Umansky, neither dead nor alive, sank down onto a chair opposite the Emperor. Molotov was also there. There was a long, unnatural silence.

Finally the Emperor unsealed his lips: return to America. Umansky must have felt like an animal let out of a trap — all thrilled muscle and releasing intestine: yes!

For appearance's sake, they also talked about the war in Europe, and the return to the Empire of its lawful lands. Umansky missed how it happened, that an unassuming black-haired person appeared at the table. Umansky choked with outrage: the time allotted to the meeting had yet to run out, it was still a long way until the concluding minutes, when the most important things coming from the heart are spoken, when he could say what he had been nurturing, so close to tears: my gratitude, Sovereign! I quite understand… And hear the forgiving fatherly reply… This was his time! Blinded, he raised his eyes to the eternal polar radiance.

"Allow me to introduce you. This is your new counselor. Comrade Gromyko. He's going with you."

Umansky composed himself and turned a grimace of sudden pain into an amiable smile: this was the end, he'd never be the man he was. Shortly after one a.m., he left the Emperor's office forever, dragging his new comrade behind him like an iron ball chained to his leg, clanging and ringing. He was convinced it was his death dragging behind him, his canceled future, as he walked toward the Belarus Station, whining: with what avenging precision did Troyanovsky's fate repeat itself.

Kostya was left to mix and drink the bitter dregs of his demise before turning into recalled trash. Having reached an agreement with the Germans, the Emperor wrote something conciliatory to Roosevelt, but the Empire invaded Finland, which never did grasp its own significance. The Americans took the side of the Finns, the "moral embargo" buried our aircraft orders, congressmen demanded that the U.S. Ambassador be recalled from Moscow, or that his salary not be paid, and Umansky was no longer received anywhere; there was no one with whom to commiserate.

His duties, as the Ambassador of the Muscovites, consisted of praising the successes of the Red Army in Khalkhyn-Gol within the earshot of employees of the German embassy, denying the union with England and demonstrating his faith in the German-imperial friendship. As France was crushed, and the 22nd of June and Pearl Harbor loomed clearer, the Ambassador, suppressing a yawn, penned missives such as, "Comrade Tchuvakhin, enclosed please find the skull of a Neanderthal child for Professor Khordlik" (and Khordlik, at the nearest opportunity proclaimed from his scientific podium: "The USSR is the only hope for humanity!") and boasted of the good life of deaf-mute people (all one hundred and thirteen thousand of them) in the Empire: "Under the socialist system, deaf-mutes have for the first time the opportunity to show their abilities creatively in various fields of socialist organization, and have won the trust of the people, who elect these deaf-mutes as their representatives in the organs of power." It was only on the 1st of March, 1941, when England, by common opinion, was dying under bombardment, that Commerce Secretary Wallace remembered the Russian Ambassador, called him for a private meeting, and ("I will be quite frank with you, Mr. Ambassador. What you are about to find out...") reported "top secret and absolutely reliable information": first Hitler would finish off England, and then he'd go after the Empire. Umansky — you couldn't sell memoirs without these details — "turned deathly pale," "was silent for a while," but "gaining possession of himself," passed this disinformation prepared by the Germans up his chain of command. Russian memoirs also don't sell very well without fake blood: here's the same tune played by the Museum of Jewish history: "The authority of Umansky's report was on par with Richard Sorge's reporting (*a lie*). At the end of the war (*a lie*), Umansky was recalled to Moscow (*a lie*) to receive his Letters of Credence(*a lie*): in addition to maintaining the post of the Ambassador to the USA (*a lie*), he was appointed Ambassador in Mexico. At the airport, he was seen off warmly (*a lie*) as an honored diplomat. The plane took off — and crashed. This was undoubtedly a flight of special (*so far uncertain*) purpose."

On June 22, the USA heard about the catastrophe of the German invasion into Russia. The numbers of casualties and those taken prisoner came with six zeroes after them, but the Russians died and fought with the ferocity and determination of early Christians. In the diaries of Hitler's generals the customary self-admiration began to be mixed with dark, disdainful incomprehension of the unexpected resilience of these Soviet earth-worms.

Andrei Gromyko received his long-awaited telegram, and without sympathy informed his Ambassador, frayed by the constant need to be prepared for the worst: "You are being recalled." Umansky got up heavily and vacated his position, hoping for a retirement pension, anything but a camp, anything but death.

Another retiree, the sixty-five-year-old Litvinov, also bet on the war and wrote to the Emperor: please put me to work, Sovereign, *any* appointment. He dreamed at his dining table of managing an orderly evacuation of the population to the East. He sent another letter to the Institute of Hematology volunteering himself and his wife as donors. The Institute responded warmly; the Emperor did not reply. The thunder of war, however, began to reach him: Maxim Maximovich, could you write an article for the foreigners in the West? Would you be available for a radio broadcast, in English? There's a vacant office at the Foreign Affairs Committee — please feel free to use it, how could you work without a desk? Litvinov read the application essays for the diplomatic academy, writing down particularly striking inanities in his own collection of anecdotes ("I offer myself for travel to warring countries at war in order to sort out the causes that make them fight"). Then, the lightning struck him with its usual transforming force, and on the 12th of November Litvinov found himself on the runway in Penza, flying to Kuibyshev and beyond, to the United States of America, as the Extraordinary and Plenipotentiary Ambassador of the Soviet Union. At the airport, Litvinov, sensing his old iron core inside him, turned to the manager who lurked behind him, yearning, but not daring to speak to the legendary peace-maker, and asked: "Where's the bathroom?" "We don't have things like that," the manager replied, embarrassed. "You'll have to step out on the back porch, and, you know..." Litvinov laughed, for the first time in three years.

The Empire required tanks, planes, vehicles, non-ferrous metals, gasoline, boots, SPAM, everything that Roosevelt could give, and the Emperor concentrated all his (irresistible) force on his push in this very necessary direction. And for this, everything in the sixty-five-year-long life of Maxim Litvinov was useful, including the iron core: a personal acquaintance with and the personal sympathy of the President (Roosevelt believed the disgraced People's Commissar to have a "Western mindset"), his Jewishness ("Maxim Maximovich belongs to an ethnic group that has gained fame on the commercial stage"), and even his English wife, who had twice been officially declared the most tastelessly dressed woman of the year in Washington.

Litvinov, like all those graced by the light of the imperial flame, left his trace not only in unreliable documents, but also in legends, which actually contain more truth. One of these holds that the first person he saw at the Kremlin after his moth-balled storage at the dacha, was Kostya Umansky.

It seems that Umansky saw Litvinov first, and continued to walk down the marble steps, along the red runner, without any particular hurry, with his charming customary smile, almost without losing his composure: perhaps Maxim Maximovich didn't know that the imperial falcon Umansky would no longer be taken to hunt, that he was now a ruffled, faded, small man, father of a young beautiful daughter, who had pointlessly waited in Kuibyshev for an order to return. Umansky, so hungry for power, had been crumpled and was about to be tossed into the trash. Maxim Maximovich? In the Kremlin? Who are you seeing? I see... Perhaps something for me if it turns up... And his boneless hand stretched out, the hand of a person no longer made of steel:

"Maxim Maximovich... Perhaps I deserve amnesty?" He understood everything, giving himself away, he realized how little he could expect — a small mercy perhaps, for old times' sake.

"Whatever for?" Litvinov chuckled; starved of playing with mice, he wasn't about to pass up this chance. "You broke no law." And he moved down the corridor, leaving Umansky behind.

Umansky was retained as a member of the Executive Secretariat of the People's Committee of Foreign Affairs, and in December he was once again entrusted with press monitoring, a dishonorable pension. He, once called a virtuoso of schemes, returned to Kuibyshev to drink vodka with foreign correspondents at the Grand Hotel, to wait to see whether Moscow would fall, and tell his new friend Ehrenburg about the childish simplicity of Americans, while Litvinov took off to serve the Emperor for the last time, and did everything that was required exactly as was required: "When he finished the official remarks, there was a standing ovation. This was the first time in my life I had seen anything like this. Litvinov spoke bluntly, it was true realism" wrote Sheinis, and the day after Pearl Harbor, on December 8th, he met with Roosevelt who greeted him with open arms. Even Umansky, in the biographer's hands, becomes another flashlight trained on the spiritual magnificence of the impeccable old man: in San Francisco, Litvinov was met by Gromyko, who had flown from Washington, and, disappointed that he himself had missed out on the ambassador's chair, said by way of greeting: "Our Embassy did not have a mature leader. And now we have received an outstanding leader." Litvinov nodded and replied: "Yes? But during a meeting with me, Comrade Stalin highly rated the work of my predecessor Umansky." Gromyko swallowed hard and led the new Ambassador to the airplane that was waiting for him.

If only Nina Umanskaya had stayed in the States for just a bit longer — she would never have met Volodya Shakhurin, a boy with strange quirks and a gift for languages. Two more months of carefree summer and she could have slipped into the seventh grade of the embassy school. Why this urgency, why was it necessary to uproot the child and drag her on a month-long trek via the Hawaiian Islands, avoiding the German submarines, through Singapore, Thailand, India, Baghdad and over the Persian plateaus? For what? She could have stayed back in the States, until the Emperor suddenly demanded information about Mexico and remembered someone, this fellow

Umansky, well-versed in Western Hemisphere affairs. Then the girl could have gone directly to Mexico City, bypassing the fateful school #175 altogether. But Roosevelt decided in May of 1942 to talk to the Russians.

He had spent a year watching the distant glow of war from his plush seat. Then it became clear that although the German armies were streaming towards Stalingrad and the Russians were starving, Moscow had not fallen, and the Soviets would retreat to Siberia and rest, but would not surrender. It was time to start talks. So Molotov flew to the USA: he was nervous, it was the first meeting — how would it go? He drooped and could only marshal granite-hard stoicism for brief moments, when Litvinov appeared. The Ambassador would grimace scornfully and make a show of obvious boredom. But whenever Litvinov was sent away, the American President found before him a vulnerable, sincere man, just like him (or so it seemed to Roosevelt), a suddenly comprehensible particle of the terrifying imperial might who astonished his interlocutors with his "unexpected openness and kindness." And Roosevelt himself was extremely nervous, he couldn't find the words to fan the flickering (or so he imagined) flame of human warmth, so vital at the very start of negotiations. They talked, they twitched, as if scuffling in the mud, and the interpreters had extensive arguments about what, exactly, had just been said, and in what sense it was uttered. Molotov whispered: things are very complicated, we may lose Moscow, Baku and Rostov. Roosevelt touched wounds: how is the food supply in Leningrad? Molotov winced from inner pain, from this intolerable directness, the idiotic desire for clarity, and nodded: yes, there are difficulties, especially in winter (there had been cannibalism — how could Roosevelt understand? That's not the way to ask!). They ate in mutual torment, throwing each other mute well-wishing looks and clinking their glasses, and the meal was coming to an end, with the prospect of finally getting up and stretching one's legs, when Roosevelt's aide Hopkins, this son of a horse-tack peddler, decided to start a conversation about something "in general" to lighten the atmosphere, but about what? It had to be a general subject, familiar to both the hosts and the guests, a social conversation, about the health of mutual acquaintances, to wish them well, how hard it was with these Russians, it was quite an ordeal… and… well at least he came up with:

"How's Umansky? Is he still working at the telegraph agency?"

Molotov did not liven up. He did not believe in idle conversations. He wondered about the malicious subtext of the question, sensing a trick… Was this a way for the American President to bring up the Russians' legendary stubbornness in the late 1930s? Or does he think it appropriate to touch upon the disappearance of some diplomats who'd been recalled from the US? From there, it's just a skip and a hop to a request that a number of Russian wives of American citizens be released from prison camps (he probably has the list at the ready!). Molotov replied with evasive dryness:

"He's working at the People's Committee for Foreign Affairs," and didn't give further details. "The Soviet government believed it was necessary in the new situation to replace him with a more authoritative person as Ambassador. Umansky was very young."

Roosevelt shook his head cunningly (he thought that Molotov was joking — the human *warmth*…):

"… And he sometimes showed excessive enthusiasm," he put his cup down on the tablecloth, meaning, we can be honest: we all know it's not about his youth. "And incidentally," he went on, fully believing his guest to be as susceptible to the simple joys of carefree conversation as himself. The next thing that came out of Roosevelt's mouth was purely (in his mind) a vacuous, harmless, meaningless observation — he was oblivious, this self-satisfied American, to its punitive essence:

"Do you know that Umansky's wife and daughter are living in Washington?"

The Americans did not understand the Russians, but the Germans did.

The talks between Roosevelt and Molotov were successfully concluded, the Germans did not take Stalingrad, Field Marshal Paulus, who had crushed, in forty days, a France that was prepared for invasion, surrendered at Stalingrad, and two hours later, trying to fall asleep on boards, suddenly said to his aide in the icy darkness, about one of the iron men he had seen passing: "What terrifying eyes that major had!" "Like everyone in the NKVD," the aide replied without thinking. After taking their first step across Russian land, the Germans understood everything. Umansky's wife and daughter are living in Washington?

Could the Emperor and his leaders not know something necessary about their own people, including their childhood nicknames and favorite songs?

Could a member of the State Committee of Defense who was sent by the Emperor himself not know something during talks with the American President?

Could he have said, "I don't know," if he really did not know?

Umansky's wife and daughter are living in Washington?

Molotov did some mental math: on 24 May 1941, he, the People's Commissar, had lectured the American Ambassador Steinhardt, who had begged to evacuate his family (the war was then imminent), with the polite loathing reserved for a coward:

"Quit your whining! Your fears are groundless. There will be no war. Our own nerves are quite strong, we don't intend to send our wives away from Moscow," and here was Roosevelt, informing his guest with a quiet little smile that hid a great deal, that the wife and daughter of the Soviet ambassador had been hiding for a year from the war, from the starvation, from the Empire, where until recently life was good — even for deaf-mutes! But, then, people constantly disappeared, such that even in the best years there was no hurry to send the family back until the fate of a recalled imperial falcon was clear. How's that for strong nerves, Vyacheslav Mikhailovich? Time, time, it makes both you and us wiser. I hope we've started to understand each other — here's to your health!

Roosevelt had spoken.

Molotov looked at the American President without warmth.

And then nodded: yes.

Yes. The authority, as always, knows who is where. Including Umansky's family.

That was all, they finished eating; the men moved to the soft couches in the living room (Roosevelt was solicitous of Molotov: sit here, let's sit closer…). Hopkins, moving on from the unpleasant subject of Umansky, asked, do you know why Americans don't like the Empire, but the Brits do? (Because in America most Communists are Jewish, pedantic people who do not connect well with the common folk, and how could you expect the average American to really appreciate the Soviet values and patriotism, if these are the only Communists around.) And by the way, shouldn't we bomb Romania from the Syrian aerodromes? We started sending bombers to Japan, and you know, we're satisfied with the result…They finally struck the right tone and the great talks began, changing history, and Nina Umanskaya's fate was decided.

Molotov's second cable to the Emperor, detailing additional agreements and a list of topics touched upon by the President, in paragraph eight said: "Roosevelt asked whether I knew that Umansky's wife and daughter were in Washington. I confirmed that I did." In the published text of the cable this sentence is followed by parentheses, indicating text that was omitted by the censor for reasons of secrecy.

I was unable to find any person who had seen the telegram in its entirety.

The Emperor read the cable, taking in the totality of things and making decisions at the same time. On the 1st of September 1943, a new girl came to the seventh grade of school #175, and Sveta Molotova acquired another friend.

Umansky moved from his bachelor room at the Moscow Hotel to the House of Government by the Great Stone Bridge, and probably, after a sad, exhausted silence (did something happen to you? tell me!) admitted to the woman he loved so madly (if we are to believe Ehrenburg): "We cannot go on now like we used to. My family has come. That's the way it is."

FISHING

THE BEGINNING OF WINTER IS ALWAYS A JOY, THERE'S AN insuppressible hope in the first snow on the ground.

I held a thick edition of *Sport Express* under my arm; soon a balding Major with ginger eyelashes joined me at the bar and placed his hands with their hairy wrists next to mine.

"I didn't order anything, I was waiting for you," I said. "What will you have to eat?"

"I'm sorry, Alexander Vasilievich, I just had a hearty get-together with the family troops," he patted his stomach. "What about you? I'll have some tea."

We got a pot of tea, the major smoked, I listened to him retelling the plot of an excellent movie he'd just seen with the feigned delight of a children's optometrist:

"The hero dies. But it's like he is born again. But not in the future, in the past." He paused, agreed to ice cream, two scoops. "A revolution, Alexander Vasilievich, is regression. It's stopping the train! And politics is everything; you and me talking — that's politics. The snow on the ground — politics!" and he added, quieter: "And the fact that representatives of the special services go into government, that's also politics, that's a sign!"

I had heard that he spent his evenings training canaries to sing, in special singing schools.

"What kind of singing school is yours?"

"Alexander Vasilievich, after the fall of the Soviet Union and the collapse of the Soviet system, singing schools for canaries were divided by state borders, and I…"

I dropped the subject and just sat there, sweating in my boots, waiting for a chance to go to the bathroom.

The major picked up the tea pot, and I placed the *Sport-Express* on his side:

"That should cover November."

"Thank you. At the risk of repeating myself, I shall reiterate, Alexander Vasilievich, that our relations are very important for me in themselves. Without the economic component. I simply find it pleasant to solve problems with you. To assist national science. I feel your understanding. And respect," his blue eyes looked at me seriously. "And the relations. The relations are the main thing. They remain forever. This," he quietly placed his hand on the newspaper, "is not the main thing. So, about your last question: Umansky's case will not be given to you."

"Why not?" He acted like he didn't hear the question. I went on, "It's not a classified case. A seventh grader was killed, fifty-nine years ago. All the relatives are dead."

He unwillingly came to life, shrugged his shoulders and looked gloomily out the window, at the lights heading into the underground parking.

"I don't know. Formally, it so as not to allow an invasion into private life. But really — I don't know…. You know what we say: if a case isn't given, then that means there is nothing in it."

"Have you seen the case yourself?"

"No. I just confirmed that it existed. I barely touched it. It's not the way we're accustomed to do things, you know, Alexander Vasilievich. It's you scholars who are a free people. But we… We work strictly on a need-to-know basis."

"How many volumes?"

"Well," he put away the cigarettes and his eyes searched out the clock on the wall. "Four. I think. The investigation proceeded, it seemed to me, within a narrow protocol. Rather formally. But, I don't know, I'm afraid to mislead you. In short, the law does not allow us to familiarize you with the case. In the archives department I have connections and resources… but — the law! We're people of the state, after all. I don't know whether this will come in handy for you…. Write this down…" He dictated in a whisper from a scrap of paper: "Case r-788, July-October 1943. Military board 4n-012045/55. Walter pistol, number 227841k."

Then he let out a long-suffering sigh and burned the note in the ashtray. "Here's what they said to me: you give someone this case, and the entire Caucasus will get up in arms!" He lifted the *Sport-Express* in both hands, like an icon, and placed it in his briefcase. "Alexander Vasilievich, I have a request, next time, if you can, let's do this in euros. The exchange rate is jumping all over the place at the moment, you know… I'd just feel more secure with euros. Well, thanks for the tea! I want to catch the news. I start at nine and go until half past eleven, I'm a total wonk: ORT, NTV, Dispatches, I don't even answer the phone. My wife knows — I'm to be left alone after nine. There's so much information nowadays…"

We went out to the street; it was snowing, there were lights shining, and we warmly shook hands.

"Could you perhaps consider the possibility," I said, "of — on some separate conditions, so as not to break the law, not to touch the case — of making an excerpt from the protocol of the examination of the crime-scene. I'm interested in the recorded position of the bodies, the arrangements of the shells and the position of the blood stains from Shakhurin. It could be a diagram. I think I could find," I mumbled, "two thousand euros."

"Alexander Vasilievich," the major said with feeling, and pressed the hand that was not holding the briefcase to the right side of his chest. "I can't! I can't! You'll have to look for other ways," and he pointed somewhere above his head. "But believe me, there's nothing in the case."

I was already feeling very cold, and tried to guess where he would go, so that I could turn in the opposite direction: every time we met in a new place.

"I didn't even read it. Just a few excerpts… For example, I remembered, I don't know if this will give you anything: one of the first people to the scene was the traffic policewoman Zinadia Stepanchikova and she testified about," — he emphasized the words — "a very beautiful woman. The woman cried louder than anyone else. And she only looked at Nina Umanskaya. She pushed everyone out of the way, saw the girl, started crying, said something like 'Kostya!' and quickly left. They never did identify her. She wasn't a relative. Evidently, there was some personal story involved." And then he added, as though he were reading a file, "A well-dressed lady in a gray overcoat, hat and blue shoes."

We said goodbye, and he spoke again, drumming his fingers on his forehead to jog his memory:

"A brunette. She was biting her fingers!"

I found what I'd been looking for. Umansky adored his daughter, his family life only held together because of Nina, but — remember Ehrenburg: "I knew that in his life there was a great emotion, that in 1943 he had suffered the torments described by Chekhov in his short story, 'The Lady with the Lapdog'. And here was an unexpected conclusion of the drama."

A very beautiful brunette who cried on the Great Stone Bridge over the dead girl, but for some reason repeated the name of her father. Umansky, at forty, had been screwing ballerinas and secretaries; he was a "big charmer," a "fop," or in Russian *"fat"* from the Latin *fatuus* — a self-satisfied, vulgar dandy; a coxcomb, a ponce. And this was a man who suddenly came to know a Great Feeling. He experienced torments. He suffered so much that the hollow Ehrenburg used the word "drama." He could leave his family, but what about his daughter? Had he left, right away, the girl would have stayed in Moscow with her abandoned mother, and would have lived, I could have run into her at the Crossroads supermarket on Osenny Boulevard, she would be shopping for chicken breasts, say, and I could see the remains, as it is customary to say, of her former beauty. But there was this nameless beauty — and the girl was killed for good, and the beloved Kostya stayed with his wife, and perhaps he did not suffer all this much, but screwed his wife regularly, as husbands do, and simply put on a show for Ehrenburg. And the lady on the bridge cried because the girl was dead and there were no more obstacles, and still she knew she would be left with nothing but would never stop loving her Kostya, Kostya... She grieved for her own love.

"Alexander Naumovich, I want to find this woman."

"Good night. Do you mean to say: find her grave? To establish the identity of a person with whom Umansky was potentially in love sixty-one years ago? Let's think about it: you hope that in the thirty-six hours between the murder of his daughter and the flight to Mexico, Umansky found an opportunity — on the ride from the crematorium to the airfield, perhaps? — to go to his abandoned lover and share his suspicions about the true identity of the killer? Or do you think that she killed the girl?"

"The details are not important. Although she did have a motive. I think she is the key. If we can dig her out, everything will become linked together, and we will be able to get out of this. Why aren't you asleep, by the way?"

"I just saw Masha off. She cooked for me. She tidied up."

"Who is this Masha?"

"Masha is our secretary. You know, she's a very warm, bright person. You should be gentler with her."

"She sounds like she'd make a good wife for your son."

"I've already written to him. Perhaps he'll visit in summer. Although she doesn't want to get married. How did the meeting with our friend go?"

"Our friend is afraid of his own shadow. We won't be given the case, but we already knew that without him. He tried to tell me something important. Two things. And I didn't really understand either of them. He can't talk normally, you know, it's all code with him. The first is that the case was opened in July and closed in October. But that's bullshit: the murder took place on the third of June. Why was the case only opened a month later? And why did it take four month to investigate a case that was deemed a clear murder-suicide, and why did the sentence come from a military board? Was someone sentenced? The kids were dead. What sentence?"

"That means there was another case, a second one, and this is what he was trying to tell you. The murder-suicide was closed, but later the same incident prompted another investigation. Question is, who's in this second case?"

"The actual murderer? I don't know. He also kept saying, the case is empty, there's nothing in it, blah-blah, but if it were made public, the entire Caucasus will howl."

"Information that implicates people of Caucasian origin? Still alive? Relatives?"

"But there isn't anyone like that among the ones we've investigated. The only thing I understood for sure: the pistol was found, it really was a Walter. But the moron wouldn't tell me *where* it was found. I haven't slept, my head's killing me, it all seems wrong... but what if something different did happen on that bridge? You, comrade major general of state security, what does your operative intuition tell you?"

"We got through to Fisher. Or rather all that was left of him."

When the investigation asked the broken-toothed Koltsov what they could use to incriminate Umansky, Koltsov — his best friend, his almost-brother — spoke (as best he could, seeing how the interrogators had knocked out most of his teeth) about the American journalist Louis Fisher who used to have great sway over "his Kostya" and said things like "My Kostya is lost without me." Based on this, I concerned myself with Mr. Fisher's humble existence, and learned that he and his German wife took an apartment on the Sofiiskaya embankment, and that he sent his son to the Red Army to please the locals, but then his son was not allowed to leave ("What are you moaning for *here?*" Litvinov whispered. "Ask them *there.*"). Fisher went to beg *there*, Roosevelt's wife took pity on him and asked Ambassador Umansky: there's this man named Fisher. He has a son. Give him to us.

Fisher's gait gave him away as a man of truth or a sold-out bastard; the views in his writing coincided every day with the written recommendations of the People's Committee for Foreign Affairs (from the untroubled look at the arrival of the American delegation to the Comintern Congress to the justification of criminal prosecutions for abortions); Ambassador Bullit (and several other officials) treated Fisher with a deep distrust, Trotsky called him a "Soviet prostitute," the columnist Klimov called him an "old Trotskyist," and the satirists Ilf and Petrov, suddenly losing their teeth, only noted his "very black and very kind eyes." Fisher finished his days as the lover of the exiled writer Nina Berberova, an icy, highly polished dame who somehow did not notice the victory of the Russian people in the Great Patriotic War as she moved from one university town to another, and enjoyed meals cooked on campfires. In her own memoirs, she praised the "time spent with Louis," and concluded, with a melancholy hint at the credit she was due, "he died a wonderful death, swiftly, during our trip to the Bahamas" — he croaked in heaven, basically. But we discovered a Fisher Jr., born in 1923, a Sovietologist, who still gave signs of life in 1999. Might the son perhaps remember his father's friend Kostya? And Nina, a girl of unforgettable beauty? Her publisher did not have his address or telephone number, and the only way to reach him was through a friend: Nikolai Troitsky, ninety-nine years of age, a member of the White Guard or a defector.

I rang in the morning, Moscow time, and reached him in the middle of the night. I waited until late in the evening, dialed again, had time to doodle a sketch of a cruiser with five cannons while the phone rang, and then forced myself to utter from Moscow, where it was night, "Good morning."

The man spoke slowly. You could make a home in his words. You could stretch your legs there, and then lie down again. His words were slow and capacious, a train crawling along towards the station.

"Fisher? You need Fisher. But he doesn't talk to anyone. Fisher is suffering from a serious demotivation. Only his wife holds him back, in the sense of moving even deeper in this direction."

"Why doesn't he want to remember? Is he afraid of something?"

"It's not that he's cautious… but it's a challenge to get through to him. What do you want from him? Umansky? I don't know, I don't know… Who was Umansky close to? Litvinov? And what do you want from Fisher? He has rejected the past. He sent his father's papers to me — Umansky's name isn't mentioned in them. Berta Fisher would have been helpful perhaps," there was suddenly the warm, full-blooded flow of something that does not get old and is least deserving of death, in the old man's wheeze, "but unfortunately Berta Fisher is no longer alive. And her son has chosen to minimize his memories to an extreme. He said to me: I even sacrificed talking to you in order not to talk about what I prefer not to talk about. And what do you want from me? His telephone number? But you will find it very difficult. I'll go and get the telephone number, why not? My memory is old too. I move slowly. I'll hand the phone over to my wife and start moving. When you rang, I was sitting and listening to Voice of America, or rather Voice of Russia. Well, OK. I'm starting to move."

Silence set in, and I heard heavy shuffling footsteps moving away from me and towards death on another continent.

I waited for a while, and then for some reason I hung up the phone.

Z

"Tatyana Litvinova, Brighton, England: during the war, my husband and I often visited Kostya at the Moscow Hotel — we went to use his bathtub. When Raisa Mikhailovna and Nina came, the Umanskys moved to the House of Government, and our bath-and-laundry visits continued there. We gossiped with full mutual trust; we used to get letters from my parents in America through Kostya. Once, I remember, Kostya said about Dad: 'The old man's gone mad. His replies to Stalin's telegrams are pure obstruction.'"

Sometimes he'd call from work, late at night, around two, and we'd jump up and drag ourselves to the phone across our unheated apartment on Pervaya Meshchanskaya, shivering, there was frost in the corners. Kostya called when he was bored — officials of his rank used to spend nights on end in their offices in case the Boss called. This rule did not apply only to my father. They said: only Litvinov can argue with Stalin. And Mikoyan.

"Do you think that Umansky could truly love?"

"He had affairs left and right… I didn't see any great feeling in his life."

"We lived very sheltered lives, and didn't think about morals. Once Misha and I got into Dad's desk drawers and found pictures of naked women. We didn't know what they were for. We put them back, of course, father noticed every little detail, you had to be careful.

"Dad was a glutton. He was fat. He used to love green onions — he'd dip them in sour cream, then in salt, and eat them with rye bread and butter, and with cucumbers, always peeled and sliced lengthwise.

"Once, Misha came back from a walk, and told Mom with great surprise that he'd seen quite grown-up men looking into the crack in the fence around the women's swimming pool on the Moscow River. I didn't tell Mom that one of these men was my Dad.

We simply lived. There was a certain freedom in our relations. No one made drama out of anything."

"Litvinov," Goltsman said, "was recalled in early April of 1943, he arrived in Moscow on the sixteenth. He flew through Africa — the allies by then had finished off Rommel's group. You were right, Litvinov did not return alone."

"But not with his wife."

Goltsman confirmed grudgingly:

"Correct. M-me Litvinova stayed in the States. He had a secretary with him. I asked my old comrades in Veterans' Affairs to take a look at the travel documents: the secretary's gender is not indicated, only the vaccinations — plague and cholera."

"I think he returned with a beautiful woman. The one who cried on the bridge. The one we're looking for."

Goltsman turned off the overhead light, turned on the radio and sat closer to me. It was just after one in the morning; streetlights bloomed outside, and we sat by the radio watching the green digits of the frequencies glow in the dark and listening to songs.

"One of our witnesses gave us the whole problem. In Kuibyshev, in late October or early November, Kostya complained: X has left, and taken Z. I believe Z is the woman. It's unlikely he would have been unhappy if X had taken Z to Moscow. Planes flew to Moscow every day… Where else could she have been taken? To the front? To Siberia? That's unlikely. We shouldn't complicate things: this X is some old acquaintance. Umansky had only been back for two months, he hadn't had time to make new friends, and we know what his old circle was — diplomats. Then we recall that on the twelfth of November, Litvinov flew from Kuibyshev to the States to replace Kostya, which already ruined his career. But what if this Z also flew with Litvinov? Then his only love was also ruined. Then, from Ehrenburg, we know: Umansky was going through his drama *on the eve* of his departure to Mexico, April-May, he was scheduled to fly on June 4. Accordingly, Z — if this is Z — should have returned from the USA by this time. And you just confirmed exactly this last part: Litvinov's secretary returned on the sixteenth of April, they had forty-nine days left for explanations, sex and tears. Ehrenburg had it right: his friend was on fire, the love of his life just came back and now they had to part again, there was *little time*, everything had to be decided, for their entire lives!"

"Perhaps this is a chain of coincidence."

"Of course," I raised my eyes to the secretary who had frozen in the doorway. "It is always the coincidences that leave their mark, coincidences sometimes also referred to as fate."

Goltsman rustled the pages of his notebook where he recorded the names and contact information of individuals involved in our investigation.

"We will find out the identity of this secretary," he said. "We know where Litvinov's children live."

I knew: Goltsman did not enjoy the prospect of hunting down some imaginary brunette beauty. He would have much preferred to keep to the trail of the boy cremated at the Donsky cemetery and buried next to the stone pioneer Dimitrov. He wanted to look closer at Vladimir Shakhurin, he wanted to clear the junk from the surface (the common versions of schizophrenia and a smothering mother): there was Empire's cruelty — the war, the executions in basements, the NKVD's impunity, the Caucasian high-landers, with their habit of cutting throats, in the corridors of power. Did the boy turn violent in a violent time?

What happened, we ought to consider, to all fourteen-year-olds, at the school #175, in 1943?

The historian Eidelman, who was briefly famous in the last third of the last century, took his own stab at Stalin: "During the war, Stalin did something unheard of (and if one takes into account that the country had military and restoration needs and colossal losses, this step is outright unimaginable): with one stroke of the pen, tens of thousands of schools were segregated by sex; it was said that the reason for this was the murder of the daughter of the diplomat Umansky by the son of the Minister Shakhurin. The separation meant that from now on there would be no love or jealousy and thus no murders."

The hard truth was that Stalin segregated schools in order to raise boys into soldiers, but Eidelman wanted a prettier story and a chance to spit at the Emperor who thought he could cancel love and jealousy with his pen. In fact, however, school #175 was segregated right after New Year, long before the event on the Great Stone Bridge. Then the Empire, it would have seemed, was striving for equality ("Brothers and sisters," said the emperor into the microphone), but in that summer, the boys of the accursed school #175, on the contrary, *furiously separated* themselves, not only according to the titles of their absent fathers, but also according to their *possibilities*: who had more, who was tougher, who could show more to women.

To fill up the boys' classes, common parents' sons were transferred from school #636 on Uspensky Lane, which was being renovated. The wives of imperial falcons, under the leadership of Mrs. Zhemchuzhina, collected old clothes for the new pupils, and someone was lucky to receive a magnificent gray Boston suit, and someone else got something else, and ended up wearing the same old jacket, hand-made by his own grandmother, until the age of fifteen, until a rich man donated a bolt of fabric to make the boy a suit — and the boy suffered for the rest of his life, never mind that he made it to the Central Committee of the Communist Party.

At fourteen, as many doctors will tell you, boys feel their inadequacy most acutely. In the winter of 1943, when at Stalingrad the soldiers of the Empire, with brute fury, fought for the outcome of the war, and the children of commoners manned the factories, making shells and chasing pigeons in their lunch breaks, and school pupils received fifty grams of black bread and one piece of candy per day, the upper classes of school #175, lived in an atmosphere of *a-normality*, a lack of any norms. The bookish boys Sergo Mikoyan and Volodya Shakhurin felt their inadequacy most acutely, in the shadow of the dandies, operetta lovers, limousine owners, sons of buxom Caucasian mothers, who even at funerals did not forget to wear gold jewelry and paint their lips. Perhaps Volodya Shakhurin did not live to become Vladimir Alexeevich Shakhurin because he suddenly, awfully felt his insignificance, he saw himself through the eyes of an incredible Americanized girl in nylon stockings: to her he was a *nobody*, a shadow on the pavement, and that's why he put a gun into his pocket when he went to meet her at the bridge — at least *this* might impress her.

One last question remained, for old Goltsman:

"How come he wasn't afraid of killing himself? Boys are most afraid of death at the age of fourteen," I frowned, thinking.

"Investigative practice does not confirm your observation," Goltsman rustled. "The threshold for resolving to kill oneself is very low in teen-age boys and girls. Children are incapable of comprehending the finality of death. For them, everything always lies ahead. Death does not in fact exist for them. Nothing bad can happen. They have the wish to scare others and draw attention. Teenage suicides are often sudden. I doubt he planned it at all," Goltsman abruptly stood up. "The decision is made quickly and put into practice almost immediately."

Shakhurin may have killed himself. But first he shot the girl.

FEMME FATALE

I HELD ALYONA'S HAND AS WE WALKED DOWN RED ARMY STREET, past the sidewalk meat-pastry sellers, with their wares bulging under cloths on aluminum trays, like tiny dead bodies, past the old ladies with jars hand-labeled "Amazing Pickles" and "Incomparable Mushrooms." Someone had a bathtub, filled with water, and was selling live fish; nearby, a Tajik beggar kneeled on a piece of oilcloth and crossed himself left-handed when a black man dropped him a coin. I thought about how warm the breeze could be in spring, and was trying to conjure up the smell of unpaved dirt.

"You should go to England," Alyona said. "See Tatyana Litvinova in person; she's a complicated person, she won't tell you everything she knows until you find a way. Or — just think about it! — I could come up with something, and we could go together!" She pressed herself against me, breathless with the gleam of bliss.

We hugged, eyes closed, and stood like trees in Petrovsky park, letting the dog owners walk their mutts over our feet, and our bags, waiting on the bench behind us, also leaned against each other. A long curving snake of Airforce Academy cadets ran through the park, the battalion windmilled their arms as they ran.

"I have to know why this is happening to me," Alyona whispered.

Why? Because you've been on maternity leave so long, you lost touch with reality... or your husband found a kindhearted girl and neglects you... or just because you're bored, and it's a whim, you want something "different" but not too much, but you got wrapped up in all this stuff, and it's long crossed the line to too much. Or you want to chase the ghost of your own youth, before your skin rots and your backside sags, you want to relive it again, shamelessly, as if none of it ever happened: the children, the wrinkles, the weddings, the acquiescence to time and the funereal order of things.

I breathed into her temple, and she heard my unspoken answer and smiled, so brightly that I thought she was going to cry.

We kissed and got into separate cabs.

"And this is Ivy Valterovna's chair."

It was large, taller than me, with eagles' heads in the armrests; an Irish terrier jumped around by my feet. Litvinov's daughter-in-law (I wasn't prepared, I didn't know anything about her) was waiting for a question, Litvinov's son Mikhail made no sound. He scared me: he stood for a second in the doorway and then distractedly walked out. Later we established: he was educated, healthy, just a bit weird. I thought immediately: I will never see him again.

I pretended to be curious about everything.

"We just lived… We fell in love. We raised children. That's life. Life is everywhere. This woman I know was in Auschwitz, she has a number tattooed on her arm. She was given work in the gas chambers: to sort through things, people only brought their best things with them — and the things remained. She got dressed up with her friends, in others' dresses, and they had dances, knowing full well the next day they could be sent to the chambers and into the oven. And our life — the members of the families of the leadership — was good, but harshly determined: school, institute, family, work, retirement."

I noticed she hadn't mentioned death. Her gaze was fixed in the middle distance.

I probed: "Did Litvinov fly to America alone? Was there anyone else apart from Ivy Valterovna?"

She replied obediently:

"His secretary. Anastasia Petrova."

This name would never disappear now.

"Did Petrova have a family at home? Children?"

"I think so…. Initially she was married to the son of the People's Commissar for Food, Tsurko. And then she moved on to his brother, which was *mauvais ton*. I think she had a daughter called Iraida, I think, from the second Tsurko. And a son, a lovechild. He was handicapped, but she tried to raise him, give him the kind of education healthy children do not get, she took him to museums, to the theater…"

She would have been around forty at the time of the events on the Bridge. Was the daughter alive?

"Where did she come from?"

"I don't remember. For a time she worked at the League of Nations as a typist. Maybe she came from there."

"Was she pretty?"

"Not exactly, but there was something about her. She was very quiet, with a Russian face, and she dressed modestly. She hardly used any make-up. She brushed her hair back smoothly, put it in a bun. She was very restrained." And here she glanced at me, before saying: "But she was a kind of *belle femme*."

I hesitated. I couldn't see my way out; if I put off asking the question for another week, someone would croak on me again.

"Did Umansky love her?"

The old, bleached woman considered how much to tell me, went through some mental inventory and finally released a part of it:

"Umansky wasn't the only one to fall for her. She inspired romantic aspirations among men. She looked off-limits, almost like a nun, but evidently possessed a sort of quiet, but very strong…" She finished wish sudden clarity, "Sexuality. A *femme fatale*. Many people fell for her. Some were her lovers. Umansky proposed to her several times."

I got up to leave, thinking, Geneva, early 1930s, a disarmament conference, the first contact we recorded between Litvinov and Umansky — and next to them a typist, perhaps, the secretary Anastasia Petrova? Did it start then? I turned back from the door— what about a photo, I asked. We would return it, of course. But there was none to be had; the old woman did not ask why we were so interested in her, she did not find this surprising.

I left, waited a decent amount of time, and then called back. As I had calculated, I found Mikhail Maximovich Litvinov at home alone. Why hadn't he said anything when I talked to his wife?

He was not happy to hear about Petrova.

"I can't say anything about her. She wasn't a beauty, that's an exaggeration," he said feebly, cautiously, slipping into forgetfulness. "Just a charming woman. And Umansky? Just a pleasant and charming person. He went to Cuba, I think, that's where his daughter died. So sad."

"Who was Petrova friends with? Who could know something about her life?"

"She died many decades ago," he said and concluded with unexpected youthfulness and satisfaction, "Everyone who knew her has been dead for a long time."

I had nothing. Almost nothing: the apartment directory for Serafimovich St. 2, apartment 306, registered Petrova Anastasia Vladimirovna (born 1902), Tsurko Iraida Petrovna (born 1928), Petrov Vasily Petrovich (born 1937) (this would be the son), then a move to apartment 499. The Museum of the House of Government had Anastasia Petrova working "as a lecturer in the English Department of Higher Courses of foreign languages at the Ministry of Foreign Affairs. Died in 1984." Iraida Petrovna, the daughter, was alive, but didn't answer the phone, the neighbors said she was abroad. How many children did Commissar Tsurko have? *Five* biological and *three* adopted ones. Four sons: Dmitry, Pyotr, Vadim and Vsevolod. I just had to choose a couple who were the right age, I'll figure out later who married Nastya first.

Pyotr, described as "selfless and fearless" — girls at dances were proud to have such a partner — joined the party at the age of seventeen, was one of Lenin's bodyguards, suffered from severe short-sightedness(he wore glasses), and worked as an agitator in the ferocious food-rationing days (and what did he, selfless and fearless, do for twenty years before the war?). In 1941 he joined the Moscow militia, commanded an anti-tank artillery unit, was injured in both legs at Spas-Demensk, and was captured in an attempt to break out of the encirclement.

He died of starvation on April 12, 1942, in a concentration camp at Molodechno. They didn't permit for him to be buried separately. He was thrown into a common grave, with another six hundred people, most of whom were shot for digging tunnels.

He reportedly told his friend, "Kostya! Kostya, if you survive, go to Moscow, and tell my children that I haven't forgotten them, that I will soon return." Why did he want to leave hope for his children? To extend his life with vain expectation? And why "children," in the plural? We've got one daughter accounted for, Iraida Petrovna. She's still not answering (it's been three weeks), but we'll wait.

Mitya, Dmitry, older by a year, was a member of the party from the age of sixteen. He volunteered for the Red Guard; he fought Ataman Dutov. As part of the special forces, he took part in suppressing the rebellion of left-wing socialist revolutionaries. Proceeded to serve in the underground in Ukraine. Was captured by the nationalists there, then broke free and fought Batko Makhno and his so-called green army. Graduated from the officers' courses of red commanders of heavy artillery. As a communist who knew foreign languages (where did he learn those?), he was mobilized into the People's Commissariat for Foreign Affairs (where Ms. Petrova may have made an impression on him with her strong sexuality), served as the secretary of the consulates in Finland, Japan and China — it's fairly clear what he was doing there with his background in the underground and the special services — but then suddenly came an inexplicable turn of events: at the age of twenty-seven, Dmitry became a private of a cavalry battalion. Something must've happened.

Dmitry duly served in the cavalry, spent two years in Spain, was distinguished with the order of the Military Red Banner, went to the military academy, and in the Second World War resurfaced as a division commander holding the Minsk-Slutsk highway against Guderian's tanks. They were outnumbered and surrounded; Dmitry broke the encirclement, and ordered his troops to disperse. He was left alone with his comrade, reached a river crossing, and asked a boatman to take them over. In a rather symbolic gesture, Dmitry paid with his personal watch; the boatman took the two men straight to the Germans.

And then silence. Were they shot? But then, whence the story about the boatman?

"Did you read this?" Borya hadn't answered the phone in the morning, then showed up late and stinking of a hangover, and was now all but screaming into my face in a compensatory show of enthusiasm. We were at Serafimovich Street again, first in the elevator, and then on the landing. "Did you read about those Tsurko kids? It's pure operetta! The children of a hero on an ice floe! These are myths of the indigenous peoples of the North! Wait! Where are we going?"

"What do you want?" I hoped there was no video surveillance and tried to turn away from the stench. "I'm going to follow-up on the case."

"I want to work on the *case*!" he shot off, offended. "This story is starting to frighten me. It's all *wrong!* We're shown something, but I know: it's all wrong," he chopped the air with his hand. "And everyone died a long time ago. And many were killed. Although some of the dead are still walking. We've spent three years all the time thinking we're connecting the dots with straight lines, but somehow we are moving around something else, something *completely different!* There is nothing to lean on, just open doors, and behind them more open doors, and more doors after that — are you listening to me?"

"Doors."

"And behind each door there's a shadow, but — whoosh! — and then it's gone again. I don't know what we're looking for anymore. They" — he gestured vaguely — "want us to investigate the girl, but we no longer give a damn who killed her, right? We're just gonna plow through, aren't we? It's up to you, of course, but I can't imagine how we'll put it all together… But!" Borya shouted, winding himself up. "Here's what I do know: as soon as you zeroed in on this woman, everything became ten times darker! Everything that she touched simply falls apart in our hands. Umansky, the plane crash… and all of these thirty-three brothers with their biographies, and the retarded kid, and Iraida, and that brunette on the bridge… Your Nastya is going to get us in trouble, you just wait. And there's not a single photo of her, you notice? Doesn't that bother you? It certainly bothers me. Here, let me tell you one truth: You'll also get bothered soon! You just thought you came up with her, like a toy, like a turbo-charged and multi-purpose super-whore on a hover-craft, who *could have* been the key to everything — and bang! — there she is, right where you drew the cross on the map for her. She just turned up there. And it gets worse: now you've lost it and you've convinced yourself that this incomprehensible *something* we can sense on that bridge was this woman, and everything that's *in addition to* the murder, *above and beyond* the murder and *in* the murder, is all connected to her… Like, she was the only person whom Kostya told who killed Nina. He told her, and flew away and then he blew up and she's the only one who knew, and told her people…"

"She had to have known! Nina ruined her life."

"I'll tell you something else," Mirgorodsky looked around, recapturing the train of his ideas. "She won't take us anywhere. Everything that she touched takes an irreversible shape, it is left hanging forever."

"I understand." I led him to the door and pressed the doorbell. Borya shook his head regretfully, and when the locks started clicking in the door, I whispered the outlines of the role to him: "Tsurko, Marianna Alexandrovna. The Commissar's grand-daughter. The niece. Of those brothers. She lives alone. She limps."

Marianna Alexandrovna's appearance had the quality of being completely unmemorable. I am almost certain that her gray hair was brushed smoothly and pinned into a bun at the back of her head, and that she wore glasses. She looked like a retired teacher. The two of us, feeling like C-students re-taking an exam, exchanged furtive glances, elbowed each other, and sat down at the bare table.

"Before we begin our conversation," she smiled sternly (meaning, we would certainly start a conversation, but she wanted to listen to us lie to her first), "I must understand the motivation of your interest in the People's Commissar Tsurko. Are you after more grist for the mills of those writers who doubt that the People's Commissar for Trade Tsurko did indeed faint from hunger at the Council's meetings, and would like nothing more than to publish the Kremlin rations for the sole purpose of defaming certain people's memories? Will you contribute to the effort to rename the town of Tsurkovsky in Ukraine back to Aleshka and to abolish the guided educational tour 'Sailing to the Birth Place of the People's Commissar'?"

Borya smiled ruefully.

"Do you really think that the life of your grandfather, the first chairman of the State Plan, could give the slightest cause to doubt his high moral reputation? Even a biased view cannot find anything which could throw the smallest shadow on his biography. Marianna Alexandrovna! Our club, 'Know about your Homeland', which my colleague and I," he pointed at me disdainfully, "created for the schoolchildren of Saratov, has not chosen to begin with the study of Commissar Tsurko by accident. Who else should we begin with? Seven toponymic objects are named after him!"

She laughed with relief.

"I'm tormented by journalists, you know: did your grandfather really not leave you anything? But he pointed to the Constitution of the RSFSR: that's my will and legacy! He was fifty-seven when he died. Stalin probably had something to do with that." She got up and went to put on the kettle. We would be here for hours, I knew.

"Our family was large…. They're buried at Novodevichy — eight people in one grave. Commissar Tsurko is in the Kremlin wall. I tried for a long time to get my mother reburied next to him. I wrote to

Gorbachev twice, I paid for the urn to be kept at Donsky. They checked my mother's moral standards in secret from me, but fortunately the institute of Marxism-Leninism gave a positive recommendation, here, look at the photographs..." There were birches, corseted ladies, manor house porches, gentlemen in bowler hats, boys in sailor suits on wooden horses, university students with large foreheads in long coats, horses, carts, bald dolls. In some photos, there were gaping holes, the size of fingernails, where the faces of the enemies of the people had been cut out. These were well-known photos; I should have known whose faces had been cut out, and yet I couldn't remember.

"There were so many children, so many grandchildren," the old woman was saying. "But you know, there is not a single great-grandchild. The line broke off. Only Iraida had a girl, Olya."

I took note of her use of the past tense. Borya pulled himself together like a Polovets scout on the steppe; he poured tea into himself with painful medicinal gulps, and waited for Marianna Tsurko to finish saying: "We lived as a large family until 1930 in the Kremlin, in a three-story building on Kommunisticheskaya Street, with another family above us. They had terribly ill-mannered children. There'd be toys flying out of windows. The street had a deserted look, one mostly ran into honored widows — Dzerzhinskaya, Ordzhonikidze, so on... Eventually we moved to the House of Government, apartment 311, fifth floor."

That's when he moved in on the target:

"And Iraida, you said, is the daughter of...?"

"Pyotr. Here he is."

We both clutched the picture the size of a Soviet greeting card: there were about thirty people lined up for a group shot in the Kremlin apartment of the People's Commissar. I stared at the women's faces — there had to have been something special, I would recognize her.

"Pyotr is in the seated row, on the left, wearing glasses. He's holding someone else's child. They're receiving a delegation."

"And there was also another brother... Dmitry, wasn't it?"

"There, in the bottom right." Something thawed inside her. "Light-haired with gray eyes. That's him. People said he looked like the singer Lemeshev. All The sons had strong characters and tender souls."

"And what happened to Dmitry?" Borya asked quickly, deciding to dig where it was softer.

"He retired in the rank of colonel. He brought a really fancy doll from Spain for me, and paraded around in a Spanish suit. And at the age of thirty-eight, right before the war, he suddenly married a twenty-two-year old," she pronounced with loathing, "female. She turned out to be a bitch. We hate her."

"But *before* this woman — was Dmitry ever married?" Mirgorodsky tested the soil with the resignation of a hastily trained mine sweeper and blurted out: "To a woman with the last name Petrova?"

"To Petrova? Yes, he also managed to marry Petrova. I don't know where he found her — supposedly he brought her with him from China. She was a cultured sort of woman. I called her Aunty Tasya. So many ambassadors came to her funeral... No, I don't have any photographs of her left. I don't know why — there used to be a lot of them. She later became Pyotr's wife, and they continued to live in the same apartment, but everything was already so calm that no one noticed the awkwardness.

"But before the war, something happened to Aunty Tasya and Pyotr. His illegitimate daughter Masha was born. He went to the front and was killed. And she gave birth to an illegitimate son, a retard, from some German man from the Comintern, Wendt I think. The German was arrested. She went to America, and sent Iraida and her brother to a nanny in Ryazan. Dmitry's fate remained unknown. There was a letter from another man saying that their division had been surrounded. We tried to find out, but someone," she rolled her eyes at the ceiling, "up high, advised us: better not."

We spent another half an hour covering up our tracks, and only on our way out, as he was putting his feet into his shoes, did Borya try again:

"And the boy, the son of Petrova and the German, where is he now?"

"At an institution. And of course, he doesn't remember anyone, doesn't recognize them."

"Thank you," I said, and I also decided to try my luck: "Have you heard anything about the diplomat Umansky, he lived in your building, on the first floor."

"Yes, he used to visit our family. He was friends with Aunty Tasya." She thought we were leaving, she relaxed and continued, not understanding why herself: "Close friends. Very close indeed."

The German man with the last name Wendt, Wend? Vend? It would've been awkward to ask again.

I called Goltsman: anything in his index cards?

"The Comintern personnel registry lists no Wendt, Wend or anything similar. Nothing among the illegals either. From the arrest lists: a Wendt, Vladimir Vladimirovich, born in 1892, a native of Latvia, a mechanic. Arrested in June 1938, shot by a sentence of the NKVD, article 58, sections 10 and 11."

"Do you think that's him?"

"There's also a Bruno Wendt, a radar operator, member of the German Communist party, graduate of Moscow radio operator courses. Petrova may have been his English language instructor. This Wendt was a member of Sorge's intelligence group in Japan. In 1936 he was recalled to the Soviet Union. His subsequent fate is unknown."

A radio operator of Sorge's group! A man in headphones in a Tokyo basement. We were looking into the darkness. So, Iraida Tsurko sent her retarded brother to an institution, cleared herself some living space, no mother to take them *both* to museums anymore — and she was currently living abroad. Suddenly, I knew what the most important question was.

I found Shtein's daughter. He was Ambassador to Italy, and when the Emperor died, he reportedly sobbed like a child. "I am mourning my ideals," he said then.

"Petrova? I remember. No, that was not her maiden name. People couldn't stop talking about her: what a woman! She had so many men... "

Twenty.

"Gnedin was also in love with her. And my father. And Rubinin. But she seemed *completely charmless* to me. She was short, with a very thin face. She had wide hips — I don't like that, but she was smart, there's no denying that. She had a son with a German communist, an incredibly handsome man. The child was a retard. For her relationship with the German she was expelled from the party while she was pregnant."

"When they went to the USA, did Litvinov know that Umansky was in love with Petrova?"

"Yes, and he made a lot of fun of Konstantin Alexandrovich."

"I have a strange question, perhaps. Why did Petrova live… like that: from brother to brother, and then… Was she looking for something? A level of comfort?"

"She wasn't looking for power and wealth, if that's what you mean," the ambassador's daughter looked at me with helpless sympathy. "There are simply women who are like this." The question remained.

"Inna Borisovna, I've read Litvinov's biography…"

"It was written by Sheinis."

"Yes. In the book there are two places where, for some reason, Umansky is mentioned and the situation is described in considerable detail. But Sheinis did not meet Umansky or Litvinov."

"Only Petrova could tell him. I know that they met; Sheinis wrote down her recollections."

FREEDOM OF SEXUAL LOVE

WE INVESTIGATED THE SHEINISES. EVERYONE RELEVANT HAD died, the family archive had vanished, the distant relatives replied rudely. On a Tuesday in February, at 10:15 a.m. I gathered everyone in the office, and Borya read aloud:

"We're looking for Anastasia Vladimirovna Petrova, born in 1902. Petrova may be her maiden name, or she may have been married to a Mr. Petrov before she became Tsurko's wife. She met Dmitry Tsurko while serving in the diplomatic corps. Later, she moved on to his brother Pyotr. With Pyotr, she had a daughter, Iraida. Subsequently, there was an affair with a German national known as Wendt not later than 1937. Petrova gave birth to a son, a retard, from the German. The boy was registered as Vasily Petrovich Petrov. At the same time," Mirgorodsky blushed slightly "there were also affairs with an uncertain number of men. With a high degree of likelihood, we may assume that these included diplomats of various ranks. One of them, Konstantin Umansky, proposed to the woman on several occasions, and once, in late April-May of 1943, she, from all appearances, expressed her willingness to accept this proposal. That's all we have as of last night. Thoughts, everyone?"

"She didn't love him," Alyona spoke, clearly addressing me alone. I lowered my eyes. "Kostya asked her to marry him more than once, but she only agreed in the spring of '43, right? Well, that's because by then she had had a chance to live comfortably in the States for two years, and she wouldn't have minded spending another few good years in Mexico, instead of being stuck back in the USSR with a mentally challenged child. A cold calculation. On the other hand, if Umansky had known her for more than a decade, I can't imagine he wasn't informed about her other affairs."

"Well, maybe it was passion!" Borya threw up his hands, hiding a smile. "Yes, he knew! So what? He just took his turn and waited for a chance to get her for his undivided use — he'd have heard of such stories in Hollywood. Then when he finally got her, he dropped her — why mess with it? And to her, he must have said, I can't get divorced, my daughter needs me, bla-bla-bla. Right? Alexander Naumovich!" he turned to Goltsman for support.

"I'm thinking. One thing we mustn't forget: Petrova in her personal life was a kind of mirror reflection of Umansky himself. Perhaps that's why he understood her so well, and she understood him: they could forgive each other. Plus, it's hard for us to get a feel for their time, the ideas that were in the air. They are both old enough to have grown up in a radical era, when Bolsheviks wanted to destroy the bourgeois morals, as they called them — family, traditional marriage. Young people went to live in communes, tens of thousands of them. Only the State Political Directorate knew what went on in those communes at night. Alexandra Kollontai was publishing at the time, about the freedom of sexual love. We're not just looking at a pair of unfaithful people."

"I don't disagree necessarily. But if two people of mature age experienced a deep feeling and suffered because they couldn't be together, then this... somehow — " Goltsman drew a squiggle in his notes and looked at me: "But as I understand it, something else has appeared? What happened overnight?"

"Nothing that's totally new to us. But I read a little, with a different perspective. Litvinov's first biography, written by Sheinis, is a regular Soviet book. But everything that concerns Umansky is described in a different voice — we noticed this immediately." The team sat in silence, scrutinizing my face. "Why is Umansky mentioned at all? The man was forgotten, for forty years no one mentioned him anywhere, and Umansky's role in Litvinov's life, strictly speaking, barely merits noting. And still, he was included. So there must have been a reason, a personal motivation — but whose? Sheinis did not meet either Litvinov or Umansky. Yet this intense personal interest in Umansky is so important for the author that even the key scene of the biography — when Stalin and Molotov receive Litvinov in the Kremlin, dust him off, and send him to the States — is described by Sheinis as if the whole point of the meeting was that Litvinov moved heaven and earth to preserve *Umansky's* life and freedom. And nothing else, if we were to believe the biography, worried the old man. But this is nonsense! What does Sheinis want to prove?"

"Go on," said Borya. "Although I can see where you're gonna end up."

"Sheinis was writing from someone else's words. Shtein's daughter told us that he met with Petrova, and she was the one that told him about Umansky and Litvinov. I think Sheinis unwittingly reflected in his writing *her* perspective, her personal motives, although he himself may not have known what it was."

My investigators shifted and whispered to each other. Someone asked:

"So, what was it?"

"Let me try to show you. Try to hear this scene in Anastasia's voice — we can bet Sheinis used her version of the events. The three of them in a room: Stalin, Molotov, Litvinov. Suddenly Litvinov asks an incredible question: What's going to happen to Umansky? It looks like he's setting a condition: I'll go to the US and do the work that's critical to our victory, but spare Umansky for this, I don't ask anything more. The leaders are at a loss, they avoid making promises. But for Litvinov — this must be what Anastasia wants — there is apparently nothing more important, so he risks his winning ticket and *dictates* directly where to appoint Umansky, this is his price. Anastasia knew where Umansky was ultimately appointed, but somehow it was important for her to represent that it was not Stalin's mercy, that it was all arranged by Litvinov. So her Kostya owes not only his life, but also his position to the self-sacrificing old man. But when she finished weaving the web, dictating to Sheinis what to write, Tasya felt bitter about the fact that in *that* previous life she was present everywhere, but no one from the present day sees her, nothing will be left of her, now an old woman. An uncharacteristic weakness overcame her, and suddenly she added: write this as well. Litvinov, in the meeting with Stalin and Molotov, asks, who can I take with me? He isn't asking about the wife, he is asking about her, Petrova. And Stalin could answer calmly, without a single clarifying question — take whoever you want — only if he already knew..."

"...If he had information about who was concerned," Goltsman finished for me.

"Yes. An ordinary woman would have said, so he took me. But Anastasia just stopped talking — it was enough for her to indicate that Stalin knew who she was. And Sheinis just followed suit, although it would have been more logical for him to elaborate and to describe in the book who Litvinov chose given such freedom. Petrova's motive is now open."

I stopped talking. My voice was getting shaky.

"She was justifying herself!"

The secretary, who had come in while I was talking and was lurking in the doorway, seemed shocked by her own outburst, and clapped her hand to her mouth. Alyona shuddered hideously from the unexpected interruption, turned around and barked:

"Shut the door! It's none of your business!" She looked around, searching faces for approval, shakily took out a cigarette and turned back again: "Mashenka, please forgive me, you gave us such a fright. Please, don't do that again." She rubbed under her left breast, forced herself to laugh, and lit up, glancing around to gauge the shift in the mood of the room.

Mirgorodsky studied me as if I were a bubble floating in a glass of water, nodded mournfully at something outside the window, then grabbed an apple out of the bowl and bit into it with such ferocity that a burst of juice ran over his chin and sprayed onto the table. Goltsman finished drawing arrows and rectangles in his notebook, put his papers into an old-fashioned cardboard folder, tied it shut (he would seal the knot with wax later in his office), rose and left to say something encouraging to the secretary, mumbling what sounded like "I'll report the thoughts" or "I'll have a quick look."

"Let me give you a ride," Alyona offered. Not hearing an answer, she hunched her shoulders and asked pitifully, "Mirgorodsky, my dear! You're the only nice person here. Please explain to me too. What happened to this Anastasia?"

"She was justifying herself." A bit of apple flew out of Borya's mouth. "Don't you see it? Kostya kept jerking her around, with his, I love you, but I can't marry you, I couldn't do that to my daughter. And then — voila! — the daughter gets killed. Now she's like, oh poor Kostya, will you marry me now? How could he get out of that? Well, he'd say, and where were you, my dear, back in '41, when no one was in our way and the kid was back in the States? You were free, and I was in Kuibyshev waiting for an appointment — or to be shot. But you turned around and flew off with Litvinov, you didn't want me then, who would, right? So here's our Tasya, answering through Sheinis — maybe it took her a while to come up with this, hindsight's twenty-twenty — how dare you compare yourself to Maxim Maximovich? Litvinov saved you, Kostya! You betrayed your teacher, and he forgave you. He laid it all out to Stalin, and wasn't scared, he did it for my sake, don't you see? Like hell would you get posted to Mexico if it hadn't been for me, sweetie. So don't you get all morally superior on me. That's what she's saying in that book."

I could see Alyona didn't quite know how to respond, but Mirgorodsky needed no encouragement.

"She slept with Litvinov, the People's Commissar for Foreign Affairs. And not just that. Our fearless leader here," he pointed at me, "believes she *loved* him."

"But that's… Borya, in '41 Litvinov was *sixty-five* years old!"

"So what? I also worked that out. So he stayed potent. A lot of guys screw their secretaries. It's very convenient."

Alyona sat down in front of me on the floor in a disgusting cinematic pose:

"Tell me it's not true."

"You know it is."

"No, I don't know that. I don't believe it," she sniffed. "You can't just do that... You can't just go around cracking people's lives open like sixty-year-old oysters."

"As a matter of fact, we can. I'm leaving."

"Can I give you a ride?"

"I want to go alone."

She shook her head, silently, and indicated: go, goodbye. I heard her behind me draw in her breath sharply and begin to wail, out of swollen throat, the sound precisely calculated for me to hear all the way to the elevator. She'll shut up sooner or later, I thought, resignedly. Or would she would jump up and run after me?

The theorist and practitioner of liberated love, Alexandra Kollontai, served the Empire as its Ambassador to Mexico, and was friends with Litvinov until she died. Kollontai advocated for communal child-care — children would gain the skills of communal living from an early age and not distract their parents from work and sexual relations.

We must, she wrote, focus on the most important things, so people can live the midsummer night's dream, be in love, be ever on the wing — this is the moveable feast. It doesn't matter with whom one is in love, the important thing is to be in love. For two or three days, or years, it depends on strength, deceit, self-deceit. I am against asceticism, she wrote, I wish to be drunk on life. Mutual understanding? It's impossible! Fight against the desire to possess another. Demand self-delusion, delude each other, stay in love.

Tatyana Litvinova, Brighton, England: Our vile and happy childhood.

We watched a parade from the seats on the dais for the diplomatic corps, on the Mausoleum, and I didn't understand why people were crowded down below, when up here there was so much space. I had heard about class division and poverty, and without understanding, I had already accepted a lot.

We weren't ever punished at home. Once, for fun, we intentionally flooded the family of the stoker Anton — they lived in the basement below our apartment. We hid and watched the water rise. If we were friendly with ordinary people and they complained about their lives, my father believed that we had simply met spiteful losers. Mom stayed apolitical, she focused on creative things and didn't read newspapers.

Almost every evening, Mom was occupied with receptions or accompanying important foreigners to Swan Lake. The mornings — we all got up at seven — were her least favorite time. I can see her now, sitting in front of an underwear drawer trying to extricate a pair of intact stockings for each of us. She's pulling, and it's a knot, a garland of underpants, bras that were forever missing hooks, socks, all falling out onto her lap from the drawer, and suddenly she just folds over, puts her head onto this underwear amoeba and cries, sounding just like me, "Silly Mom! Stupid, stupid Mom!"

Mom was fundamentally in favor of free love, she had affairs, various admirers came and went.

I don't remember when I first saw Petrova. I feel like she was always there. If anything happened — well, we'll have to ask Petrova! She always knew everything. I can't say she was a beauty. She had an elongated face like you see on the icons, eyes set close together. She always had her hair pulled back. She wasn't plump, and wasn't tall. She clearly had Jewish blood. She behaved like a woman of the Party, and deported herself very demurely. She dressed with taste. She adored my father.

Her being a *femme fatale* is a sort of family legend. She had affairs, and quite a few, if you believed the rumors. But some of those were circulated on purpose, so that people would think she was someone else's whore — not my father's.

With Mom she was very frank, she talked about her affairs. Once she said, "Do you know why men love me? Because I am different with each one."

I listened to the recording of this conversation over and over, and felt really irritated at this point.

There it is again: "Do you know why men love me? Because I am different with each one."

I don't understand. What does that mean? Was Litvinova lying in her feeble old age, or did Petrova really produce the kind of banality they print in every women's magazine? Or did she want to say that she was capable of changing, of shedding her old skin, and that she needed a new man for every season? Or did she have another trick? A married woman was a moored ship, a thoroughly charted and conquered territory, but a man can look at another woman and think: *this one* could've been mine. But Petrova, with her bends and twists, made it clear to every man: no, you can forget about what you see now, what I give to this man is only for him, with you I'll be different. Is that right? Or will we never be able to understand you, Tasya?

PERSONNEL FILES

"**B**UT WHERE IS THE PHOTOGRAPH?" "Someone removed the photo from Anastasia Vladimirovna's file."

For two hundred dollars, we obtained the identifying idiosyncrasies of relevant lives. I forced myself to look at Dmitry Tsurko first and soon had him fully inventoried and indexed: small, neat letters, featureless handwriting, but look at the signature: with curlicues like these, the twenty-year-old son of the People's Commissar must have had a complex vision of his identity.

I had his personnel file, listing Dmitry Tsurko as a cleared employee of the People's Committee for Foreign Affairs, "without right to publish," born on December 29th (old style) of 1900, in the city of Kherson. He did not possess expert written command of a single language (there was no doubt that the job in China was his old man's friends' doing); his mother was a former noblewoman, but he claimed no knowledge of the precise origins of his father (the son of a People's Commissar, he could afford this vagueness); "the family experienced major material difficulties," but Dmitry, it seems, was still able to "study while being maintained by his parents"; occupation — none. At the age of seventeen he joined the Red Guard in Ufa, "was on the staff" of said guard (we were already pretty sure that the stories of underground work in Ukraine, the imprisonment, and the battle with Batko Makhno were all smoke and nonsense). Home address: Kremlin, Cavalry Guard (or Cavalry) corpus; then he served as duty secretary, manned the reception desks of Lev Karakhanov and Georgy

Chicherin, after which Karakhanov, a dandy with a love of white trousers, navy blazers and two-seat Packards, who lived with his ballerina mistress in a mansion on Smolny Lane, found him a spot at the mission to Japan, and then in China, where there were lawn tennis and simple joys, *femmes fatales* and bourgeois pleasures, so that by the age of twenty-seven, without any education or accomplishment, no assets whatsoever apart from rather vacant gray eyes and a home address at the Kremlin, as a pathetic secretary in the office of public law, Dmitry Tsurko sat down and wrote: "Owing to certain circumstances of a personal nature, I consider it necessary to change the nature of my activities and hereby request a reassignment from the Foreign Affairs Commissariat."

What happened? The date — 23 July 1927 — fits: you, Mitya, just learned that Nastya Petrova, your love and passion brought from China, is five months pregnant with your brother Pyotr's child, and *everyone knows*. You must have surprised yourself with this new insight, this feeling of sudden loathing or desperation, and you decided to change. You asked for a fresh file, a new biography — and you started from scratch. Only you wrote "single" in the marital status box for the next ten years until you met that bitch the family hated — that's how long Tasya burned you and did not let you go.

I called Goltsman and Borya, so we could all be there together, ripping the sheet off the corpse of the mysterious Anastasia Petrova in the form of the autobiography she had submitted to her personnel files.

Party ticket #00131681. Female.

I was born in May 1902 in Moscow. I spent my whole life in Moscow. I grew up on Krasnoselskaya street, by the bridge. Then lived on Sytinsky Lane and the Small Zlatoustinsky. My current address is Serafimovich Street 2, apartment 36.

In my childhood I had the surname Flam, from my father. My father, Vladimir Pavlovich Flam, born in 1870, a legal consultant, died in 1936. My mother Sofia Alexandrovna Topolskaya lives at Yermolaevsky Lane

18/31 in Moscow; she has been divorced from my father since 1908. Before the revolution she worked as a typist and saleswoman, her last job was at the Moscow Evening newspaper. I had a brother, Kirill Vladimirovich Topolsky, born in 1904, a student — he died in Moscow in 1924.

I graduated from the gymnasium, and worked for five months as a clerk at the Central Print office. In the spring of 1919 I went to the Penza district, as a stenographer at the district committee in Kerensk. I joined the Party at the age of seventeen. I was not in the Komsomol. In August 1920, I voluntarily went to the front, and served as a record-keeper at the headquarters of the First Polish Red Army command. After the war I was a stenographer at secret police courses and under Comrade Voikov.

In the summer of 1923, I went to China, where I worked at the Legation until the summer of 1925. Then I worked as a stenographer for Comrade Litvinov, and at his secretariat for three more years. I attended the Institute of Oriental Studies, but did not graduate for family reasons. Instead, I graduated extramurally from the Institute of Foreign Languages. I made two trips to Geneva. I also went to Glasgow, to visit my husband who was working there. At the Community of Foreign Workers Press (subsequently Progress publishing house) I edited English translations of Lenin's and Stalin's works. I also served as a member of the party committee.

At the end of 1936, after the arrest of one of the heads of the publishing house, I was removed from the committee for lack of vigilance. Subsequently he was released and rehabilitated. But I had to resign and work as a teacher while my case was being considered. Three times I was elected secretary of the party organization at the extra-mural Institute of Foreign Languages, and I wrote an English language textbook. I went to the USA as the secretary of the Ambassador.

I'm a widow. My husband was in the Moscow militia, he was captured by the Germans near Yelnya and died on August 14, 1942.

For twenty-five years I was a lecturer at the English department. At the age of seventy-seven I retired, and lived for another five years as a distinguished pensioner. Height five feet four inches, eyes — brown, hair — graying black, no special features.

Was awarded the Order of the Badge of Honor and six medals including "For Valiant Labor in the Great Patriotic War" and a special badge for 50 years of service in the Communist Party.

That's it. It wasn't even her. Someone really cleaned things up well.

"It's not her," I threw the file aside. "You can't even tell from this why her last name is Petrova!"

Mirgorodsky replied angrily: "What did you expect? You should've known we'd get this as soon as we realized all her pictures were gone."

"I don't believe that we have made no progress here," Goltsman said carefully. "Take note of the twist in her biography: a seventeen-year-old girl leaves Moscow for the Penza district, for Kerensk. Surely, she's not doing so merely in order to work as a stenographer? Taking into account her... er... subsequent biography, we may assume she went there to be with a man. Or together with a man. Petrov, if indeed he was her first husband, may be found in that district committee in Kerensk. We also now have more clarity about Mr. Wendt, the father of the handicapped boy — he worked with Petrova at the publishing house."

"Alright then," Borya clapped his hands together. "So we'll find the German. We'll dig up Dmitry Tsurko's bitch of a second wife — she had to have known Petrova. And we'll finally find this Iraida, her daughter..."

"Also Pyotr Tsurko had a daughter from his second marriage, I believe," Goltsman suggested.

"And her too! She was born before the war, she should be alive. Someone should go to London... But I want to hear it straight: what do we want to find?"

"A living person! Petrova lasted eighty-two years and died free of dementia a mere twenty years ago. I could have met her! You could have met her... I want a witness! Petrova couldn't have kept silent all her life. She must have sat down once and told someone her story. Old women like to remember the same things over and over again. She had to have sat with someone in the kitchen once a month, had to have drunk tea and droned on: I loved Kostya, he loved me, but he didn't get divorced because of his daughter, and then Nina was killed… And she was killed *like this*… Petrova is the only interested witness. She could have seen the scene of the crime."

"Fine," Mirgorodsky waved me off. "You wanna spend a year screwing with this Tasya because you think it's all because of her, fine. What do I care. Just tell me who's going to London."

A month later, Borya called: "Write this down. Pyotr Tsurko had a cousin, Olevinsky. Pyotr left Tasya for this Olevinsky's wife. He had a thing for his relatives' wives, the freak. Zina was her name. She was a singer in the Bolshoi Theater Choir. At the Museum of the House of Government I was told: Zina and Petrova were very good friends. Zina and Pyotr Tsurko had a daughter Masha, and this Maria Petrovna just came back from the States to visit, she's leaving again soon. She'll see you tomorrow. She, by the way, is a PhD in Chemistry, a perfect listener for old ladies at kitchen tables."

I was definitely hoping for something when I crossed the threshold of another childless apartment of the Tsurko family and said hello to a pleasant woman.

"Well, my father was cheerful, he enjoyed life. He liked to eat, drink and hit on women. Whatever work he did, he always rose quickly. He didn't join the military because of tuberculosis.

"Before the war, Dmitry married an unpleasant woman, I don't want to talk about her. They had a son, Alexander, a copy, incidentally, of my mother's first husband. No one in the family believed that he was Dmitry's son. But he doesn't have any children either."

"Only Iraida had a daughter, Olga," I said, demonstrating my interest in the family circumstances.

The Doctor of Chemistry gave me an unpleasant look, and after a lingering pause, inquired:

"What exactly are you interested in? Petrova? She was very smart. An exceptional woman. It was a joy to be around her. She and my mother liked to reminisce about my father together. They did not feel they were rivals, and that's a sign of exceptional women." And she fell silent. That was all that she knew.

"What did she like to remember from her past?"

"She didn't talk about anything from her past. She once mentioned that Dzerzhinsky liked to grope her knees when she was young. But I didn't hear anything else."

I asked twenty more questions (Umansky, Umansky's daughter, the Great Stone Bridge), and received instant dead-end answers: "no," "she didn't say anything," and "I didn't even know that."

"Photos?" She got up and brought an ancient purse of white leather with scratched metal corners. "I found this after you called, it's all that's left."

She wasn't curious enough to look through the relics herself before my visit, and now she laid out the items on the table, far enough from me to nip in the bud any notion of my touching them. There was Anastasia Petrova's diploma (Why didn't Iraida have it?), certificate of defending her dissertation, two work records books, Pyotr Tsurko's death notice (Didn't she know that her father's death notice was in this purse?), someone's cross in a box with the inscription "Veteran of Labor," and a velvet drawstring bag with the monogram VF and the date 1884 embroidered in tiny beads.

"I don't know what this is…"

That, my dear, is the monogram of Tasya's father, Vladimir Flam. Something was given to him as a present at the age of fourteen or around that time, perhaps for his Bar Mitzvah? Or perhaps the future legal consultant finished a school year with straight A's.

There was also a watch with a braided string instead of a strap, a foreign watch, and another watch without a strap, of the Victory brand; keys, telephone numbers written on scraps of paper. I sat opposite the stern elderly woman, and thought how meaningless these clips that hold our lives together — savings books, birth certificates and boxes with medals in them — would seem when the time came to prepare for the last journey; nothing would be needed apart from a cross, but that wouldn't save her either, and her hair would be tousled by the cold railway wind.

"No, you see, there are no photographs or letters," Maria Petrovna tossed everything back into the purse and went to put it away, and I quickly reached out and grabbed from the edge of the table one forgotten scrap: a piece of brown paper with two holes in the corners for a string, a number (26) written in chemical pencil on the back, and the inscription, "Maternity hospital Grauerman Anast. Vladi. Petrova, boy." This was an old-fashioned tag used by maternity wards — it was tied to the leg of Anastasia's new-born baby and it was what she thought necessary to preserve for her entire life, for her son.

"How can you explain that Petrova was so secretive? Every person likes to pour their heart out once in a while."

With this I finally, somehow, struck gold. The woman burst out:

"Don't forget, she lived with Vasya, her lunatic son! From the end of the war until her death. She lived with him for almost forty years, and she didn't get married again because of him.

"The boy seemed perfectly healthy when she left for the States, and just eighteen months later, when she returned, he was already ill. After making rounds to the doctors, she said: I can't make him healthy, but I can make him happy. And she laid down her entire life.

"Vasya's development stopped at the level of a five-year-old. He could put a piece of aluminum foil into his mouth and swallow it. But he had a great memory, took music lessons and could read music, although it was torture to listen to him play. He was of medium height, and his face was quite handsome, but his eyes were clearly insane, you know? He was on the heavy side, he liked to eat, and there was no point in trying to restrict him. Whenever he took a bath by himself he wouldn't stop until he rubbed the soap bar completely away. Sometimes he was completely serene, but he could also get very agitated, and that was scary.

"My mother tried to persuade Anastasia Vladimirovna to put Vasya in an institution. But she immediately said: no, don't even talk to me about that. She let him go out by himself. When they went to the Baltic Sea in summer, she let him swim as far as he wanted.

"She bore everything on her shoulders. When she couldn't do

everything herself anymore, she hired a woman, Anna Ivanovna, who got on well with Vasya, she sang with him in the kitchen, and stole from the family. My mother got angry: Tasya, don't you know she's stealing your sheets? But Anastasia Vladimirovna put up with it: where else am I going to find a sitter who gets on well with Vasya?"

"How did she die?"

"She was retired and worked at home — until her last day. She was editing Galperin's two-volume Russian-English dictionary, no signs of dementia whatsoever. She used to go to church at Yakimanka.

"Before her death she received the sacrament of extreme unction. She wasn't afraid, she said, soon I'll see Mitya and Petya. My mother demanded of Iraida: never, ever promise that you'll take Vasya to live with you, even if your mother demands it on her death bed, don't promise something you won't do. Iraida didn't say anything, and Anastasia Vladimirovna, of course, knew what would happen to him.

"What else do I remember... She used to say, she couldn't stand party meetings, she'd sit in the first row and sleep with her eyes open.

"She didn't like household chores, she didn't like to talk about Vasya, she didn't like to talk about illness or any weakness, or ever anything personal about herself. Books and films, she was glad to talk about them. But that's it. And that's all. So goodbye."

I looked at the last reports and handed them over, but the secretary didn't leave.

"What?"

"Alyona Sergeevna called twice this morning."

"Yes."

"I also meant to say... I decided... To help, I contacted Vadinsky."

"What's that?"

"It's a town, formerly called Kerensk, Penza region, where Petrova went to work. I spent Sunday in the archives, and I wrote down everyone who could have worked with Petrova in the party district committee. There are no Petrovs in the district committee. But there are twelve Petrovs among the Communists of the district, I'm thinking of going there again…"

"Masha — what's your full name?"

"Maria Nikolayevna."

"Maria Nikolayevna, dear, don't waste your time. You should only do what I tell you to. Do you have a passport to travel abroad?"

"Yes."

"Go to England to see Tatyana Litvinova. Find her phone number, make friends with her, ask her to invite you to see her. Borya will help you come up with a good cover."

"Thank you very much," her voice trembled with excitement. "I won't let you down!"

"What's she so happy about?" Alyona looked over my desk, my face (especially my lips), the monitor (whether I was looking at my email) and the telephone (whether there were any messages), then walked around and leaned onto my back, sniffing for any scents of other women, and whispered into my neck, "God, how I've missed you."

Borya coughed theatrically behind the door, turned the handle and looked in:

"Not interrupting anything, am I? Iraida Tsurko's phone started working. She's back in the country, I talked to her."

I kept a cowardly silence. Tasya's daughter. Her whole life with her mother. Who else could we put our hopes in? But what if she was also afflicted by this epidemic of silence?

"You can't get through to her: she has no photographs of her mother, her mother didn't write letters, didn't keep a diary, there is no archive. Could it be that Iraida hated her mother? And now just wants to forget her? She's sleek, cold, and harsh. No response to mention of Umansky, Litvinov and Wendt. I don't know anything, she said, I just saw them twice, briefly and from a distance. She refused to meet."

I pretended that I had expected and foreseen all of this, and Borya chuckled at my cheap pretense of self-possession.

"But. She agreed to talk once by telephone. On the condition that no one would ever call her again. I'll connect you in fifteen minutes. I said that we were gathering memoirs of diplomats who worked in the US, for the seventieth anniversary of the establishment of diplomatic relations. I don't think she believed me."

"Hello."

"I was thinking about you and I realized something: it's very hard for you to get a grasp of our times. We lived completely differently. We had a school reunion many years later and I suddenly realized: Marina is a Jew, and Shamil is a Tatar.

"I remember walking up the stairs — the elevator wasn't working — and tapping my finger on the paper seals on the doors: all the apartments had been sealed, everyone had been arrested. I remembered that day forever because I got home and came down with scarlet fever. I was scared to go to school: who else in the class wouldn't turn up?

"I was born on the thirty-first of December at 11:30 a.m. at the Grauerman maternity hospital. I was the first grandchild of the Soviet People's Commissars. My grandfather was greeted with applause at the government meeting, and at home the nanny dropped china, to which my grandfather responded exclaiming: Don't be sad, Dunyasha, it's good luck!

"My mother came up with my name. My grandfather didn't contribute. I was actually lucky. One of the boys in the building got named Red Proletariat." Iraida referred to the custom of naming children after Soviet symbols.

"What do you know about Anastasia Vladimirovna's parents?"

"Her father, as you know, was a lawyer. Her brother died tragically. He threw himself under a tram, or fell under it. My grandmother was very religious. She knew many languages, went to the Lenin Library and translated Dumas' novels for me (only *The Three Musketeers* and *The Count of Monte Cristo* were published in Russian), she printed them out herself and bound them. And she also wrote fiction — romance novels. She worked as a typist and hated Stalin: they were all mortally afraid of making a typo. But she loved Khrushchev. She kept his portrait cut out of *Pravda* next to an icon. She said: first I pray to that, then to this. She was almost a hundred when she died. Whenever she'd start losing it, someone would take her to see Anastasia Vladimirovna, and grandma's head would clear again."

"First your mother married Dmitry, then Pyotr…"

"Dmitry met my mother in China, but they did not get officially married. He was crazy about me, it was an abnormal sort of love. People even suspected that I was his daughter. I remember that he came back from Spain: Iraidushka, let me read to you. But by then I could read myself! My father worked in foreign trade, he used to go to England regularly. He went to the front voluntarily, although he had a white card as being unfit for service.

"He was tall, like all the Tsurkos. He was hardly ever at home. I knew that my father and mother did not get on, I was very upset about this, but they did not suspect anything — I'm a very private person.

"Our family was large and cheerful. We played Mah Jong. The loser had to wrap himself in a sheet, go down to the street door and ask the CheKa officer on duty what time it was."

"How did the family obtain such detailed information about the deaths of Dmitry and Pyotr?"

"After the war, a man found us. He had been imprisoned in the camp somewhere, he looked like a Tatar. He stayed for a week and told my Mom about Dad. Details about Dmitry's death came from many sources. Twenty years ago a friend of ours had a car break down, and someone gave him a ride. This man actually told him that he served in the Army under Dmitry Tsurko and he last saw him wounded. But I would strongly urge you not to pry too hard into Dmitry's biography."

"Do you remember Litvinov?"

"I remember Maxim Maximovich as a very lively person. I remember I saw the movie *Secret Agent* and it just blew me away, so I had to praise it to him, and it made him laugh so hard he cried. He just groaned, 'Iraida, you're joking! You can't think that!'"

"Who did you stay with while Anastasia Vladimirovna worked in America?"

"A very devoted nanny lived with us, Yevdokia Filippovna Zulaeva. We spent the entire war with her in the village of Svobodny near Ryazan. Before she left for the States, Mama came to the nearest station, Sasovo, and brought clothes for winter. In the autumn of 1941, a man came to us: there was an order — if the Germans got close, he was to take a horse and carry us to a safe place.

"We were always hungry. The packages of food Mama sent did not reach us, and the clothes were too small by the time we got them. I worked in the collective farm, I mowed and reaped.

"When she returned, the family had lost the apartment in the House of Government — you'll have heard the story about Dmitry's second wife — so we were given a room with neighbors. Our nanny's son turned up, Mama helped him out and found him a position in the navy, and he boasted: 'That Iraida of yours has become a real beauty. Great arms! Great legs! And before, she used to be quite dainty.' Mama immediately procured a pass to Moscow for us, and moved us there. She had a new house built for our nanny as a sign of gratitude. She was a bit scared of our nanny. Our nanny was very bossy and had charge of everything in the home. Mama was no good at running a household.

"Mom did not like Gromyko. In America she once exclaimed something like, Only an idiot like Gromyko could think up something like that! Then she turned around and he was standing right there. When Litvinov retired, she was made the assistant to the deputy Minister Gusev. She was the only woman in the Ministry of Foreign Affairs who had the rank of first secretary. But she found things so bad with Gusev that she moved to the American section, wrote a doctoral dissertation and went to teach. She considered the defense of the dissertation to be the most pointless activity of her life. Her English pronunciation was only so-so.

"She was a good swimmer, and would lose a dozen pounds over the summer.

"It wasn't acceptable to raise your voice at home, but Mom was very strict. 'Mama, what does this English word mean?' 'Have you looked it up in the dictionary?' If I promised to come home by midnight, then I had to be home by midnight.

"When I got my first gray hair, she said: dye it immediately, don't let anyone see it. Don't repeat my mistakes.

"Of course she wasn't a die-hard communist. Especially when you remember how religious she was.

"She once said to me: you know, I can't allow myself to get very attached to Olya — Olya's my daughter — because there is Vasya."

"About what about you yourself?"

"I worked at the UN, and spent a lot of time at disarmament talks: Helsinki, Vienna, Geneva. You can make a note, Gorbachev gave me a medal, and Yeltsin mentioned me in a decree and gave me a cash award. Gromyko also encouraged me, even knowing whose daughter I was.

"But I'm a person who keeps to herself. Mom didn't know my life at all.

"She had the last rites read to her in hospital, at that time it was already permitted. She was buried at the Vagankovo cemetery, not far from the church. 'I want to die now. I have such a humiliating disease (colon cancer), I'm tired of myself.' She said this quite calmly, and with complete confidence, she added, 'I haven't seen them all for a long time. I'll see everyone.'"

"All your relatives have rather unpleasant memories of Dmitry's second wife."

"She lost the family apartment, she was eighteen years old at the time. Valentina Ivanovna Romodanovskaya. I won't say anything bad. All I'll say is: she was incredibly beautiful, with dusky, unusual skin. I think she worked as a fabric dyer.

"And that's it now. Goodbye."

Mirgorodsky turned off the recorder and gave it to the secretary, to download the file for our archive. To me he said:

"I'll bet your Tasya is just the same — cold and dry. She never let anyone get close to her, and never cried. Did you notice how this lady talked about her half-brother Vasya: in the past tense… Where did he go? Who had him committed? I suppose you want me to find this fabric dyer now. What are you thinking about?"

I was thinking: the Tsurkos were strange. They had eight children apiece, took in foster kids, lined up in three rows at the Kremlin apartment — and suddenly they were cut off, at the same time, in one cursed generation. Only Iraida had her Olya. All that was left of this large, many-branched Communist family, dozens of handsome people, was this one girl Olya. And we had not yet found any traces of her existence, and her mother had just talked about her as if the girl had long ceased to exist.

THE LIST

"Everything worked the way you wanted," Borya whispered. "Remember that Chukharev character we tried to find? His wife turned up and brought us a little something." A sheet of paper danced in Borya's hands. "Everything he knew about Umansky's case. Here you are."

I looked at the paper. It read:

6th grade
Mikoyan, Sergo

7th grade
Bakulev, Pyotr
Barabanov, Leonid
Xxxx, Xxxx
Kirpichnikov, Felix
Redens, Leonid
Khmelnitsky, Artyom

8th grade
Mikoyan, Vano

"Six weeks after Volodya Shakhurin and Nina Umanskaya died, eight boys from school #175 were arrested. Six weeks later! Your major from the FSB wasn't lying: the case was opened in July. They were held in prison for half a year, and then sent to remote regions. Would you like to know who these boys were? Alexander Naumovich, tell him."

Goltsman leaned in and began talking, quiet, almost gentle in his persistence, as if coaxing a child out of bed on a winter morning.

"Barabanov is the son of Mikoyan's assistant. Khmelnitsky is the son of Marshal Voroshilov's special aide. Bakulev is the son of USSR's Surgeon General. According to the Kremlin guards, Bakulev senior was the only doctor Stalin trusted, he even took him along into the box at the Bolshoi Theater. Kirpichnikov is the son of Beria's deputy. Leonid Redens is the son of Stanislav Redens, from the NKVD, who by that time had already been executed. And Sergo and Vano are the sons of Anastas Mikoyan, he Special representative of the State Defense Committee."

I wished for this to end — for the names to stop dropping into my lap, under my feet like litter, all these facts.

"Do you see what is happening here? By July of '43 Mikoyan's eldest son, Vladimir, had already been killed at the front, and now his two younger boys are arrested in Moscow. They take in Leonid Redens — his mother's maiden name is Alliluyeva, he's Stalin's own nephew! Two important conclusions become rather obvious: there was only one man who could make the decision to arrest *these* boys at *this* time."

"I'm with you."

"And secondly: the boys must have done something out of the ordinary indeed to prompt Stalin to intervene," now Goltsman sounded ready for a fight. "And whatever they did is not a story of unrequited love. Or not only a love story."

"We're near the target," Borya announced. "We can drop Petrova. Let's sort out these boys and go after them."

I stared at the eight names and did not see anything.

"What about this Xxxx Xxxx?"

"I hear Alyona Sergeevna is resigning?" Borya said, in a non-sequitur. "You drove her to it. She was irreplaceable in field operations. What are we going to do without her?"

They'll be in their seventies now — are these boys even alive? They lived in the shadow of their fathers, no one knows where they made their own little lairs.

I set out eight tin figures on my desk.

There are seven fathers. Almost nothing on Barabanov, not even initials, all I found is that he at one point "sat at the reception desk for Anastas Ivanovich Mikoyan," "was very lively," stout, short, a good fellow and a simple man, a non-entity. Stanislav Redens, the son of a Polish boot-maker, eventually rose to the position of the People's Commissar for Internal Affairs of the Kazakh Soviet republic and married the kind Anna Sergeevna Alliluyeva, the older sister of Stalin's second wife, the suicide Nadya. Redens was the kind of man who dined with the Emperor in the family circle and destroyed many people in his name. He orchestrated Crimean purges, starvation in Ukraine in 1933, his signature unleashed the deaths of many thousands in Belorussia. In the spirit of the times, he was made a Polish spy in 1938, and was treated in the manner reserved for generals and leaders: he was escorted from his cell into the yard of an internal prison, driven in a black van onto Malaya Lubyanka, across Dzerzhinsky Square (they said, incidentally, that Dzerzhinsky died in his arms) to Ilyinka street, into the courtyard of the terrifying building 23 (next to the pharmacy); brought up the back staircase to the second floor, before the sleepless eyes of the Military Board of the Supreme Court of the Soviet Union — for exactly as many seconds as it took to hear the sentence — and down the stairs again into the basement where the duty officer shot him in the back of the head.

They removed the shoe from the still warm right foot, tucked under the collapsed body, and tied to the big toe a cardboard tag with a number written in ink-pencil (do they still make these? They did when I was a kid) — a name was no longer needed. Redens' wife several years later was sent into exile to lose her mind somewhere obscure; his younger son wrote a book about the greatness of the Emperor and the Zionist conspiracy, but the elder, Leonid, was still playing hide-and-seek with us.

The biography of Rafael Pavlovich Khmelnitsky, aka Ruda, has been well publicized, in scandalous detail, in the books of that bastard defector Rezun who writes under the pen-name Suvorov. I wonder if Ruda himself adorned his story, or if his son Artyom, the biggest day-dreamer and fabulist of the school #175 lent a hand? Khmelnitsky, Voroshilov's special aide, was reported to have been given by the Emperor himself a Parabellum pistol (there's our weapon!) with the inscription *To my friend Ruda* from Stalin along with an eight-seat Packard. After injuring his spine (he and Voroshilov fled a bombardment on a handcar), Khmelnitsky left the front and went to work establishing an exhibition of trophy weaponry at Gorky Park. Later he took on the soul-rotting job of redistributing personal automobiles of conquered armies to Soviet officials. The old ladies at the museum of the House of Government promptly identified his kid. The seventy-year-old Artyom had made a fuss about his name not being included on the marble plaque commemorating residents who were victims of Stalinist purges (And what were you in prison for, Artyom?). Could Ruda have intervened for his boy with Voroshilov? After all, the Marshal was the only man who addressed the Emperor with the informal *you*. Anyone else who did so had been killed long ago. But Voroshilov's cavalry with its lances was wiped out as far back as the Finnish campaign; the fall of Leningrad and the Volkhov front increased the Marshal's shame tenfold, and in order to avoid shooting him in front of the troops with his shoulder-straps torn off, he was given a pencil pusher's job in the rear. Would he have really come begging back to Stalin for someone else's kin?

Would Bakulev seek favor for the boys? The head surgeon was born in the Vyatka region and was school friends with Alexander Poskrebyshev, Chief of Stalin's Personal chancellery; he played pool with Communist aristocracy: General Khrulyov, Admiral Kuznetsov, Vasily Stalin and Nikolai Vlasik, head of Stalin's personal security. He had plenty of connections, but still — who was he? A mere doctor, there were plenty of doctors, he wouldn't get a favor in return for a past enema.

Mikoyan — and only he — could have found a moment, late at night, in the imperial office, after the discussions and meetings, having honed his words over a month of suffering, having sterilized, steam-ironed and polished them to a pearly sheen — he could have said, Father! One of my sons died at Stalingrad, and two are in jail, they are schoolboys, Iosif Vissarionovich, an eighth and a sixth grader… He could have asked a question (he could not beg), and he would have been given an answer, but it is unlikely he saved anyone. He would have shown: I am weak, I am not completely made of steel, there is still something living inside me. What did that FSB Major say? If we open the case *the Caucasus will howl.* This is what he meant, here's one piece of the puzzle coming together.

Only once does the black shadow appear in the margins of the innumerable memoirs penned by the many members of the Mikoyan clan: "The children went to walk by the river. And they did not return. That was how Beria took his revenge on Mikoyan." They certainly had enough to bring out under Khrushchev, or better still — in the latter-day wave of scandals when their ancestor's hands were publicly dipped in innocent blood, that would've been the time to come out and say, our Daddy's not guilty, he did none of that, and we also — how does it go? — we drank so to speak, with the people, from whatchamacallit, the bitter cup… in short, it did not pass us by! But the sixth and eighth grader remained silent, as if preserving the *shame,* and everyone around was silent too, as if it were a *secret* shame.

But how did all that fit onto the Bridge, next to the murdered Nina, I thought again, standing over the papers, feeling the hunter-victim shiver tickle my spine from the neck down to the tailbone. What were these Mikoyan kids up to? Sergo was a scholar, for some reason he studied the life and work of Konstantin Umansky. Vano joined his uncle's aircraft design bureau. Relations inside the family, according to various people, were vacuous: obligatory gathering for meals, no one contradicted father, the biggest threat from the mother was "I'll tell Papa!" There was nothing more terrifying than father's wrath. The four surviving Mikoyan boys chased all their unrestrained desires, they lived loudly and broadly. Aleksei Mikoyan got mixed up in love affairs, his father took away his Kremlin pass and thundered, "I'll have him demoted to a lieutenant! I'll send him to Siberia!" But they got away with it, *they always got away with everything.* Except this one time, apparently, when the Emperor suddenly turned his gaze upon them. Someone mentioned a TV show about the wayward children of the Kremlin elite, on which Sergo Mikoyan suddenly mentioned Shakhurin and twirled his finger by his gray temple, saying only, "He was a nut." But he did not finish the thought and say, myself and seven others went to jail because of him.

I was processing all this and getting ready to go to bed when Goltsman called.

"I asked our people to look at the Interior Ministry database. With a high degree of probability, we can say that Barabanov, Xxxx and Kirpichnikov are dead. Five of them are alive."

Lying on the couch, under the blanket, with the light off, I thought about Wendt, the German Communist whom Petrova reportedly "loved very much." If the German wasn't executed, hadn't he ever wanted to see his son at least once? It seemed not; only the mother stayed with the halfwit. But still: not to live in the same room necessarily, but to see him, to bring him a toy from the German Democratic Republic, to explain why the sun goes to sleep at night. To run his hand slowly over the fragrant head of his son — his own invalid, pitiful attempt at immortality — silently to say farewell to Petrova, pressing his face into the tears on her cheek. Or he could have written at least, asked for a photo. He may have stopped loving this *femme fatale*, hated her for cheating on him, at the interrogation she may have saved her own skin and betrayed him, but what about the boy Vasya? I imagined how it was for him now at an institution, where they feed people like him semolina and buckwheat porridge and strap them down to beds so the staff can take a break.

AS A MATTER OF FACT

THE SENIOR ASSISTANT TO THE PROSECUTOR OF THE USSR, THE Empire's best detective and the author of thrilling mystery novels Lev Romanovich Sheinin ran the first investigation into the Umansky-Shakhurin case swiftly and without a fuss: the children were cremated, the surviving Umanskys flew to Mexico. The school principle Leonova, a few teachers and several classmates gave testimony about the culprits' lack of discipline and teenage love. The case was closed, Shakhurin's ashes were buried at Novodevichy, and Nina's remains sat in storage in a ceramic urn for eighteen months at the Donsky crematorium. The seventh grade of school #175 was assigned to educational agricultural labor at the Irrigation Fields collective farm in Lyublino to pick vegetables and strawberries and hoe beets; the kids were allowed into town on weekends — to bathe.

The class fell distinctly short of fulfilling the picking and hoeing quotas they were set, but no students were reprimanded, and in fact, the kids each were given forty kilos of vegetables to take home. Then something unidentified happened, and eight boys were arrested, all of them (apart from the youngest) on the same day — the ones who are still alive cannot agree to this day whether it was Saturday or Sunday.

Vano vanished from the dacha. The family called the morgues and hospitals: Had he been hit by a car? Where was his bike then? The police searched the ravines along the river. Did he drown? Until the *pater familias* himself called the dacha and told everyone in an unfamiliar voice, *there's no need to worry*, Vano has been arrested.

Artyom Khmelnitsky received a call from Galya Lozovskaya: she asked if he wanted to go see an American movie, *His Butler's Sister*. Artyom agreed to meet her at the theater; while he waited, a black GAZ-M pulled up to the sidewalk, and no one ever saw him again.

Surgeon Bakulev's widow wrote in her diary: "Nine boys were arrested in the middle of the day on the city streets without the parents being told anything. Among them was our son Petya."

Petya was also called: someone from the building administration wanted him to come down to the office to check a receipt. As soon as he stepped into the yard, Petya was grabbed and lifted into a vehicle by skillful hands, and the car roared off, across two lanes of busy traffic, which made it clear it belonged to the Power. The boy only dared to say one thing: "Tell my parents." At the first interrogation he lost consciousness.

Bakulev, desperate, called the head of the Kremlin's medical unit, the father of the beauty and soul of the class Busalova (the one whom we eventually located at the City Hospital #67, to be regaled with tales of old times — the indoor skating rink at Petrovka, pilot-suitors dipping their plane wings over Papa's dacha). Bakulev mumbled to Busalov over the telephone: my son has disappeared, completely without a trace, I am scheduled to operate on an NKVD General first thing tomorrow morning, and I don't know how I'll manage — my hands are shaking, and the case is quite serious, his life is in danger, I'm afraid I may have to withdraw. At six the next morning Busalov called back: there's nothing to worry about — your son has been arrested. Go and operate in peace.

Leonid Redens, whose pedigree made him Emperor's nephew, wearing a T-shirt under an unbuttoned shirt, a pair of shorts and sandals, went to visit Vasya Stalin in his new apartment, to see how the remodeling was coming along. Vasya, his cousin, was ill-disposed due to a battle wound (a rocket he was trying to use as a fishing tool blew up at close range). Redens saw a car parked next to the building entrance, and a man approached him and started talking, very solicitously, until Leonid was in the car, and then was being relieved of his belt and shoe-laces, and then, almost as a joke, finger-printed, and a camera flash went off playfully, impressing Redens into the Lubyanka files forever.

His distraught mother Anna Sergeevna called everyone: find my son! And stopped when she heard the reply: *he's with us.*

Two weeks later, Sergo Mikoyan was hanging out at the gates of his dacha, when another black sedan pulled up and a familiar Cheka officer got out (they played dominoes together, and he had taught Sergo to shoot a pistol at a shooting range): "Hop in, let's drive to Moscow, we'll bring your brother." And off they went. For the first time in his life, Sergo saw the perpetually closed gates of the Lubyanka open.

The mothers of the arrested boys gathered close to the top, at Ashken Mikoyan's. In the vain hope that no one knew and no one would read the reports later, Ashken secretly ran to the Novodevichy Monastery to see a Tarot reader and have a séance with the former court poet Sadovsky and his mistress, a former lady-in-waiting at the Tsar's court.

Anastas Mikoyan risked everything and *asked* about his sons. "Beria will sort it out," the Emperor replied indifferently, and there could be no further discussion on this Earth.

Why were they arrested? Why only the boys? The Mikoyan brothers were not in the same class with Nina Umanskaya — why them? Why were they released half a year later, but exiled? Why didn't a single one of them ever talk about being arrested — with anyone? And why were they arrested six weeks after the murder-suicide on the Bridge?

Something must have come up in those intervening six weeks. Someone did not believe that Nina was killed by Shakhurin.

Tatyana Litvinova, Brighton, England: Nina was quickly accepted at school. Kostya talked delightedly about Mikoyan's sons escorting her on motorcycles, all but with machine guns, to Molotov's dacha — she had made friends with the People's Commissar's daughter.

However, that relationship proved to be a typical Kremlin friendship: sometimes Nina was suddenly not invited and then again she was.

When my brother and I became students, we got a housekeeper, Dusya. Before us, she had worked for the Mikoyans, and afterward she became a junior lieutenant of the KGB. Once Misha and I asked her to wake us at a certain time. She knocked on the door in the morning, and I said "Thank you." Dusya suddenly burst into tears. It turned out that when she woke up the Mikoyans, they threw boots at her.

"I'm flying to England on Saturday," our secretary said when she came in. She did not bring a notebook and sat down without being invited. After waiting pointlessly, she added, "Litvinova lives in Brighton, a sea-side resort in the South of England known for its historic boardwalk."

"What isn't clear to you?"

"Everything's clear," she recited indifferently: "I am to prepare for the conversation, write reports every evening, make regular contact. The Great Stone Bridge. The circumstances of the teenagers' death. Umansky. The main target is Anastasia Petrova. Are you now in love with her?"

I gave a nervous laugh and snickered, unsure of what to say.

Outside my window were clouds, dusty wind, the inexplicable wind of spring. Yellow flowers poked up through the rotting grass on the side of the road, cars passed by. The monotonous seething of birdcalls.

"Everything depends on you, young lady."

The secretary sat, leaning forward, without raising her eyes. The way a person waits at a doctor's office, when they have reason to be anxious. I went on:

"Kuibyshev. The start of the war. All Commissariats, most government agencies, main factories and hospitals have been evacuated there.

"All our characters suddenly come together at this geographical point over the course of *three weeks,* from October 16 to November 9. Shakhurin arrives around the 20th along with Molotov and Mikoyan.

They are accompanied by a convoy of fighter planes. Molotov spends the entire flight reading Chekhov in silence.

"Shakhurin Senior works around the clock at aircraft factories. Sofia Mironovna is busy with her social life at the dacha with the other evacuated aristocrats.

"Litvinov lived on Frunze Street, on the corner near the statue of Chapaev, five minutes' walk from the city garden. There is nothing in his rooms but a table, a cupboard and a bed with squashed springs.

"I think Petrova came alone. And I believe the people are correct who say that she lived with Litvinov in an apartment right above Shostakovich's — the composer was finishing his Seventh Symphony, he was taken out of blockaded Leningrad, and allowed to take only eight kilograms of luggage with him. They promised to bring out his wife and sister, but could not do it.

"Umansky arrives. He lived across the road from the Litvinovs, some say. He drank vodka with foreign correspondents at the Grand Hotel, say others. What is indisputable is that he is a winsome man who has lived abroad, had a radiola, and good suits in addition to Stalin's autograph on a photo in a fake birch-wood frame. But he cannot hide his internal upheaval: Umansky doesn't understand why he was recalled. He never lived in the empire for very long, and it's war-time now, rationing, bed-bugs, outdoor privies, no one to talk to about Picasso. He starts to suspect that something is wrong. His best friend Koltsov had already identified him as a German spy. Umansky considers his life — at thirty-nine. What does he see? Nothing that is solid enough to hold on to. And then he suddenly understands *why* he has returned, why all of this is happening to him. Kostya understands: it's all fair, he has lived wretchedly, he lied, he betrayed his teacher, he treated women like they were disposable, he chased after his appetites. He served the Emperor poorly, But he has the chance to save himself. Kostya suddenly understands that there is only one woman in his life whom he has really loved. And everything is collapsing, perhaps, only in order to show him that she is the one, the real thing, only that. Go to her. There won't be any other chance to save yourself. Soon will come old age and death… He is convinced of this," I drew a line in front of me with the tip of my shoe. "This is Umansky's position."

I walked behind the secretary's back, and she straightened up, as if expecting me to touch her.

"Now you are Petrova. You're thirty-nine years old. You are incredibly attractive, fabulously beautiful. Also, you have two children to look after, a mother and a nanny. Dmitry Tsurko is MIA. Pyotr Tsurko vanished without a trace. The German Wendt is in prison. Umansky will go to jail tomorrow and die, or he'll breathe archival dust at a desk job as the deputy secretary of the sixth department of the ninth regional directorate, screwing secretaries until he retires, because he won't be able to afford actresses anymore. He doesn't even have an apartment! And your Maxim Maximovich is received by the emperor! He will perhaps rise to be a People's Commissar. This is your chance. You could wear evening gowns and ride around in open cars, you could leave the kids in a safe, remote village with the nanny and be young again, flirting with the members of the Politburo. That's your position."

It was as if I was balancing two stones in my hands as I moved to the doors.

"And there is also another factor: the country. The deciding conversation, dates, nights, walks, hysterics, all this is happening in terrifying times: the Germans seem to be inexorably moving towards Moscow. And any day something could happen to change the lives of hundreds of millions of people, and all of your and Umansky's desires and passions — everything, you understand — will turn to dust. All we will want is to survive, to eat. We understand this very well and hurry to seize and devour our piece of happiness as soon as we can, right? This is the position of the country, everyone is waiting. Every hour, everyone is waiting. For an order, a flight, a victory, a catastrophe."

"Well, first of all, I know what you are worth," the secretary shifted, as if a photographer had permitted her to change her pose and rest, and she spoke with effort, an old person, she was Anastasia now. "You're a superficial, frivolous person — flighty, they called you, Kostya. Now you feel one way, but tomorrow you'll feel differently."

I suddenly choked, expelling the words from my throat, trying to hold back tears — I was Konstantin Umansky:

"I was prepared to abandon my family… To take you, your children… Knowing everything that happened to you, everyone you have been with — didn't we talk about this before? Didn't we? We must have…. And you said: Maybe. *Maybe!* I love you. You're the only one. I could change."

"And I want to say," she got up. "You outlined my position, and your own… But in Kuibyshev another person was also waiting for the future. You're forgetting Litvinov. In Kuibyshev, I loved him. And I loved him in such a way that I thought it was going to be forever."

I rubbed my cheeks with my hands, thought about happiness, looked around, and happiness embodied itself for me in a liter bottle of freshly-squeezed orange juice that was waiting in the fridge.

"And where is your love, Anastasia Vladimirovna? Are you even capable of it? You returned from the United States with your lover…"

"I may have become disappointed, I may have changed and understood many things," she said quickly.

"What's that? *Disappointed?* Are you sure it wasn't me you came for, across Africa, knowing full well Litvinov may never rise again?"

"We may have corresponded."

"So I knew about your retarded son."

"Not necessarily, it wasn't clear yet that Vasya was ill."

"And I may have realized how much my wife actually meant to me."

"Oh, yes, the insane and graceless Raisa, on whom you cheated at every opportunity."

"Above all, my daughter…"

"That's for sure — so many useful connections you made through her!"

"I lived for Nina's sake, you know what she meant to me!"

"Uh-huh. Especially what your new post meant to you! You just didn't want to bother with a divorce. Molotov wouldn't have liked that."

"Ehrenburg wrote: 'Umansky experienced a drama'…"

"What else could your friend have written? That out of boredom you gave it a try for the last time with a woman who was in love with you? That as always, you didn't miss your chance for one last tryst?"

"I really did love you, Tasya." I paused. "But I loved Nina madly." I couldn't wait. "You should say: but when Nina was killed, what stopped you? And I would reply: I couldn't abandon my wife who was mad with grief. Together we would have reminisced about things. I felt I was to blame for Nina's death. And in order to somehow make up for it, although that's impossible, I should now give everything to Raisa… Perhaps at some point later, I thought, after some time… In another city. We would meet on the bridge and go walking in the evenings, joining our gnarled, dry hands. We would care for each other… We would be happy… And we would miss each other if we were apart even for an hour. This all happened in our life for some reason, something held us, although so many fates and bodies passed by, and together we somehow… connected. Perhaps I even wrote to you about this from Mexico. But then the plane blew up, and Nina was reunited with me and Raisa. She wasn't buried for such a long time, as if someone knew that nothing would work out with us. And I became a slab on the wall of the Pokrovskaya Tower, 27 on the map of the Novodevichy Monastery."

The secretary unexpectedly raised her eyes and looked at me, trying to catch a mocking smile.

"The briefing is over. Now you know what to look for in Brighton."

"I'll try to become like you. I can't say I enjoy experiencing things this way. But I tried. I asked Alexander Naumovich to show me the papers. I tried to see Umansky and Petrova. I sat there and stared at their records until it was late, as if at a wall. And then I placed their forms next to each other on my desk and suddenly it was if I saw a weak light, from the other side… As if the stones did not fit tightly, but you could only notice this at night. I was lucky. The forms intersected at the same time and in the same place. You didn't pay attention to this because it happens at the very beginning, right after the revolution. When she was sixteen, Petrova worked as a clerk at the Central Press office. Umansky, who was seventeen, also worked there, as the secretary to the Chairman of the Board. He saw her, and she saw him. This means they go way back. This means, as you like to put it, that with a high degree of certainty we may assume they were each other's first love, and everything that came afterwards — Kuibyshev and Moscow — were only attempts to step over everything that followed, everything that was outside, that was in the way, and return."

BAD OMENS

Tatyana Litvinova, Brighton, England: after hitler attacked the Soviet Union, my father found things completely intolerable, and he sent a letter to Stalin asking for an appointment. He was given an office at the People's Committee for Foreign Affairs — without even a typist! — but they sent Petrova to be his assistant.

Dad sent Mom into evacuation, to Kuibyshev. Mom corresponded with Petrova regularly and once received a postcard: I have a new lover. You'll never guess who. The woman was writing about my father.

I think their affair began as a result of Dad's radical isolation. He couldn't have done it with anyone outside the Commissariat. He was terribly lonely; he felt that he had robbed his children of their mother (because a real mother should be home with the kids instead of going to receptions and flirting with foreign correspondents) and blamed himself for the death of our baby-brother who died of pneumonia in Oslo. He also knew he was the man who created his isolation.

Anastasia Vladimirovna came to Kuibyshev with father. He explained to Mom that he could not refuse: Petrova threw herself at his feet and begged him to take her. By then, my parents no longer slept together, but still, if Mama had known the truth before they left for the U.S., I think she would have stayed.

Instead, the three of them went to America via Teheran, Baghdad, Calcutta, Bangkok, Singapore and the Hawaii. During the journey, Mom began to suspect something and asked Petrova directly: are you a traitor? Anastasia Vladimirovna answered with the same directness: yes.

In the States, Mama went straight to New York and stayed there, even when father and Petrova returned to Moscow.

Tasya, meanwhile, moved into the Embassy, and the American septuagenarians who wrote requests to be accepted into the Red Army and attached drawings of home-crafted blades with which they would cut enemy paratroopers out of trees began to receive responses of restrained gratitude signed by "A. Petrova, Secretary to the Ambassador." Those dead Embassy papers began to be ennobled ever so slightly by her calm, domestic-sounding notation, "MM has been informed."

I tied the strings on the folder "Petrova, A. V." and went to say goodbye to the fabric dyer Valentina, a bitch with beautiful dusky skin, an old woman in a turban.

Her son was not there this time, having been convinced of my harmlessness, but the old lady sensed a bit of sepulchral chill, left alone with me.

"Petrova finally married the German Jew, Wendt, from the Comintern. Do you know that she herself was Jewish on her father's side? Her maiden name was Flam. All the Tsurkos remarried Jews, they did not like me. Petrova never got along with Zina, but they united against me. Petrova's brother hanged himself, and her granddaughter poisoned herself — she overdosed on pills because she was in love with that composer who lived next to them in Kuibyshev, and he was a disreputable man. She was buried at Vagankovo."

So that's where the girl Olya went, the only Tsurko grandchild, the only chance for the future.

"When was the last time you saw your husband?"

"On a weekend we decided to go to the forest to pick mushrooms. Suddenly there was a phone call, a summons to headquarters. He came back upset — he said I had to go to Moscow, and he had to go on maneuvers. I refused, I wouldn't go. There had been maneuvers before, and I had waited for him at the dacha. We were driven to the station, but the chief of staff took a long time with the luggage, and we were late, and also the child got food poisoning, it was very hot. When we came back and Mitya realized we missed the train, his face convulsed with anger. He sent us the next day by various indirect trains. We reached Moscow on June 21st. Then we evacuated to Tyumen. Petrova sent me letters from Mitya regularly. I realized that Mitya had disappeared when the money stopped coming.

"I came back to Moscow and found the conductor Alexandrov living in our apartment. We went to court over the apartment, because they said that Sasha wasn't Mitya's son. How could he not be Mitya's son? I looked for traces of Mitya in the Partisan movement archives — I thought he may have been hiding under his mother's last name. We lived here when Nina Umanskaya was killed — I saw it with my own eyes, I was standing on the balcony. There were three of them on the bridge, all school kids. And then there was some kind of altercation — before my very eyes! Marshal Konev's wife knew that Mikoyan was the killer. But it was all blamed on Shakhurin."

"We have a problem," Goltsman said, and paused tragically, before continuing: "The new guy…"

"Chukharev."

"Yes, the one you hired. Someone gave him access to our latest information." Goltsman took a deep breath. "And he decided to take the older Mikoyan on his own."

At this point Goltsman opened the door and summoned the offender into the room.

"Idiot! Moron! Scumbag!" Borya yelled at him with a sincerity that surprised me; he then knocked several stacks of papers and stationery off the desk onto the floor for greater effect. "Animal!"

Chukharev's mouth twitched, but he didn't say anything. I gave Borya a look to turn the sound down, and snapped at Chukharev:

"Look at me."

"I thought I'd try to find the number, his telephone number. And I found it. Then I thought I'd call and check if it worked. And he suddenly picked up — I didn't think he would."

"What did you say to him?"

"That I…"

"Word for word!"

"Hello, I'm sorry to bother you, my name is… We are investigating the murder of Volodya Shakhurin and Nina Umanskaya, would you be available to meet me to answer a few…"

"And he hung up on you."

"He first said, 'Scum!' And then hung up."

"Zero," Borya pointed to the miserable man in complete silence. "No abilities for field work."

I went into my office, where Alyona was waiting for me.

"Why did you show him the latest information?" I asked Alyona.

"I was under the impression he was working with us," Alyona answered with cold swiftness, gathering up things into her purse. "Where were you yesterday? I called."

"I'll tell you later. After I've had time to come up with some plausible details. I need to talk to Alexander Naumovich."

In a couple of nervous moments the two of us were alone. Alyona left without saying another word.

"You know, Alexander Naumovich, I don't believe that the old woman saw with her own eyes how they were killed and who did the shooting. She simply wants to live and be needed. But it's completely accurate that there were three individuals on that bridge, and the third, about whom everyone knows and no one talks is Vano Mikoyan. It's all come together."

"You don't like this?"

"Do you see how they slipped him to us on time? Just as we are trying to figure out how to link the arrested schoolboys with the Great Stone Bridge?"

"I'll write a letter," Chukharev butted in, leaning into my office. "I'll find out the address and place it in the mail box. He cussed me out in the heat of the moment, and now he regrets it. He will talk."

"Get out of here!" I roared. And then sighed. "Alexander Naumovich, is that all?"

"We have identified two people who had something to say about the boys, both of them in their sixties. One is Khrushchev's grandson who said, if you believe the family stories, that the boys were arrested for not being sufficiently conscientious — they knew that Shakhurin was planning a murder, and did not inform on him. And the second one" — he gave me a yellowed sheet headlined *Construction News* — "is the elder brother, Stepan Mikoyan."

The article in that god-forsaken paper that no one ever read chewed over the "tragic story with unclear motives" — the murder on the Bridge — and then took the inexplicable jump to the arrest of the sixteen-year-old Vano, and then Sergo. The investigator was the sinister Sheinin, later replaced by the bloody Wlodzimirski.

"Lev Yemelyanovich," Goltsman followed my index finger as it moved down. "A serious figure. Head of NKVD, lieutenant general. Convicted and executed in connection with the Beria case."

Why did Beria's henchman get involved with a teenager? "He went through intense interrogations, wasn't allowed to sleep," the newspaper said, but there was no mention of torture, and eventually Sergo was exiled to Tajikistan for a year.

"What does 'children's war games' mean?" I pointed to a phrase in the story.

"Keep reading."

Everything passed and began to heal, but in the terrible year of 1949, the Emperor, who forgot nothing, suddenly looked at Mikoyan, pulled out his moist, quivering soul and smoothed it out on his rough palm.

"Anastas" — I'm sure Mikoyan only told his close friends, and only shortly before his death, about the Emperor suddenly calling out his name, and maybe even imitated *the way* that special voice asked: "Anastas! Where are your children?"

The ones who played war games. Sergo was at an institute. Vano was at the Academy; there was nothing to add here.

"Are they worthy of study in Soviet universities?"

The question required an answer, and for several paralyzed weeks, Mikoyan waited for an answer — was life getting too crowded for his boys? Was there still room for them?

THE PLAYERS

The investigation found Stepan Mikoyan an old man, gray-whiskered, a small brush under his nose, wearing a short brown shearling coat. He was small as a boy, and he waited for me at the entrance to an unidentifiable aircraft component factory. He did not have a place to receive guests, and we sat down on squashed chairs, joined in threes, opposite a little window with the sign "Cashier" above it; Stepan Anastasovich resorted to a whisper whenever an employee walked past us.

What I had before me was a handful of dust, mere remains. Yet there had been a time when this diminutive, eagle-nosed old man had been a master of life and had inspired holy fear by the mere mention of his father's name. One old woman had told me that the strongest impression in her life was when Stepan Mikoyan stepped into an elevator with her, and she was breath-taken, she saw *him* next to her, he was incredibly handsome. When they reached his floor, and he went out, she couldn't move, she just stood there and breathed in the scent of his cologne!

I believed him when he said:

"Vano never told anyone why he was arrested. And I didn't ask. They say that he was playing war games. I don't know anything more than that. In our family, everyone kept silent about it — both my mother and father. Do you think that my brother's arrest is somehow connected with the murder of Nina Umanskaya?"

We also got Petya Bakulev, the son of the Surgeon General, on the phone; he said his mother had just passed away. Chukharev, trying to make up for his earlier blunder, obediently read a bunch of solicitous lies we prepared for him off a piece of paper, stopping to allow Bakulev to respond where appropriate, and then hung up:

"He agreed," he said.

"And remember," Borya (sober this time) instructed, "never ask too much. For one person, there are just a few questions which have meaningful answers. It doesn't matter if the person thought about these things a lot or if they never even occurred to him or her until you came along. It is just a coincidence. You need to guess. If you ask less than necessary, there will be something he forgot to tell you. If you push him, he'll start lying and believe what he says himself. Any questions?"

"He *wasn't surprised*," Chukharev said. "If I were him, I'd think this was a joke, or something. It's like he'd been waiting all along for someone to come after him."

An early-Spring snow had fallen, a lot at once, and it clung to tree branches in thick, lopsided slices of white. Children came out, rolling up strips of white with greenish underside into balls to make snowmen. The sun gleamed off the icicles. In the sky, vast stretches of blue opened up and then vanished; the water in the ponds of the Troparev park looked solid under a heavy chill. Up from the ponds, from the rickety old footbridges, a path led up the stairs to the Olympic Village — the 1980 sports complex — where, last week, an unknown individual had shot a 30-35 year-old man of Caucasian origin with a shot to the head. Inside Bakulev's apartment building, a set of iron bars divided a hallway that led to three apartment doors. Before opening the grill, the gray and wrinkled old man looked for a moment at Chukharev through the bars, as though he lived in a prison.

"What can you say about Nina?"

"She was calm, attractive, well-dressed. She was kind. She had quite a figure — very well nourished by comparison to others."

"Did you consider your friend Shakhurin to be insane?"

"Volodya was a very strange boy. He always wanted to impress people, and did a lot of unusual things. 'If I come to power, I will walk down Gorky Street, and a battalion will walk behind me and play a march!' That was what he dreamed of. He would say things like 'My parents are going out tonight, I'll just sit there with a loaded pistol, all alone and sad.'"

"So he had a pistol? A Walter?"

"I don't remember. Many boys at our school carried pistols.... I knew that Volodya was madly in love with Nina, but her parents didn't approve of him. When he wanted to call Nina to come out, I would be the one to call from the pay phone; I'd tell her parents who I was, then say to her: I have a friend here with me, and give the receiver to Volodya. She answered him indirectly, with hints, so that her parents wouldn't know who she was talking to. At school he didn't even go near Nina, so he wouldn't be mocked for having a crush on her."

"Do you think they... is there a chance they were intimate?"

"It's unlikely. Sofia Mironovna watched his every step and ran a tight ship at home. She wore a leather coat. Girls didn't invite boys to visit. Maybe at the dacha... Sofia Mironovna thought that Volodya should be friends with the other boys from his class, so she invited them to their dacha at Nikolina Gora. There was skating and skiing. But Nina did not go to visit them. Perhaps they kissed..."

"What games did you play?"

"War games, as boys will. We thought up secret organizations and military titles. We wrote orders. The most envious thing was to wear an American military pin on your coat. We really just wanted to impress the girls. We pretended to argue, someone would pull a gun, others would rush to take it away — the girls gasped!"

"What were you arrested for?"

"Sofia Mironovna cooked it up. When that whole business on the bridge happened, she was incensed: how is it that all the kids are good, but my Volodya is bad? So she called Stalin, and he said, go get those bastards. When the thing... when Nina's murder happened,

I gathered all the guys together. I thought everyone in our class would be questioned anyway, so I said we should destroy Volodya's papers lest something come up. And we shouldn't say anything about our games."

"Was that your own idea or did someone advise you to do that?"

A pause.

"No. It was my own initiative. And everyone promised me they would do as I said, but… Let's stop. I'm tired."

"Did you hear anything about the circumstances of Konstantin Umansky's death?"

"Someone probably told you already: my mother worked as an X-ray specialist at the Kremlin hospital. In the 1950s, she talked with a patient who was on that plane. The woman survived because when the plane fell apart, her seat landed in a bush. I don't know anything more than this story."

"Did anything connect Umansky and R, the composer?"

"They were friends. And neighbors, I think. Why do you ask?"

Chukharev said goodbye and left. Outside the apartment he stopped and looked at the city from the eighteenth floor, at the sweaty, murky city, the patchwork of roofs, the wet grass and paths trod through it. Down on the street he was captivated by the tall saleswoman he saw through a shop window, so he went into the shop and bought two apple turnovers, carrying in his pocket a telephone number written on a canceled cheque — for a moment he felt happy and young; he rode on the metro, ate a turnover, looked at the protocol of his first interrogation, and sized up the people boarding the train. Opposite him a serious-looking woman was reading a book: *Cancer — Tactics for Healing.*

What the hell was that game the boys played?

Artyom Khmelnitsky was remembered at school as a dreamer and a liar. "Don't believe him, don't believe him," Chukharev repeated Mirgorodsky's parting instructions, as he entered a five-floor apartment building in Cheremushki. The lanky son of the aide of Marshal

Voroshilov's aide led his guest to the kitchen, and without sitting down suddenly whacked his palm on the table:

"What was the weapon that killed Nina Umanskaya?"

"A Walter."

"And whose pistol was it?" Khmelnitsky whispered, stretching his lips in a mocking grin. "You don't know everything, do you? It's not working out for you, is it?" and with a creak he sat on the stool; he was amused and happy: here was a person who would respectfully listen to him and carry out his orders — that was what he, Artyom Rafailovich, had lacked all his adult life.

"Did you have a pistol?" Chukharev asked, determined not to believe a word he was about to hear.

"I'll whisper into your ear: I had a Mauser! Not a new one, mind you. The boys in our class were officially entitled to weapons. You know, as the mathematician Yulik Gurvits said: I'd go to school and all the boys would be sitting with their elbows on the desk, a dagger with a swastika under one arm, a pistol under the other. I'd turn my back on them to write on the board and shake all over: what if they shoot me in the back!" And he chuckled with satisfaction.

"What were the games you played?"

"War games," his voice dried out and withered. "We dueled with shells from incendiary bombs — you know, like the clubs of Russian heroes. We split up, the Reich division against the NKVD division, or the Death's Head battalion against the Siberian guards. Here, I have a picture to show you," Artyom Rafailovich changed tack suddenly, steering away from the topic he didn't like. "Here's Nina at the exhibition of trophy weapons at the Park of Culture and Leisure, that's professor Shchusev, Marshal Voroshilov, Colonel Boris Sergeyevich Sakharov, and there she is."

"Did the girls play with you?"

"Not a single one," he mumbled without pleasure, and skipped to the next square. "Umansky, I remember, lived in room 550 of the Moscow Hotel, and then moved to the fourth entranceway of the House of Government, first floor, he worked basically around the clock.

Nina's mother had to think what she wanted to say in English first, and then translate it into Russian. She was friends with my mother, and Mother told me the secret" — the gray-haired Artyom leaned over to Chukharev and exhaled — "Nina was pregnant."

And nodded emphatically, *yes, yes.*

"Did you tell the investigator?" Chukharev asked mercilessly.

"My father told me to stick to the facts. Later, when they arrested me and trumped up charges of anti-Soviet activity, who cared if she was pregnant?" The prisoner of Stalinism dolefully raised his eyebrows. "I'm telling you: there I was sitting, studying for my exams, and suddenly there's a phone call and it's Raisa Umanskaya: Nina's been killed! We ran to the bridge, but it was already cleared, we gawked for a bit and went home."

"Who told your parents you had been arrested?"

"Stalin told my father himself!" Khmelnitsky snapped. "And I was released personally by Lavrentiy Pavlovich Beria. There was such an uproar… Teachers were dismissed, three classes were dispersed among nearby schools. I had that arrest shoved in my face all my life," this would be the painful truth bursting forth now, Chukharev thought. "I could have been an admiral…"

"They say that Volodya was really interested in girls."

"I don't remember him being overly hung up on sex. There was a lot of talk in the class about who had their eye on whom, he was close friends with Nina, but nothing more…"

"Why were you arrested?"

"I need to go cash my paycheck," Artyom Rafailovich stood up and began to get ready, grabbing a jacket, boots, other things. In the dark hallway, he pressed close to Chukharev and whispered: "You've got to know this. If we really wanted to," completely speechless, he blinked with the effort to speak. "S-s-st…in," he couldn't pronounce the name. Chukharev realized later what this hissing and whistling meant, "Killing…him would have been easy. He used to come to our home."

"Kill him? What would you kill him for?"

"To take revenge!"

Chukharev had asked all the questions on the list, but to avoid falling silent, he fired off one of his own:

"How come after…that, you never got together again, all of you, and never talked about it?"

"We were made to sign a non-disclosure agreement," Khmelnitsky weighed his statement, and decided to add: "And an obligation not to meet — for thirty years."

In the courtyard, Khmelnitsky reported that he worked at a service garage and made good money. He had just bought a car, he said. A Volvo. A new one. For forty-two thousand dollars. With armored windows. Chukharev kept a respectful silence, looked at the foreign cars sprinkled with melting snow, and contemplated asking for a ride, but Khmelnitsky marched straight out and they walked together to the trolleybus stop. Both rode to the Profsoyuznaya metro station.

Chukharev got off at Kievskaya station, and changed trolleybuses. It was spring now, and he put his head out the window. It was good to ride along the embankment, putting your face to the wind, glancing at the thoughtful, light-haired girl by the window, to breathe in the forgotten smell of river water and see the leaves by the streetlights shining with gold.

We were afraid to spook the youngest, Sergo Mikoyan, as Vano could have warned his brother. We looked for him for a long time; we were told he was not in Moscow, then not in Russia. Chukharev, lying in great detail that he was preparing a museum exhibition of school #175, left his telephone number with Sergo's daughter, and a month later Sergo called.

In the building on Rublyovsk Road, a thin and formerly tall man, his hair forming what used to be called a thatch, was paying the repairman who had installed a new door:

"Oh yes, I also owe you for the delivery. Well, let's say one hundred and fifty rubles. Is that enough?"

"Sure, it's enough. I wanted to ask you for your autograph, even just on a piece of blank paper, for my daughter. She's nineteen years old. I said: you do know this surname — Mikoyan? And she remembered it!"

"Right, I'll find a postcard... how old did you say she was? Shall I address it to her?"

"Write 'To Yulia'."

Chukharev sat down at a low table and examined the rocking chair, the pussy willow branches in a tall vase, and an African drum with two drumsticks. He picked up an enormous sea-shell, turned it over in his hands, held it to his ear, looked inside and read the inscription: "To A. I. Mikoyan from the fishermen of SRT-R-9000 Omar, Havana, 25.11.62." Flattened silver spoons and forks were hung on fish line under the chandelier; these twisted slowly with the movement of the air, and made a sad chiming sound.

"We lived in the Kremlin, opposite the Troitsky gates." Sergo, well-trained by television appearances, knew what to say. "Kommunisticheskaya 3, opposite a special purpose garage. Today, the Kremlin Palace of Congresses stands on that site."

He stuttered slightly, and got over the difficult syllables on the outbreath. Chukharev waited, opened his notebook with its reassuring blue lines, and nodded in encouragement.

"We saw my father at six in the evening: he would come home for dinner. He never hit anyone. He seemed gentle, but he was terribly strict. Once he didn't speak to me for four months, when I, er, did not accurately report the outcome of one of my exams at the end of 8ᵗʰ grade. What was your question?"

"About Shakhurin."

"Oh, he was a crazy, pathological sort! He would gather us, pace around the room, and mutter into the air, 'The weak have no right to live! The weak must die!'" Sergo got up to show how the crazy Shakhurin walked, and threw his arms up in the air so wildly that he hit the floor lamp. "He'd read too much Hitler! He knew German excellently... And then that awful business with Nina. Stalin was informed, and he wanted someone punished. Who was left? We were the ones who got caught."

"You know, I heard that when Shakhurin killed Nina Umanskaya and himself, there was another person nearby on the bridge."

Suddenly, Sergo seemed to discover that he was not talking at a television camera or the brainless daughter of a door installer. He looked at the creature sitting at his table, and twice tried to adopt a more comfortable pose.

"Your brother," Chukharev hinted with pleasure.

"Vano? Vano came running home. His hands were shaking, his teeth were chattering." Sergo frowned as he spoke, as if recalling a dream. "'I was on the bridge! I saw the consequences.' Shakhurin told him to leave, that he would be the odd man out. Vano did as he was told, then heard the noise, turned around: the two were both on the ground."

Chukharev felt lifted up by a wave of monstrous force that set his blood racing and pushed him against the wall. Stuttering himself, in a shamefully breaking voice, he barked something incredible:

"Why did Vano take the pistol? The Walter."

"The pistol?" Sergo faltered under this direct attack. "Well, Volodya first asked for the pistol himself, to scare her a little… So she wouldn't leave. Of course, Vano was stupid to give it to him with the cartridge. Then Shakhurin drove him away, he told him to leave. Vano turned around — they were both lying on the ground… He grabbed the pistol and ran."

"But some people say that Vano killed both of them. With his own pistol."

Sergo gave a martyr's sigh, nodded and weakly squeezed out:

"Yes. Sofia Mironovna, Shakhurin's mother, thought that was the case. That Vano killed them both. Out of jealously."

And asked, belatedly: "Excuse me, I forgot — who are you?" Chukharev should have replied "the scourge of God," but he was intent on finishing as quickly as possible.

"What you do you think, could Shakhurin or your father intervene with Stalin directly for you?"

"Impossible. These people never spoke of personal things."

Chukharev's hands shook, for the first time he felt the pleasure of reeling in the big fish — he'd done it, he was now in the big leagues. He now moved among the ordinary, digitized people, he passed through their biographies, photographs, property disputes and inconsistent testimonies with no need to concern himself with food or shelter — he brimmed with that exalted power that elevates a man the moment he lifts the yellow ribbon around the crime scene where life has shown its essence, steps in, flashes his badge, and everyone instantly knows: here he is, the one who will tell us what to do, he is the one with the burden of knowing, of finding out exactly what happened, and he will carry this burden alone for none other can shoulder it.

Chukharev wanted to rush into the office with his incredible news, but he didn't recognize Moscow when he stepped into the street: this was conquered land, which belonged to him and a select few. He didn't want glory — his power came on the condition of remaining invisible — all he wanted was to cast his net again, to pull it in, to turn over more rocks, not to stop.

We caught up with Redens in a high-rise building on Kotelnicheskaya embankment. The day before meeting him, Goltsman and I went to look at the building and the courtyard, and then walked from the Illyuzion movie theater up the Tagan Hill, until Alexander Naumovich got tired, and we went back down. I had been in the neighborhood before, in the two-story building on the corner, in a nondescript office that took calls about death from all over Moscow and dispatched agents and plain coffins. Redens, who did not use his mother's surname on principle (then there would have been another Alliluyev), was the one out of the group who resisted being found the longest — a year, an entire year, four calls in different voices, I was afraid that he would die.

"Leonid Stanislavovich," Goltsman said to him on the phone gently in his role of the director of the MFA veterans' archive, "We've already asked all your classmates, and all of them, of their own motivations, ah, don't exactly accuse you, but... who better than you could address the gaps and weaknesses of other people's memories? We wouldn't want to publish anything without your input."

Redens fell for it. They had all been waiting for someone just like this, they were all thrilled and heart-broken to learn that someone still needed them.

"The boys are a waste of time, Alexander Naumovich," I said while we walked. "No one but Vano knows anything about Nina Umanskaya's murder: they all heard about it from their parents, they came running, the bodies had already been taken away, and someone had spread sand on the pavement to soak up the blood."

"But why did they not see each other for so many years? Was it really because one of them betrayed their games? They still don't know who it was, and the arrests ruined their lives, they would have been admirals and had better apartments, or so they think… They don't think of their lives as their own. They had to lead lives forced on them, and all because of Shakhurin?"

"You have to remember: they were children, and they were interrogated by experts. They piled all kinds of blame on each other — I bet they were simply ashamed to look each other in the eye after that. That's it," I stopped and grinned at the cold, attentive eyes of the gray-haired, elegantly withered Goltsman. "*They're ashamed!* They're ashamed of their games. Not one of them came out and told us what it was, how this was connected with Nina. It wasn't the possession of firearms that got them — Mikoyan could have been arrested for that, but not the others. And there are rumors about some lists that were found…"

"You're just waiting for our agent in England to receive information that will change everything."

"It will show us a way out. The way I see it."

"Do you want my opinion?" Goltsman asked. "Don't wait. Petrova is a beautiful woman, and nothing more. Our secretary is a good, hard-working girl, but that's all she will find. Chukharev will make a good agent too, with time. I believe it was Redens that turned the group in: he was the most vulnerable, his father had been executed, and Stalin

did not like his mother. As soon as Bakulev demanded of the boys —
swear that you'll never tell anyone — Redens knew perfectly well
where that would take them, so he got up and ran. Talk to him."

"Come in! This is my grandson Vasily."
The grandson, who I assumed was named in honor of the Emperor's
son, was sitting at a computer wearing earphones.
"Let's sit down, here, these are good chairs…"
"I came to Moscow at the end of 1938 from Almaty after my father
was arrested. The apartment had been sealed, but my grandfather was
able to register it in his name. Don't call our building the House on the
Embankment, we all knew it as the House of Government.
"When the war began I went to Sochi with Svetlana Stalina
and Yakov's wife Yulia, and then we drove to Sukhumi, Batumi and
Tbilisi; we lived in the same hotel as Jose Diaz, the secretary of the
Spanish Communist Party, have you heard of Jose Diaz? By the
way, the polar explorer Papanin wrote about my father in his book
of memoirs. Have you heard of Papanin? From Tbilisi we went to
Krasnovodsk, then Tashkent, and then by rail to Kuibyshev. We got
there in mid-November, I went straight to school. I quickly made
friends with Sergo.
"All we were interested in was pyrotechnics, we'd find some
gunpowder, stuff it into used up carbon dioxide cartridges and blow
them up. Of course, we all dreamt of weapons! But only Vano had a
real pistol.
"I found a pistol frame in a rubbish dump; I made a mood, cast
the rest of the shape in lead and carried this toy around. Sergo found
a low-caliber revolver somewhere, a starter's pistol. To try it out, we
hid in the attic of a house next to the school, and in the darkness we
pressed the trigger — it didn't fire. Sergo turned the pistol around,
pulled the trigger again — and shot himself right in the hand! Ashken
suspected that I had shot him with my fake lead pistol. She blamed all
her sons' shortcomings on bad company. Sergo stuttered, so she told
everyone that my brother Alexander had taught him to stutter.

"I became even more friendly with all the Mikoyans at the Gorki-2 dacha in Zubalovo. They lived noisily: once they stole a rifle from the commandant's house, sawed off the barrel, and when their defenseless father was driving out of the yard (the guards' car was waiting outside the gates), they fired a shot into the air from the mansion tower! The Checka guys ran around like chickens, they thought it was an assassination attempt!

"We once went to visit Molotov, and Vyacheslav Mikhailovich suddenly and ceremoniously sat everyone down to eat and announced: now everyone has to propose a toast. Svetlana Stalina said something short and very good. I was so confused I couldn't squeeze out a word. Don't be shy, Molotov said, just say: to the cutlets! And the people who respect them!"

"When you were around them, did you feel less privileged?"

"You know, times were different… Everyone had seen someone close to them arrested. My Dad had been arrested too. But deep down I never believed that he was an enemy. My mother also believed he was alive, and forever rallied people to search for him. And most importantly, everything in our lives depended on Stalin's attitude toward us. And Stalin treated us well. Take for comparison Jonik Svanidze — he was a very smart boy, stayed away from our games, and he had a rough time. Both his parents were executed, and he was left in a room in a communal apartment, with a strange family, and lived in great poverty. You can't compare him with me."

"Some of your friends call Shakhurin crazy."

"It was politics, he was being nerdy. Everyone gets weird about something. For example, my brother sees Jews everywhere. By the way, do you know that Khmelnitsky's father introduced himself as Rudolf Pavlovich, but his real name was Rafail? So, for Volodya it was politics… I remember him and Sergo walking down Tverskaya, waving their arms and talking about what they would do when they came to power."

"What did they plan to do?"

"I don't remember. When I hung out with him, he'd show me his copy of *Mein Kampf*, he also read *Hitler Speaks*, other German books, but I was more interested in cars. Volodya's father, Aleksei Ivanych Shakhurin was driven in a Graham, an unusual car for those days. I loved machinery, and didn't care about much else, and Volodya was also so wrought over Nina. He was terribly preoccupied with sex! He could barely breath when he talked about her: 'I stopped by, and there she was, just in her house-dress, and *nothing else!*' "

"Do you think he was telling the truth?"

The old man fell silent, then repeated stubbornly:

"He really wanted her. When he found out Nina was leaving, he said: I'll kill her! I'll kill her!! I blamed myself later: how could I hear all this and not tell anyone? It was a real obsession!"

"But why would he want to kill her? Did he give any explanation?"

Redens fell silent again and mumbled discontentedly:

"He didn't explain it at all. He just attached himself to me, when I came to the school, and made me a confidant. He often talked about how he ran away with another girl to an island in Kuibyshev. In February, he gave me his diaries and correspondence with Bakulev for safekeeping. He was afraid that his mother would find the papers, Sofia Mironovna was constantly on the look-out for something, she watched his every movement."

"And you handed the papers over…"

"*Because I considered it to be my duty!* I didn't know myself what I was giving them! We were going to Volodya's funeral, and my mother said, you should at least read what you're carrying first, but I didn't read them, yes, I went to the apartment and gave the papers to Volodya's father. Aleksei Ivanych went into his office to read them and when he came out his eyes were this wide!"

"Chukharev demonstrates extreme zeal," Goltsman was tired of waiting for me and suppressed a yawn. "I can't get him out of here. His wife calls every half hour."

"Yes, I heard him yelling at her: don't interfere with my work! And then he hangs up… But why Vano, really?"

"You don't believe it?"

"That a pregnant girl was killed on orders from a secret organization of oversexed teenagers who were preparing to assassinate Stalin? No, I don't believe it."

No one could remember Nina's funeral, only that it was wretched and horrible. Nina lay in an open coffin, no one came from the Defense Committee or other Commissariats, there were no ambassadors or members of the Central Committee. Umansky was restrained, he went up to each person and shook a teacherly finger at them: don't you slip up on me, Raisa Mikhailovna is supposed to think that Nina was killed by a car, that she hit her temple on the stone pavement. It seemed to some that only a few of Nina's school friends had been invited — Umansky couldn't stand to see them.

Raisa Mikhailovna, when she was finally pulled away from the coffin, took the watch from her dead daughter's wrist and put it on.

The Umanskys were taken to the crematorium by Ruda Khmelnitsky in a twelve-cylinder dark blue Packard (there were just two of these cars in the Empire, the other belonged to Vasily Stalin, but here we have a significant discrepancy: another source maintains that there were actually more than two Packards with armored windows in circulation, but they were only allowed for members of the Politburo, and precisely at the time of the funeral, Vasily used a Willis or a Canadian Graham). The same Packard — at any rate, the same vehicle — took the Umanskys from the crematorium to the airport. Whose decision it was — Umansky's own or someone else's — is not clear, but he buried the girl and ran, before the interrogations began, before people could blame him. He grabbed his orders and flew to Mexico, hoping they won't find him and Raisa there.

Everyone remembered Raisa Mikhailovna's feet — she couldn't walk, and was more or less dragged to the car: her feet drew two gently curving lines in the path leading from the crematorium.

Many believed Volodya and Nina were cremated on the same day, in the morning (which wasn't actually the case). Sofia Mironovna, in contrast to the Umanskys, wanted to see everyone, making it clear: she had nothing to be ashamed of, her son *did not kill*. She called everyone, the class left the lessons and went to Granovsky Street to stand by the elaborate coffin — the boy who showed incredible abilities for languages lay in flowers, covered by luxurious shrouds. Sofia Mironovna moved about with a deliberately tragic air (except, as Kirshon's son remembered it, she lay prone and half-dead on a daybed, alone in a small room, and all he could think to say was, "Don't beat yourself up like that, Sofia Mironovna"). She embraced Bakulev and pulled him towards the coffin, like a dear guest to a banquet table. Another friend, the boy Yuri Kuznetsov — who, like a puppy, was taken to Volodya at his dacha, so they could run around together — remembered: on the day of the funeral he suffered from diarrhea.

Someone noticed that Redens arrived with his mother and carried some papers, and everyone had their own idea of what they saw: *a folder, an envelope, a notebook, lists.* Each person fantasized in retrospect. Rich with knowledge of the consequences, each wanted to say, I saw destiny, it was all in front of my eyes, and I, I was also a participant, and not just a prop.

Goltsman called me at night: Wendt had been found, the retarded boy's father.

"It's night time, Alexander Naumovich, why aren't you asleep?"

"I was listening to tapes from Brighton. Masha came back."

THE MUTE ONES

THE SON OF A BUTCHER — OR, ACCORDING TO INFORMATION WE received in exchange for two hundred dollars, the son of a small-time retailer — Erik Rikhardovich Wendt was born on the 29th of August 1902 in Leipzig. He worked as a type-setter at a printing house and joined the communist youth union when he was sixteen. Subsequently, he was arrested for involvement in plotting a coup. Fleeing persecution, in June 1931 he came to Moscow. There, he became deputy chairman of the board at the Publishing Guild of Foreign Workers; Anastasia Petrova at the time was one of the editors at the same publishing house. She worked on the translations of Lenin's and Stalin's works, including *Marxism and the National-colonial Question*, and participated in the meetings of the Party committee. In August of 1936, Wendt was arrested for spying for Germany and expelled from the Communist Party of Germany. The pregnant Anastasia (it couldn't have been more than two or three weeks) was removed from the Party committee for lack of vigilance, but this proved to be a lucky break in the end — the following summer the authorities arrested the Chairman of the Board, Bela Kun, one of the Emperor's falcons, famous for purging the Crimea of the counter-revolutionary elements, an operation in which he ordered 1,634 people executed in one day. Kun was made to stand on one leg while he was interrogated — for twenty-five hours straight. Whenever he would lose consciousness and fall, they'd him douse with cold water. Kun named many people. He was tortured for two years; if Petrova had not been kicked out earlier, Kun would have dragged her down with him.

Wendt spent two years in a Saratov prison, and was released on another summer day for lack of evidence. He was restored to the Party; after the pact with the Germans he was allowed to teach schoolchildren his native language in a remote village. When the war began he was deported, along with most Volga Germans, to the Krasnoyarsk region where he served as an accountant's assistant at the Mayak collective farm. Eventually, it was decided he could be trusted, and for five years he worked as an interpreter on the radio (Did he see Tasya? Did he know his son?). In 1947, he returned to Germany and lived out the rest of his life without further upheaval: he rose to the rank of Deputy Minister of Culture (Did he ever come to Moscow, did he write to the woman he loved?) and died quietly in the spring of 1965, receiving mention in two reference books as a member of a government delegation that negotiated with the Senate of West Berlin for permission to allow family visits to East Berlin during Christmas.

Suddenly I thought of something else. I called Goltsman:

"Where is his case?" I asked.

"In the archive of the Saratov FSB. They won't give it to us without power of attorney from his relatives."

"Now you're going to tell me that Wendt didn't have anyone after Petrova…"

"After her, no. *Before* her, it appears he had a wife, Lotte Kuhn. The Party sent her in 1935 to be a secretary to Walter Ulbricht at the office in Paris. And she… well, she became close with Ulbricht, in a personal sense. But she was still classified as Wendt's wife. After Wendt's arrest, Lotte was investigated by the Comintern's international supervision commission and received a reprimand. Ulbricht married her, she was his third wife."

"So that means that…"

"Yes, Wendt's wife — either he abandoned her for Petrova, or she left him, became the First Lady of East Germany, and died recently, in

March 2002, at the age of ninety-nine. She lived as a recluse, without any contact with anyone. She was known as a women's rights advocate."

"Children?"

"None of their own. They adopted a two-year old girl from an orphanage in Ukraine, Beata. She died in 1991. In the protocol of the first interrogation, Wendt said he had a brother Kurt, residing in Berlin, unknown, another brother Fritz, whereabouts unknown, a sister Johanna, married, residing in Berlin, address, of course, unknown, and his wife, Anastasia Petrova, Serafimovich st., House of Government, apartment 311. It is not clear why he included her if their marriage was never official."

Goltsman waited for a while, then asked wearily, "Why do you need his case?"

He waited some more and continued, bitterly, "You want to know what Petrova said about him, don't you? You think she betrayed him and saved herself."

"No, no of course not." I felt a dull hostility that resembled serious jealously spread inside me. "No," I broke off hoarsely, really uncomfortable with myself. I didn't want to think about Anastasia betraying her lover, but life is so wretched and boring, it has a way of knocking everyone down to a common denominator, everyone needs to eat, especially with a small child who doesn't understand anything yet, anything, except that he's hungry. "I just wanted to see what she was called in the case… Her code name: Bertha? The Englishwoman? Agent Flame?"

"You must…" Goltsman pointedly did not say "be an irretrievable idiot"; instead, the gentle old man went on, quietly, as if I had offended someone he loved, "you must think Petrova was a secret employee of the NKVD?"

"And you don't?"

He paused, considering the facts, then said:

"No. But you seem to find this frustrating."

"Alexander Naumovich," I said, "Last week I sent an inquiry to the Foreign Intelligence Service from our local organization of young historians. The inquiry was whether Anastasia Vladimirovna Petrova, aka Flam, appeared in any of their cases."

The old man already knew what he would say, but he kept a dead silence, pretending to be uninformed, letting my receiver fill with the rustling of dust between the stars. "No, Alexander Naumovich, they don't have anything about her."

"You see then."

"But they wrote back to say that over the last three months, this is the second inquiry about Petrova-Flam, and the first one also came from our address."

Somewhere out there, in the night, in an empty apartment on the corner of Leninsky Prospect and Universitetskaya Street, the old man covered his eyes with his hand, sighed and said:

"I only wanted to… check."

"I think you also realized that Tasya was one of us. That her life should be looked at differently."

"No. I just wanted to check."

"And you didn't tell me anything. You taught me yourself: don't believe anyone. And you didn't send an inquiry to the FSB archive because you know as well as I do that the NKVD never reveals the identities of the foreign section agents. Never. Especially not agents of the Second department. I think, and you also think, that she was in the counter-intelligence service. I just don't know why you would imagine I would find it painful to find out that the beautiful Tasya did more than love men."

"That's not what I think," Goltsman said more firmly, for himself as much as for me. "You suspect everyone. You have not been getting enough sleep. Give her a chance, let's continue treating her as we have been." Indeed. I really wanted to do just that; I wanted to leave her where we placed here, and I wanted her to stay there. I did not want to think about Anastasia carrying out missions while men confessed their love for her, when she kissed someone for the first time, and later, on sheets in dacha bedrooms, in stuffy, stealthy breaks between taking dictations, when she'd drop her steno pad and listen to the sounds behind the door, and then smile tensely to someone's aging wife, secretly picking up torn-off buttons from the floor and once more assuming a working appearance. I didn't want her steering the conversation to a pre-assigned topic and filling out a report in her tidy handwriting once a week.

"Remember her personal file," I said. "She spent more than a year as a stenographer at Checka — clearly, that was where our people found her and took a firm hold of her. She didn't go to China on the strength of her stenographer's skills alone. At the publishing house, what was her job?"

"An editor?"

"That's what she wrote when she filled out the bio sheet in 1943. But if you look at her Party record, it says she was the head of the secret section. Then, look: her husband (and he had to be her husband) was arrested as a German spy, but she" — I chuckled and shook my head — "she wasn't even expelled from the party! That's because our people covered up for her, whisked her away, hid her. And she proved useful! No one would've let Litvinov go to the States alone — he was resentful, his wife was English, who knew what he could have done, and it was 1941, he'd have made a perfect Prime Minister for a free Russia! So here's Petrova — she sleeps with him, as everyone knows, her children were kept hostage near Ryazan, and as the Ambassador's secretary she controls all his contacts. It wasn't Litvinov who requested her from Stalin. She did everything to make us think that. But on the contrary, she was brought in and introduced: why, Maxim Maximovich, you know each other, didn't you work together in Geneva? And Litvinov couldn't refuse, although I bet he could see straight through it all. He went along with it, he stroked her hair and bedded her, if he still could. After the war, where did she go? The Deputy Director of foreign language courses at the Foreign Ministry! You must remember who was trained there. Those were exactly the years when ambassadors carried out the duties of resident intelligence officers."

Goltsman answered almost plaintively:

"I just don't believe it. I can't."

"I checked the list of Soviet citizen agents who were in contact with the New York resident at the time, and whose identities have not been revealed to this day. Semyonov had a group in the early '40s: Evrika, Born, Andreev and Tasya — I bet it's our Anastasia!"

"They couldn't have given her such an obvious alias."

"The same people who referred to Yakov Golos as 'Voice' because of his last name, Bukhartsev — Emir, and Umansky — Editor. They weren't very creative."

"I don't believe it."

"What do you believe in then? In love? In resurrection from the dead? In what, besides the truth? That a seamstress was sent to work as the secretary of the Soviet Ambassador to the U.S. in the same month that her husband was sent to Krasnoyarsk as a suspicious German? That they couldn't find another secretary in the entire Soviet Union?"

"Excuse me." There was a beep, and Goltsman disappeared.

TATYANA LITVINOVA, BRIGHTON, ENGLAND: My father came back from America an older, kinder man, without his customary harshness. He brought me some clothes. He showed consideration, if he went somewhere he asked: what shall I buy? He moved into the House of Government, into a large apartment below the ballerina Olga Lepeshinskaya, with a view of the Kremlin. There was him, my husband and me and our two children, and two housemaids — both NKVD lieutenants. My father had a 450-square-foot office, and there was a room, just as large, prepared for my mother. My father asked if I would be against it if Petrova came to live with us for a while. By then, my mother had written to me about the discoveries that she had made about the two of them on the way to America. I replied: it's your apartment, you decide. My mother was terribly offended that I replied in this way. But I did not understand everything at that time. So Petrova lived with us until Mama arrived.

"Who were her friends?"

"Petrova did not have any friends. Only lovers and colleagues. And us."

"Do you think that she was connected with the NVKD?"

"I don't know, it's hard to say. She could have been. But it was obvious that Anastasia Vladimirovna did not pursue power — she truly wanted to be with my father. She loved him very much, genuinely. She really wanted him to leave mother and marry her. But he did not want to do so.

"Why not?"

"Because he loved my Mom. In America they had a talk, and my father begged her not to leave him. He loved and appreciated her very much, and she was a strong-willed person herself, so they had been through separations before. It's hard to say who was in the right. Their relationship was completely stripped of any pretense, they respected each other. But then again, when she was much older, Mom told me: you shouldn't treat men the way I did."

"How did Maxim Maximovich really feel about Petrova?"

"My father and I were talking about her once, and I quoted one English writer who said that if a woman can't be with one man, then she needs an endless number of men. He said: yes. And added: I really don't know if she's a lady or a Komsomol activist."

"But what's the bottom line, really? Was she with your father because she was on a mission for the NKVD?"

"Everything was possible back then. But I can tell you she was very devoted to my father. And she grieved for him when he died. She came to me and said: there is twenty-one thousand dollars in a Dutch bank account in your father's name. Write to the Deputy Minister of Foreign Affairs, you must try to get this money."

"Was Petrova unhappy?"

"I don't know. I just didn't think about this. You ask a lot about Petrova… But that wasn't the most terrible thing. The terribly thing happened earlier, before the war, when Ivy Valterovna took in a young girl, a little pet, and made her their adopted daughter. The girl knew English well, she sweet-talked everyone, and slowly Maxim Maximovich began to live with her, sleep with her, and then he married her off to the head of security. It was Mama's fault. Who brings a sex bomb into the house?" Goltsman turned off the recording and looked at Borya and me with the expression that said "You're all dismissed."

"Is that really all?"

"There's one more tape left. The last one chronologically. There is not much point in listening to it. It is entirely about the topic that the source referred to at the end here."

"That Litvinov screwed his adopted daughter? That Petrova had another happy rival?" Borya turned to me. "Are we going to look for her, too?"

Tatyana Litvinova, Brighton, England: The summer I was eleven, I had gone to the pioneers' camp, and Mom was left alone in the house by the Red Gates metro station. Once she looked down from the balcony and saw an incredibly beautiful girl reading a book in English. *Are you English?* She asked. The girl said yes. Mom was so happy — finally there was someone with whom she could speak English. Zina just turned thirteen.

Her Polish father, Vitol Buyanovsky, a talented worker, had emigrated to England. Zina had grown up there and had gone to a Catholic school. She was physically developed and sensitive beyond her years.

The first question Zina asked me was, what was the most terrifying thing in your life? I only read about terrifying things in newspapers. We taught her to swear, and she became one of us. Misha, of course, had to torment her, the way boys would, and they fought ferociously. Dad was initially wary of her, but then he started to take pity on her along with Mom: the poor girl! With those looks, she's sure to get married too early! She was forever getting cat-calls, boys wouldn't leave her alone, she didn't get along with her mother, etc. Zina spent more and more time with us until Mom suggested adopting her and asked me to let her share my room.

Zina's father was very angry about his daughter being taken away from her parents, he threatened to complain to the Party committee, but he was arrested and imprisoned. Zina's mother also came after her for her betrayals, but Zina was indifferent to it all, she was generally a one-dimensional sort of person.

Mama found out about the relations between father and Zina when my father was getting ready to go to a sanatorium, and said he was taking Zina with him. Mama was surprised, then angry: Why not Tanya? Why not Misha? She finally cornered him, and he confessed. Later, Mom showed me a piece of paper covered in Dad's signatures — he was so nervous during their talk, he had to keep writing something to keep his hands from shaking.

Dad tried to arrange things for Zina, he took her everywhere with him, to meetings, but it was all in vain. Finally, she started an affair with a security guard, and it lasted quite a long time. Dad was very upset when he found out, and gave up on Zina, he wanted to remove her from the family, he was so ashamed — with a security guard! — and considered himself to be dishonored.

Her terrible marriage brought a lot of trouble. The guard she married informed on our family, and really — he was just some security guard! And Zina turned into a real pest. When there was a shortage of groceries in Moscow, their table groaned — she finagled so much out of father! I remember once I was sitting and crying because I didn't have a whole pair of stockings left. Father gave me thirty rubles a month. Zina saw my tears, and went and got *one hundred rubles* out of my father! She just always got what she wanted.

Never mind, that's enough, what can you tell me about yourself? The man who sent you here… The one you work for… Do you love him?..

Goltsman clumsily hit the recorder, pulled out the tape with a crunch and stopped, having decided not to put it away as long as I could see where he stored it.

I felt my face grow hot and jumped up: I wanted it all to end as soon as possible.

"We know her name: Zinaida Vitoldovna Buyanovskaya. We know she went to medical school. I'm off to look for her."

"She's no Vitoldovna," Mirgorodsky got up, too. "If she was adopted, that is."

We headed out; in one of our nooks, Chukharev was bent over the records of the interrogations of the eight boys. The poor bastard, his wife was going to kill him.

"How's your wife? Don't get up," Borya acted the big boss. "I see you're working hard. That's good. But don't forget your wife. Work in intelligence puts a lot of pressure on the family. How's your investigation going?"

"I'm working on approaches to Mikoyan. I'm studying his inner circle."

"That's sensible. Well done, well done," Borya suddenly gave a whole-body jerk, changed in the face, and asked in a different, threatening voice: "What for?"

Chukharev touched his pencil, the armrests of his chair. He searched for clues to as to how he should respond in my face, and explained as best he could:

"So that by receiving additional information we can establish the degree of his involvement in the events on the Great Stone Bridge."

"What the hell for?" Borya swayed a bit. "It's clear anyway that Daddy covered up for him."

"You really think so, Boris Antonovich?"

"We'll prove so," Borya looked at him sadly and sternly. "Easily."

Borya's teary eyes looked somewhere into the future weeks, to the next quarter, the approaching years, perhaps discerning even Borya's own place in the cemetery. Chukharev shrank, expecting bad things.

"And what will you do next?" Borya inquired.

Chukharev couldn't answer, and touched his glistening forehead.

"You'll live. You'll keep on living," Borya reported to no one in particular. "And Vano will keep on living. And then they'll all croak one by one, and so will you. Now you know what to expect. We warned you. Get ready and come with us."

Outside, Christmas trees were being gathered, Santa Clauses with white beards were walking about, the colossus of the Foreign Ministry towered like a black cloud above the squat buildings along Arbat, and massive snowflakes slapped together like a cow's eyelashes. We walked on, and above our heads the unfamiliar sky revealed itself with black smoke and pieces of blue — the sky that was still there for us to see, not yet boarded up and hidden under six feet of dirt. It's a pity all of this was just an accident, nothing but the Universe's blind thrashing around, a collusion of atoms and molecules, that there was no higher meaning in not meeting someone, in beautiful handwriting, in one's heart skipping a beat at the sight of the year's first snow but it's too much work convincing yourself that it all can be explained by the contraction of the myocardium and the deceitful work of certain parts of one's brain.

"You drive," I said to Chukharev, as we packed into the small, warm space. "Maroseika Street. Stop opposite Devytakina Lane."

Chukharev got behind the wheel; we rode in silence. We were going to see our balding Major, the keeper of FSB's state secrets, with twenty-two years of service who paced the pavement as if it burned the soles of his boots and sweated off his ginger eye-brows. He saw our license plate and almost walked in front of a trolleybus, waving his arm — I had never seen him without a briefcase before — and restrained himself from running; the great number of us in the car unsettled him, he had hoped for a one-on-one interview.

"Flash the headlights. And open the door for him."

"Howdy," the major squeezed in next to Borya and giggled. "I don't know everyone, mind you. Alexander Vasilievich, so not according to plan, I…" The major looked for some sort of support in the nightmare and stubbornly stuck to me: a familiar face, we drank coffee together. "I need help! I have no one to go to… There is someone, but with that person — I can't! He could ruin my whole life! My career, life and family…" — he liked the word — "ruined. I never thought… that it could be ruined like this. I'm prepared to give some, er, remuneration, er, within reason… Ah, what am I saying — I'll pay anything!"

"Tell me," said Borya, without turning around to the miserable man. "What choice do you have?"

"Blackmail from a...," in his prepared phrase this was where the word "prostitute" stood, but that last word stuck in his brain with the realization of objective reality.

"Have you known her for long," Mirgorodsky was not so much asking as making statements.

"Two, two and a half... three years." The Major was happy that he no longer had to talk himself, only to answer and be honest.

"You met at her place."

"Yes, almost always."

"Does she have a video-camera at the apartment?"

"Why would she?"

"Girls like her usually do."

"I never thought of that! I swear."

"Did you pay her?"

"Well..."

"A hundred here, a hundred there, a small present."

"Yes, that's about right. No big presents. A fur coat."

"Someone else from your office screwed her."

"That's what I meant to say... there were two or three times, er, a limited number of times, nothing regular, I swear, when we went to a sauna all together. There were a few — not exactly friends, but... I can't! I couldn't possibly name them! And no one must — this can't happen!"

"What does she want?"

"It was New Year's Eve at the department, we finished early, everyone went home, and I decided to go to her, when suddenly she says..."

"How old?"

"What? Me? She? I don't know. Thirty-seven."

"Did you screw her? That evening. Did a sexual act take place?"

"Yes. To start with — yes. Then she says: Honey," the major found it necessary to imitate a woman's voice, trying hard, letting in greedy heat, "let's buy a little place for us to meet. I'll decorate it, it will be cozy, it's high time for us..."

"Had you previously talked about this?"

"No, not seriously. She would bring it up: it would be good to have a nest of my own, for some stability… My own home. You would come and relax at my place."

"What did you say? What did you say to that?"

"Well, what… that it would be good. But that it wasn't time for that yet, we should wait, I didn't make enough, not yet… Someday maybe…"

"Does she know your name? And where you work? Does she know your work phone number? Could she have seen your passport when you went to take a shower? I see. How did it end?"

"She's got hold of me and wouldn't let go! I couldn't take it and already cut it off like a man: I'm not ready! Not ready! And she… Suddenly she said.. I'll talk… about you! And who was in the sauna. Give me *one hundred and eighty thousand* dollars, and that will be enough. Tomorrow."

"You."

"I… I… To be honest, somehow… Sorry, guys, you're — guys, you'll understand, in short," he shook his right hand, "I punched her in her whoring face! Whack! And I left. But I came back. I said," he spoke it quietly, like a password, "Fifty. She said: 'for that I can only buy a one-room apartment, and not in Moscow. And I'm not alone.' I said, sixty to you and nothing else to nobody. She: 'no, but I can do a hundred now, and eighty in a month…'"

"Did you wear a condom, yesterday?"

"Yes."

"Did you throw it out yourself?"

"No, she must've… I didn't look…"

"Did the punch leave a bruise on her face?"

"I don't know, I think so… I drove off, I just drove off! I thought: she'll calm down, I'll go to her today, we'll talk again, at least by phone… I got five thousand ready… I spent the night at the dacha, and in the morning my neighbors called: the cops came to the house, and they called the office looking for me, too. She'd filed the complaint, for rape. I told my colleagues it was some joke, someone's made a mistake, I'll go to the cops, but I called you…" and he fell silent like a child, and glanced at me sleepily, as if trying to work out where the Major could be put out of the car on Sadovy Circle. "They'll fire me, of course they'll fire me… But if my daughter finds out…" the major began to cry, unexpectedly, involuntarily, not understanding where the tears were coming from, wiping the drops from his face like rain. And he fell silent.

I silently counted up to twenty-six, restraining myself: and-a-one, and-a-two… Go get him, Borya.

"A daughter, then," Borya noted with satisfaction. "For a child, of course, this is a terrible psychological trauma."

Chukharev suddenly looked at me as if something had drilled itself into his head, and pulled the door handle.

"Where are you going?" I muttered. "Sit there and learn."

The major leaned in my direction like a begging dog.

"Where does your… Tanya live?"

"Yes. She's called Tanya."

Borya replied himself:

"On Losinoostrovsky. In the northeast." And he said in a measured tone: "What difficult people work in the police there!" And to me: "How? I don't know. It's very difficult there. Are we going to solve this? For sure? Have you thought it over?" And to the major: "State security, you were asked a question: when do we get the case from the archive?"

The major froze, and then quickly thought it over and remembered:

"I said it straight away! That's not my business! I'm not in the archive department…"

"I didn't hear that, when will we get the case?"

"If only it depended on me! The only possibility is a letter of authorization from relatives."

"The declass date's long-passed. You can't photocopy 200 pages? What can you do at all? Fellas, why are we talking to this guy? Get out."

The major grabbed Borya's arm:

"There are certain personal aspects in the case, a personal secret… Let's decide things on a commercial…"

"What secret? The cops are waiting for you."

"But I don't have it in my desk!" the major was breaking into a shriek. "I'm not a thief, I'm from the FSB, I can only do things for money! Any figure. Just name it!"

"Listen," Borya said wearily. "Let him go. And we'll drive on, right?"

"And what if the police call me? What do I say?"

"Is that our problem?"

"I'll give everything. I'll sell my dacha. My plot of land. I'll close it all in a month. Name a figure!"

Borya seemed to remember something:

"Listen. Listen, what's money got to do with it? We're pursuing the truth… We understand: you won't get the case. All right then. Bring the indictment. Just two pages. We'll solve your problem in any case — you're suffering for the truth! — but please make an effort for us, OK, my friend?" Borya slapped the major on his sweaty shoulder, not removing the hostile and disdainful expression from his face.

"All the same: authorization from relatives…"

"Listen, two pages… I don't know, find some relatives, bring in your own. We've already agreed on everything. You go get the indictment, and we'll go and solve your problem."

"You mean… What about me? What should I do now?"

"Nothing. Wait." Borya sang: "Tanya, Tanechka… Tanyusha!"

The major was at a loss, in torment he turned to me. But I don't pity anyone, I just nodded out of boredom: yes. And in the eye of the major, a drop of warmth appeared and blossomed like a flower. The major pressed his palm to the place beneath which his heart was beating, and looked straight into my eyes: should he believe me? The wind was chilling him, he was already out of the car, he was already standing on the ground, and the abyss had let him go: "Guys! Honestly — I owe you one." He waved and uncertainly walked to the metro, yet believing — he was alive!

"Where are we going?" Chukharev asked "To Losinoostrovsky?"

"We're not going anywhere."

"You see," said Borya. "You said the major can't do anything anymore. But a person can always do more. And isn't Tanya great!"

A UNION OF FRIENDS
UNTIL THE GRAVE

ON THE GREAT STONE BRIDGE — I WAS NOW ALWAYS DRAWN there, wherever I was going — I really wanted to look at the landing on the stairs descending to the Popular Music Theater, but I walked along the opposite side of the street and stopped across from the Kremlin.

I like looking at the Kremlin, like everyone who grew up around here; to look at the Kremlin from drifting ice floes, from gallows stools, from cockpits, classrooms, office windows, sofas and cells — to look at the Spassky tower from which the Kremlin Clock chimes, at the brightest stars, at the place where the night does not fall. I looked at the Kremlin, leaning on the stone parapet; behind me walked lovers, vulnerable people, and tourists; below, dinner boats thrust themselves under the bridge, drunk people waving from them, cottonwood fluff went flying and dissolved in the meaningless sky, and only from this viewpoint — with the towers standing sentry before me — could one discern any meaning. I looked at the towers, the battlements and walls, at the most important thing of all — a sort of final Russian justice standing on the Kremlin hill, encircled by the red brick, and it had nothing in common with me, or with the truth of weak human organisms. I had known since I was a boy: this altar accepts no sacrifices. The wind kneaded the river water; I looked at the Kremlin and felt its indifference, and its preoccupation with deeds greater than our earthly fussing, and its malignant, long memory. And knowing about the Kremlin, and now often seeing it, I never felt fear. I even forgot mortal fear when I saw it and heard the Spassky Tower clock chimes. I am never alone, vengeance will be taken for me; perhaps the Kremlin cannot yet recognize all who are its own as its own. That's fine, that's how it's supposed to be, but what remains from us will certainly be found and reburied to the accompaniment of salutes and medals floating on red velvet pillows. Here is a place where they know everything about us, they remember us and will rewards us, eventually, and we will stand here to the end, we will do everything as it should be done.

The new watchman did not immediately recognize me, and not fully believing his eyes, shuffled behind me, hesitating to give me the key.

"Go and rest. I'll do some work, then tell you when I'm about to leave."

He stood there for a while, then crawled back to his nook by the entrance. I turned on the computer so there would be a noise, and sat down, slowing my breath, listening intently to the details of the watchman's presence: the newspaper rustled and was arranged, a chair grated the floor, a spoon clinked against the bell of a cup, in anticipation of a cautious sip. I sat there for a while before he finally turned on the television and became engrossed in the wheezing swill of the news. Finally. I rose silently and crept to Goltsman's office, fanning the keys out on my palm like a thief — which one? — and I stuck in a key, and tormented the lock, pushing on the door. The key didn't fit. I tried the next key, then the next. I wondered if I skipped one in the heat of the moment. Or maybe the lock turned in the other direction? I worked to keep myself from hurrying, and tried the keys again, one by one, and in the other direction. I glanced back, taken by surprise, into the thickened air — the watchman, gray-haired and stooped, was standing behind me.

"Would you like some tea?" he asked sternly, as if he were talking about something else.

"Where are the keys to this office?"

I got ready to lie convincingly: the computer is broken, the internet is down, I forgot something, something I need very badly... but why should I have to explain myself to the watchman?

"Your... Naumych doesn't leave me the keys," the watchman looked at me the way the owner of a burned house looks at a mounted occupier riding down the main street.

"What about the cleaning lady? How does she get in?"

Surprised by something, the watchman muttered:

"Yes. The cleaner... She must have a key on her chain," but he didn't budge.

"Give me the cleaner's keys. You have them? These? Let me, I'll do it myself, I'll see... Who are you calling?"

"Naumych can say which key it is, why go through them?"

"No need! I know which one. Thank you, you can relax," I turned around and walked away, jumped back, furious: "I said: don't call him!"

He shuddered and dropped the receiver.

Banging into the corners, I returned to the reception room, and got the key right the first time. I turned the light on; I memorized the arrangement of papers on the table, the paper clips, the pencils, the distance to the moved-back chair, and pulled the drawers out as far as I could, placing my hands under the folders, feeling the edges: there was nothing, nothing at all. Could it be in the safe? I looked over the shelves and the window sill, tried the safe's stainless steel handle, went back to the desk, looking over the disciplined arrangement of notebooks, the calendar filled out with important tasks. He could have left it out in plain view, if he had guessed that I would come to look for it — on the desk, in the desk, no, it's not there, so it must be in the safe. Hopeless. I gave the keys back to the watchman, told him to keep quiet, and took the next fifteen minutes to check all the updates on my favorite arbuzik.com site, especially "Beautiful girls. Rough porn." Then I turned everything off that had been humming, and waited for all the peaceful green and red lights to fade; I moved the protocols from the interrogations at the edge of my desk, stacked the correspondence with the Foreign Affairs archive on the rolling set of drawers, and reached for the folder labeled "Urgent!" It was stuffed with print-outs from the Soviet military toys site.

Before I put my Dictaphone in the desk drawer, I clicked it to check the tape deck, and there it was — that's where Goltsman had hidden it!

I fast-forwarded through parts of it ("Papa tried to arrange her life…he informed on our family, and really — just some security guard! And Zina became such a pest…"), until I found what he hadn't let me hear.

I prepared myself.

"All right then, that's enough, what can you tell me about yourself? That man you talked about, the one you work for, do you love him?" I listened… time rustled by, crawling ahead empty, and then… click! the recording ended.

It would appear Masha didn't reply; she may have nodded, she may have shaken her head "no," she may have kept a polite silence out there on the English shore, but what if I were to meet her somewhere by accident, and clasp her by the elbows in greeting, and brush her cheeks with my lips, and we should happily walk together for a while? And what if a few hundred yards before reaching the office I would stop and ask: "Do you care for me, even a little bit?" She would raise her eyes: "Why are you asking? You know the answer perfectly well." "Please do me a favor. My life is difficult enough as it is…" "I understand. No one will find out that we have seen each other."

There was a small art-market on the Crimean Embankment, with a good smell, the warm wood of picture frames. Artists with tanned faces, short-haired and bearded, sharpened short knives; some looked at the interested people with hard-boiled indifference, while others were anxious, the way a dog gets anxious when someone picks up one of her puppies. The thick smell of oil-paint, pictures of Stalinesque spires, churches, monasteries, large-breasted girls lying and sitting, lilacs and peonies, copies — the dark towns of northern Europe, mountain slopes, seas with sailboats, and most of all forests and village lanes, a few cubes and lines, numerous cats and slightly fewer dogs. Further on, in the Sculpture Park gloomy Georgians sawed marble, and further on still statues stood in a group like people in a retirement home: cheerless Lenins, a Stalin with a broken nose, a spittle-covered, dried out Dzerzhinsky, half a Brezhnev, the freezing Sverdlov with a turned-up collar, and Kalinin who was placed in the shade — all of this was suggestively surrounded by barbed wire and concentration camp floodlights with the inevitable "Lyusa was here" carved into their wooden based.

She was walking next to me, and I found myself remembering a feeling that I had thought I'd never feel again: when you look from a distance at an unfamiliar, beautiful young woman who captivates everyone, and does not belong to ordinary life, and transforms the street she walks along, transforms the weather, the room she is in, wherever she goes...

"I am ready for a new task. I can work a lot. I will pair up with Alexander Naumovich. You don't notice anything, but it is hard for him. Elderly people don't have enough energy in the spring, he gets tired, but he tries to make sure that no one notices. I made him an appointment with a therapist, they can prescribe vitamins for him — it took me a month to persuade him! Just like a child. In England I — did I do everything right?"

There was tension in her voice, a need for praise. She was confused by my silence.

"Boris Antonovich told me you'd send me to the asylum, to talk to Petrova's son, as soon as we locate him. But what can he possibly remember? I bet he died a long time ago, anyway, and Boris Antonovich just wants to scare me when he tells me retarded people are especially attracted to young women, because, he says, they have this sexual drive. May I request someone else goes?"

We had already reached the office. I squeezed Masha's elbow, without looking her in the face: from the office window, Alyona looked at me and made as if to pull the curtain, but changed her mind and waved with tensely spread-out fingers.

"Maybe you won't even have to do it anyway. We haven't tried everything yet. First we'll find Zina. If we can."

Two months later we found Zina.

Everyone we contacted about her said the same thing: she had passed away a long time ago. But it turned out Zinaida Levashova was still fighting a good fight against her ninth decade and arthritis, and took twenty-six seconds to get to the phone. One just had to be patient.

"I called her again," Chukharev announced as soon as we had entered the office. He held up the telephone receiver as proof of his efforts. "For the third time."

Masha remained at my shoulder, as if she wanted to stay near me a little longer. Alyona was still standing by the window, not looking at anything, just parked there.

"She said that she worked as an announcer on the radio for fifty years. She doesn't remember things. She said that Sheinis wrote a wonderful book about Litvinov. No one could say anything more about Litvinov after that book."

"If you can't talk to the old lady, give the phone to Masha here," Borya said, pointing at the secretary and mysteriously walked around the room in a circle, dressed in a camouflage hunting jacket.

"She said she had waited for me for two days. But we never agreed to meet! And now she's tired of hearing my name. And won't say anything. She said: I'm an old, sick woman. And hung up."

"Give Masha the phone, you idiot. And watch — they'll be fast friends."

Alyona turned to me personally.

"Tell me, have you ever actually loved anyone?" she asked. Then she collected her things and left.

"Everyone come here! Alexander Naumovich!" Borya shook with excitement as he pulled two photocopied pages out of his jacket. "Here it is! The Major got us the indictment."

For a moment Borya held a nauseating, theatrical pause.

"That game the boys played? They pretended to be Nazis."

"On the 18th of December 1943, we, the People's Commissar of State Security of the USSR, Merkulov, and the Prosecutor General of the USSR, Gorshenin, having examined the materials of the investigation concerning the arrested persons Vano Mikoyan, Sergo Mikoyan, Leonid Barabanov, Pyotr Bakulev, Leonid Redens, Artyom Khmelnitsky and Felix Kirpichnikov, conclude the following:

"In late 1942 and early 1943 Vladimir Shakhurin, a student of the 7th grade of the Moscow school #175, proposed to several of his classmates and friends that they establish a secret organization. Initially this association and its activities were pursued as a game, but gradually, under the influence of Vladimir Shakhurin, who had read many translations of Fascist books, it became a clearly anti-Soviet organization. The members of the organization praised the Nazi Army and the German Nazi leaders in conversation. The members of the organization were assigned titles borrowed from Nazi hierarchy, such as Reichsfuhrer, Feldfuhrer and Feldmarschall; they named their organization The Fourth Empire. The members of the organization frequently discussed such topics as methods of carrying out propaganda directed towards undermining the Soviet system, and overthrowing the Soviet regime after the war.

"Some members of the group pursued their sexual impulses and engaged in what they called 'romancing' female persons of comparable age. The result of their rampant criminality and moral corruption was the incident on the 3rd of June of 1943: the ring-leader, Vladimir Shakhurin, shot and killed Nina Umanskaya with a revolver that belonged to Vano Mikoyan, after which he shot himself.

"Vladimir Shakhurin's accomplices, understanding the anti-Soviet nature of the organization Fourth Empire, did not inform anyone about the existence of the organization and kept it a secret. Vano Mikoyan failed to report the murder of Nina Umanskaya by Shakhurin.

"The behavior of the participants of the organization is all the more criminal because it took place during the Great Patriotic War, when the entire Soviet people battled German fascism.

"We consider it necessary to exile these individuals from the city of Moscow to various cities in Siberia, the Urals and Central Asia for one year. The term of exile will be calculated from the day of their release from custody.

"People's Commissar of State Security of the USSR Merkulov. Prosecutor of the USSR Gorshenin."

"No wonder everyone wants to blame Shakhurin for everything," Borya said. "Maybe we shouldn't have... er... pushed our Major as hard as we did. There's nothing about Umanskaya in this document. Although," — Borya glanced at me and all but winked — "Comrade Chukharev, in your opinion, why didn't Mikoyan stay on the bridge? Why did he not call for help? He ran away. And as we now know, he didn't say anything to anyone."

Chukharev kept silent, waiting for Mirgorodsky to produce a miracle.

"Because it was his Walter, you see," Borya narrated, didactically. "And the boy was afraid of his Dad. This boy, you see, was still young, and he just witnessed the agony of two beautiful human beings, a girl with her head blown open, her skirt up... So he ran off. That's what he was taught to say to the investigator Sheinin. And Sheinin, just a cop, basically, could not quite up and ask, of Anastas Mikoyan's son — I would, but he couldn't — so you got scared, but what about an hour later, a day later, why did you not go and report what you'd seen? And most importantly, how come you were this scared, but you still had the guts to unclench Volodya Shakhurin's cold, dead fingers and pull the gun out of his hand?"

"What if he didn't take it!" Chukharev jumped up. "What if he was the one who shot both Nina and Volodya, and ran away because he hoped that no one had seen him?"

"That's smart of you, Chukharev! But someone did see them on the bridge — the *three of them*. And what motive would he have had? Jealousy? That's doubtful. What should we do now? We need to look at the scene of the crime and question the witnesses. We need authorization from the boys. And it's obvious now they'd never give us permission, and neither will their relatives. Never. "

I followed Alexander Naumovich into his office and asked him as casually as I could if he'd gone to the doctor. Goltsman sounded as if he'd suddenly landed in a really uncomfortable hotel room that just had to be endured:

"It was a waste of time. They told me to get a blood test and referred me for an ultrasound of my internal organs."

"Did the doctor say anything?"

"He said my scleras look yellowish."

"What's that supposed to mean?"

"Sometimes the whites of your eyes do that. He asked if I ever had hepatitis. I don't think I did. But I can't be sure about when I was little — it's not like I can ask my parents. Regina would have known."

"But something's bothering you, right?"

"Nothing's bothering me," he said glumly. "It's all Masha's obsession, she thinks I've lost weight. Occasionally I get a pain in my stomach, here — but I've had this before. It's all nonsense. I just regret the waste of time. I'll get myself checked out, it won't hurt, I suppose, and it might get Masha to back off."

They created a secret organization to seize power, they played at being Nazis and kept minutes of all their meetings. It all makes a certain amount of sense: their fathers became iron men and lost their tongues and their personal lives, they rose and walked on air, without leaving behind ink traces. But Commissars' children, the pupils of school #175, grew up the only way they possibly could: without fear of the camps, police or hunger, they sent honest letters unaware of censorship, they kept diaries without concealing them, they aped the mores of films about Ancient Roman history, in which the heroes win and rise above the mob. They mimicked what they saw: the life of adult conspirators, and they did it with a corresponding amount of paperwork. These children loved paperwork, documentation. The emperor's daughter from a young age preferred to compose action memos rather than verses about the sun, and attached these, and other decrees, to the dining room door with thumbtacks. In these writings, she counted Lazar Kaganovich, Molotov, Kirov, and the Emperor himself among her secretaries. And the school's first secret organization wasn't thought up by the seventh-graders — a Mr. Skryabin (Molotov's nephew), from the eighth grade, Vano Mikoyan, and the aviation boy Kuznetsov, who is mentioned in our case, thought up A Union of Friends until the Grave, compiled a list of members and created a cipher. Except that Molotov happened to find out about it and nipped the conspiracy in the bud.

Why did they plan to seize power? What else was left to them, the offspring? Their fathers had already done everything: the war was supposed to end in victory, a great victory. They had to think of something bigger. The offspring were not left a better future. There could not be anything better than what the Emperor and their fathers had accomplished. But the Emperor would pass into the earth, and their fathers into retirement where they would keep silent, not complaining about the meagerness of their pensions, thanking the party for not killing them, writing their memoirs; the offspring would be cautiously handed dachas, cars, savings accounts, diamond earrings — but not glory, not power, not the ultimate self-erasing devotion to the Absolute Power. They could see their future, the seventh-graders: they were to eat and drink, to drive foreign cars, marry Marshals' daughters and retreat into oblivion under the burden of their fathers' perfect and complete accomplishments. There was no way out of the shadow, no way to become anyone but a Commissar's son; their single and eternal accomplishment was to be their name, so they were to fade, finding jobs for their grandchildren as close as possible to the diplomatic service, and boring their neighbors at the dacha: my father was a saint, and do you remember the Emperor… They were not Yakov Stalin, who perished in a concentration camp, but Vasya Stalin, the twenty-four-year-old general, a hooligan, looser and patron of footballers. And if Volodya Shakhurin wanted a different fate he would have to gather his own loyal pack and bite off his own age of glory, he'd have to learn how to rule the human dust, the masses, how to rise on an idea (like Hitler), how to charm the people. So the boy read — *Mein Kampf* and Raushchning's *Hitler Speaks* — but he wasn't the only one who did. These books were translated and published in Russian for Stalin's Falcons, and the Empire's best and brightest had been watching the Third Reich with painful attention, having suddenly discovered a whole crop of maddeningly strange-looking kin to their own Third Rome. F Molotov wrote to his wife: "Polinka, darling. I'm writing to you briefly, as I can hardly manage the huge pile of things I have to deal with. I only managed to steal a few hours on Sunday night to read Rauschning's *Hitler Speaks*."

Why did the boys take on Nazi ranks? Why, you would ask, while their entire country was bleeding in the fight against these very uniforms? The uniforms indeed. As one graduate of school #175 admitted, even in our propaganda movies, the Germans looked incomparably batter than the foot-wrapped and baggy-coated Russian soldiers, these rag-tag savages. The victorious, terrifying, elegant Nazis offered a vision of a cruel, unimpeachable masculinity. It was the beauty of the enemy, the beauty and cultural solidity of their civilized life, with hot baths and precisely followed schedules that intoxicated the boys of school #175.

THE GIRL

"LEVASHOVA AGREED TO LET ME VISIT HER. TOMORROW. I TOLD HER I worked for the social services and was delivering gifts to veterans for Victory Day. It's very shameful to deceive her. Perhaps I can take some money and buy her an electric kettle?" the secretary suggested. And then she asked, "Do you like movies?"

What a stupid non-sequitur.

"Would you like to go to the movies with me?" she clarified.

No, not really.

"I'd like that very much," I said, instead. "Go out and walk towards Sukharyovka Market. I'll catch up with you."

Outside my door, in the shared office, Alyona handed me a sheet of paper:

"Please sign this."

"Your fourth resignation letter? You could have left it with the secretary."

"Nothing personal, just need to get this done. I do have a life. I've been offered a job. I've had three interviews and I passed their tests the first time."

"As a merchandiser? A traveling sales rep?"

She waved her hand, meaning, oh, I so knew you would say this, and fussed with the signed paper, unsure where to put it. Then still leaned down for a cold kiss and whispered through tears:

"That's how it should be. It will be better for us. I have to try," and added a line from American films: "I love you."

Then she left.

I sat in my office, moving around the unlovable Bryansk toy soldiers on my desk: the early ones are coarse and fat, as if they had been made by children, especially the grenade thrower with his squashed face. I wondered if this was really it with Alyona, would I want to see her again?

I locked up, left the keys with the guard and went down the stairs. Alyona stood with her back to me; she must've been there for a long time, pretending to search for something in her bag, and rehearsing a look of surprise when she saw me.

"I thought you were gone," she said. "Your car isn't here. Are you walking to the metro?"

"I'll walk by myself."

Alyona squinted into the invisible space between the garage and the Komsomolskaya station, then the other way — to Sukharevskaya, saw what I'd expected her to see, flashed her eyes at me with hatred, hunched over and walked away at a pace resembling a run.

I hadn't been to the movies for a long time. At the Almaz movie theater everything had changed so much — there were lines for the ticket office, some screenings were sold out, the place was packed with blond sharp-kneed girls and loud, swearing boys in baggy pants. It took me two minutes to study the seat with all the gears and engines that lowered its back and raised the footrest, like at a dentist's. Suddenly Masha touched my elbow with a strong, sincere grip:

"Why doesn't Alyona Sergeyevna want to work with us? Because of me?"

"I'll tell you a secret. She has a flabby ass — it's absolutely shapeless, neither large nor small, just nothing. And I like big asses. That's the only thing that I'm really interested in. I can take you as a replacement, if you want. But it'd be a waste of your time."

"I see. My ass just isn't big enough for you."

The lights were lowered, and the ads began to thunder. I got up, saying I was going to the bathroom, and left. Outside, I asked the dark-skinned girl who sold pop-corn for her phone number and went out into the fresh air, onto a threadbare green rug laid out to the sidewalk. There was a taxi waiting at one end of the rug, so I got in and rode home. I didn't want to eat anything, I didn't want to talk to anyone; how does anyone go to the movies? I heated water in a bucket, washed myself, opened the window wide, threw a sheet, pillow and blanket onto the couch, took my clothes off, read three pages of Poznyakov's *Soviet Intelligence in America*, and turned off the light.

Tatyana Litvinov: "I saw the Litvinovs on TV the other day. Misha was just sitting there, resting his head on his hand, while his wife did all the talking, and he just nodded, yes, yes. Did he have a stroke or something? Is he on a military pension? Petrova told me: Misha graduated from the two-year aviation school and started in the Mechanical and Mathematical department at the university when the war broke out, and everyone was evacuated to Kuibyshev. They enrolled him in the pilots' school, but Petrova says he never saw any action — he'd get sent to the headquarters whenever things got hot. He didn't even get a whiff of what war is! But according to the documents he took part."

"How did you end up in this family?"

"I came from England and lived in the diplomats' house by Red Gate. Khoromny lane, do you know it? A gray building, as was fashionable back then, in the German style. Divilkovsky lived there, so did Noiman, and Karakhanov, a terrible poser, and Umansky. On the third floor, the Stomonyakovs. Rubinin on the fifth floor. The Litvinovs were on the fourth. My mom, Ivy Valterovna, heard me and my sister speaking English all the time. I hated my sister, she's nine years younger than me, I was forever baby-sitting her. I don't even talk to her.

"I was very bored, I tried to get to know Moscow — Myasnitskaya, Sadovaya, Basmannaya Streets, the Sukharyovskaya tower was still there — I walked around, but not in the evening, because men were constantly bothering me. No books, no newspapers, and every yard you went into stank. No one rode bicycles.

"Out of boredom I went to visit the English lady — Ivy Valterovna, that is — she'd been asking about me. She was delighted to meet me.

At last! She was talkative and charming, she could really draw you in. 'I'm alone, my husband's in Geneva, my children are at camp...' She got me when she said, 'If you want to read newspapers come here, I receive them, and you can borrow some books too.' She was lonely, chatty and interesting — I was hooked.

"In September, Maxim Maximovich came back. I was so innocent, I didn't understand who he was, what a Commissar was. It was all Greek to me. Tanya came after him, and we became friends. Mishka liked to swear all the time. And he pulled me by my braid. Every time he walked past, he'd give it a jerk. One day I got so mad at him, I grabbed the first thing I could reach, a stick, and slammed it on his head. I still remember the sound it made. He left me alone after that."

"How old were you?"

"Fourteen. I started to come over for sleep-overs on weekends, and then the Litvinovs moved to Spiridonovka Street, I went to visit them, and Mom was ready: this is Misha's room, and you'll sleep in the same room as Tatyana — that's how I became part of the family. When Dad turned sixty, Stalin gave him a Cadillac, a blue one like Chkalov's car, only Chkalov had a Packard. And we were moved to Morozov's mansion — the rooms were enormous, there was oak everywhere, we occupied the entire upper floor."

"Is your maiden name Buyanovskaya?"

"My maiden name is irrelevant. When the time came to get my passport, Maxim Maximovich said he had to talk to my mother, my birth mother. 'Girl,' he said, 'You would be better off changing your name. Who knows what's coming.' And what was coming? My father had been arrested in Murmansk and executed as a spy, but I understood nothing.

"I called my mother: you know, they want to talk to you. About what? I don't know, just to talk. I wasn't present. They talked about something. My mother went away. I didn't even see her.

"Maxim Maximovich says: 'Now you'll be Zinaida Maximovna Litvinova. It's better that way.'

"So I was saved, there are plenty of stories like this — children had their names changed, they were taken away beyond the Urals, it was an incredible time! And for some reason all the leadership took in adopted children: Stalin, Kalinin, Ordzhonikidze. Rudzutak had an adopted daughter. Or a niece?"

"Your new parents."

"Oh, they were such different people. Dad liked to dance. At every reception! And even with me. He brought a lot of records back from abroad. Dancing is exercise, that was very important to him, we were forever taking walks, two hours every day, even in winter. I taught him to ski, cross-country, he was fairly good at it. He was a decisive, very firm man.

"At ten in the morning he went to work, on the dot. At five o'clock, he went to have dinner at the Kremlin dining room and received a ration for supper: French bread and caviar — we got everything.

"He would come home and ask, first thing, who's home? He would check all the rooms, then go to his office and change, he had this cardigan with triangular buttons. Then he'd lie on the couch and take a nap. In the evenings he came out to have supper.

"Mom lived her own life. She and Dad were friends, but they had nothing in common. She was bored. Her husband went to work, her children went to school — what was she to do? She translated a lot, but she was still bored. She was only friendly with Americans, but Dad didn't approve: 'You must understand, I can't invite foreigners to my home,' he said. She didn't do housework. I don't think she even once in her life put the tea on to boil. The woman Afanasieva, who lived off the kitchen, did everything. The whole family met only at supper."

"Why was there no love between them?"

"Mom never graduated from school, she had to take care of her half-sister, and she went to work, at some office. She hated it. Then somehow she met Russian Bolsheviks in London. The Bolsheviks were also pretty tedious: they just sat there, waiting for the revolution, and they all thought it wouldn't happen for a long time yet. Dad was almost forty, but had no family, everyone was bored, and here was Mom, this chatty English woman with a beautiful singing voice — and that's how it started. And also, she helped him to translate letters. Dad often talked about it, how much help she was to him, and then he'd add, 'But she changed so much when we came to Moscow!'

"I didn't know what he meant, but I understood that there was nothing for her to do in Moscow. She created her own world and inhabited it: she liked to go to exhibitions, she was mainly interested in abstract art, in modern art. She was interested in R-ov, he had only just appeared back then, she had lovers. I didn't know this, I really got it from Umansky."

"You knew Konstantin Umansky?"

"He was in charge of the press section, and all of Mom's foreign correspondent lovers were accredited through him. Once she took an American correspondent with her to the dacha. Umansky called me: 'Zina, are you out of your mind?' 'What did I do?' — 'Why do you allow your mother to take foreigners to the dacha on her own? Don't you know anything?' — 'What am I supposed to know?'

"I remember one case. Do you know Vozdvizhenka Street? The Central Committee Presidium is there, and the Kremlin hospital is a little further on, and on the corner there is a shop where second-hand books were sold. And once Mama took me to Vozdvizhenka: "We'll go to visit someone." Her, me, Umansky and a correspondent, Kenneth was his name. We went up to the third or fourth floor, Kostya opened the door with his own key, we sat and talked a little. Then Kostya got up and nudged me in the side: 'Well, Zina, we're leaving.' — 'What about Mama?' — 'That's none of your business doesn't concern you.' And we left, but Mama and Kenneth stayed. And it turned out that this place was an inn for the NKVD!

"I heard Dad yelling at Mom many times: 'I can't convince them that you don't know anything! They think I tell you about my work.' "

"What changed in your life after Maxim Maximovich's dismissal?"

"I remember it was May 1st, the International Day of the Solidarity of the Working Class, we went to the parade, and then, like everyone, went to our dacha. We came back on the 3rd, the next day I came home from the university, and heard Dad's car outside at four in the afternoon. I knew something was wrong — was he ill? He came in and put his briefcase down. 'You can congratulate me,' he said. 'I'm no longer a People's Commissar.'

"But we continued to live as we had before: we didn't pay for the apartment or for food — we were sent everything, from fruit to caviar. We went to the dacha as if nothing had happened, but at the dacha conflicts began: everyone wanted different things — Tanya met young men, she gave up school and started to paint, Misha wanted to go to a concert. Everyone went their separate ways. It ended with Dad and me at the dacha by ourselves in the evenings. That was how tamed and domestic I was. Like a cat. I was always at home. If I went to the theater, I went with Papa. And he had terrible pneumonia, he'd cough over the toilet until he threw up. And only I was with him. I made hot milk for him…"

"Some say he was in love with you."

"That's not true. Of course he felt warmly towards me. Perhaps because of my attention. He spoiled me, I won't deny that. We walked together. He always walked, he liked to walk, and in his pocket he had a Colt, a big one. And in his briefcase, there was a revolver in a holster. 'Why do you carry that?' — — 'Just in case. I won't give myself up to them alive.' He asked me to find a person to clean the revolver, and I couldn't think of anything better than asking the head of Dad's security, Levashov.

"Levashov and I sort of fell into it. He was charming and charismatic, he grew up in a university town, Tomsk. He was different from all the other NKVD men. Dad used to tell me I was naïve and stupid, and I had to know Levashov had been sent to watch him and report about what he did. I just laughed it off — what would he report, that Dad went on a walk? That he put on a record and danced by himself in his office? Dad wanted me to become a doctor. But because I got married, I had to give up school, although I was done with all my exams except surgery.

"I married Levashov, and then the war began. Mom, Flora and Pavlik went to Kuibyshev, and I went with my husband far away, to Siberia, beyond Novosibirsk, to a village. I was eight months pregnant, my birthday is on the 15th of October, and I had this obsession: I wanted to celebrate my birthday in Moscow! Everyone tried to talk me out of it, my husband said it wasn't a good idea, but I went to the railway station and showed them in my documents whose daughter I was, and they immediately gave me a ticket.

"I traveled in a strange, half-empty carriage, without mattresses, without any light, the conductors wore gloves, all the passengers were from the NKVD: coats, belts, revolvers — there was incomprehensible talk about 'the Big Land' — I thought maybe they were partisans. Germans bombed the train at one point — everyone jumped out, but I stayed. When it was over, they came back; there was a doctor with them, and he asked, 'How could you stay on the train? In your condition?' I said it didn't matter where to die.

"From the train station in Moscow I called Dad. He answered in a funereal voice: 'What have you done? The Germans are closing in!' — 'Really?' — 'We're leaving for America via Kuibyshev.' — 'But I came here for my birthday!' — 'You're insane.' He sent a car to pick me up. I wasn't afraid, I don't think I went to the bomb-shelter once.

"But he insisted I go to Kuibyshev with him. He sounded sheepish when he asked if I minded if Petrova came with us. 'But Papa,' I said, 'What is Petrova going to do in Kuibyshev?' He quietly and calmly replied: 'She's going with us to Washington. I made her my secretary. Mom told her to watch over me when she left Moscow, so Ms. Petrova has taken charge.'

"If she's going, she's going, but when I tried to fall asleep I noticed that the light was on the whole time in Papa's compartment. I got up and crept along and saw that he was lying there. And she was sitting next to him."

"Was Ivy Valterovna upset about the relations between Maxim Maximovich and Petrova?"

"No, not really."

QUESTIONS TO ANSWERS

After the boys were arrested, they were treat according to a certain plan. For the first three days in jail, they were fed thin soup with sardines, but then they were fed as if being fattened up for slaughter.

During the day, they read. Sergo Mikoyan was absolutely captivated by Dostoevsky and du Terrail's Rocambole series, after discovering that like Rocambole, he was being held in cell 413. Khmelnitsky was put in cell 91, a good cell with a toilet and sink, and he waited every day for the library cart — in six months, the boys read more than they ever had or ever would. Redens' cell mate introduced himself as the projectionist Masterkov (allegedly arrested for letting a film projector catch on fire), and this Masterkov would entertain the boy by retelling movies, only occasionally slipping in a probe: 'Perhaps someone taught you to play these games?' They were interrogated at night.

Volodya read somewhere about the Jesuits' political machinery, and liked their methods: deceit, cunning, intrigues. He especially liked the dictum: the younger member of the order should be a corpse in the hands of his superior. The boys even wanted to call their organization The Order of Jesuits of the 20th century, but argued over it. They created a ruling extraordinary council. Redens was the head of the Foreign Affairs, Khmelnitsky was responsible for agitation and propaganda, Barabanov had arms and finances. Shakhurin was the leader, the Reichsfuhrer. Vano was the boss and patron. Everyone contributed ten rubles a month. For what purposes did they gather funds? The money was to purchase weapons for their future army. Shakhurin had a broken Bulldog pistol, a Walter pop-gun and a large knife. Sergo Mikoyan had a small five-chambered revolver, and Kirpichnikov had an old bayonet and knife.

Redens' legs, when he sat, didn't reach the ground, and at the first interrogation the investigator suddenly said, distracted from the pursuit of truth: "You're almost an adult, quit dangling your feet."

The boys were questioned by the Empire's finest masters of the pre-death conversation. The famous Sheinin, a monocled detective whom even people who hated him described as "highly sophisticated," came from a large Jewish family personally recruited by Kaganovich. Sheinin was the only one the boys were not afraid of: he smiled. Sergo Mikoyan remembered this false truth all his life: if the interrogator smiled, you would go free. There was also Bogdan Kobulov, the deputy head of the NKVD, Umansky's friend, a man with the large head and full face of someone who liked to eat and drink, bulging eyes, large hairy hands and short, crooked legs. The terrifying, tall and handsome Lev Volodzievsky paced during interrogations; he was later entrusted with cleaning up the cesspit of Vasya Stalin's debauchery in the Moscow Regional Air Force command.

The man who inspired the greatest fear in the boys was Lieutenant-General Nikolai Sazykin. Sazykin did not smile, and did not hide the disgust that all of the investigators felt towards this bunch of Nazi-aping kids. That particular summer Sazykin also headed the Fourth Department, the secret political department which investigated the rust and rot of the iron people: lust, predilections for vice, drunkenness, idleness, arrogance, penchants for shiny trinkets, anything the Emperor needed to know. He was tired of baseness and for that reason didn't deem it necessary to smile at the Commissars' sons.

The investigation found that Shakhurin received German books from Vano, keeping them secret from his parents. Did anyone encourage or advise him to read them? No one knew. He said that he liked some of Hitler's principles. The enemy should be received warmly and offered poisoned sweets. He said: when we grow up we'll hold leadership posts, and will conduct our own policy. What kind?

The teenagers were play-dough in the expert hands of the NKVD, they could have been turned into anything. But the investigation, following the plan, did not want *anything*, so it returned to the same question: Weren't your games led by an adult, a visiting American perhaps?

Volodya planned to come to power with the help of Japan, which would provide weapons and in exchange receive the Far East. His favorite phrase was "When we come to power." He planned to build villas in Australia and other parts of the world. He pointed to an island in the Indian Ocean — our nation will be here!

"He said he would legalize private trade and private property, would open luxury restaurants with music and dancing, fashionable cinemas, and everyone would do whatever they wanted."

"What was the practical activity of this 'Fourth Empire' organization of yours?" the investigators asked.

"We fired slingshots at each other." Silence fell. The boys did not think about death. They remember that clearly.

"That's enough. I don't see anything there anyway," I said, squinting as the suburban train pulled out of the station. Borya and I, planted among weekenders, were going fishing. "Their plan is clear. The boys say what the investigators tell them to say: Japan will give them weapons and receive the Far East in exchange! It's all for the Emperor, in a language he can understand. So he won't touch their fathers."

"They all blamed Shakhurin. Convenient, seeing how he was dead," Borya muttered.

"Note there's not a word about Nina. The Great Stone Bridge is their weak spot. They hope that the Emperor will believe the story of unrequited love, he's a Caucasian, he's hot blooded, he has to believe it: be mine or I'll kill you! Borya, we won't see a damn thing from here. We need to go to the scene of the crime. To the third of June, 1943."

"And the authorization?" Borya munched sunflower seeds and spat the shells into a rolled-up newspaper. "The boys won't give it to us."

"In the indictment there are eight people. We've only found five."

"And the rest are no longer alive. I think," Borya leaned over to me, talking over a loud salesperson peddling tea in the aisle, "we should buy our permit. We should find someone serious in the FSB — a hundred grand oughtta' do it. But Naumych won't go for it. He says the *rule* must be observed. And the rule is that someone has to let us in himself."

In the end, I decided not to fish with Borya, and just came back to Moscow by myself. At night, I followed the hunchbacked shapes of dacha gardeners back to the station, with their charitable escort of stray dogs, listening to the wheeze and creaking of hand-carts loaded with vegetables. Everyone carried flowers, as if going to a funeral. The people climbed to the platform in a single line and stood still there, in its almost-primordial dark, waiting for the blinding headlight of the engine to give them form and definition. In the light of the approaching train, I could see the people's steaming breath and a thin wisp of smoke rising from a dropped cigarette.

The boys were released shortly before the New Year. Only the dreamer Artyom Khmelnitsky remembered the exact date — the twenty-second of December. Three years later, to the day, his mother was sent to prison for ten years, and his father said, "I'm not going to get involved" as if he *could have*, but his duty did not allow him. Why they were released, why none of them gotten five year in jail, when common people would get ten for having a Nazi leaflet in a pocket, no one knows.

Upon walking out, Redens saw his mother. She looked at her well-fed son and turned in surprise to Kobulov in shock. The boy had some papers shoved at him: sign, here and here. "And what if I don't?" he asked. "Be quiet!" his mother snapped. And he signed. It was only then, after all was said and done, and they could go, that Redens' mother, Anna Sergeyevna, a woman of strong character and endless kindness, suddenly felt compelled to draw herself up fully and look at her son's former jailers and ask, "Now, if you have no more questions, I have a question *for you.* How did my son behave? Is he a scoundrel or not? Isn't he an honest Soviet youth? I'm taking my son from you, and I must know this!" She was assured that the boy was quite alright and gently maneuvered towards the entrance.

Redens was sent to Omsk by train, it was the first New Year he did not celebrate at home. From the loudspeakers at every station he heard the new national anthem — it had just been adopted.

Sergo was told to gather his things, and for the last time he was led down the prison corridor past the wooden booths — people walking in the opposite direction were hidden there, so that the prisoners would not see each other. In an office at a desk with a standard green cloth, he was given papers to sign: I took part in a fascist organization, I repent, I ask to be released. "I won't sign this! I didn't take part in anything *like that!*" the boy balked. Take it easy, they yawned, it's just a formality, your mother and brother are waiting for you next door. Sergo could hear voices in the next room, free voices, unconstrained by the protocol — but still, he didn't recognize them. The fear struck him then: what if he'd sign and they would grab him and take him to a cell, this time for good? But he signed anyway.

In the next room he was embraced by his mother and Vano. Armenian relatives were visiting them at home, and Sergo announced from the threshold:

"I was imprisoned in cell 413. Like Rocambole!" Suddenly he saw that the guests were wearing epaulets, recently reinstated by the army. "Epaulets! Like in the Tsarist army?"

"Shut up!" his uncle yelled. "Haven't you had enough?"

The Mikoyans had to pick between Siberia and Central Asia, and chose Stalinabad: Kurbanov, the chairman of the Tajik government, happened to have just been at a reception with Mikoyan, so Sergo was dispatched to a two-room apartment in Stalinabad for the duration of his exile.

Bakulev went off to relatives in Guryev.

Vano Mikoyan marched to his father:

"I'm not guilty of anything."

"I know. If you were guilty, I would have killed you."

And the boy vanished, leaving a handsome trace in the documents: "was sent to the front to service the planes of fighting brothers."

The boys were not let out of sight. When they applied for admission to universities, their applications were returned to their home addresses without further explanation. Bakulev worried for his son and applied for his rehabilitation — no reply. After the Emperor died, someone from the Supreme Court called and asked for Petya by name: you have been acquitted, they said and added sternly, but don't play these games again! Sheinin became friends with the Bakulevs, visited often, and gently made fun of Petya; he died on the same day as Bakulev senior, and they were buried next to each other.

Redens wanted to go to the Moscow Economics Institute, so his mother went to see the Rector beforehand and was told that with a conviction like this her son could only be admitted to the Department of Electrical Mechanics. Redens was admitted, but expelled later, when Anna Sergeyevna was arrested. A year after the Emperor's death, he received three official papers: your father was shot without justification, your mother was imprisoned without justification, you were sentenced without justification.

Kirpichnikov graduated from the Moscow Higher Technical Academy and defended a dissertation at the Institute of Metallurgical Machine-building. He remained a very taciturn man for the rest of his life.

They never met again. Redens once saw Kirpichnikov from a distance, and another time he ran into Khmelnitsky at the service station.

"What do we have about the dead boys?"

"According to the Interior Ministry database, Kirpichnikov has a son still living — Alexander Feliksovich. He's registered at Maria

Ulyanova street, 6, apartment 39. He doesn't answer the phone, I've been calling for two weeks. Barabanov has a son, Alexander, and his wife is even alive, Nina Gedeonova, Rostovskaya embankment, 5, apartment 146," Chukharev reported. He chewed over something unspoken, briefly glancing at Goltsman.

"Start with Barabanov."

"There is a note in the database that either Barabanov or his wife are our people. And if we raise their suspicion — we'll hear about it."

"Listen, what the hell difference does it make? Your business is to set up a meeting. Tell them whatever you have to tell them. We only need one person to give us permission — a nephew, a sister, a grandson, anyone. Can you get that much done?"

Chukharev went away to sulk and toil.

"Alexander Naumovich, have you been to the doctor?"

"I'll go next Wednesday. I had the blood work done, and I've been to the ultrasound people."

"And?"

"I don't know about the blood tests," Goltsman paused. "The ultrasound nurse took a long time. Asked me to turn this way, then that. To hold my breath. She said she'd send the results directly to my doctor." He paused again. "But she said there were changes in the liver. Maybe it's just my age. She also asked if I'd ever had hepatitis."

"You shouldn't brush it off," I said.

Goltsman got up as if he hadn't heard me.

"So are you going to the third of June?" he asked.

"What choice do we have? The survivors won't talk. Let's go together."

THE 3ᴿᴰ OF JUNE
(BEGINNING)

ALL REPORTS OF THE INCIDENT ON THE GREAT STONE BRIDGE stated that it happened 'in broad daylight,' but that wasn't true: Nina Umanskaya died early on a June evening, which was almost as bright as the middle of the day. Double-decker trolleybuses with open upper platforms had just appeared in Moscow, and there were two routes that passed over the Great Stone Bridge. There were few passers-by — in 1943 people did not just go strolling at leisure near the Kremlin, and the stairs that led off the bridge to the Popular Music Theater were generally little used. The scene of the incident was deserted, only the House of Government stared at it with all its windows.

The first thing that was made up *post hoc* was that Nina was shot with an exploding bullet in the back of the head, and Shakhurin got an ordinary bullet. No, the bullets were identical.

TROYANOVSKY: We occupied two rooms at the Moscow Hotel. On the 3ʳᵈ of June, Nina came to say goodbye, made her farewells and left. Later on the same day, Konstantin Alexandrovich stopped by, and Nina called to catch him. She told him that she would be late, and he shouldn't worry. Umansky gave his permission for her to stay out longer, "as long as a boy walks you home." Vladimir Alliluyev:

I was playing with the other kids in the yard, and suddenly we heard two shots. We ran out to look, but by the time we got there the bodies had already been taken away. But my aunt managed to see them.

Leonid Redens: I also ran out onto the stairs that day, but I only saw bloodstains.

Pyotr Bakulev: My mother called me from work, "Do you know what happened?" In the evening, my father said: it's a hopeless case, most likely he'll die. The bullet passed from one temple to the other. If he survives, he'll be an invalid.

Unidentified Witness #2: I remember Kostya in the apartment, quite out of his mind. Raisa, his wife, was at the dacha at that time, and Kostya told her that there had been a car accident, and told everyone who came to see him, "Don't let anything slip!"

Unidentified Witness #3: They took Raisa Mikhailovna to the Troyanovskys' apartment, where things wouldn't remind her of what happened — she was completely distraught. She lay motionless on the bed, like a rolled-up rug. The doctor asked Troyanovsky's son not to leave her side. Polina Molotova came there too. Umansky looked in on his wife, and quickly went away to consult with Sheinin. He returned with a strange phrase on his lips, *"It's amazing how differently you can see things after you've talked to an intelligent person."* He may have asked for advice as to whether to cancel the flight. I don't know what his words could have meant.

Unidentified Witness #4: Sofia Mironovna believed that the incident was the work of German intelligence. Shakhurin seemed completely calm and walked about the apartment. Later, Sheinin said that Mrs. Shakhurin wanted the case to be treated as a political conspiracy, but it was merely the result of her son's bad upbringing.

Everyone was frightened — the parents of school #175, the "accursed caste," as the Emperor put it, circled their wagons for several hours around the stairs, stained with blood and sprinkled with sand, while the city cops were still calling their bosses, before the NKVD arrived. They had to work out how to present the whole story to the Emperor, in order to save what could still be saved, to prevent the earth from cracking open and devouring everyone around. By the time Lev Sheinin, this hyper-effective tool, arrived at the scene, he had already been told *what happened:* a mad passion, Iosif Vissarionovich, the Shakhurin boy shot the girl dead, and put the gun to his own head.

They counted on the Emperor's own past: his oldest son attempted to kill himself, his wife Nadezhda succeeded (she also used a Walter), plus in this case the culprits were children: the Emperor and his circle didn't seem to know what to do with children, they didn't want the fuss, there were already six hundred juvenile delinquents in Moscow. The Emperor would not be surprised that pupils of the best school in the country shot each other. And also (everyone thought) he wouldn't question the love angle: he didn't consider love to be worthy of imperial attention, "that's for women," but he kept having to deal with it in most unexpected ways: it hadn't been three months since he had slapped his seventeen-year-old daughter twice across the face for her "I love him!" engendered by the forty-year-old screen-writer Aleksei Kapler, who had decided to take the shortest path to the top. The Emperor demanded the love letters, and discovered, that he, a man who could tilt millions of lives into death, could do nothing about this love — he was as awfully powerless as any father in the face of kissing doves and hearts pierced with arrows drawn in the margins of notebooks. Thus, he would not look too deeply into the matter. That was what they hung their hopes on: the Emperor would not want *to know everything in every detail.*

And indeed he said only, "Wolf cubs." With a hint of surprise. Or perhaps despair. No one remembered. Is that really what he said? Who got the task of delivering the news to him?

There's a record of Molotov and Beria meeting with Stalin on the 3rd of June, but earlier in the day.

On the 4th, the calendar lists Beria, the People's Commissar of State Security Merkulov (was he the one to report the incident?), and the sniper hero Lyudmila Pavlyuchenko, back from her very successful tour of America.

The 5th of June must have been the day the Emperor was served the main dish. By then Volodya had died, Umansky had flown to Mexico, and Sheinin had written his tale. At 22:35 Stalin received Mikoyan. Five minutes later the Emperor called the head of the main department of military counter-intelligence SMERSH, Viktor Abakumov. They talked together for an hour. Abakumov was the first to leave, and fifteen minutes later — at midnight — Mikoyan came out.

Shakhurin, poor Shakhurin, the lover of beautiful ties, who had buried a ceramic jar with the remains of his only son at Novodevichy cemetery, does not appear on the calendar until June 9th, when he sat in a meeting with eleven other people, demonstrating with his diligent note-taking: the most important thing was to triumph in the war with the German Nazi occupants, and the rest was just insignificant detail. And, no doubt, he smiled when necessary to Mikoyan, who was also present, but was seated much closer to the Emperor; and he also went to see the Emperor on the 10th, 14th and 15th of June — days when he could still dare or expect (and fear) the sympathetic (or reprimanding) question: "I heard that your son…" The one person the story-tellers forgot was Sofia Mironovna Shakhurin, whom her son had called "the black bomber" — she knew *her own* truth and would shout it on every corner, she did not care for anyone else's deals, schemes or desires to live a little longer, other people's maneuvering away from Lubyanka Square or Kolyma camps. Sofia Mironovna, an absurd woman who wore outrageous hats and collected porcelain, defended her young, her blood, her fledgling son — what was left of him, at least a kind memory of him, an echo. When the frightened Redens turned over to her the papers of The Fourth Empire, Sofia Mironovna knew how the swastika games could be used: they would force the Emperor to look at the Stone Bridge again. A new truth had to be put together, a truth full of holes, with a baggy fit, a truth no one believed, but a few people finally learned about the slime that had appeared in the empire. Eventually, the moment came when the Emperor suddenly looked up and asked, "Anastas, where are your children?" and Mikoyan gasped for air. And so it came to an end. Life was over.

It can't be said that we were getting closer; we were sinking deeper, with the dead, whose number was limited and who were not interested in talking. Vano knew something, but we wouldn't be able to get it out of him. Anastasia Petrova knew everything, but she was born in the time of mutes, and her time made sure she did not talk heart to heart, open her heart, lighten her heart, or pour her heart out; I suspect that even at her deathbed confession Tasya unburdened herself in rather general terms. There was no one else for us to talk to, it was time to see it from their point of view.

"Who are you talking to? I can't see…." Alyona and I were walking above ground towards Pushinskaya Square, along the boulevards, and finding ourselves very close to spring. In clear weather, if you were to get on a hill and look far into the distance in the direction from which the spring would come, you could almost see it beyond the white houses and the black branches, you could catch its breath in the wind, the dense, volatile scent of damp earth.

Mr. Kirpichnikov's phone rang and rang without answer, so Chukharev went to his address: Maria Ulyanova street, six. Apartment thirty-nine.

The sun was shining. He entered a damp and icy courtyard, and with a business-like, unhurried pace he walked alongside the building, looking for the right entrance. A young mother returning from a walk just then let him in — he helped her to carry in the stroller. Chukharev went up to the second floor.

The hallway leading to apartments thirty-nine and forty was blocked by a solid iron door with a solid iron lock. There were two doorbells. The top one had a piece of tape stuck to it, with the number 39 written in ink. The lower one was blank.

Chukharev stood for a while and listened. From behind the

door he could hear kitchen noises. He pressed the upper button. He didn't hear a bell ring, and pressed the button harder. Suddenly, he heard the door of apartment thirty-nine, in which no one answered the phone for three months, including this morning, open and a domestic shuffling of slippers approach the peephole in the iron door.

Chukharev felt fiery energy flowing through him, the introductory "Hello, I am…" rose up to his throat. He stood up straighter, with an entreating and kind expression on his face, he looked and felt confident…The steps moved away again, and the door of apartment thirty-nine was locked with a click — everything became still.

Did the person on the other side look in the peephole and walk away? Perhaps someone had come out of apartment forty to put out a vacuum cleaner bag for taking to the trash in the morning on the way to the bus stop? Chukharev rang the doorbell of apartment thirty-nine again. And again. For twice as long — again. Nothing happened. He took out his cell phone and called the telephone number of the apartment. No one answered. He jammed his finger into the doorbell of apartment forty. Nothing. Still, he had just heard someone come out of apartment thirty-nine. Who was the inhabitant afraid of? Why didn't he pick up the phone? Chukharev waited by the elevator, but then got worried that the neighbors might call the police, seeing a man in black just standing there and waiting. He went down to the street door and sat waiting on the window sill, himself ashamed of his trick. No one came out. He walked back and forth in the court-yard, waiting for residents.

"Do you know anyone from apartment thirty-nine?"

A man with a battered face looked at Chukharev in horror. Yes, now it's going to seem like that all the time. When you're searching for someone, there are no longer any accidental passers-by or by-standers — everyone has a *role*.

A girl came out of the building.

"What about you? Do you know anyone from apartment 39?"

She turned away fearfully and walked on.

Chukharev could not restrain himself, and did something that his teachers would not have praised him for: he stopped, and tilting his head back, looked straight at the windows of apartment thirty-nine. He looked fixedly, rolling back and forth on the balls of his feet, showing himself, hoping that someone would looked out from the safe height to check out the man who'd rang the doorbell.

One window was open. The window next to it was cracked, and the crack was covered with scotch tape. Was he an alcoholic? Constantly drunk? Did he need money? What about throwing a pebble at the window?

Chukharev turned away and went out of the yard.

ICH HATTE EINEN KAMERADEN

First the snowdrifts began to get covered with a dirty gray stubble, and then during the day when the sun was shining big chunks of snow started slipping down from the roofs and cornices with rustling, muffled sounds. Bulging green garbage bags appeared on torn-up black lawns, scrawny crows jumping about between them, and finally the tiny sabers of grass pierced through the ground — the cheerful spring cavalry. I stood among mournful people who held obediently still at the street crossing, and sneezed with great pleasure. An old man next to me held an ice-cream cone in both hands, and whenever he tried to bite into it his hands shook. The cars drove by, and then the light turned.

I was in a courtyard on the outskirts of Moscow, the 5th Magistralnaya Street or some such, a place where the city suddenly grew tired of spreading and ended with a four-floor red brick building, separated from the busy by-pass road by rows of garages. I sat on a bench among piles of poplar fluff, the ground around my feet littered with fish scales and jagged fish skeletons, and stared at the laundry, informative as ancient parchments, hung out on the balconies. Children had accumulated in the sandboxes. Pale, skinny women with drab white skin came out in satin dressing gowns with necklines that plunged far beyond common sense. Cars of indistinguishable makes stood wrapped in rags like mummies awaiting resurrection, a black terrier ran around, and a large-bottomed woman called after him without conviction. A white cat slunk past the building; the small feathers of a mangled pigeon clumped on the pavement and it was clear they would lie there until autumn. In another corner, on a bare spot, sat the rusty frame of a railroad car.

I remembered how anxious I used to get in these terrifying moments — a long time ago — sitting, waiting for the magic door to open, to be invited in. Waiting to follow a backside, in low-cut jeans which, with their low waist, revealed pale skin and a transverse of bluish veins.

First the words began to repeat, the language became thin and worn-out, limited to a readily available collection of niceties. The stories I told became all one story, a muttering, automatic progression from point to point: "your hands are cold," "it's amazing, I feel like I've known you all my life," "are you married?" And then places began to repeat, too: new women did not take me to new places, but for some reason kept leading me to old, familiar haunts, as if insisting on getting into someone else's bed, someone else's life, taking on someone else's warmed-up and well-worn shape. After that, death came even closer: I saw bodies and poses duplicated, the words were the same in bed, after sex, and life stopped changing — everything was polished and rolled into the featureless smoothness of a coffin's lid. Nothing grabbed at me, nothing held me, nothing promised to warm my last days (weeks, hours?) in the hospital bed. I couldn't find what I needed and could not even imagine it, could not imagine anything different, people or circumstances, even when I closed my eyes with the women I didn't need. So what? What was the whole point? Was I just to bear it and wait, and not make a fuss? But somewhere, somehow, I'd had it — in my dreams, perhaps. In my dreams it was exactly the way I wanted it to be, like the first time: with a shy hope, with a thrill, and the bliss of the first penetration, a tender acuity with someone unbearably intimate. But it only happened once. And a very long time ago. And that's the way it is for everyone.

I sat on a bench, with *The Sport Express* unfolded in front of me like a screen and felt like I was about to fall asleep.

I looked up dully at the sound of someone running towards me: Alyona, somehow emaciated and glum-faced. She ran up and dropped her news like an unwanted baby into my lap:

"I got divorced."

She screwed up her eyes, grabbing me, witch-like, having decided to play out the proper sequence right there on the stairs, but I maneuvered her into the building and stroked her sympathetically. Alyona picked up on my tactic, and confidently pushed me up the stairs to my door.

Inside the apartment, Alyona was beside herself, muttering, "My love, will we really be together?" I hugged her and manhandled her, like a doll, pushing her away from my face, and that's when I suddenly saw it: the door to the bathroom was outlined with sharp lines of electric light. I felt my palms turn clammy — *please let me have forgotten to turn out the light!* — but then the door *opened* and a very real, wet-haired girl, the one I brought home with me last night, held out her presumably dusty shoes to me with a question:

"Would you happen to have a shoe rag?"

I was led along the icy street down from the old KGB building at Lubyanka, and we walked, it seemed to me, for a long time, before coming to a building whose street entrance was studded with many plaques ("Administration of High-rise Buildings" and "Telecommunications Monthly" was all I managed to take in). We climbed the stairs to the second floor, to another door marked "Reading Room"; my companion rang a perfectly ordinary round door-bell, and I was let into the place where the truth was kept. I looked around: there was varnish on the cheap parquet floors, dust on the window-sills, flower pots. Ficuses. Old external electrical wiring. Narrow runners between the desks. Cheap pictures of Russian nature on paper posters. A clock that ticked above my head.

"Here's his diary. It's absolute rubbish. And here," the NKVD man who guarded the truth fingered a piece of paper that was glued into a thin exercise book, "is his or her father giving his view of this… er… incident."

I wished for him to go away and not touch these people. This was mine.

I felt the notebook: there were two exercise books bound together. And both of them were thin, damn it, very thin! The first was a home-made school diary. The second the author had titled "Notes".

Under *Homework* on the first page of the diary, Volodya Shakhurin had entered "History of the Italian renaissance" — is that what Soviet sixth-graders studied in the autumn of 1941? (What did I study in sixth grade? Brutal serfdom and the growth of revolutionary inclinations among the peasant masses? Kondraty Bulavin? Stepan Razin?) Or was Shakhurin showing off to the Kuibyshev rednecks?

He then applied himself to writing down German poems; he copied many of them, he worked very hard at it. I leafed through the pages, then stopped — one of the poems was called "Mexico." Where Nina was going. It was probably just a coincidence. A stroke of fate. I looked at the other poems. I only worked out the author in a few of them, Heine. I did not find the poem "Mexico" in the volumes of German poetry approved by the Empire (including the sonnets "The Party" and "The Unemployed Man"). The four-volume edition of Heine contained an extremely long opus about the war between the Spaniards and the Aztecs, titled "Vitzliputzli" after the bloodthirsty man-eating God, something along the lines of "The terrible day passed. Now / The wild night of triumph began…" I leafed through Heine again, trying to guess what Vladimir Shakhurin could have copied into his exercise book, what Heine could have written about a sixth-grader who fled from Kuibyshev with his beloved girl, then moved into the seventh grade, completed it and shot himself or was killed. I tried to read with the eyes of the boy… Maybe this?

> *Let's run away! You'll be my wife!*
> *We'll rest in foreign realms.*
> *In my love you will receive*

> *A homeland, and a home.*
> *If you won't go — I'll die here,*
> *And you'll be left alone,*
> *And home will be as strange to you*
> *As a far-off foreign land.*

This was followed by a solved algebra problem crossed out diagonally with red pencil. The boy did not write anything more in the first exercise book.

I tossed it aside and carefully opened the "Notes." If anything was destined, it was here, and I reached inside, under the trembling arch of Shakhurin Sr.'s lines,: *absolutely everything, that you read here* (the father was in a hurry, sweating, he needed to tell everyone at once — from an unknown NKVD lieutenant to members of the Ministry of Defense, to the Emperor — whoever got a hold of the book, he was only concerned with his own skin; his son had already become the flying dust of the crematorium, the frightened Redens boy had given the "Notes" to the father at the funeral) — *all of this is pure invention*. Volodya wrote it in one sitting, he made everything up about the Autumn of 1941, "to show the boys what Volodya could be like," and there's no truth in any of this. I would argue with you, Aleksei Ivanovich, lover of singing, former People's Commissar for Aviation Industries, about the truth, about reality and the authenticity of these inventions, about what really moves the young and old — but there is no longer any time.

For the epigraph, the boy chose these lines: "*Being always on one's guard, catching every glance, the significance of every word, guessing at intentions, frustrating their plots, pretending to be tricked, and suddenly, with a shove, upturning the whole enormous and arduously built edifice of their cunning and schemes — that's what I call life.*"

Right away I thought I had heard or read this before — this was smooth, literary diction, you wouldn't say it aloud, what sort of nonsense was this? I would look for the quote on the Internet later and figure out where this crap had come from. Alright, Volodya, speak for yourself.

We were evacuated to Kuibyshev. There is an asylum here. All of its inhabitants think they're living in Paris.

Tomorrow I'm going to Engels. I want to meet a German girl.

*I didn't meet anyone, there was no convenient opportunity, but the German girls are **charmant** — almost all of them.*

20 September. A German girl appears in Volodya's notes, blonde, with blue eyes, Zoya, then on 22 September: *Today Moscow was bombarded for the first time. I feel quite strange…* ("Bombarded" and then a mannered ellipses, plus the correct date of the first bombing — did he remember things well enough to compose this a year later?)

29 September. *We went to see Zoya (in German she's called Zenita). I can't believe I was unsuccessful. All of her cheerfulness vanished in an instant, her gaze expressed the sadness that is usual under such circumstances.*

I squeezed her hand — she responded by squeezing mine. A beginning was made. On the way back, at the dacha, I met Valya — never before did I think village girls could be so beautiful. She placed her hands on my shoulders, and said directly, "Why waste time on talking? Act! This is wartime." I made sure she wouldn't have to ask twice. 5 August. (Why? It was just September…)

6 August (Why did he return to summer?) *I went for a boat ride with Irina. Today there was a great victory. Two little tears rolled out of her charming eyes (just like in Mr. Voskresensky's novels).*

Mikhail Voskresensky, a priest's son, was dubbed "Moscow's own Walter Scott" and died in 1867. While alive he keenly captured the preoccupations of the middle class: called by critics "a flea-market scribbler," he was wildly adored by readers, who loved the "heaps of passion, licit and illicit, events piled on top of events," demonic heroes, and a sensitively elevated diction of his novels. Who gave Volodya Voskresensky's books? Sofia Mironovna, who hired cultured staff? Or did he pick up the reference somewhere else and just insert it into his notes for posturing's sake?

"It's strange," she said slowly and thoughtfully. "We never talked about this, and suddenly… This is so unexpected."

The best answer was another kiss!

10 August. I went to see Zenita. The sun seemed to me to be the 'Sun of Austerlitz.' We met strangely and strangely we'll part.

Only in the evening I felt ill at ease when I caught the song on the radio, 'Ich hatt einen Kameraden'

What radio station did the young pioneer tune in to, that he could listen to *The Good Comrade,* that old and well-loved lament of the German Armed Forces, while our own soldiers were dying heroically by the hundreds of thousands on the western border?

I am doing psychological improve with Militsa, Klava, Galya, Marta and Nelli.

I started to read Notre Dame *in French but I feel that I've let my command of that language slip considerably. Maman called me: "March to the bomb shelter!"*

10 September. Jose Diaz has come to Moscow (I've seen this name somewhere before). *Pops* (this is how he talks about the People's Commissar — Pops, Maman — he's not one to write about his father slapping him in the face!) *brought him to us for lunch. Diaz promised to give me books to read in Spanish.*

12 October. I fought with Yura. He says that Moscow won't withstand the attack — is that the Russian spirit? Yura is Yura Korenblyum, the son of the executed Kirshon — and the boy wasn't afraid to say such things? He mustn't have been the only one who said such things in Kuibyshev in '41. And apparently, the Emperor wasn't the only one invoking the Russian spirit, either.

So. The boy liked his classmate Galya Kuibysheva (in the city of Kuibyshev, the daughter or niece of Kuibyshev? This is the girl he would hit in the face later, during a geography class back in Moscow, to stop her babbling about the escape he was planning for Nina. Nina Umanskaya went to see her before she died). Another classmate, Romanov also fell in love with Kuibysheva. Volodya moved indirectly and came up with a plan: *I want a resolution soon. I will meet her as a go-between, laughing at the actions of my friend a bit, finding him childishly stupid. We'll see what happens. As always, I am certain of victory.* And the number 6. November, perhaps?

Today Galya received a note. 'Galya! I have a great deal to tell you, and as it is quite urgent, my friend will talk to you, Volodya Shakhurin, as unfortunately I do not have this opportunity today. G. Romanov. Find a way to let me know today, if you'll come to the statue of Lenin at 8:30.

But it's totally dark at 8:30 at night in November — who would let the girl go out, when it was impossible to see? Did they go to school in the second shift, in the afternoons?

At the next break, she nodded to me with a charming smile. I'll keep Romanov near me all the time, to stop anything from going wrong. At 8:15 I went to the appointed place and hid. My heart was beating rapidly in spite of myself.

The girl arrived, he presented himself, apologized for being late, and described his friend's passion, "expertly portraying him as a dupe," and asked if he could see her home. She told him she lived close by, and he responded with an *experienced* (as he put it) move: *All the better, I don't have much time myself. In continuation of all of this I observed her attentively and saw that I had won. Finally I lowered my head as a sign that my thoughts were finished, and thanked her 'for giving me the honor of talking to her.' Then I took the simple girl, who would never comprehend the scheme, by the arm and led her in the direction she indicated to me.*

By the house he played out the finale: *Galya… Is this really the end?* She could not hide her emotional upheaval: *'No, no! Just don't let it be the end!' Yet another fortress fell to the force of our weapons.* The writing ended.

"Hand the documents over, please."

"Yes, just a minute. Sorry."

Those were the diaries he kept and gave to Redens to keep: read and tell the rest of the class! Talk about the girls he screwed — those were his "lists." His father wrote again with a quivering pen: "On the 11th of June 1941, my wife Sofia Mironovna, her sister Anna Mironovna and a friend, Rakhil Gurevich came to Saratov. They lived at a dacha by

Saratov, without coming into town." Why are you making excuses, iron man? Your boy has died. And who are you crying to? "Volodya was a talented, good, well-behaved boy, but these qualities could not make him popular in the Moscow school, in the circle of his comrades. He always remained the same boy at home, but for the kids at school he invented all kinds of stories, ashamed of his good behavior." *He wasn't the killer*, the People's Commissar wrote, solemnly, as if whispering. *Look close by.*

DARKNESS

Lev Sheinin led the Soviet prosecution team at the Nuremberg Trial (later people would write: a hangman judging hangmen!). When a truck completely accidentally ran over Solomon Mikhoels, the chairman of the Jewish Anti-Fascist Committee and friend of Konstantin Umansky, the Jewish community, not understanding the demands of the time, called for not only the renaming of Malaya Bronnaya Street to Mikhoels Street, but also an independent investigation (the Emperor read in reports), which was to be carried out by the Empire's best detective Sheinin, a fact that Lev Romanovich found suicidally flattering right until December 1949, when he was dismissed for absolutely juvenile reasons: he was said to "embellish" and to "pursue" headlines. On the wave of this flattery (and few were clear-eyed enough in the three or four years right after the war to see things for what they were becoming) Lev Sheinin turned down the offer to become the Head of the Criminology Institute and was awarded the Stalin Prize for his screenplay *Meeting on the Elbe*. In 1950, however, his fellow writers detected in Sheinin a developing cosmopolitanism as well as an ineradicable Jewish nationalism. Lev Romanovich slipped and, after a short slide over the ice, crashed into the hole cut in it, and at the first interrogations could not even muster the strength to deny having been a ringleader in a "group of nationalist dramatists" or to attempt to disprove the claim that one morning at the dacha, in late May, he had walked as far away as possible from the house, stood for a long time alone among the blossoming apple trees under the eternal, mute sky and, having looked around three times, all of a sudden quietly muttered words unexpected for an old bloodstained party member: it would be good to move to Israel and live out at least these last years without fear… His cell mates recalled him as being stingy.

Sheinin did not bother to deny the petty details: conversations, moods, "Jewish dominance," but his friend and co-author Mikhail Maklyarsky was determined to drag him down and incriminated him in a conspiracy, even an underground movement and ties with America. The two men fought for life, each for his own lie, but then the Emperor died, the times changed, and they were released on the same day, and walked out into the street together, and — as the legend has it — agreed to write a new script, *The Night Patrol* — in the taxi that took them home. In 1967 Sheinin died of a heart attack, although he had never complained of heart trouble before.

After the Emperor's funeral, his most gifted apostle Marshal Beria, who had discovered *everything* about the case of the boys in school #175, reached for power, but on June 26 he was arrested and promptly executed for "sheltering agents of imperialist intelligence," and for "capitulation and moral decay." It is also a fact that two more investigators of the Forth Empire's case were executed for their association with Beria, Bogdan Kobulov and Lev Volodzievsky.

One person survived — Nikolai Sazykin, a peasant's son. He was merely demoted from his rank of lieutenant general, and after some contemplation expelled from the party. He taught for a bit, and then went off to earn his retirement at the Ministry of Medium Machine Building. He died in 1975. Once, when he ran into Sergo Mikoyan at a bakery, he gave him the usual gloomy glance, and — without a word — passed him by on his own business.

Without noticing, I had developed the habit of thinking about the secretary before I fell asleep, it somehow happened imperceptibly, although there was nothing unusual about it — a person needs to think about something before going to sleep in order to make the next morning even a little inviting. I would wonder what the secretary would *be like* tomorrow. It's hard to live without being in love with someone, but there was nothing left ahead but death, and so I suppose this was me, picking up the last crumbs from the floor. Goltsman hired her, I didn't notice her to begin with, there was just a girl sitting there, with a skinny back, straight, at the computer. There was a new voice asking me on the phone if I would be coming in. You look pretty today, I'd say. Thank you, she'd say. She never answered if I asked questions not pertaining to work — Alyona, having been burned many times, made sure to warn the girl, unless, of course, as Alyona would have put it, she wanted to swallow sperm and be thrown out of here with her mouth still wet. I lay in bed at night, and told myself a bed-time story: *Not once — not with a word, not in any way — did the secretary let him know that she wanted to be closer, to stay longer. Their fingers touched once or twice, when she brought him a full cup of coffee. Early, when the office was still mostly empty, he would ask: Who are your parents? The secretary answered briefly, nibbling a cookie, they divorced…*

Is your mother also a beauty?

Yes, the secretary nodded.

When everyone thought that he wasn't at work, and Alyona wasn't patrolling her territory, protecting her prey, the free and cheerful voice of this strange tall girl, bubbling over with life, floated in from the reception room — she only became a secretary when he was around.

This is how it began. Later, I started deceiving myself: let her help the investigation, I thought, she seems capable. What I wanted was not to admit that I just wanted to see her more often. Now she came into my stories every night: *she listened to him and answered with something that he had not dared to hope for, and they sank down onto sheets, as if into water — he seemed to be rummaging with his fingers in the darkness, and now when it was time for him to sleep, and then be left without parents and then to disappear off the face of the earth, he thought that he wanted not just her, but a total, devouring, self-erasing intimacy with her — he hadn't wanted anything like this for a long time.*

Why did this secretary, this girl, move me like this — me, a man with gray hair? Do I really want her to be attainable?

What was I going to do next? I decide just to watch from a safe distance. Notice that she didn't wear skirts often. And didn't wear skirts above the knee. I couldn't imagine her underwear, or her small and probably modest, pathetic breasts, and what was between her legs, it seemed unimportant — the greatest thing I wanted was to walk with her among the oaks, hearing the voice addressed to me, to take her by the hand to help her across something... let it be autumn there, puddles, rotten leaves, and once to hug her, brush my lips against her skin as she stepped closer. And not to get hurt.

Chukharev was screaming into the phone: He left the letter to Kirpichnikov in a post box! But last night, just as he, Chukharev, lay back in a dentist's chair and Dr. Karnaukhova all but draped herself over him, Kirpichnikov called! He lived in Germany. He was leaving for Germany the day after tomorrow, but when Chukharev asked if they could meet, Alexander Feliksovich replied, sure, any time, starting from this minute! Could he, Chukharev wanted to know, go to the meeting?

Of course! And further: Kirpichnikov had been doing some research himself, and he was willing to show us his materials, and maybe even to sell them.

I put several photographs of Nina Umanskaya in a folder, and found a blank sheet of paper. While I was writing, Alyona stood behind me. Now she'd hug me. As if this were our shared happiness.

"I, Boris Antonovich MIRGORODSKY, having received authorization from Alexander Feliksovich KIRPICHNIKOV to familiarize myself with the materials of case r-788 in the archive of the Federal Security Bureau of the Russian Federation, undertake not to mention members of the family of Alexander Feliksovich KIRPICHNIKOV in the exhibition prepared by the museum of school #175 without his consent, and further, not to make public any facts in the biography of the KIRPICHNIKOV family under any circumstances." Now we just had to make sure to include Kirpichnikov's passport number in the authorization.

"Is that it now? Kirpichnikov will sign the authorization. On the third of June you'll go to the Great Stone Bridge. You'll find out who shot Nina… And it will all end," Alyona did not seem as if she were about to cry. "Are you going to let her go right away?"

"You think I only need one thing."

"No, I'm starting to think that you don't even need that." She was silent for a bit. "Aren't you afraid of being alone?" And silence again. "What are you afraid of?" She didn't even hope that I would reply. "Kirpichnikov is the last person who could give you the authorization. I simply can't fathom what you would have done if you hadn't identified him."

What would I have done? I would have gone at it from another side. The person who shot Nina Umanskaya refused to settle for what was measured out, allocated, with what was appropriate. The Emperor sensed the greed that split the imperial armor from the inside, spilling out the corpses of seventh-graders on the bridge, the wolf cubs — the greed was the *rust* of his iron falcon tribe. They crested the summit — the war — and ahead, on the far side of victory, they saw their sunset: after a sea of gruel poured by nurses into their dentured mouths and the pointless battle with bedsores they would go into the Kremlin wall, or into the ground under the walls of the Novodevichy cemetery, beyond the tarnished iron gates, like a conveyor belt, riding in wooden coffins amid the red foam of cushions with the golden droplets of their medals, without any rites for the dead. The key machinery of the iron people seemed to wind down; they, still young, felt the stirrings of their mother's songs, grains of the petty bourgeois black earth swelled under their fingernails, their blood filled with the now foreign whisper of their ancestors, their feet got tangled in the roots of their lost kin, and there was nothing anyone could do about it. There would come a moment — unannounced, little-noticed — when they would want to live *common* lives, the lives of the weak. It wasn't Nina Umanskaya's bullet-ridden head, the death of the girl who wore American stockings, that bothered the Emperor. No — it was the number of those who needed him to respond to it. Everyone.

CURLY FORELOCK

THE TIME "AFTER THE WAR" BEGAN. IT SUDDENLY SEEMED TO THE Empire that it had conquered something greater than what it actually obtained. Both the iron men and the masses were possessed with desires; the Emperor contemplated distributing bread for free. In Ogaryovo, at the former estate of the Governor General, Grand Duke Sergei Alexandrovich, the elites gathered on summer evenings in the manor house: secretaries of the Moscow committee of the Communist party, the secretaries of the All-Union Central Council of Trade Unions, the boyars and sextons of the Moscow region and city Councils. They played dominoes and volleyball, and some attempted to follow the example of the first secretary of the Moscow city Council Shcherbakov by mastering lawn tennis. There were family-style meals at a common table, and Sofia Shakhurin, who had stopped by Ogaryovo on the way from her dacha (still a year to go before the victory), was moved to exclaim in the middle of the social gathering: How can this be, victory is near, and we still live so poorly! So uncomfortably. It's time to think about the conveniences that would measure up to our standards. To build mansions, you know.

The truth of these words was all the more urgent for their having been pronounced by the woman who was famous for her profiteering schemes, wherein she traded food from the reserves of the People's Commissariat for Aviation Industries for fine china of which she was a passionate collector.

Shakhurin, according to one biased person, was told to be quiet:

so many people in Moscow still lived in squalor! But everyone was astounded a how cheerfully *alarming* this furious, repressed desire sounded in the summer air, how it grew stronger once voiced; after she had dared to say it, the others felt like they, too, could speak of it. Obviously, Madam Minister, as Sofia Mironovna was addressed by Westerners, was not alone: the Emperor's own daughter dreamed about oak doors with gold handles and a noiselessly efficient staff: "People want happiness, egotistical happiness. They want life to become European, finally, for Russia too." People's visions of the future had nothing to do with the Plan, or Communism; it appeared that the earthly paradise had not come about so it was time to divide into new teams and rethink the game.

Aleksei Shakhurin — a simple soul! — mobilized the best carpenters and cabinet-makers from the People's Commissariat to work in his new apartment. The Shakhurins made no pretense at humility: there was a winter garden, a pool, a cavernous massage room, two levels, adorned with custom-cast bronze busts. All of Moscow knew of Shakhurin's apartment, and the Emperor muttered: "Shakhurin lives large. Shakhurin lives badly." The People's Commissar read about himself in the newspaper and held receptions: Commissars, marshals, secretaries of the Moscow city committee, artists, the bass of the Bolshoi Theater Mark Reizen and his wife. A relaxed, comfortable atmosphere, jokes, a grand piano.

Not long after, the grand apartment was divided up: the aircraft designer Lavochkin and his family moved into one half, and the other became part of a government hotel.

Sometime in November, the Emperor invited Shakhurin to his dacha in the Akhun Mountains to celebrate Mikhail Kalinin's 70th birthday. The People's Commissar was received hospitably by the Emperor, who even ordered Poskrebyshev to accompany Shakhurin to the train station. The Emperor was considered a sadist because he would smile at people he was about to destroy, and talk to them about future work. He was gentle in the last hours with people he no longer needed — many were given hope right before they died. But who knows what the Emperor felt: Did he enjoy the gullibility of his rats? Or did he separate himself personally — a man of flesh and bone, a man with pockmarks — from the terrible, great service of the Russian land to immortality, service clothed for the time being in the common cause of the Communist party and the Soviet people?

The train (Poskrebyshev, one of the thousands of the Emperors' eyes, would have waved his hand or his cap as it departed) took the carefree Shakhurins north, back to Moscow, and Poskrebyshev, returning to the Emperor, reported a detail he had noticed — a personal car returned with the Shakhurins to Moscow, on an extra platform attached to the train. Aleksei Ivanovich, who always sought the greatest comforts, came on holiday with his own trophy car. Shakhurin would have years ahead of him to remember the escort to Sochi, and this wretched car.

On the far side of everything that happened afterward, in old age, Shakhurin ran into Molotov on a winter road between dachas — Molotov was creeping along with the measured stubbornness of a clock's hand, tapping the ice with his cane.

"You ask me what I went to jail for," Shakhurin mumbled having just been asked this idiotic question again by a small-time bureaucrat, someone else's descendant, who had no notion of being burned by the flame of the great. "Ask him." He pointed to Molotov who was just drawing abreast, his joints creaking. "He put me there."

"You should be grateful you didn't get more," Molotov advised without any silly greeting or introduction, as if no time had passed between then and now, as if nothing had ended. Then he crawled off, while Shakhurin with his tearful sincerity embarked on a long reflection on the great state mind and unique natural abilities of the Emperor.

What did he go to prison for? The People's Commissar for Weaponry, Boris Vannikov, believed that Shakhurin changed the design of aircraft-mounted guns for thin-walled shells without the government's permission. Others talked about leaking fuel tanks. Of poor ingredients: during the battle of Kursk plywood panels kept getting torn off the Yaks — glue, the chemists sent an inferior glue that dried out in the sun. Others have written about fuselage stringers, which were unilaterally added or removed; they've written about the Union falling behind in jet propulsion technology. The surrounded and doomed Germans were flying planes with early jet engines in 1943, it wouldn't do to inform the world about any backwardness.

The Emperor let slip once: "Combat pilots from the front helped us in unmasking this case." Most likely, it was Viktor Abakumov, the head of SMERSH in the Commissariat of Defense, who was first to hear from these "combat pilots from the front": the planes were low-quality, pilots were dying, and the information on the causes of accidents was distorted, the People's Commissar for Aviation Industries and the marshals were hiding the truth, all they wanted was money and medals. And apartments.

The Emperor heard Abakumov's report (at the interrogations later, Abakumov wheezed: It's nothing to do with me! The Emperor *ordered* it!) and nodded: yes, it's time we dealt with these people, but we must, in short, observe, certain things… Vasya Stalin threw himself into the task of gathering signatures (seventy-five) for a beautiful, fatal letter, trying to get as many Heroes as possible. It quickly turned out that the airmen did not like Shakhurin.

That's what could be intuited at the intersection of what had happened and what was still being imagined: even as the Emperor was pampering Shakhurin at his dacha table in the Akhun mountains, Aleksei Ivanovich no longer existed.

The Emperor rested and returned, the war ended, and he seemed to grow more aloof, there were fewer conferences, reports, meetings. The calendar shows Shakhurin was received on December 18, and on the 27th he visited the Emperor for the last time in his life. The meeting lasted one hour and forty minutes; it had been at least six months (perhaps Aleksei Ivanovich noticed it on that day), since he stopped receiving private appointments with the Emperor. The one hour and forty minutes ticked away, and Shakhurin was let go forever.

Four days passed, and on December 31, as the Shakhurins were greeting their New Year guests, Merkulov brought the Emperor a sheet of paper: having received a signal through the appropriate channels, we have investigated what was going on at the People's Commissariat for Aviation Industries with trophy transport. Madness, in short, like everywhere else. First, there was a list of 41 people who were to receive foreign cars. Then they cut the list down to twenty-one names. At that point, there was no work, only talk about who was going to get what. In the end, Tupolev received a Mercedes, Ilyushin, Lavochkin, Myasishchev and Sadler (the deputy supply head) each got a BMW, Yakolev, by the way, got a modest Hudson, and so did Shakurin's deputy, and Dementiev got a Wanderer. Now about Shakhurin himself. He was assigned a five-seat Buick and a LaSalle (manufactured in 1940, delivered from the USA), a seven-seat Horch, an open-roof Auburn roadster, an Opel (registered to his wife, Sofia Mironovna), a Mercedes Benz and a Buick (which is being repaired at present), a Willis (to go hunting) and an M-72 motorcycle (according to our information, parked in Gorki-10, at the dacha). Signature: People's Commissar of State Security V. Merkulov. In the first days of January Shakhurin received a shocking call asking him to stop by the Party Control Committee, an organization that at his rank had no relevance, did not exist. No, they said, we're not asking you to join in a meeting, just come see such-and-such — the name was unfamiliar and also meant nothing. The People's Commissar hinted, by way of warning the caller: I'm busy, I'm preparing to report to the Emperor, perhaps one of my deputies can attend? We're expecting you in an hour, they said, and an hour later, in a small office, a petty, badly-dressed louse, who had never seen a People's Commissar in the flesh before, announced to Shakhurin that the case of the personal immodesty of Comrade Shakhurin had been referred to the Committee for consideration, and specifically what could Comrade Shakhurin tell the Committee about the eight automobiles of foreign manufacture that are registered in his name, no, go on (the louse said "Go on" to *him*), in writing and in my presence… The Commissar was being spoken to as if he could not get up, curse them out and leave, as if they would now be giving permission to *him!* Aleksei Ivanovich, the Emperor's favorite (only a week ago they had last shaken hands), attempted to restrain himself, told himself to go along with this, sat and wrote things on a piece of paper, things that were poorly judged but now appeared in his own hand. He almost laughed at the gall of it all, already wondering who would stop and punish this insolence, who should be called about this unheard-of nonsense.

On the same day a document appeared in the Secret Archives: "Top secret. Shakhurin A. I. Party card number 0473630, active in the Party since 1925. Document 473, #1 of January 7, 1946. Comrade Shakhurin had 8 personal automobiles for his own use. This act shows a lack of Bolshevik modesty in personal behavior. Ruling: 1) He is to receive a formal reprimand, to be recorded in his personnel file; 2) 6 of the cars in Shakhurin's personal use to be sent to the reserve fund of the USSR Council of Ministers, leaving him two for his personal use." Sent: to the People's Commissariat, Bulganin, Khrushchev, Merkulov, Poskrebyshev. After signing the document, the Chairman of the Party Control Committee Shkiryatov (who put the fear of God into many who learned that if he addressed a person as "dear," things were bad indeed) penned a four-line explanation to Comrade I.V. Stalin: "Comrade Shakhurin sees nothing illegal or wrong in his actions. It appears that he has forgotten the old Russian bit of folk wisdom 'Know the edge, so you don't push over it' — it is especially apropos in his circumstances." Shkiryatov knew what was expected from him — Shakhurin was dismissed on the same day.

Aleksei Shakhurin's life ended at the age of 40. Everything remaining was only made tolerable with vodka. He is remembered as a man who enjoyed singing and had a beautiful voice. He especially liked the song Curly Forelock.

One night in April Colonel Gordeyev came to the Shakhurins' apartment on Granovsky street, with his arrest squad. Gordeyev's job was to arrest the Emperor's former favorites.

Sofia Mironovna was in a hospital at the time. Soon after her husband was arrested, she seemed to forget about her weak heart and other maladies, asked her friend Henrietta, who was a tailor at the

Ministers' Council, to teach her to make bras, and quickly developed a circle of devoted clients.

In May, the Military board of the Supreme Court delivered a verdict on the charges of "knowingly sending defective air-planes to the Armed Forces, which led to a large number of accidents and deaths of pilots." The seven accused received decreasing sentences — seven, five, four, three, and two years, a fact some observers found amusing. Shakhurin got seven years with confiscation of personal property in the equivalent of 520,031 rubles that was to cover the damage his actions had caused.

THE GRANTOR

IN PRISON, SHAKHURIN SR. SURVIVED SEVERAL HEART ATTACKS; HE complained of a bad heart, and poor circulation in his feet. To keep from going mad, he copied out poems and talked to a spoon. His cell mate, a technician at a documentary film studio (this was how Ilyin introduced himself, the head of the third section of the secret political department, who had been in prison since '43 because of mutual jealousy between the NKVD and SMERSH, and lived for a long time afterwards until he was hit by a car) did not like Shakhurin: Shakhurin had food delivered from a restaurant but "didn't share the grub," and cursed his accomplices.

What went through Shakhurin's mind during this time remains unknown, and he only wrote: "Only my faith in the Party saved me. The faith in the Party, my own innocence before it, and the fact that in the middle of torture and humiliation I did not, for a single hour in these difficult years, feel myself to be outside the party — this is what saved me."

When he came out of prison (something mysterious happened to the souls of these iron people in prison — many of them resurfaced as strong and handsome men, at the height of their 40s and 50s, but completely incapable of action), the first thing he did, in the sanatorium, was write a petition to be restored to the Party membership. To his brothers he said (repeating word for word Marshal Rokossovsky, my grandmother and several million other people): "We will *never* return to this question again."

And he took to drink (of the iron people, those who went in to the Emperor every day by one door and could every day leave through another, many drank). He was taken in by the People's Commissar Dementiev as a third-tier deputy. Colleagues greeted Shakhurin with applause when he came to meetings, and at his own 50th birthday he made such a self-congratulatory speech that Dementiev got up and walked out, after which the celebration died down of its own accord. Shakhurin thought up his own action plan at the ministry — and was reassigned to the lowly Committee of External Economic relations at first opportunity. Two years later, he was asked to retire, and found himself, at the age of fifty-four, only asked to carry out an occasional task for the Soviet committee of war veterans, the USSR-USA friendship society (he was remembered as always willing to help out and forever excluded from the lists of those authorized to travel abroad) and the party organization of the Manometer factory as well as being photographed with cosmonauts on holiday in Bulgaria — with Sofia Mironovna at his side, grown even stouter, in an open swimsuit, a little taller than her husband, an arm flexed in a weightlifter's embrace.

They went into a hospital at the same time, to rooms on different floors. Sofia Mironovna was diagnosed with intestinal cancer, and her husband's heart condition had worsened. One evening he visited his dear Sonya, who was recovering after surgery, and went back up to his floor. He called his niece, asked her to call back in the morning. The next morning, he didn't answer the call. Several hours later, a woman picked up and told the niece to come collect his body.

The date was July 3, 1975. Sophia Mironovna calmly considered several proposed designs for the family grave marker and chose a set of polished tall stones, under which they would finally come together, all three of them. She had a very sensible attitude towards life, without undue anxieties. Not a single person could recall ever seeing her cry.

She said, "I won't die until I finish his book," and went to the desk covered with photographs, notes, and bookmarked volumes of documents to finish *Wings of Victory* for her husband. She understood that the book was his best chance to overcome death.

Volodya Shakhurin was never mentioned in connection with his father's case which became known as "the aviators' case."

April. Heavenly colors the names for which have not been invented yet by the human race graced the tips of tree branches, and girls found that portions of their bodies could be revealed to the world — pale strips of bellies and knees, patches of chests.

Borya fought with his fake beard: the beard stuck out ferociously around his ears and seemed to extend to the back of his neck where it sank into the collar of a gray tweed sport coat. Under the studious coat, he wore a colorful home-knit thing, meant to imply a mother's care for her weak-lunged and nerdy offspring. He had a tiny illegible pin on his lapel and spoke in a high-pitched priestly voice with an occasional pious bleat.

Armed with two bottles of vodka in a bag from Seventh Continent supermarket, the two of us headed to number 9, Maria Ulyanova Street, second floor, and rang the doorbell to Kirpichnikov's apartment.

"Ahh," he said when he answered the door. Fat arms, glasses, a face bearing a faint resemblance to Isaac Babel's — "Don't take your shoes off, I live in Germany, people don't take their shoes off there. A friend of mine was staying here, he says someone rang the doorbell, he didn't open the door — was it you who came?" He was lying, there was no friend. It was him at the eye-hole, looking at Chukharev.

"This apartment is quite, uh, historical — before Alexander Galich's departure I had the honor of hosting his last concerts in this apartment. In fact, I had the privilege of organizing those concerts."

There was something familiar about him. I heard bottles clink together in Borya's bag. Why was he not asking us who we were?

"Shall we go to the kitchen?" A round table, a box of Stratosphere chocolates, cognac, an Easter *kulich* bread. "You know, I've no interest in the dirt in the case of Volodya and Nina." He turned to pour coffee into cups and instructed us, over his shoulder: "So, do tell!"

I opened my mouth and saw that Borya was grinning. Before I could get a word out, though, Kirpichnikov went on: "Umansky belonged to the fourth echelon of power; he didn't even have a personal vehicle. Yes, it's a unique story: the children were arrested, but the parents weren't touched. My grandfather worked on the third floor at Lubyanka, and his son was in prison on the fifth... Here, have some sugar. My grandfather was a handsome, prominent man. He had a beautiful voice — Levitan, the radio announcer, would say to him, quit your nonsense, come work for the radio! He reported to Beria three times a day."

I kept pushing the authorization paper toward him, but he didn't see it.

"My father died in Germany. Three years ago this May. Of cancer. Over two months. It metastasized to the brain. He didn't feel pain. In February I couldn't keep up with him on the skating rink, and in May he was dead. He never told me anything. I asked him once, Dad, how come you know so many poems? And he said, I learned them in prison. I found the indictment of the schoolchildren among my father's papers when I was fifteen. Father, once he climbed into his shell after the shock of being imprisoned, never came out. Oh yes... the charisma of power can affect people in a certain way. No, I don't believe it was a murder for love. Neither Shakhurin nor Mikoyan would have fallen in love with a bow-legged girl. And Vano was the sort of boy who had to fight girls away from his doorstep. But who can really know what's going on in the mind of a fourteen-year-old? I certainly can't! It's easier for me to understand Stalin. Do you know how Stalin reasons in my story? 'Great sacrifices are justified. And if they are not justified, that means they are not great sacrifices.' And suddenly!" Kirpichnikov shouted this last word; Borya hid his chuckling face in his cupped palms, "It was as if I had woken up: I wrote thirty pages about the story of the arrested boys. Initially it came out as a romantic story. Then a psychological thriller. Then I wrote a third version, and I knew it was the right one! I spent two months editing; I slept less than two hours a day. I just nailed it! I'm sorry, am I boring you?"

We shrugged, and he went on:

"I know this will be a bestseller in Russia, three hundred thousand copies, easy... I reached incredible psychological insight in my dialogue, and overcame what I hate most — logical gaps and lack of authenticity. Stalin! For him, people simply did not exist. He's the one who destroyed everybody. I would read you the manuscript, since you're so interested, but I have to get to the airport."

Kirpichnikov smiled at me in the new silence. He frowned. Then he smiled. Then wondered out loud:

"Do you think three hundred thousand copies will be enough?"

Borya took a deep breathed and groaned a little. He put the vodka on the table, close to the letter of authorization, and made gestures at me to communicate his urge to leave.

"Alexander Feliksovich," I said as Kirpichnikov got up to see us out. "We would like a letter of authorization from you. For the sake of your father. We need access to the archives for our research, you understand, for the authenticity of information. Of course, we won't publicize anything without your permission." I must have sounded miserable.

Kirpichnikov listened dismissively: No, he could not sign anything without his mother's agreement, and his mother was in Germany, he would talk to her, he didn't want any dirt, he was primarily interested in psychology, *the truth of life*, a depth of artistic image, the insight. A master like him had no need of documents; a fleeting impression was enough to get to the heart of the matter instantly!

"Alexander Feliksovich," I was soft as the poplar fluff, I was unobtrusive and gentle, "We have certain information — the serial number of the murder weapon, the records of the interrogations about the Fourth Empire — that would lend a certain charm to your amazing, incredible book." Kirpichnikov froze, as if he had heard a secret code word. "Your *amazingly incredible* book. We can easily get authorization from another member of the Fourth Empire group — we have found everyone, we have addresses, and imagine what may be revealed. Anything at all! They were children! They blamed each other at the interrogations, they protected themselves, and what if this is made public? And if *you* sign the letter of authorization, then you will personally decide what to make public, and what not to. You will determine how your father is remembered."

Kirpichnikov considered, ran some mental math: no. No, we should wait until the book came out, he was already sending the manuscript to publishers. But he would certainly give us free copies of the book, we shouldn't worry about that. We would be among the first.

We left. Outside the door, Borya leaned on the staircase railing in exhaustion.

"Your face," he groaned, stifling another fit of laughter. "I thought you were going to strangle him right there." He blew his nose and added in his normal voice: "I hate writers."

At the office Borya gave me a salami sandwich.

"I get fed at home."

"At last!" Borya clapped and turned to Goltsman. "Alexander Naumovich, I've just been waiting for him to start boasting. How he gets fed at home! How neatly his bed is made! Do you think he'll tell us about his new mother-in-law, too?"

Goltsman was dressed in his best suit (someone's birthday? A reunion?) and in contrast with the dark fabric his hair seemed especially white, bone-like. I noticed for the first time how thin it had become; one could glimpse his scalp, pink raspberry-spotted. Goltsman, his face to the window, shifted in his favorite chair. I wasn't sure he heard me when I told him we couldn't get Kirpichnikov to sign the letter.

"Alexander Naumovich!"

He gave a start and blinked, his eyes teary: yes?

"I think we should go to Mexico," I said. "We may not get very far there, since people don't speak Russian, and probably have their own stories to hide, but with your experience... It would be helpful if you went."

Goltsman shrugged, non-committal.

I left, and went back to my own office. The secretary came in to straighten up the chairs and collect the glasses.

"Do you ever wonder how they might feel?" She asked, without warning, and gave me an uncomfortably penetrating look. I could tell my answer was important to her. "To have someone else, from a much later time, investigating their lives? Collecting the bones? Inventing what he can't prove? And feeling no sympathy?"

How would I feel if someone studied my life? What was so special in my life? It might as well not have been. I couldn't think of anything to reply.

"Also, I wanted to remind you: Alexander Naumovich went to see the doctor," the Secretary said. "Please talk to him when you have a chance."

I stopped by Goltsman's office again later, at night, and found him in the cool semi-darkness, freed of his tie and suit-coat, reclining on the couch. He was leafing through folders labeled Mexico; it was clear he hadn't expected me to come back, but he smiled gratefully:

"You shouldn't have… Everything seems to be all right. I had to have a colonoscopy. The procedure is painful. The doctor said there's nothing there. 'I don't see anything wrong here,' he said." Goltsman smiled with satisfaction. "I must say, I felt much better. I didn't want to say anything, but you know, when everyone is asking, When did you start losing weight? When did you first feel weak? When this? When that?" Goltsman sat up straight, as if to prove a point. "I am not feeling weaker. The physician frightened me. There was low hemoglobin in my tests. He said it looked like a liver disorder."

"But now you know there's nothing to worry about, right?"

"Yes. I eat pomegranates for hemoglobin — Masha brought them. I'll buy iron supplements. But the doctor advised me to go to the district clinic and get a more thorough examination."

THE FATHER

THE PLANE CARRYING THE NEW IMPERIAL AMBASSADOR LANDED in Mexico City on the 17th of June. Umansky, after slaving away for two years as a board-member of the People's Commissariat for Foreign Affairs in charge of censorship, was reinstated by the Emperor as an iron man, impervious to fire. He had left behind the woman he loved. He cremated his daughter, murdered by a perpetrator who was unknown at the time and has remained so to this day, and rushed from the crematorium to the airport, saving the remains of the future.

A witness who knew Kostya superficially told us: "A *different* person came out of the plane." In the photo it is easy to recognize Umansky — he had put on weight, had a short neck, and was wearing a fine coat; he stood above the sea of navy caps, and observed the fussing people who were there to welcome him with disdainful curiosity, looking away from the newsreel camera and ladies with complicated hair. Next to him was a woman with a crooked nose wearing a hat with black ribbons — Raisa Mikhailovna?

"In six months I'll speak Spanish," he promised, introducing himself to the President. In October he made his first speech on the occasion of presenting the score of R's 7th Symphony to the local conductor. "The Seventh," he said, "is a message from the fields of battle, full of faith in humanity and its great future." Umansky was sent by the Empire, and now he would squeeze water out of stones.

Three years before the flowers and the welcome at the airport in Mexico City, the Emperor gazed somewhere far into the future and suddenly ordered: Bring me everything we have on Latin America. Especially Mexico. They brought what they could: diplomatic relations were broken off in 1930, Trotsky was killed by a man who refused to give his name, they hated the Empire; population, area, political parties, major industries — numbers on the page, the Americans' underbelly — but it was enough for him. The Emperor never took his eyes off *that* continent, as if he had decided: *we're going there*. And Mexico (referred to as "the Country" in the reports), *suited* the Russians surprisingly well, and no matter how many times the Emperor ordered his people to forget about the world revolution, every Muscovite (Chicherin, Pestovsky or the apostle of free love Kollontai) who found themselves in Mexico sent back intoxicated cables: the Russia of the American continent! These are the people to take the lead in the battle against imperialism! This is where we can set fire to the USA, here's a revolutionary situation, everything is white-hot: the Catholics, the military, the nationalists, the refugees from Spain (our own trustworthy people), Polish emigrants, hunger, poverty, a handful of rich people... Mexico ships strategic raw materials to the States, and its proletarian masses are becoming engaged. Let's nationalize the oil companies; Lieutenant Rojas has already attempted to shoot the President; one and a half million vote for the fascists, but there's a whole kennel of lefties… What are we waiting for? In nine months Kostya was the most popular diplomat in Mexico; three months later, the Americans were convinced the Mexican President was entirely carrying out the orders of the charming Konstantin Alexandrovich, received during horse rides together — the symphony made itself heard.

The United States had just begun to recognize itself as the co-owner of the Earth, but it already understood the Russians — a stubborn, impenetrable, harsh, devious, uncouth breed, a tribe of two-faced paupers, that was utterly utilitarian and yet drawn by revolutionary magnetism, that exported the red plague everywhere it went, canceled any agreements, laughed at the rules of the game and all known games generally. And it was one thing to suffer all this in Moscow or at a distance, over Uncle Joe's cold and unpleasantly pedantic telegrams, and quite another to watch the persistent encroachment of this foreign power right in one's back-yard, a breath away, in Mexico. The Americans already knew that no one in the empire did anything on their own; the ironmen were moved by the Supreme Force. Umansky had been chosen as the spear tip and there was no more death for him.

The wife of the Embassy's First Secretary Lev Tarasov, translated press clips to send back to Molotov — on cigarette paper, with a pencil and ballpoint pen alternately: "The most outstanding propagandist of the land of the Soviets has established himself in Condesa in Tacubaya, in the former house of the Perada family, the descendants of Spanish grandees, a large building with a magnificent park, with a large hall in the Spanish colonial style. Above the front stairs leading to the large salon, a quote from Stalin in gilded letters. Umansky, a former railway worker, is now an aristocratic, an impeccably dressed man with an acute sense of protocol and manners. There is also a small cinema at the Embassy (its walls were painted with scenes of Russian folk life) where they screen Soviet films for important guests.

The guests are entertained by famous violinists; the local *prima donna* Miliza Korjus sings selections from Mozart, and in conclusion there is a film about the victories of the Red Army, or a lecture by the master of the house." Time magazine, after begging without success for an exclusive interview, was left to note the Ambassador's sociability that was somehow combined with a great skill at staying behind the scenes and "getting others to do his work for him." He was described as a "major political figure," and the "representative of the government of the USSR in the Western hemisphere." Words no one would dream of saying about Ambassador Gromyko — Kostya got everything he wanted, but also paid a great price.

Did he remember his daughter? Did he blame someone for her absurd death? Did he miss the woman he loved and had abandoned in Moscow? Guests noticed on the Ambassador's desk a small photograph of a girl next to the famous signed photo of the Emperor in a fake birch frame. Did he talk to the photographs, was that why he placed them next to each other?

In his long speeches, Konstantin Umansky often said, "There is not a single family left in Russia that did not lose one of their loved ones. I had a chance to experience this first hand in the months I spent close to the front." He did not like places where there was shooting and one might get killed; it is doubtful Umansky ever went to the front — he was speaking about something else entirely.

One woman told us, "You seem to think he was indifferent. But that's quite wrong. He worked heroically, but at night he wandered like a ghost around the Embassy. He couldn't sleep. After Nina's death he had no peace anywhere."

It seems that Umansky indeed did not sleep at night — *things were piling up*: couriers carrying nuclear secrets from the States back to Moscow; the first secretary Tarasov dispatching his army of illegal agents to pick apart the nuclear project — the Embassy in Washington was no longer used for important communications, after its cryptologist was picked up in a bar by the American police, piss drunk. Mexico would be the staging ground for the third world war;

it was from here that military groups would march into the U.S. under the guise of seasonal workers who settled in Latin America with the documents of Czechoslovakian emigrants. Mercader, Trotsky's assassin, waited for Kostya's actions — the Authorities wanted him out of the Lecumberri prison. Mercader's escape was planned for Christmas: he would lie low for a while at a safe house and then be whisked to Havana (his Cuban passport was lying in Umansky's safe) — but in the middle of December Mercader's mother descended on Mexico. Beria failed to keep the woman in the Empire; in Mexico she refused to meet with her fictional "daughter" (the intelligence officer assigned to be her liaison), pestered the resident agents (both the legal and the illegal ones), demanded to meet with the Minister of Defense and got admitted into Palacio de Lecumberri for a visit. The woman was mad, had been to an asylum at least once, was known as an anarchist, and eight years prior bought small arms in Mexico for the Spanish Republicans — the light finally went on: the Soviets are preparing a prison break. The Soviets want this man.

Sometime in January, people from the FBI told President Roosevelt, "Mexico is the focal point of the Russians." And on January 25, the plane carrying Konstantin Umansky, aged 43, exploded at takeoff on its way to Costa Rica, and ahead of the sickening condolences sent to Moscow, two Americans wrote the truth: "He gave tractors to Mexican peasants and now he is dead, and a long time will pass before a successor comes and gets up to speed on the entire spying web." This is what one gets for possessing too much zeal.

On the eve of his departure for Costa Rica, the Ambassador hosted a boisterous celebration of the liberation of Warsaw at the Sans Souci restaurant, toasted the free and prosperous future of Poland, and returned to the Embassy around midnight. There, he received welcome news: his main rival, the Ambassador of the Polish government-in-exile to Mexico, had just died of a heart attack in New York. Umansky sent a thank-you note to the Mexican President for letting him use a government plane (instead of flying with a commercial airline) and left for the Balbuena airport.

I finished reading about Umansky's career in Mexico, turned on my phone, deleted the text messages that clogged the screen, and called the office. I was lucky: the secretary picked up.

"Why are you at work so late?" She did not respond, so I asked, stupidly: "Are you alone?"

"I'm alone."

"How are things going?"

"Chukharev is calling the Xxxx family. Few people pick up the phone. Probably a lot of them are at their dachas." She was silent for a moment, then suddenly said: "Maybe you should look for people from your own past?"

"Do you want our operation to come to a screeching halt?"

"No. I don't know. Although when I am alone in the evening, I get scared among our folders. Especially when I look at photos. Let me finish now. Everyone remembers people they lost. Childhood friends. Just interesting passers-by. Fellow travelers. Attractive but far-away people — all of those with whom you think you might have fallen in love, had you not been too shy to come up to them and ask their name. I'm sure that even the happiest men don't forget these people who remain unknown. And when I found out that you can find dead people, I thought: you've also had these people who seemed to be something to you. But it didn't happen. With your abilities — …"

She thinks I have *abilities*.

"… — you can concentrate on yourself: you could live your life several times, to make sure you lose nothing, you give nothing away. You could leave nothing behind." She was speaking these words into the darkness around me, herself sitting somewhere in a dark room; she was calling me from the far side of the river, over the black water, trying to intuit things, to charm things into a semblance of order in her crooked, merciless life.

I said with conviction:

"Nothing like that has ever happened to me. I have no past."

Before falling asleep, though, I remembered a seventh-grade girl from the town of Odoeva whom I saw five times — twice on a train and three times in a camp on the Black Sea shore. She had dark straight hair. What happened to her? What year was it? Did I know her name? She wouldn't even have noticed me, a fifth-grader in a cap, or maybe she would have, and did, or I thought she did... And the girl from Tiraspol called Marina — I was embarrassed to ask her address, she said she lived on Lenin Street and her last name started with an S... I remembered thirty or so of them; I knew I could remember more of these people — the ones who didn't remember or notice me.

MEXICO

WE WERE GOING TO LEAVE FOR MEXICO EARLY, SO THERE wouldn't be so much traffic, but I didn't go to bed for a long time, trying to outlast Alyona: I told her I would work a bit more, I had to get ready. Whenever I heard her schizophrenic scuttling — bedroom-bathroom-toilet, would she ever go to sleep? — I'd turn off the feebly moaning erotica on the STS channel with the remote control, and re-read, frowning affectedly, the investigations of a Z. Sagalevich. Mr. Sagalevich maintained that Umansky was known as a friend of the great master of the Jewish stage Solomon Mikhoels. He did not live to see the nationwide Judeophobic campaign of '49. And still, Mr. Sagalevich wrote, "His tragic death in a plane crash was, as it is now becoming clear, not a coincidence, but was a planned operation carried out by the state security bodies of the USSR. Umansky took part in a rally at an enormous stadium held in honor of the Jewish Anti-Fascist Committee of the USSR. A simple solution was found: no person — no problem. Only those who knew him in Mexico truly mourned his death: the entire staff of the Soviet Embassy came together for a memorial ceremony, including Colonel Tarasov, the NKVD resident agent in Mexico who had to have been the one to carry out the mission."

A few more hours and what would we learn? It is terrifying to learn *everything*, and I knew Goltsman wasn't sleeping either in his apartment on University Avenue. How many of these shared days, early mornings would we have left? I shaved to pass the time, but

Alyona came after me as soon as I lay down — to empty me, to mark her territory, make sure I was hers. I felt like a dying fish, turning away from her arms.

I rose early, grabbed my toothbrush, and a few minutes later I was walking out of the elevator, into the yard, and, yawning mercilessly, across the street to the Sberbank branch where an army-marked UAZ flashed its lights at me. I walked through the night and felt it thinning, slipping away around me.

Borya, at the wheel, had already had a chance to get pissed off.

"Whose idea was it to get up so early? Was it you? It's a twenty-minute drive, and it's so dark you won't see your frigging float. You don't give a damn, and Borya has to get the car, Borya has to pick everyone up, and Borya doesn't get to sleep at all!"

He tossed my things over the back seat, past Goltsman who looked cowed.

"Where do I turn off Kashirka?"

"Take a left at the first traffic light, following signs to Molokovo, through the villages of Ostrov and Volodarskogo, to Misailovo," Goltsman read out of a notebook shining a flashlight onto the page.

"Follow the signs! There's no frigging signs there!" Borya drove angrily, cursing at every car he saw. I was cold and yawned.

We turned off the ring-road at the Kia dealership, went through a completely wooden village and followed a dirt road through a field. On the right, I saw a smattering of unfinished cottages in red brick; on the left stretched a thick forest. Our car rocked — the road dipped suddenly, zigzagged between the trees, and I saw water ahead, behind a wire fence. We were not the first: there were three cars and a motorcycle already in the parking lot. In the guard booth, two very sleepy camouflaged characters were filling out permits and issuing firewood to a pair of well-informed tourists in Chelsea hats; the tourists' wives — big hair, sweaters — were loading a portable grill into a boat. Goltsman took a footpath to the outhouse behind the smoke-shack; I waited for him and looked around. I could see shadows moving on the pontoon, from which they fed the fish; someone or something splashed in the water. A thin plume of smoke rose from the far shore, and I could hear people I couldn't see cast their spinning poles with a quiet whistling sound.

The tourists finally left. I asked about our reservation.

"Yes, cottage number six. Please pay. The boat will take you over."

In the boat, Borya, who had been commenting on every sight and sound, finally stopped talking as if he'd run out of battery life. Goltsman and I sat on the stern, facing the boat-man — an Asian-looking kid in a black raincoat. The kid rowed, frequently looking over his shoulder to make sure he didn't miss our dock — a pair of boards on small pylons. Where the lake grew narrower and more shallow and gigantic gray reeds rustled on the marshy shore, seeds swirled on the surface of the water and I wanted to drop my hand into the stream and spread my fingers to comb through them.

The boatman stopped rowing, let the boat drift for a bit, and grabbed at a pylon. He pulled the boat closer with his strong arm and looked at us expectantly: here you go. We climbed out.

In the cottage, Goltsman touched the radiator — there was no heat — touched, remembering this place, the log walls and the window, finally sat down on a coach and looked at me pathetically. He didn't want to change his clothes.

"Is it OK that the windows are plastic?" Borya fretted, following behind the guard on duty. The guard was also sleepy. He rolled up the mattress from the bed and opened the windows to air the place out. "I saw a TV show: even flies die of plastic," Borya added and sat down to change.

The guard stepped out to smoke. I could see him through the window: he splashed water at his face from the bucket on the porch, then took a piss under the fir-trees where we had picked mushrooms last year.

Quickly, I stripped to my underwear and dressed, choosing from the clothes piled on the floor, in navy britches with red trim, an undershirt, and a matching navy single-breasted mess jacket with the hammer and sickle insignia on the sleeve. I went to the mirror and put on the red-and-navy cap. Borya was right there with me; he put on a gray woolen overcoat on top of the uniform and walked back and forth across the room checking himself in the mirror.

"Could I please not change?" Goltsman pleaded.

"At least put on the overcoat and the cap. Or else they won't understand us."

"You wouldn't happen to have a paper with a crossword puzzle?" the guard came back and yawned threateningly. He walked to the elevator shaft concealed behind an old wardrobe, and pushed a button. The winches came to life with a whine, the ropes coiled. "Don't worry about your things," the guard said. "I'll be here, and I'll look up if I step out. How long are you going to be? Fourteen hundred? No problem."

I knew he would go back to sleep as soon as he sent us off.

I wanted to go outside, to look if it was light yet — but these clothes held me, the seams held me in, I could not, I was on duty. Goltsman placed the cap on his gray curls — he could have gotten a haircut, but didn't — and suddenly looked taller, stood up straighter and gave me an emptied, steely look. That's what he used to be like, then, an officer of State Security.

I shuddered when the prehistoric worn-out lid of the elevator cage appeared in the shaft. It rose, lined up, and came to a stop. We opened the grated door (I always remember the round black knob on it) and quickly, as if it were a race, piled in, into the small lit box. We shouldn't rush, I thought. We should think, make sure we remember who is who: Embassy staff, air-field crew...

"Let's go."

The wooden doors slipped shut and the guard, looking upward, as if waiting for an order from above, pushed the button. I squeezed my eyes shut as if we were about to drop, uncontrolled, into a long and terrifying fall through the void. The morning light flickered and vanished, and without delay we descended, held in a loose clump of trembling electric illumination, which was flickering evenly, measuring time or depth. Borya, as if remembering something forgotten, squirmed and, without looking at anyone, took out a TT pistol with corrugated wooden pieces on the handle from under his coat, and put it into his trouser pocket.

"Why did you bring that?" I grabbed Borya by the shoulder (the cage shook) and pushed him against the door: "You drunk animal! How many times have I told you! You'll trap all of us there!"

"Go to hell!" Borya pushed my arms away and adjusted his cap. "Uncle Borya knows what he's doing. Don't yell, you got it? I outrank you."

Outside the cage, red brick arches ended; strips of lighter and darker clay alternated as we slipped lower, and water occasionally splashed on the glass and trickled down — we were going to the bottom, and there was nothing more to talk about. I felt sick, my knees felt weak, as before an exam, and my stomach churned as if in anticipation of a fist-fight. The cage shook and stopped with a crack, a little lopsided, and I had time to think — we were stuck, I was sure — although I could already hear voices outside: Mexico. Borya, trying to be the first, to anticipate the unseen people, pushed the wooden shutters with his fists and let in the noise of locomotives releasing steam, their shrill whistles, and the hot, unfamiliar air. I focused on the foreign bluish asphalt under my feet, on the heels of Borya's shoes in front of me, and did not attempt to make sense of the voices speaking all around me.

We went out under the enormous membrane of the train station's dome and followed the rail lines out, to the dead-ends. Borya gloomily nodded to a bespectacled guy with a fine brown head of hair — a tall man in a warm ginger-colored jacket with patch pockets, his face ashen, as in a sepia photo, he leaned over to Borya, clutching a notebook and pen, as if asking a question. The platforms were full of people, the asphalt was barely visible under their feet; all warmly dressed in the heat, hats, coats, children being held, children running, mountains of suitcases and bundles. I stared at the old clothes, at the unfamiliar, non-existent, long-vanished faces with sunken cheeks, so as not to look at the children — only the children were shouting and babbling, and the remaining grown-ups looked at our coats and caps, making room for us with difficulty — they were already crowded, but they opened a patch of emptiness around us, retreating from each step we took. There were only locomotives on every line, parked at dead-ends without cars behind them; I didn't see pigeons, trash or grass in between the rails either — there was only asphalt and black dirt soaked with fuel oil. What were these people waiting for? We stuck to Borya's navy back. Borya listened to the guy in glasses, not taking his hand out of his pants pocket, and scanned with the crowd, the walls of humanity around us, with a displeased expression. Finally he decided to point to his ear for the man, meaning *can't hear*, we must get out of here, and the man nodded eagerly and put out his long arm pointing to the underpass. Borya, who really didn't want to let the elevator out of sight, moved cautiously down the stairs; we were followed by some civilians. All men, they looked into our faces anxiously, they nodded and made signs, as if they didn't speak Russian. I looked straight ahead and listened to the trains whistling and the steam hissing; we walked down a long corridor, to a grated door, and a small room on the other side, with a desk and a couple of stools and a portrait of an unfamiliar person on the wall. Now things were becoming clearer: the young man did speak Russian, I could catch individual words, they just refused to add up to a comprehensible whole.

Borya came to an abrupt stop and turned to the accompanying men:

"Right, comrades, our time is limited. Let's not waste it. Who is the senior in rank here?"

"Ambassador Kapustin. I replaced Comrade Umansky," a faceless man announced, coming forward.

"After you then," Borya pointed to the small room. "The others — please do not leave," he commanded and gave the bespectacled character a meaningful look. The young man was now silent, but watched Borya's every motion, admiring the way his overcoat draped over his shoulders and how neatly the cap fit on his head. Ambassador Kapustin readily sat down and rubbed his hands. We could hear the train whistles even here; they marked time, spurred us on. Borya sighed, walked behind the Ambassador and looked obediently at Goltsman: He would be the one to ask the questions. Borya positioned himself by the door, making sure that the rest did not leave and did not get close.

"Comrade Kapustin," Goltsman said in the grating voice of a pencil sharpener. He was in no hurry: we'll dig right through, we'll sift off the sand. "We are a field group of the NKVD State Security Directorate's fourth department." Kapustin nodded with deep gratitude and relief — perhaps he actually knew what the fourth department did.

Question: Comrade Umansky did not live to see our nations triumph over the Fascist scum, and was killed in the line of duty by our enemies. The Soviet government accepted the condolences expressed by the American government, but only in order to make our work here, Comrade Kapustin, easier. Were you shown the official results of the investigation at the defense ministry?

Answer: Yes, It appears the plane was cleared for takeoff at almost exactly 5:30 and blew up four minutes later, breaking into two parts. The pilot executed a textbook takeoff, two-thirds down the runway. The signal lights went off on the wings, which happens when the plane leaves the ground, and the pilot retracted the chassis. Experts estimate that the aircraft reached the speed of 75 knots and the altitude of eight to ten meters. The flight continued for about 25 seconds.

Question: What did an examination of the accident scene show?

Answer: The Defense Ministry's investigators found a piece of barbed wire wrapped around the fuselage. Several fence posts were also broken and knocked over. On the ground, inside the airfield fence, traces of the propeller blades were found — the plane plowed into the ground with one propeller for about seventy meters, and then for a little distance with the other. The investigators established that the plane's engines were running at full power. Traces continued again 160 meters beyond the fence, where the plane hit the ground again after apparently bouncing up, and stretched for 93 meters more. At that point, the aircraft caught fire and blew up there. When the plane hit the ground, the fuselage split into halves in the area of the cargo hold. The fuel tanks on the right wing blew up, the fuel leaked out and caught fire; flames engulfed the left wing, and the fuel tanks on the left wing exploded. The official conclusion was pilot error. Evidently the pilot decided to reduce the angle of takeoff to gain speed more swiftly, and lost his bearings in the darkness. The electric lighting at the airfield had not been working for around two years because of the repair works, but the runway was lined with lit kerosene beacons every 30 meters.

Question: Who examined the bodies?

Answer: The forensic experts of the Interior Affairs ministry. The remains were placed in large baskets and taken away. Raisa Mikhailovna Umanskaya's body was the most badly burnt. She was identified by the wedding ring on her finger. They also found a revolver in her purse.

Question: Did they perform autopsies?

Answer: Comrade Kasparov, the Charge d'Affaires, made an official announcement that the Soviet side did not wish to have the bodies autopsied. At the funeral, the deceased were in closed coffins.

Question: That's not good, Comrade Kapustin. How did that happen?

Answer: I arrived in Mexico when…

Question: Yes, we all know when you arrived and what you did. We will certainly talk about this. We want to question the employees of the Embassy who escorted the ambassador at the airport and saw the plane fall, and especially Mrs. Troinitskaya, who was on board.

Answer: There was also a crew member who survived — the flight engineer, junior lieutenant Morales. Captain Velazco Queron died…

Question: We have Ceron in our records…

Answer: A transliteration mistake, I'm sure. Also killed were Captain Martinez, junior lieutenant Guzman and the radio-operator sergeant Roman.

Question: Did the resident agency's staff question the Mexicans who were at the airport?

Answer: Yes. The testimonies are contradictory. Nothing is certain, everyone repeated rumors: The plane blew up because someone was smoking on board, or the passenger seats had been replaced just before take-off. Someone allegedly saw suspicious people getting into the plane and loading some boxes into the tail section. Supposedly the mechanic had said there were malfunctions, and the pilot turned off the main ignition system. Supposedly the aircraft itself was replaced by another plane at the last minute. We could not confirm a single one of these statements. The plane was provided specially for Comrade Umansky by the President of Mexico — a C-60-01 of American manufacture, new and in excellent condition. The payload was normal. This aircraft can take 18 parachutists with full equipment, and there were only nine passengers on board. Shortly beforehand, the plane had been tested on the ground and in the air by Captain Queron. He had considerable experience of night flights and flying blind, a total of 3,755 flying hours, and not a single reprimand. The date of the flight was kept top secret, no press, of course. For added security, two identical planes were prepared for flight. At night the plane was guarded by a reinforced army detail.

Question: How many people guarded the plane? Were they able to get inside the aircraft?

Answer: Eight soldiers of the eighth infantry battalion. They did not get close to the plane — there were two airport mechanics on board, guarding the plane in two-hour shifts.

Question: And yet Ambassador Umansky was killed! Our comrades were *burned* by Trotskyists! Don't waste my time on these platitudes about the excellent pilot, and a fine plane, and the vigilant guard. Who do we trust? How can a Bolshevik trust his enemies? We need facts! The burnt bodies of Communists — these are facts. The joy of our enemies is a fact, and so is your blindness," Goltsman droned. "We will make our own conclusions."

Answer: I want to add: Comrade Umansky insisted that the Costa Rican Ambassador to Mexico fly with him. But the man refused, giving various excuses, until Umansky really pressed him. I checked: his car really did arrive to the airfield at 4:30, but returned to the residence soon after. The Ambassador explained that he had been misled: apparently he was told that Umansky had already taken off."

Question: Comrade Kapustin, you said that the Umansky's plane took off immediately after another plane. What does "immediately" mean?

Answer: I don't know. It's what everyone says: immediately, in dangerous proximity… This happened because Umansky's flight was delayed for unknown reasons.

We were done with Kapustin. The man walked out on unbending legs and Borya had to steer him to the door with a few gentle shoves.

"Who accompanied Comrade Umansky to the airport?" I heard Borya ask of the people in the corridor. "Quick! Names and position."

They named the Embassy's secretary Kasparov, assistant to the military attaché Pavlov and the couriers Isachenko and Melnikov. I decided to try Melnikov.

Question: Comrade Melnikov, we read your report in Moscow, but we have a few follow-up questions. Please be succinct. On the day of the accident, you went to the airfield, correct?

Answer: We did.

Question: You were to escort the Ambassador to the plane.

Answer: We did.

Question: And what, for heaven's sake, can you tell us? What did you see?

Answer: It was very dark. I saw the plane taxi away into darkness.

Question:: There was another plane there, correct?

Answer: Yes, some other plane took off. We ordered a cup of coffee at the bar, right there, with windows looking out on to the runway. Before the barman could even pour it for us, the siren began to wail *in a special way*. I looked out — the window was large: there was a fire in the distance, but a large one… Everyone seemed to have the same thought at the same instant. We ran to the blaze. The barbed wire fence had been torn down, and the two iron posts were also torn out… The plane was in two pieces. The front section, where our people were, the Soviet delegation, was burning so fiercely that you couldn't go near it…. It took an hour to put out the fire. The bodies were barely recognizable. They had to identify them by the buttons."

("He's lying. He didn't run over there," Goltsman said quietly.)

Question: Comrade Kogan, how did Umansky behave before the flight?

Answer: He behaved quite normally, comrade major of state security. His wife, Raisa Mikhailovna, was very nervous.

Question: But what did she have to be afraid of? She'd flown over three oceans and wasn't scared, and here it was just 40 minutes to Costa Rica.

Answer: She said: Ah, Kostya, you're constantly dragging me along with you. We'll perish one day.

Question: And what was his reply?

Answer: Raechka, you and I have both lost the dearest thing to us. But now there's a war on, and millions of people have been killed, millions more will be killed. And we've already suffered our personal sorrow, and you ask what's going to happen to us?

Question: How did you remember that, comrade sergeant? It's quite a long passage.

Answer: I wrote it down on the same morning.

("He's lying. He didn't hear anything. *Raechka... Kostya... Our personal sorrow...* He made it up afterward," Goltsman whispered again.)

Question: Did he talk about his daughter, Nina?

Answer: I don't think so.

Question: Is the surname Petrova familiar to you? Anastasia Vladimirovna Petrova.

Answer: I don't recall it.

Question: Why was the flight delayed?

Answer: I didn't see it myself. But... The Mexican officers saw it... After everyone got on board, and the engines were started — you couldn't hear anything over the engines — a person got off of the plane, a man.

Question: From the Soviet delegation? Who exactly? Umansky himself?

Answer: It wasn't Umansky. They don't know who it was, they could only recognize Umansky. The man was wearing a black coat. He ran to the waiting hall. And he was away for a long time. Then he returned, also running. And the plane taxied to take off… That's what delayed it.

Question: Are you sure that the same man who left the plane returned to it?

Answer: I didn't see anything myself, Comrade Major.

Goltsman sighed. He was done with this question and answer business. "Off you go, Comrade," he said. "Do what you're supposed to."

"Comrade Major of State Security…"

"Speak."

"You didn't give the password."

"The password, Comrade Kogan," Goltsman said, unblinking as a toad, "was given to you by the Authorities for communicating in the course of carrying out your tasks and duties, and we are carrying out a special mission, the goals of which are vastly beyond your pay grade. Is that clear?" He paused. Then said to Borya, "Comrade Mirgorodsky, please prepare Ms. Troinitskaya and the Mexican from the crew who survived… What's his name?"

"The password," the diplomatic courier asked again in desperation.

"Junior lieutenant Morales," I shouted at Borya, jumped up and slapped the diplomatic courier on his cloth, doll-like. "You're free to go."

"The password!"

"Why isn't anyone coming?" I yelled at Borya and hit the courier in the temple; he fell off the chair, but immediately got up on all fours — silently, without shouting, as if he knew very well how these things went. I kicked him in the side, and again, hating myself for this, I kicked his compliant, fleshy ass. Goltsman, rifling through the drawers of the desk, threw out other people's junk.

"Are you looking for a rope, Alexander Naumovich?" Borya jumped up with a cheerful and dazed look. "Take the belt. Don't you watch action movies? Stop hitting him! Just stuff some socks into his mouth and let's go!"

"We can't! What about Troinitskaya?"

"The Mexicans and Comrade Troinitskaya are upstairs. They're scared to come down."

We almost ran up the stairs, to the train whistles, to the glassed-in stuffiness. I glanced over my shoulder once: two of the civilians in hats stayed by the door and pointed their fingers at the man I left behind, but did not go in, waiting for us to get away. On the platforms, there seemed to be more people, and it seemed darker, as if it was about to rain. I looked towards the elevator — would they let us get to it? Borya cupped his hands over his mouth, grew a head taller and yelled,

"Comrades! We're from Moscow!"

Then he caught the tall bespectacled man in the ginger coat — he was still following us with his notebook — in a drunken embrace and inquired: "And who are you, my friend?"

"The Embassy's interpreter, Pavel Lvovich Goncharov," the man stammered, almost dropping the notebook.

"Fine," Borya said, breaking into a wide smile. "Are there guards here from the eighth infantry battalion? The ones who guarded the plane? Don't fuss, Pasha, we don't need all of them, just grab whoever's closest!"

The interpreter dove into the crowd, and heads swarmed around him in a whirlpool; there was a vague buzzing, and he returned with a triumphant look:

"The plane was guarded directly by Jose Guidinos Herrera," he waved a page torn-out from his notebook. "The day after the accident he went AWOL and was subsequently deemed a deserter."

"Well done!" Borya praised him. "Smooth. Ask if Jose did his AWOLing alone."

"He did not. Two more guards left with him," the interpreter tried to stand at attention when he replied, and barely concealed a proud smile. "They deserted because of the onerousness of their watch duties."

"What about the mechanics who watched in the plane, are they here? Just one."

The interpreter led forward a shabby little guy. "What's his name?" Borya asked.

"His name is Alfonso Baca Hernandez. He's 22."

"Tell me then, Baca, mechanic," Borya for some reason turned around and winked to Goltsman. "Tell me how you and your friend kept watch. First you for two hours, and then him for two hours. Or was it some other way?"

The interpreter translated on the fly, obviously proud that he had intuited Borya's train of thought at once, and showed something on his palm to the mechanic — the mechanic shrugged his shoulders and said something inaudible.

"Both of them were asleep all night," the interpreter exclaimed. "He admits it."

"What would I do without out, Pashka," said Borya in surprise, and chuckled happily. "I'll have to mention you to Comrade Stalin in Moscow. And what about him, who's that enthusiast?" Borya mocked the swarthy boy, who stood with his raised hand in the front row, like at school.

"Ramon," the interpreter beamed. "The nephew of the second pilot Captain Martinez, who was killed. He wants to tell you what he saw."

"Tell us then, please," Borya suddenly squatted down, and the swarthy Ramon also squatted; the interpreter followed suit, and translated shaking his brown curls and drawing a squiggly line on the asphalt with his finger.

"He is a driver. He was at the airfield. Ramon saw the plane taking off. Close to the other plane. After it. The signal lights of the tail moved away. And then these lights started to drop gradually. They came way down, and then there was an explosion. An enormous flame burst into the air. Everyone went running. The people who came with the passengers, the airfield crews, and he ran too. When he reached the plane, it was all on fire, it was impossible to get close to it. And there was a very strong smell of burnt meat."

"What about the firemen?" Borya asked. "Didn't they call the ambulance, the Red Cross?"

"An ambulance with fire-extinguishers was called immediately, but it got stuck in the gravel in the ditches — there was repair work underway at the airfield. And the junior lieutenant Morales came along, and Mrs.," the interpreter checked his notebook, "Miriam L. Troinitskaya."

"Miriam L.," Borya bent over, sighing in exhaustion, as if something upset him, and called weakly, "Where are you, sister?"

A bony woman in a hat crookedly placed on her red hair shifted from one foot to the other in hesitation — the beaming interpreter gently nudged her closer. Junior lieutenant Morales, who looked like a drawing of an American Indian whose tongue had been cut out by the Conquistadors, nursed one arm in a cast. Troinitskaya (the interpreter mumbled something encouraging to her) put out her hand, protected by a shabby glove, and Borya grabbed it so hard that the woman gasped.

"Miriam L.," Borya hissed. "Who called you that, my dear girl? You're Marina Leonidovna or Maria Lvovna."

"I... I don't know," Troinitskaya tried to pull her hand back, but Borya wouldn't let go. "That's how it was written down."

Borya dropped her hand, wiped his palm on his coat, straightened up, ran his hands over his face, adjusted his cap, and everyone saw: the officer was crying. Borya sobbed out loud and squeezed words out in-between the paroxysms of emotion:

"Look what we got here, comrade major of state security! What can we report to the People's Commissar for Interior Affairs of the Soviet Union? A 15-year-old girl was killed on a bridge by unknown assailants. And maybe she was even pregnant." Borya cried throatily, swaying as if over a coffin. "And someone brings explosives onto the plane. The guards are paid off and sleep all night. Other guards run away altogether. A man in a black coat delays the flight. Someone tips off that Costa Rican bastard not to fly. Someone digs up roads so the ambulance can't get to the scene. And our comrades" — he lost his voice here and merely grimaced for a bit, shoulders shaking — "our comrades are *burning* alive." He raised his blinded, tear-filled face to the sky, reporting to someone up there. "And it smells strongly of burning meat. And no one speaks Russian!"

Borya sobbed, slowly moved his right hand holding the pistol to the side and with a brief glance, shot the interpreter in the head.

The Mexicans, howling with terror, scattered as if from an explosion. The emptied asphalt spread around us like a gray tumor, and I — where was I, what was I doing? Goltsman, his face full of patient suffering, held the silently squirming junior lieutenant Morales in his arms, and I focused on not letting Troinitskaya break free from my grasp — she stamped her heels on the asphalt, trying to crawl away; she lost her hat, her red hair waved in disarray, and I repeated, not hearing myself because of the howling and sirens:

"Don't be afraid. It will end soon. You'll be let go. Don't be scared."

I couldn't look at the interpreter's legs, which were still twitching, or at his hands pressed against the hole in his forehead as if he had suddenly remembered something, while blood spurted out of his mouth at regular intervals. Borya unbuttoned his coat, waved his pistol and bellowed:

"Now do you all understand Russian? We've punished the provocateur! The Trotskyist! The fascist bastards!"

With one jump he flew over to the cowering Morales and asked, "Who are you?" Borya gently stroked the man's hair. "Let's talk."

"Don't! *I didn't see anything!*"

"Don't howl! Speak to the point!"

"I was put with the second pilot, in the passenger compartment, in the back, for balance," Morales put out his shaking hand, fingers splayed, covering his face. "The second pilot was overweight. But I immediately felt a slight tilt forward, and then the left wing hit the fence posts and I saw sparks."

"I understand that," Borya grabbed him by his sore arm and pulled him down. Morales howled, and froze with his mouth gaping. "See, how it hurts?" Borya inquired, and gave me a jolly look. I got up and dragged Troinitskaya after me closer to them. "Who inspected the luggage?"

"The captain. He actually packed it. At dawn, when they tested the engines. When the plane hit the posts, the passengers shrieked in terror. The pilot instinctively pulled the lever towards himself, lifted the plane and hit the fence with the right wing this time. The plane rose up a little more, then tilted on to the right wing, as if doing a right turn, and then quickly slipped down. The passengers screamed again, the plane was plowing through the ground, scraping it with its right wing. The screams were heart-rending…"

"What did they scream?" Borya asked again as if he hadn't heard a part of the story.

"I don't know! *I'm not Russian!* My arm hurts. Please!"

"You tell me, woman," Borya turned to Troinitskaya.

"I heard a noise!"

"It was the propeller hitting the ground!" Morales interjected.

"Be quiet," Borya snapped.

"And a sudden slap. I said loudly: what's that? And no one had a chance to answer because there was an explosion right then! Everyone shouted at once. There was a terrible panic. The plane sort of just jammed into the ground, then lifted up again, and fell finally onto its right wing. I sat in the fragments, in the burning plane, alone… And I saw a man running away and shouted, *Help!* He didn't even turn his head."

"Is that right, Morales?" Borya feigned surprise. "The Mexican air force?" And he lightly hit the Mexican across his face with the pistol.

"No! Don't shoot! The woman is in shock! She doesn't remember! After the plane hit the ground the fuselage exploded, there were bodies all around, the floor tilted, and I crawled holding my broken arm, and I heard a woman screaming in pain. She was stuck between the seats — I couldn't help her — my arm was broken. I pushed her into the hole with my foot as best I could; she slipped through and fell down among the wreckage of the right wing. And evidently she lost consciousness. I only just managed to follow her, my left leg got stuck between the pipes, the wing was burning, my face, my left leg and arm were burnt, and broken, but with my right arm I dragged her out of the plane… I saved her! And then shooting started! The bullets from the crew's pistols started exploding, fifty or so 45-caliber bullets. And then the fuel tank exploded. And corpses went flying into the air."

"Corpses? But what if someone was still alive? And you didn't drag them out?"

"I didn't hear any other voices."

"Was the flight delayed? Did anyone come out of the plane after the boarding?"

"I didn't notice," Morales' knees and arms shook, his mouth gaped, he closed his eyes as if he were falling asleep, but he kept closer to Borya: he needed to, he knew that was the safest thing to do.

"What about you, Miriam L.?"

"When the m-mo-mo-mot… star…"

"Speak!"

"When the engines started… Raisa Mikhailovna Umanskaya shifted in her seat and started looking for something by her feet."

"Where was she sitting?"

"In the front. One doesn't get quite as sea-sick there."

"Where did she look? Maybe she just noticed something under the seat?"

"She kept repeating: Where it is? Where?"

"What did Umansky do?"

"Konstantin Alexandrovich helped her look."

"A small thing then, but something that belonged to Raisa Mikhailovna, correct?"

"The military attaché Vdovin started to help. They didn't find anything in the plane. Vdovin went out and ran to the parking lot, to ask the driver to look in the car. He was gone for a long time. When Raisa Mikhailovna saw Vdovin waving his hand from a long way away, meaning no, he didn't find whatever it was, she sat back down and said: we won't have a good trip today. And that's exactly what happened. Let me go! You're our people!"

"On your knees," Borya raised the pistol at Morales, moved his lips soundlessly and aimed, turning away a little and grimacing, as if he was aiming at the sun, or was afraid that he would be sprayed in a moment.

Goltsman took his cap off, and whispered:

"I don't feel very well. I'll go and lie down." Holding his side, Goltsman went to the far wall, to the elevator shaft.

"Sit down."

Morales closed his eyes, and blindly, warily, as if his skin was grazed, he sank to his knees and hung his head. Troinitskaya, feeling that her turn was coming, thrashed in my arms:

"My dears... Dears... Don't kill me!!"

She writhed wordlessly, trying to scratch my neck, and I pushed her arms away. She scratched my cheek to make it bleed, suddenly jerked away and fell on the asphalt — Borya fired a shot above her head.

"Borya!"

"Go away," he seemed to be thinking hard about something.

Troinitskaya cried without wiping her face, but kneeled down just like Morales, as if they had been taught to do so somewhere. I followed Goltsman — the old man was sitting in the opened and lit-up elevator, with his face thrown back in pain, but without unbuttoning his coat, so he wouldn't give anyone away. I covered the scratch on my neck with my hand which was dotted with blood — it would heal, everything would heal, only for Goltsman would it not. I walked toward him, and as always I tried to guess if there would be an odd or even number of steps to the elevator — if I were right I'd make a wish, but I couldn't think of anything to wish for. For everything to end well? But what did 'well' look like? Everything ends in the same way. Borya fired a shot, then another shot, and without looking around I ran and jumped into the shaking elevator. Borya shot again, and I turned to look: he was standing alone, Morales and Troinitskaya had already been carried away. Borya shot into the air, aiming at something only he could see there. He wanted to hit the sky, to break the glass that covered the train station, he wanted to let air in here and real light, to receive proof that the sky was *there*, for the shards to scatter and ring out. But the bullets hit nothing, the shots rang blank. The last shell flew out, Borya dropped the pistol without disappointment, kicked it away, spinning, like a puck, and came towards us, hunched over and with his hands sunk deeply into his pockets, as if he'd just sent his entire family away on vacation and had to stay behind alone: there was nowhere to hurry to, he was alone in his emptied life, he had to return to an empty apartment, where toys were scattered…

We squeezed tighter; Borya shut the elevator door neatly, pressed the button, and, elbowing us unceremoniously, threw off his cap, took off his coat, his mess jacket, stepped out of his shoes, wiggled out of the trousers and covered everything with the undershirt. When the doors opened back in cottage number six, Borya stepped out in his boxer shorts.

Borya walked straight past the guard, hit the door and walked across the grass straight to the dock. Without bending his back he pushed off and leaped into the water putting his arms in front of him at the last possible moment. The fishermen looked up together, surprised and angry. Borya surfaced twelve feet farther and swam to the other shore swinging his arms wide and strong. On that side, smoke was rising from the grills and people pulled bunches of gold-scaled carps out of the boats for the wardens to weigh.

THIRST

GOLTSMAN SIPPED SOMETHING OUT OF THE THERMOS MUG. Without taking his eyes off the surface of his drink, he said:

"It's obvious that Umansky's plane got caught in the stream of thinner air left behind the aircraft that took off before it. They flew too close together. A few seconds. If they hadn't been late for take-off… Is that enough for you?"

"We have to find out why the flight was delayed. What did Raisa Mikhailovna lose? What was this thing without which she wouldn't fly?"

Goltsman did not reply. Perhaps he wanted me to leave, wanted to sit by himself, but he had to work and to remember who his commanding officer was and who paid his salary.

"How do you feel?" I asked.

"Sorry about that back there… I think my blood pressure shot up. But I need to get checked up."

The Emperor had to swallow the Umansky's coffins like bitter pills, a few more among many. He could only offer eternal memory in response to Death, but at least he, better than anyone else, knew what could be done with this memory. An American military plane brought the urns with the ashes to Moscow on February nineteen; the obituary ran in *Pravda*, signed by Molotov, Litvinov and Gromyko.

Umansky died, and the spring that he had coiled too tightly flew away: the very next day unidentified persons searched the apartment of the Embassy's administrative officer Peter Kirmasov, and three days later the first secretary Grebsky found his own door forced open. Thugs regularly ambushed and beat up diplomatic couriers; the new Ambassador Kapustin kept low and concentrated on a rural water supply project; visitors to the Embassy were publicly called spies, the police and courts descended on the Mexican Communist party; the Slavonic club and the Society of Friends of the USSR were reduced to next to nothing. Trotsky's works and defectors' memoirs were published in great numbers. Every month, as many as two hundred and fifty FBI and CIA officers came to the country looking for the paths by which nuclear secrets leaked out. All of a sudden, in the matter of weeks, a break in relations was in the air again and even the Eastern bloc diplomats avoided the Soviet Embassy like a lepers' colony.

Only legends remained of Kostya: the saddles he rode in, the bowling alley he built, the 15-ton underground cistern for deficit petrol (the Ambassador only had to complain about the lack of it), the tram line moved to the neighboring street (the noise of the tram disturbed the Ambassador's rest) and the love affair — Umansky's personal secretary fell in love with the aide of the Mexican president.

It is somewhat possible that she did so without being instructed to do so, but there's no reason to believe this.

Even fewer facts survived in Moscow: Nina's classmates believed for the rest of their days that Ambassador Umansky was killed on his way to the USA, and that the urn containing Nina's ashes fell into the ocean.

In summer, Chukharev fell ill and was left behind in Moscow while his wife and daughter moved to the dacha twenty miles outside the ring road. He went to see them on weekends, taking peaches, apples, plums, apricots, grapes and strawberries in tall plastic pitchers. At night he couldn't sleep because of the humidity and his obsession with the last boy of the Fourth Empire: he called potential children and grandchildren, everyone with the right last name in Moscow, the Moscow Oblast, the Russian Federation, and, just in case, in Israel and Ukraine. The office was empty, except for Goltsman who felt the need to present himself somewhere every day by ten o'clock in freshly ironed trousers.

Then one day Chukharev called a meeting: he had *found* someone and had to work really hard to pretend it wasn't a big deal.

"All the Xxxxs I talked to by telephone denied being related. For $350 our people at the Interior Ministry checked the fresh database of residential registration, but it now only lists initials, not full first names and patronymics. So they found an Xxxx V. This V. is registered at two addresses: Pilyugina Street 14 and Frunzenskaya embankment, 24/1. Neither phone number answers," Chukharev reported.

"At the dacha!" suggested Borya, dressed this time in a motorcycle jacket. Goltsman didn't say anything: he sensed there was more.

"I went to the housing administration complex at Khamovniki and bought an excerpt from the house book: the people they have registered on Frunzenskaya are Victoria Xxxx, her six-year-old son, and her mother Nina Vasilievna Pirogova, who, by the way, was born in Kuibyshevin 1908. She died in 1990. Victoria's surname and patronymic match our information: it's obvious she is the daughter of our Xxxx."

"Our savior!" Borya said happily. "Well done. Is there anything else?"

"I went to the municipal board on Frunzenskaya, 26, and met two guys in charge there, quite sociable, they like money. They got me past the front door and up to the apartment, but no one answered when I rang the doorbell. The two neighboring apartments didn't open either. At the account's office, I was told that no one had paid the rent since April. I think that we should send a registered letter, so that the mailman rings the apartment doorbell from time to time. And in a week the technician supervisor Yelena Vladimirovna comes back from vacation — we'll inspire her to ask the neighbors what the family is like, where they may be."

I listened as if half-asleep and let the realization sink in: we were close, we were a train pulling into the station. Almost ready to go back to the 3rd of June.

Alyona was waiting for me, with her unnecessarily long legs. Her face looked very calm.

"I forgot to tell you," she said, "it's Seryozha's birthday today. I'll go now, OK? You keep working, if you want; it'll be nice not to have me hovering around. But do wait for me for dinner, I'll be back by then: Seryozha invited his friends to go bowling. I have to spend some time with them." She frowned; her eyes were glistening again. "And it's his birthday. I thought about it, I didn't want to say it, but I will: perhaps later, not now, not even soon, much later, maybe — I'll introduce you two?"

I nodded. She hugged me, quickly, and ran to the elevator.

I became aware of a senile voice croaking in the background. I looked: the secretary was playing a recording of an old person talking, perhaps to draw my attention to her achievements and herself. I listened for a minute and recognized the voice of Litvinov's adopted daughter, the sex bomb Levashova. Indeed, we weren't done with her yet.

"These are the last tapes of conversations with Levashova. Would you like to listen? Would you like some coffee?"

She brought the Dictaphone and coffee, then sat down in

anticipation of us listening together, uninterrupted. I could tell she was put off when I said:

"Go home. You won't be needed anymore today. I'll listen by myself."

I came back from Siberia in 1943 with two children, and in '45 I had another child. I did not see anyone again. My father couldn't forgive me for marrying Levashov.

If I needed anything, I could call Petrova and Maxim Maximovich would order things for me at the distribution office. He wouldn't order cigarettes, though, he wasn't about to do my husband a favor.

But I had my own honor: love me, love my dog. I didn't think that Papa was right.

Then one day we had an argument about something, me and my husband, and I must've said something especially sharp to him. All of a sudden, he burst out: you cosmopolitans should all have been packed off to the taiga a long time ago! That's when I started to think. I watched him and waited.

While we were in the process of getting divorced, he went to live at the dacha, and I stayed in our apartment. One Sunday, the doorbell rang, a man. Open the door please, I'd like to see Levashov. He's not here, I won't open the door, I don't know when he'll be here. I've come to see him from Tomsk. And my husband started his career in Tomsk, he was in CheKa there. I opened the door. A man came in. He was terrifying. Such eyes he had. I want to see Levashov! He said. I said, I understand, but he's not here, he may not come today at all. He's retired, I said, he doesn't work anymore. It doesn't matter, he was in charge of my case, the man said, and I've come to settle scores with him. I'm going to kill him. Please, forget about that, we're divorcing at the moment… Let me divorce him, then you do whatever you want. The man said he was beaten and tortured when he was arrested, and Levashov was smart — he didn't do any of it himself, just stood there and gave orders to the others. Where is he? I said: at the dacha, and I gave him the address.

Late that night I heard the door opening — it was Levashov. I locked myself in my room and listened. He was rushing about in his room like a tiger, and groaning, Oh God, can this be the end? I realized that something had happened. Evidently the man from Tomsk had found the dacha.

I don't know how he died. He went to see our daughter at Rossoshanskaya with some wine, he drank, but it wasn't enough, so he went to get some more. His niece, the daughter of his second brother — by an incredible coincidence — was walking past the shop and saw her uncle lying on the sidewalk. He had had a heart attack. By then, we hadn't talked in a long time, I severed the relationship. I didn't make it to Maxim Maximovich's funeral, they told me too late — he was buried at five o'clock, I was at work and couldn't get time off.

Petrova — I remember one time I called her just because I was bored, and she sounded so happy to hear from me. Come and visit, she said, only I am very ill and am not working. I went. She was lying on her couch in her room. Vasya, her ill son, was doing something in the kitchen. We talked about the old times, how Gromyko spied on Maxim Maximovich in America, how he got a matching set of keys for Papa's desk even.

And then I found out that Petrova had cancer.

I didn't keep in touch with her daughter, Iraida. She is just as cold and unapproachable as her mother.

I looked at the recorder's timer — the recording was almost over. Suddenly, the secretary's voice came in: very clearly, she asked the last question of the former beauty Zinaida Maximovna Litvinova, Levashova, nee Buyanovskaya: *Tell me, what is love for you?*

The silence hissed and screeched, new rustles and outside noise grew louder, and then the old woman spoke. *Love… A conglomeration of feelings, I would say.*

MM

THE EMPEROR RECALLED HIS AMBASSADORS TO THE USA AND England at the same time — in early April 1943.

Recalling Litvinov, just like appointing him, was a forceful statement in the ongoing conversation with Mr. Roosevelt. The Emperor showed that he was tired of the uncertainty about the second front, of the inclination of his temporary friends to pay for everything with Russian blood, and their lack of desire to guarantee the western borders of the Empire. After recalling Litvinov, he left a pawn in his stead — Gromyko.

Roosevelt, reportedly, responded to Maxim Maximovich's casual, "Well, I guess, it's good-bye" with a direct (and for the Russian, therefore, unbearable) conclusion:

"You will never return."

Maxim Maximovich and Anastasia Petrova got vaccinated against plague and cholera and embarked on their twelve-day journey through Africa (the Americans had already defeated Rommel) to Moscow, where they arrived on the 21st of April. Umansky, Litvinov and Petrova, all residents of the House of Government, all neighbors, had six weeks to tell each other things and to determine their fates.

They returned to the tiny office of a deputy People's Commissar and idleness — only the foreign press corps still thought that Litvinov mattered. They rode in a government open-top limousine in the First of May parade, and no one recognized Litvinov, in his diplomat's uniform with elaborate shoulder-straps.

On July 18th of 1946, when Litvinov turned seventy years and one day old, he was summoned to the office of another Molotov deputy, Dekanozov, and informed that he was being relieved of his duties. The old man begged not to be thrown own, to remain anywhere — in the complaints office, or foreign trade — but eventually accepted his *sinecura* as a deputy of the Supreme Council of the USSR. He never met with voters because of poor health and spent the Council's plenary sessions doing crossword puzzles. At home, he did not miss a chance to talk about the Emperor condescendingly: "He doesn't know the West. If our enemy had been a few shahs or sheiks, he would have outsmarted them."

Left on Maxim Maximovich's office desk was a pile of papers, a page from a 1948 calendar with a scribbled note "85 rubles" which was then crossed out and "156 rubles" written over it. On the reverse he wrote, "Politics is the ability to make use of people's stupidity and gullibility." Maxim Maximovich attempted to write memoirs (and swore: "I'm not mad enough to be writing"), only to tear up in the evenings what he'd written in the morning, never getting past his escape from the Lukoyanovsky prison. He was alone, like a thousand other iron men, all those marshals and commissars who survived long enough to experience an irrelevant and cruel existence after they had been used, after the glory they achieved despite the oppression of facilities management boards and residential Party organizations, a common existence.

Two years before he died, Maxim Maximovich, as befitted an Emperor's loyal lieutenant, his faithful dog, wrote a farewell to the Emperor on a mockingly small form reserved for deputies of the Supreme Council: I appeal to you in this deathbed letter with a last request... Dealing with the approach of the natural end of my life... Don't leave my wife and children in need. He closed with, "I will die with a clear conscience, with the knowledge that I did everything I could for Communism and my dear homeland to the extent that my energy, knowledge and skills allowed, and it was not my fault that I did not do more. With parting greetings, I wish you health and longevity."

Litvinov would not have any boot-licking or drooling. He signed in a large, swift hand.

He went to die, after his third heart attack, to the Kremlin hospital — this man who hated open doors, who had been cheerful and often quiet, who liked to dip sprigs of green onion in sour cream and ate with an easy, family-man's grin. He lived for a while on oxygen and morphine, with two nurses always on watch. On New Year's Eve he started to choke, a nurse rushed for the syringe, but his wife, Ivy, stayed her hand, asking:

"What would this accomplish?"

"A few more days."

"It's not worth it."

Someone heard Litvinov sigh, "I wish it were over."

Ivy Lowe went home on New Year's Eve a widow.

The next day, people who said they were from the Archive Service searched the apartment. The family had time to throw down the trash chute a bundle of U.S. Dollars they found in a desk drawer, lest they be accused of working for the Israeli special services as was the custom of the day. They asked if the family wanted to buy the furniture from the government.

They found his will: make peace with Austria, become reconciled with Yugoslavia and lift the occupation of East Germany. The funeral was modest, although many came (others remember that the guards didn't let people into the ceremony), and everyone remembers Petrova crying. An official read the *Pravda* obituary out loud in a stifled voice over the coffin set in the middle of the ceremonial hall at the Ministry of Foreign Affairs. Outside the coffin was opened for people to say goodbye, and snow fell onto Maxim Maximovich's gray suit and his face, and stayed there. The money from his savings account lasted for a year; his biography was published under the title *Stalin's Standard-bearer of Peace.*

Ivy withdrew, suddenly and completely, into complete self-containment. She told her daughter, You know this is the first time I've encountered death. She instructed her son to move into his father's study so that the room wouldn't sit vacant, and she did not seem to need anyone's sympathy. She wasn't allowed to go back to England for a long time, and then finally she was. When death neared, she wrote to her daughter, I need you — and kept writing (her daughter came and put a typewriter in front of her). When she could no longer write, she read, reading was like her breath, and her last word was *ink*.

Among her papers was an envelope inscribed with the words "Concerning the body." It contained detailed instructions about the medical center to which she wished to donate her corpse. The envelope did not contain instructions to bury her ashes alongside her husband in Russia.

Anastasia Petrova, a functionary of the Foreign Affairs Ministry, found herself without anyone to love shortly after she turned fifty. She had a very sensible view of human abilities to withstand time and understood correctly the words that accompanied her everywhere, "You look incredibly young!" Before she returned to Soviet Union, she had an elegant Karakul fur coat sewn for her in America — everyone came to remember this coat in the poor times, when women dreamed for years of having just *one* new blouse. As she walked around her beloved Riga, Petrova wondered at how poorly and tastelessly the people were dressed.

She held important positions in the Ministry and at the diplomatic academy where her students remembered her as stern and demanding, a woman who had a way of pinning one down with her eyes like a bug. She had the profile of an antique statue, incredible skin, high forehead, gray hair gathered in a French knot. She dressed simply; she had few clothes, but they were all expensive and of highest quality. She never mentioned Litvinov. Once, casually, she said she had worked with him, he was a good sort...

If younger female colleagues came to ask advice on personal issues, Petrova listened to them in silence, not once uttering the words "love" or "passion" in reply, and always gave the same counsel: defend your dissertation, don't waste time on making preserves and baking cookies. She despised any urges to redecorate. She never complained. She never told anyone anything.

She was diagnosed with cancer in the last stage, and was not even offered chemotherapy (or she was offered it, but a doctor she knew advised her: go home and live another three years in peace, chemo kills faster than your cancer). Her cancer developed slowly, and Anastasia Vladimirovna never took drugs in her entire life, so she was able to rely, until her last three weeks, on simple pain-killers. Finally, she went into the hospital for old Bolsheviks on Shosse Entuziastov; she called her daughter at work and asked to see Nonna Nikolayevna, an old friend. They spoke English all evening in her hospital room (supposedly so as not to disturb the other patient). We looked for this Nonna Nikolayevna, but couldn't find her. The following night, Anastasia Petrova died.

I crossed her off the list and suddenly thought: How was it when they took Vasya away, her son, her doom, the one who took everything from her? He would have been taken in a car, with a few strong men for company. Could he have understood that his mother had died? She died — that meant she went away, she would come back later. He would ask, as all children do, practical questions: Who will take me to concerts now and feed me? How will these people know what I want? Who will be proud about how well I read music? But something, undoubtedly, must remain, the traces of something elusive and warm. How difficult, surely, it was for him to understand the asylum's *routine*, its *food, wards, head doctor*, fences and locks. He probably waited for all that to end and for people to come and take him home, and probably talked about this for hours on end with whoever was assigned to keep him company, while something was taking shape in his mind, an Idea of his own existence. Somehow, he must have found a way to explain everything to himself: I'm like this and I'm here because… Or perhaps everything was swallowed by the chewing-gum of existence, everything except *Mother*.

I really think he talked to her.

Anastasia Petrova was buried at Vagankovo, not far from the church. She was silent about her life and those she knew until the very end; she did not betray anyone. Her daughter was cool; her son was uncomprehending; her grand-daughter, reportedly, killed herself out of unrequited love. We could not crack them open; Tasya Flam was beyond us. I threw the folder with her name on it across the room.

In the reception room the light was on.

"How long have you been working for us?" I aked Masha. I offered to walk her to the metro.

"Four years."

"Who are you? I, for example, am an empty person. What about you? Tell me briefly about yourself."

"Why are you being like this? I don't know about myself. I don't know what I want. I'm confused. I know what I want, but I can't say. It's impossible anyway. I bought you an icon," she reached into her purse and shyly offered me a small wooden rectangle. I thanked her. "I went to church," she went on. "To my priest…"

"Do you believe in God? Do believe that we can expect a transformation into something unknown?"

"If you get the authorization, can I come with you to the 3rd of June?"

"No, of course not. Only men will go."

"How does it usually happen?"

"Truth is established at the location. Those present at the scene of the incident talk, their memories are clarified — we help them a little with this, we make sure that no one is deceiving themselves. Everyone talks in turn about what they saw and what they *thought* they saw — adding their desires, their life, their fear of dying — everyone wants to remain, to put in more of themselves even in other people's stories. We don't spare anyone, we only take the truth with us."

"Why can't I come?"

"E-mail me a picture of yourself." Someone may have warned her about me, but she still said:

"I don't have any good ones, I'm not photogenic. But I'll find one for you if you tell me why you want it. "

"It's simple. Your life."

So I don't waste questions, so I can study you, so I can look at your body in calm solitude, when I want, when no one can take it away and time won't change it. "Better in a swimsuit. Or without one."

"I don't have any pictures like that."

"You're so beautiful. Are you just embarrassed? One of those people who doesn't get undressed with the lights on?"

After not saying anything for a while (autumn had begun, it had fallen on us, as always in our city, brutally and for a long time):

"I don't mind having the lights on. The question is who for. And I may allow myself to be photographed."

"If you trust the photographer?"

"I would have to love him."

"And you would have to be sure that he really wants this," I suggested by the gaping maw of the metro. We shook hands; I waved. Pretending to be sad, I thought, now I've got her thinking. And suddenly for an enormous moment, I felt my past right there with me the way you feel it just a few times in your life — something from the outside, like wind: iron barrels with boiling water, laundry lines rolled up into balls, the melted lead settling in the mold for a Little Octobrist's star-shaped badge with the curly-headed infant in the middle, a black-and-white television set, and the terror of the tube in it dying; how people all of a sudden pulled up and left the barracks, the crackle of newspaper torn up in the toilet, a satin cap, the horrifying language of funereal and congratulatory telegrams, printed on ribbons of brown paper without commas or prepositions, the stuffy phone-booths for intercity calls, the poster on the street-car "A Passenger's Conscience is the Best Controller," end-of-school year ceremonies, exams, shooting tests, words and analyses, many rusty shell cases… I took out my cell phone, pressed the buttons, and informed Alyona:

"I won't come home tonight. I simply don't want to."

Then I put it on "silent" and went to Shchelkovskaya street to see a music school principal — I knew she had just remodeled her kitchen and put heated floors in the bathrooms.

EIGHT UNANSWERED CALLS

My phone showed eight calls, all from Chukharev — Victoria Xxxx had returned from the dacha, flown in, arrived, was seen by the maintenance crew supervisor, was spotted by neighbors, so tomorrow could be the day she would give us more clues to another day, many years ago.

"Come in."

Victoria Xxxx studied my face on the intercom screen. She was a tall, sturdy woman in shapeless pants and a long tunic. What she saw was a sleep-deprived, carefully shaven man in a clumsily ironed T-shirt and well-worn jeans, with sandals on his bare feet and a backpack. I had brought a camera, people trust a person with a big camera. I shook off the sandals at the door and walked across what felt like a whole field of hardwood, after her, barefoot. She couldn't imagine how many years we had followed her, all for the sake of the keys, the keys to the 3rd of June. This was the woman who could unlock for us the name of Nina Umanskaya's murderer, but she did not know this and could easily say no. But I was not worried; it would be hard for her to refuse me, it's hard to send away a smiling beggar. I suddenly felt like an old man. I had grown old, but we had gotten a lot done.

I placed the camera on the table that was suggested for this purpose and laid out two prepared sheets of paper (her authorization, my non-disclosure affidavit) face down next to it. She glanced at it all distractedly. I showed her my fake ID — a new photo and a stamp. She listened to the lies about the museum of school #175 with a sympathy that I could tell did not come easily to her. She delivered stories about her father from a metaphorical tray, laid out neatly, picked over and deemed fit for public consumption, and then found it hard to stop talking — it is very hard, when someone looks you in the eyes, shares your sadness, smiles at the funny parts and just the right questions that touch you just so. I could tell no one had asked Ms. X such questions for a long time. There are so few really warm people, and even relatives don't really feel sorry for anyone — so there she was, almost unwittingly opening up to a stranger, to my accidental warmth: I doubt this'll be of use for your museum, but you just choose what you need, I never told anyone about this, and you don't tell anyone either, I just… I want you to understand, to imagine what it was like. Her voice washed over me like waves, and I looked at her dark, sun-burnt face, at the cloud of her black hair — the kind that could only be called lavish — at the well-appointed expanse of her luxurious apartment, and did not remember anything she was saying. Then, I put out the human warmth in my eyes, stopped feeding the questions that stoked the flames — and Victoria Xxxx immediately came back to reality. Distinctly, louder than usual, I said in the voice of a person in charge:

"Do you know that your father was arrested in July 1943 for his involvement in an underground organization, and was imprisoned for six months in an internal NKVD prison at Lubyanka?"

She knew and hid it. Or she didn't know. Or she didn't want to know. She was completely at a loss, and looked convincingly dumbfounded. Or she knew everything herself, and had read the certificate of rehabilitation.

"My father," she said, "was not a particularly brave man. Now I understand why he never felt completely at ease in this country."

"It was schoolboys playing a game," I went on. "Nothing serious, but they used Nazi titles in their so-called organization. Then, their *Reichskanzler*, Volodya Shakhurin, shot and killed a classmate on the Great Stone Bridge. It was called the case of the wolf-cubs, haven't you heard about it?"

Victoria Xxxx kept a disgusted silence. I didn't say anything more either, making it clear: I wouldn't say the most important thing, *there was a lot of dirt involved*, but we could just make a deal quickly.

"You must understand," I leaned in. "We cannot ignore this case, especially as some wild rumors are coming to light now, the tabloids are about to blow this out of all proportion. To stop the lies, I must have the actual case files in hand. FSB has been very cooperative, it's all unclassified, and they've shared a lot, but for the rest of the files the archive requires authorization from the boys themselves, or their relatives. I made inquiries, the boys died a long time ago," I said, knowing that if she'd called even one of them, even once, I'd have to get up and leave, but I sensed that her father had led an alien, marginal existence at school, and fear had driven his family as far away as possible from all the others. "The relatives have all dispersed, I was only lucky enough to find you… Your father's role in the boys' so-called organization, as I learned from the archives, was minimal. Accidental. If you were to give me permission to access the archives, I will sign this non-disclosure agreement to guarantee that neither your father's name nor any facts of his life would appear in any exhibitions, scientific or journalistic publications. Ever. And I will make sure that the pages of the case with his testimonies are destroyed. As if Xxxx had never been part of the Fourth Empire."

I slid the non-disclosure note towards her, together with my real passport and the authorization letter, with a conspicuous gap for her signature.

She read the note attentively, and took the authorization letter out of politeness, only to hold it in her hands.

"But it's…. You need some information about me… My passport number?"

"It's all been filled out."

Victoria Xxxx chuckled bitterly, as if she had expected something like this, warily picked up the authorization letter and checked it twice, digit by digit. Series, number, home address, telephone numbers. It only cost us $100 for the passport clerk, but it made a great impression.

I passed her a pen with black ink, not leaving space for a no.

"Just your signature."

"But these authorization letters… I've never seen one before. Don't they typically get certified? Do I have to go to a notary?"

"Nothing more is required of you. Just sign once. We will talk to the notary. He will certify your signature without your personal presence."

We — that's what infuriated her — *we*. We were making her, the owner of a good apartment, work for us. She felt disgusted by her own sincerity, she hated herself for revealing small details of her childhood and her Daddy's death, she hated the way she let herself be lured into warmth, into trust, into letting a stranger in, and hated her own intolerably foolish eagerness to respond to human interest, an interlocutor, despite knowing full well that no one, really, ever gives a damn. The only thing she could do to rise above us in cynicism and cool — exactly what I counted on — was to take that pen and scribble her signature broad and careless at the bottom of the letter. She shoved it towards me with a gesture that said, out of my house.

By the door I gave her the chance to win a little back:

"Would you like me to make a copy of your father's testimony?"

"I don't need anything."

I ran down the stairs, leaping over two at a time, away from there, forever. I broke out into the daylight, and raced across the street not waiting for the traffic light, to the two people waiting for me a little to the right of the Andreevsky Bridge. They already knew it — I waved the white piece of paper in the air above my head, and it flashed in the sunlight, turning them into a photograph, a sharp and permanent vision: an emaciated stiff-backed old man in gray, precisely ironed trousers from his only suit, with wrinkled, spotted, already inhuman extremities, the halo of white hair around his head, his eyes both sad and stern, and his lips tucked into a merciless fold, and a cheerful, ruddy-faced, untidy Russian with a peasant's thin cow-lick, an avian, eager head and a kind, short-sighted expression, caught in the middle of an urge to run, to exclaim, to crumple me in a bear hug — so scared was he to stop for an instant and take it all in.

I ran across the road, and we walked towards the bridge in silence.

THE YEAR 1943

THE COMMANDER ISLANDS ARE OPENED TO THE HUNTING OF THE arctic fox. The snipers Dadashev, Bogdanov and Dzhabrailov eliminate 66 Fascists in 17 days. In Moscow, snow removal services are inadequate; schoolchildren on winter break spend their time repairing the shoes of Red Army soldiers. In a building on Gorky Street, a few individual citizens violate the decree of the Moscow city council and proceed to chop firewood right in their apartments. Epaulettes are re-introduced in the Soviet Army: the infantry receives a raspberry color, the artillery red, the air force blue, and the cavalry bright blue. The Stanislavsky Theater buys castanets and Spanish ruffs from the public.

Factory school students master the proper technique of throwing grenades while on skis: the left leg forward on the knee, the right ski perpendicular for support, the grenade swinging, two sticks in the left hand. Marina Raskova, one of the first female combat pilots, is killed in a training flight. Soviet writers hold a workshop, "Tips for Writing Defense Songs." A Mr. Zenov wins 10,000 rubles in the lottery and requests that the money be used to build an extra Air-force squadron.

On the 9th of February, Soviet forces capture Solntsevo station, liberating, presumably, my father and grandmother. An exhibition: presents made by children for the soldiers at the front. There's a little case for two spools of thread and a needle, a case for a comb, dominoes, an envelope holder. "Dear Mr. Soldier!" a child writes. "When you go to battle, kill the Germans dead. I am brave myself, although I'm a little boy."

Spring comes early, with forecasts for flash floods which threaten to wash away the stockpiles of firewood placed on the ice of the River Moscow. Rzhev and Vyazma are liberated. Sergeant Vasiliev calls artillery fire on himself when his dug-out is surrounded by Germans. Middle school workshops repair tables and stools. The manufacture of the Tula accordion is resumed. Postwoman Shalayeva delivers only some of the letters on April 7th and flushes the rest down the toilet; she is sentenced to four years of labor camp. Five days later, Kalinin accepts letters of credence from the Ambassador Extraordinary and Plenipotentiary, Minister of Mexican diplomatic service Luis Quintanilla. Collective farmers hitch cows and bulls to the plows and begin to work the fields.

A letter from the front: "You know what I dream about at night, or when I'm alone? Firstly, of course, about victory. Then about you. I dream that I come to Moscow, and get off the train. The sun is shining, the trees are murmuring. You come towards me with your friends. And I haven't come alone, I'm with my comrades. We walk along the wide street, talking and laughing. Everyone is happy. We go in to a restaurant. You know, I've never been to a real restaurant before. We sit down at a table, there are marble columns and crystal chandeliers around us. There are bottles on the table — yellow lemonade with bubbles and all kinds of multi-colored things, pastries and sweets. I read you poems."

On the 20th of April, the Mexican Ambassador is received by Comrade Stalin. On the 18th of May, the Presidium of the Supreme Council of the USSR appoints Konstantin Umansky Ambassador to Mexico. There are major air battles over the Kuban.

On the 2nd of June, gardeners begin to plant raspberries. Young people help the families of soldiers fighting at the front to work the gardens. On the boulevards, stands sell carbonated water, mors, kvas and a pine-scented drink that has five times more vitamins in one glass than an entire lemon.

The 3rd of June is a Thursday. At the Udarnik movie theater, the film "She Defends the Motherland" is playing.

THE 3RD OF JUNE

FINALLY, I WAS SEEING IT FOR MYSELF: MOSCOW HAD EMPTIED out with the throat-catching brief emptiness of New Year's Eve, its buildings had sucked people in, and if you stopped (I could not — I was propelled by the power of a young, incipient love) you could glimpse a few living shadows on the far side of the river, in the distant windows of the House of Government on Serafimovich Street, behind innocent-looking curtains in crayon colors. We were outside — alone with motionless cars and streetlights, so no one would interfere. I hurried to the Great Stone Bridge, high above the black water sprinkled with silver pinpricks of reflected electric lights, glanced happily at the Kremlin, and turned right, on to the stairs that lead off the Bridge toward the Popular Music Theater. On the landing where Nina was killed, someone had sprinkled sand to cover the blood, and bouquets of flowers lay in the corner.

"People took care," said an old man coming up from down below, with heavy steps, tightly clutching the rail. "Sand, flowers… To recreate the scene, they said. I told them to toss the weeds." He finally came up — my contact — a red-faced veteran, retired to teach physical fitness, stooped over, with emaciated and hollow shoulders, wearing white sneakers, blue track pants with stripes and a red tank top. A thin gold chain draped down his sun-burnt chest. He wheezed and rasped, but that was his usual voice, and I had heard this voice reach the middle of wrestling mats, the center of boxing rings, the far end of swimming pools. He drew nearer — a squashed, broken nose, an ultra-modern haircut with an immaculate part; he put out his crooked wrestler's arms, grabbed me and hugged me.

He fixed me with his tiny, half-hooded old man's eyes:

"You've changed too… Let me look at you. Not a boy anymore. Still collecting soldiers? I just went to China, wanted to buy some, but then remembered you only want Russian ones. I brought you a T-shirt, so don't say I never gave you anything. But I forgot to bring it. Look, is it OK that I… went a bit wild here?"

He frowned cunningly, trying to guess what I would say: down on the embankment lit so brightly the pavement looked white, he had placed a pair of stretchers. The stretchers were covered with sheets, and bare feet stuck out from under the covers.

"Here's what I figured," you could almost hear the iron gears grinding in his head, assembling sounds into words, until words could come out with a sticky thump. "That'll keep gawkers away. No one will know where these came from and they'll be too scared to ask. Because, you know, what if we'd lift the sheet and ask them to come up, one at a time. Everyone knows: if the murderer looks at the victim, the corpse will sweat blood. I asked a featherweight fighter and a gymnast girl, Lena, to lie down there for extra credit — they're calm sorts, athletes — they'll just fall asleep there."

It was time to go down; he crawled after me, constantly making noise like a machine crushing stones:

"I said to them: why so many seats? It's not football! Well, how many witnesses were there — ten. At the most, *twenty*," he stretched out his fingers. "There they are, being unloaded." A TV crew was taking people off a bus. Each witness was escorted, stepping over many cables and pieces of equipment, to the brightly lit bleachers that had been arranged like an amphitheater, in two semi-circles. Each was seated on a specific spot, with a blue number on it. The first rows filled up; the crew did a sound check, the light changed. They carried three small podiums down the aisle between the bleachers. I hid my hands so that no one would see them shake; once I went up there, I wouldn't be able to see anything beyond the white circle of bleachers, people's faces washed by the harsh light into blindness, turning this way and that, to follow the noise.

The coach whispered in my ear:

"Are we going after Mikoyan?"

"What do you mean? We are here to find out what happened."

"That's what I understood!" the coach wheezed, quickly looking around. "We'll establish the truth, of course, the circumstances, you're the competent organs," he nodded, and whispered again: "And then go after Mikoyan."

I turned to him:

"Don't you get it? We're after the Truth!"

The coach fell silent as if he was chewing on something, and turned away, offended:

"Can't you ever just do without your bullshit?" He snapped. "The *truth*. Of course, the truth. That's what I came here for. But I won't come again. Even if you call me, I won't come. You've gotten mean, that's what. The truth! You ever bother to ask yourself, *what truth?* To what end? You gotta have a direction. A goal. So this truth of yours can be of some use, that's why."

"Don't you understand?" I grabbed the trainer, he bitterly shook his head and tore himself away. I was left facing a new person — a shapeless, pale-lipped man with a neat Orthodox beard in a shiny suit.

"We always wait for you, *professor!*" the coach croaked. "You just have to keep us on the edge, don't you? It's almost time!"

"Good evening to you all!" said the professor hesitantly, as if he had a bad premonition, and handed his briefcase to a girl from TV. He turned off his cell phone and gave it to her too. "How long is it going to take today? I'm flying to Yekaterinburg to see a client in the morning."

We were told to get ready, the girls came over to attach the microphones.

Television is made by people I hate for people I despise. I hadn't slept, and now I had talk. The bastards would hope that we'd see only what they wanted to show us.

"Oh!" the coach raised his finger in satisfaction. "The clock is striking."

How did he hear it first? The chimes of the Kremlin tower clock, their familiar sound changed by the distance of the river, drifted out over the Great Stone Bridge.

We were signaled to walk onto the set and so moved to the narrow passage between the rows, into the circle that was eerily lit up in the middle of the blackness. I was the last, and immediately put my hands on the podium, next to the paper and sharpened pencils.

"Dear friends!" the invisible host said in a velvety voice, "to commemorate the day of victims of Stalinist repressions, and within the framework of the year of overcoming communism that was announced by the Council of Europe, today we examine the case R-788, military tribunal sentence 4n-012045 slash 55. The murder of Nina Konstantinovna Umanskaya. We must remind our respected guests of the rules: You may ask the witnesses any questions, but the witnesses only reply to the questions that they hear, understand, and which they wish to answer. Are you ready?"

The professor noted something with a pencil, and proclaimed in his customary rich voice, taking a handkerchief out of his breast pocket:

"We are ready, thank you." He ran his eyes over the rows of identical heads. "Is Comrade Sheinin here?"

One of the witnesses immediately began to speak in a mechanical, lifeless voice, as if a recording had been turned on.

"Head of the investigation department of the Prosecutor General's Office of the Soviet Union, Senior Assistant to the Prosecutor of the USSR, Lev Romanovich Sheinin. I ordered to open the investigation on the personal instructions of the Prosecutor of the USSR, Comrade Bochkov."

"The forensic conclusions. Care to elaborate?"

SHEININ:

Date stamp: June 4, 1943. The body of a teenage girl, five feet two inches in height, correctly formed, well-nourished. General color is corpse pale. Cadaveric spots of purple color, rigor mortis in all muscle groups Hair on the head is matted with blood. Entry bullet wound on the left side of the head in the area of the parietal ridge, round exit in the right side of the head. The shot, accordingly, was made *left to right, upwards from below, from the front to the back*. Not at a close distance, more than twenty inches.

The professor wrote this down, drew something and made a sign to me to be quiet.

"Are there any comrades who carried out the first investigative activities? Who was the first to arrive at the scene of the crime?"

POLICE SERGEANT ZHELEZNYAKOV:
At 20:15, as I walked my beat, I saw people running and screaming, "There's been a shooting!" I followed them. I discovered two citizens, male and female, on the stairs down from the Great Stone Bridge, with bullet wounds to their heads. The woman was lying face down, the man was lying face up. With the sentry Stepanchikova, we called two ambulances: the man went to the First City Hospital, the woman to morgue number 2 of the Moscow University. The citizens who gathered on the scene identified the victims as Nina Umanskaya and Vladimir Shakhurin. Subsequently, I accompanied Lieutenant Lokteev to the Shakhurins' apartment on Granovsky street.

"Did you question the witnesses?"

ZHELEZNYAKOV: This was not possible. No one saw anything.

"The boy was still alive. Did he say anything? No? Alright, let's go on."

SENTRY POLICEWOMAN ZINAIDA STEPANCHIKOVA, age 18 (female sentries stood guard armed with Mosin-Nagant rifles): It took me about three minutes to get to the scene.

"How do you know it took three minutes? Did you hear shots?"

STEPANCHIKOVA: No, not shots, but I heard people screaming.

"Did you try to find the weapon?"

STEPANCHIKOVA: I looked for it. I didn't find anything. And I thought that the pistol had been taken away. Shakhurin was the murderer, first he shot the girl, then himself.

"Zina, how did you come to this conclusion? Who told you that shots were fired from a pistol? Did you find anyone who saw the *moment of the shooting?*"

STEPANCHIKOVA: No one saw it. Although a lot of people were gathered there. I especially remember one woman.

"Why do you remember her?"

I thought: this must be Petrova.

"She recognized the girl. I heard her exclaim, 'Nina!' And she bit her fingers in despair. She was a brunette. Well-dressed. In a gray coat. And with a hat. I remember her blue shoes."

The professor paused and continued:

"Is Lieutenant Lokteev here? Did you go to the Shakhurins' apartment on the 3rd of June?"

POLICE LIEUTENANT LOKTEEV: At the apartment we questioned the housekeeper. We established that Nina Umanskaya and Vladimir Shakhurin knew each other. On the 4th of June, Comrade Umansky was supposed to be flying to America. Volodya came home at 2 p.m. that day, in a happy mood — he had passed a geometry exam with an A. At around four, his friend Mikoyan came to visit. At six, they went out for a walk. Comrade Shakhurin, when he left the apartment to go to work at the People's Commissariat, never left his personal weapon at home, and when he comes home, he puts it in a safe, which he always locks. While we were in the apartment there was a phone call from the hospital: Volodya has been operated on, the operation was successful, he was conscious.

"Who called?"

LOKTEEV: I don't know.

The coach croaked cheerfully:

"Father, let the cops go. You know they shut their eyes and plugged their ears as soon as they heard the names Mikoyan and Shakhurin. I bet they didn't get past the kitchen in that apartment; that housekeeper would've kept them hanging in the hallway, waiting for the NKVD. These are simple folk — let's talk to the doctors instead. Are the surgeons here?"

Vladimir Shakhurin's Chart:

Patient was delivered to the hospital unconscious. A bullet wound passing through the head, with damage to both brain hemispheres. Condition extremely serious, respiration bubbling. White brain matter coming out of the wound. The shot *was made at point-blank range*, in the temple area. The patient had 15 rubles in cash on him and a watch made of white metal with the glass broken.

Trepanation indicated. Pupils — dilated with a poor reaction to light. Light grabbing reflexes in the hands. Increasing hemorrhaging in the eyeballs. Sweating slightly. Breathing speeding up again. Small twitching of the face again. The condition remains extremely serious. Pulse uneven and extremely weak. Cyanosis of the face and fingertips. Rattling wheezing in the lungs, breathing very labored. After breathing dropped severely to 56/min, it once more increased to 66/min. Condition still extremely serious. Pupils not reacting. At 20:50, the pulse dropped suddenly and respiratory movements disappeared, heart activity stopped, despite the application of cortisol and caffeine subcutaneously and CPR. Vladimir Shakhurin died.

"God rest his soul," the coach swiftly crossed himself, moving his fingers left and right somewhat unsurely, and bent over to the faceless doctor nearest to him. "Who actually treated him?"

CASE HISTORY: Spasokukotsky, Bakulev, Burdenko, Busalov, Grinstein, Ochkin, Vovsi, Arutunian, Stefanenko, Kochergin…

"A veritable who's who," the coach said, proud that he had been answered. "Well, what do you think, *nurse*, was he killed?"

CASE HISTORY: We came to the conclusion that Shakhurin had committed suicide.

"Why is that?" the coach asked. "Was he bullied at school?"

CASE HISTORY: You see, the shot was made at practically point-blank range. Gunpowder was burned into the skin on his temple. And the wound was typical for suicide.

"Practically point-blank or really point-blank?" the coach asked, and everyone was silent for a minute.

"And when?" I demanded, and a doctor, a robot, a no-longer-existing person, suddenly turned towards me, barely noticeably, miraculously. "When was the conclusion written?"

CASE HISTORY: On the 10th of June.

"You see?" the coach chuckled. "It wasn't written on the fifth, when he died, there was no need for it, no one from the top asked for it. They burned the body first and then sat down to write stuff, when they got the orders."

"Let's assume that," the professor conceded. "Did anyone see Shakhurin with Nina Umanskaya before the shots were fired?"

IGOR TURGENEV, neighborhood boy: I didn't see Shakhurin fire shots because we ran over to ask Borya Kirpichnikov for a cigarette. Borka gave us a few drags. But I saw them walking from Udarnik to the Kremlin.

In fact they were walking in the opposite direction.

VALENTIN PETROVICH GORDIENKO, another boy: I was walking by the bridge, and saw Nina Umanskay walking with Volodya and Vano. Suddenly people ran down the stairs from the bridge. Vano wasn't there.

NURSE KHASYA LVOVNA AMITINA: I finished my shift at the Kremlin hospital and was walking to the shop at the House of Government, and ran into the girl on the Great Stone Bridge. She was walking with two or three boys. I noticed her because she was laughing loudly. And ten minutes later, when I came out of the shop, the boy and the girl were lying on the ground covered in blood. The boy was still alive and breathing intermittently.

"About what time was this, do you think? Stay in your seat, we agreed you don't have to stand up."

AMITINA: "I work until seven…. Then I locked my office, then by the time I got there… I think it must've been 19:55.

"Khasya Lvovna, as a medic, you probably registered Volodya's position? Where were his arms? Did he say anything?" The professor paused after each question, and hopelessly but confidently, as if he had received a reply, he continued: "Where exactly was the blood on the landing? And what did it look like, drops, splashes, streams? No? Ok, thank you. Comrades, has anyone from school #175 been invited?"

NATALYA MIKHAILOVNA BUCHNEVA, 40 YEARS OLD, STARPOMINOVSKY PEREULOK 5/21: I always found it very unpleasant to talk to Volodya Shakhurin, the boy behaved very arrogantly. At home he criticized his teachers. When I told him off for studying poorly in the first quarter, he brazenly looked at the clock, to time my diatribe. He was very high-strung and quick-tempered. He was in charge of the collection to support a Skholnik airplane, and when he found that the sixth grade had collected more money, he beat up the organizer of the subscription from the sixth grade, and gave up on his own collection. Another example: he publicly slapped Galya Kuibysheva for telling her classmates about the fact he had run away from home when he was evacuated, across the Volga with some girl he 'loved.' Generally, Shakhurin was very interested in girls, he had an opinion about all of them. I know that Volodya kept a romantic diary, he copied out poems in English and German. His friendship with Nina did nothing to improve his academics.

"Didn't you try to talk to Shakhurin's parents?"

BUCHNEVA: I did raise the issue with them. The parents initially felt critical, but then they made Volodya put more effort into his studies. Sofia Mironovna said that Volodya was very worried about his mediocre grades.

After the boys and girls were separated, he became quieter, he didn't seem to get excited at all, in fact. He became sort of sluggish, and we advised the parents to consult a physician about Volodya. I think he was diagnosed with exhaustion.

OLGA FYODOROVNA LEONOVA, PRINCIPLE OF SCHOOL #175, DEPUTY OF THE SUPREME COUNCIL OF THE USSR: Volodya Shakhurin exhibited signs of neurosis: his face twitched and he stuttered. At his mother's request he was exempted from physical fitness tests on the 20th of May because of a nervous disorder. I know that he used to sneak his father's car out for joy rides and that Sofia Mironovna disciplined him physically for it.

For slapping Kuibysheva, Shakhurin apologized to the majority of the girls.

Nina… She was initially rather reserved. The girl, it must be said, stood out, because she had studied outside the Soviet public school system. Her friendship with Shakhurin was noticed from the beginning of the school year *(the principle is nervous and therefore overdoing things: the kids only met in February)*, and we immediately informed the Umanskys, especially since Nina's mother had asked the school to advise her how in bringing up her daughter and what friends to choose for her. From the 1st of January, the boys and girls were separated, and on the 20th of May Nina left school because she was preparing to leave the country. I don't deny that Volodya was also friends with Vano Mikoyan, but Vano, in my opinion, was a simple, modest boy, without any conceit or arrogance.

TEACHER YULY OSIPOVICH GURVITS, 60 YEARS OLD, not a member of the Party: On the 3rd of June, Volodya Shakhurin passed a geometry test in my class. He went home happy. *Gurvits — short, thin, temperamental — was called the "school's Daddy" by Polina Molotova at a parents' meeting. Gurvits' co-author of a geometry textbook had been arrested, and Yuly Osipovich himself had much to fear, but he was the only teacher who did not talk badly about Shakhurin.*

CLASSMATE ARTYOM KHMELNITSKY, BACKGROUND — SON OF A LIEUTENANT GENERAL: Now about our organization. It was formed in December of 1942, was created by Volodya and called The Rose of the South. The members were Shakhurin, Xxxx, Bakulev, Redens, Barabanov, Sergo and Vano Mikoyan, Kirpichnikov and I. Then Shakhurin proposed the name Fourth Empire. At Redens' suggestion, Shakhurin was confirmed as the Reichskanzler, and was also the Feldführer. I was nominated to be the lieutenant general, like Daddy, and be the logistics commander. I told them: your titles sound rather fascist. Volodya said: 'If you've been given this title, you shouldn't refuse.'

"What did your organization do?"

KHMELNITSKY: We wrote to Bakulev — he split with us. The correspondence was kept by Redens, our head of intelligence. Shakhurin said: "After the war we will seize power, Providence itself is in our favor. And for the moment we need to recruit more people into our organization." From Hitler's expressions, he chose his favorite: "The greater the pressure, the stronger the response."

"What makes you do you think Hitler said that?"

KHMELNITSKY: Vano brought Shakhurin Hitler's books. I personally saw an accompanying note by the NKVD to Mikoyan. I saw the words Top Secret printed in gold letters on the book's binding.

Everyone from school #175 remembered Artyom Khmelnitsky as a charming, selfless dreamer.

"What can you tell us about the relations between Vladimir Shakhurin and Nina Umanskaya?"

KHMELNITSKY: He became friends with Nina in winter, he told me, "It's a complete mess!" And later, he said, "How do you like that, Nina's going away!" I said, "Well, that means everything's gone according to plan." That was just a thing we liked to say, "everything's gone according to plan." And he said, "No, not quite." I thought he was generally sort of secretive. No one really knew about the affair between Volodya and Nina (*Except the principal, their teacher, the parents, and a dozen of their classmates at least*). Other kids called him "psycho." He often sat there with his head on the desk. Four days before he died he said to me, "You know, Nina is going to have a child," (*You've been repeating this for sixty years, perhaps this* is *in fact what the seventh-grade Reichskanzler said*) and also, "Mark my words, Nina isn't going to Mexico."

"He said that to you?"

KHMELNITSKY: Redens told me what Volodya had said.

"Redens? You mean the one who's actually Alliluyev?" The coach pretended to be alarmed at this information and concealed a yawn, supposedly hiding profound and bitter contemplation with his palm placed to his face. From behind his hand, he whined with a snotty, child-like voice, "Give us the fathers, professor."

The professor paused, then suddenly turned to a man in a hospital-issued robe, our faceless, nondescript, adversary:

"Lev Romanovich, I understand that my question does not directly relate to the investigation you carried out. But still: did Konstantin Umansky and the People's Commissar Shakhurin interact at all after their children's death? In the evening of June third, or on the fourth, before Umansky's flight?"

Sheinin: We do not have this information. I don't think they met. Our investigators established that on the 5th of June at 1:30 a.m., Shakhurin's secretary, Comrade Protasov, took down a phone message from Comrade Umansky: "I'm flying abroad in the morning. I send my greetings and a warm handshake to Aleksei Ivanovich and Sofia Mironovna. I ask you not to dwell on the negative, as there is no time for this. Our grief and sadness are shared. My wife does not know the details of the incident. I told her that our daughter was walking down the stairs, tripped and fell, and died from a severe concussion. I ask you not to write about this incident in your letters to us. My wife is very ill with a severe nervous disorder. Umansky."

The professor looked at me with the ordinary, vulnerable face of a mortal man, mouthing a question — *now what?* — as if we were left alone and no one could hear or see us.

"Umansky called when there was still hope that the boy would survive. I think he wanted to preserve his relationship with Shakhurin, who was an influential man. He didn't call the boy a killer… He must have realized that Shakhurin didn't believe Volodya was the one fired the shots, and would demand an honest investigation. His call meant: deal with this yourself, I don't want to know anything. I'm scared," I said. "But then why did Sheinin include the message in the case file? Everyone knew who would read it. Perhaps it wasn't Shakhurin for whom the message was intended: Umansky placed his call when he knew it would be the secretary who'd take it. So maybe, the meaning of his call was different: I am to blame, I have been justly punished for failing to raise my daughter properly, my grief is endless, have mercy on me? I advise People's Commissar Shakhurin to dedicate all his efforts to the victory of the Soviet people in the Great Patriotic War. Such a message from Umansky would actually help Sheinin. I can't rule out the fact that Lev Romanovich dictated it himself. Is that right, Kostya?"

KONSTANTIN ALEXANDROVICH UMANSKY, AMBASSADOR OF THE SOVIET UNION TO MEXICO: Over the spring months I got the impression that Volodya Shakhurin was courting Nina. I must say, both my wife and I were alarmed about this; the boy made a negative impression on us, and we had heard unflattering things about him from others. *(Then why did you let Nina spend the night at the Shakhurins' dacha? Why did she accept Shakhurin's gifts?)* The boy was secretive and very persistent, both qualities that gave us pause. Nina held Artyom Khmelnitsky and Vano Mikoyan in higher regard. On the 3rd of June, she called me at work in the evening *(not the evening, and not at work, but in the Troyanovskys' room at the Moscow hotel)* and said that she was going for a walk with two boys *(and you said: just don't go walking alone).*

"Thank you."

UMANSKY: If I may — may I? — I want to make this quite clear: it is *completely impossible* that my daughter was seriously infatuated with Volodya. She was engrossed in her studies and couldn't care less for flirting.

ALEKSEI IVANOVICH SHAKHURIN, PEOPLE'S COMMISSAR FOR AVIATION INDUSTRIES OF THE USSR: My son is a stubborn, hot-headed, fierce boy. He studied well. I didn't notice that he had any bad inclinations. He behaved evenly and calmly all through the spring.

On June 3rd, he went for a walk with Vano, and 15 minutes later we learned… of the incident.

"Don't give me that crap!" the coach barked, and hobbled over to the figure that was moving its lips on behalf of Shakhurin, and extended his hand to his throat, groaning, "Speak!"

SHAKHURIN: Volodya did not keep a diary. He invented that story to make an impression at school. A boy could not become popular if he was well behaved, and I think Volodya was ashamed that, at the bottom of it all, he was just an ordinary, obedient boy.

"Something, at least! *Go on!*"

SHAKHURIN: Nina and Volodya often met after school — in my apartment or at the Umanskys' home. Sometimes at Vano's. My wife bought a bouquet for the Umanskys before they left. Volodya was happy about this, and with my wife he wrote a note to put with the flowers.

"Are you trying to tell us he wasn't planning to kill the girl?" the trainer wheezed, almost tenderly, while furiously wiping an itchy drop of sweat from his purple forehead. "That's not enough. It won't get him out of this!"

SHAKHURIN: Volodya did not have a weapon. My 6.35 caliber Mauser and my Belgian revolver were kept in my safe at work *(that's a clumsy lie, one handgun remained at home)*. And Nina was killed with a 7.65 caliber bullet.

"Ok, the weapons don't match. That's still not enough. Tell us more."

SHAKHURIN: Vano was also courting Nina.

"That's not much, Shakhurin!" The trainer leaned on the barrier that separated him from the past and tried to grab the bandaged arm of the witness, but Shakhurin pulled it away. "Tell us like a man," the coach asked simply, "while we're all here. It took us seven years to get here. You've got to give us something, a glimpse, a clue — just point us in the right direction, and we'll do the rest, we'll bite into it and won't let it go until we know what happened. Don't go quiet on me, Commissar. You know we'll have to leave soon. And no one will come back here. It'll just be you, alone, haunting this staircase. The ghost of you. Every night. You'll walk up and down these stairs and remember things. So just tell us now — say what you remember. You remember something, don't you? Not the ties and the purple suits. Not that fucking Yak-9. Tell us something. Go on, tell us."

The coach waited for a while in silence. Then he turned around and started to walk back to where I stood. Only then did the figure speak again, indifferent as before.

SHAKHURIN: From what Tanya Reizen's mother said, I know that Tanya told her mother as a secret that Vano and Volodya had talked about having a duel.

The witness suddenly raised his white bandaged arm, as if he were trying to touch his own face, and then his arm dropped. He did not have the strength.

THE KEY

I PACKED UP MY THINGS DURING THE NIGHT, HAVING RIDDEN TO the office in a crowded shuttle bus; I filled two trash cans with things to get rid of, and fit everything I really needed into a single black body bag. This I tied with a red ribbon; I still had my tin soldiers to pack — I would need two boxes, one for my collection and the other for duplicates. I chose November, a good month to end everything: nights are early, and there are days with warm wind when it's pleasant to walk to the metro thinking about the prospect of snow, Christmas tree markets, the stockings hanging in the street stalls, and the lights strung in the windows and over balconies, even though it's still raining, and the grass is thick and green around piles of dog shit on the lawn, and the forecasters keep promising either snap-freezes or sudden thaws, or a drastic drop in the dollar exchange rate, but nothing happens.

Without knocking, as if he was entering an uninhabited emptiness, Borya came in and anchored himself on a tiny window sill, blocking the light. He arranged his arms in an angular shape on his chest and stayed there, staring into nothing, adjusting his glasses every now and then — the way people wait for a judge to call them into a courtroom from a long bench filled with mad old women and lawyers.

I read the fresh piece of paper left on the desk:

VLADISLAV R-OV, CONDUCTOR.
"Vladislav R-ov, a young man then, often walked in the courtyard of the House of Composers with his Airedale terrier. I was just a

boy, and was friends with his son, so my contacts with Vladislav Dmitriyevich were limited to common courtesies. But neither then nor now, remembering him, could I sense in him the spark of God-given talent. He resembled a well-mannered and educated fixer who condescended to mere mortals out of boredom. Perhaps I am not being fair to him, but those were my impressions back then, and they have not changed."

"...He was an imitator, incredibly talented and artistic, and cheerful."

"My passport is American, but I am Russian in my soul..."

"I defected to the West from a banquet through the kitchen exit..."

I tore the note into four pieces, then into sixteen, and threw it away. Then I became aware of Borya's gaze, fixed on me all of a sudden; I fished the pieces out of the trash can and shoved them into my pocket.

Borya looked at me with eyes that had cried a long time ago, dried out and become fiery, and *saw* everything.

It was hard to be quiet. I didn't know what to do with my hands. It was dark, in autumn I can guess the time precisely. I wished the phone would ring.

"Stop," he said from a distance. "We have come to the edge, from here on there is only water. The ocean."

I heard stumbling, stunned steps, and the secretary appeared at the door. She looked furtively over the office, as if expecting to discover someone else there:

"I thought I overslept. Should I have come earlier today? You should have said something if you were going to be cleaning."

"I need two cardboard boxes," I said. She glanced at Borya's face and quietly closed the door; I could tell she remained on the other side, motionless.

"If I understand it correctly, the case is over. You don't need me anymore," Borya wanted to hear his own voice, uttering these words calmly. Now that he'd spoken the words, it was easier to be silent. I found I could move on from the piddly, secondary, frustrating things that happen to everyone and think about what might come next: Tsurko, the mother and the others would not help me, I couldn't explain an interest in Olya's suicide with my museum story. But the girl still had a father, any mention of whom was so carefully avoided in conversation that there must be relatives on her father's side and through them I could find her friends. Olya was buried at Vagankovo; if I found the grave, I would find out the girl's surname, the date of her death, the names of people responsible for the grave plot and their telephone numbers — that was my next trail, and I would follow it.

"I am very grateful to you. It was some kind of life, after all," Borya was becoming blurry in my sight, twitching, fading into a gray, flickering television speck, a glitch. "I wish that with people you would be at least a little more — " he concentrated, searching for the right word.

"I don't need your advice," I said.

The secretary appeared in the door again.

"There are people here. They say they're the new tenants and are moving in this afternoon. They asked for the keys."

"Give them the keys."

"Are we moving? Where? What should I do?"

"Gather your things, we're moving out today. Then stop by the accounting office to collect your salary and the severance pay. And write a letter of resignation."

"You don't like my work? Did you find someone to replace me?"

"Our organization is experiencing certain difficulties."

"I can work for a month, or two months, for free. Why didn't you say something? Why can't you just tell me things?"

"Maria Nikolayevna, let me tell you then: we have sufficient evidence that on the 3rd of June, 1943, on the Great Stone Bridge, Nina Umanskaya was shot and killed by Vano Mikoyan. That's all we wanted to know — so now we're closing."

"But you don't know why he did it!"

"That's not important."

"And you're just going to leave it at that?"

"Ah, you must be asking about justice," Borya said, smiling in what he thought was a soothing manner. "Retribution. But we're not the police, haven't you noticed?"

"But everyone must know that Shakhurin is not guilty!"

"Isn't he though? It all depends on how you look at it. We're all sinners, aren't we?" Borya crossed himself, reached inside his shirt, pulled out an imaginary cross from under his shirt, and kissed it.

"What was the point of it all then?"

"The Great Stone Bridge. You just didn't understand what we were doing," Borya said languidly and sadly. "We scraped up everything that was reflected in those human hearts, we calculated the balance of the testimonies — because you know, all of them, even those drawn under torture, even false ones, they all come from somewhere — and we put all this information together into our own bouquet. Except now the thorns stick out on all sides of it, and if we just take it out and give it to people, everyone will be hurt. That lot — " Borya pointed out the window and around the area" — the living, have no experience of facing the truth. You can't look at it. We've all been deformed by the protocols and records and people like, like him," Borya, without turning around, waved his hand in my direction. "And you, my dear, have had your brain sealed and packaged by the television, so now you demand that the truth be put forth and made available for public consumption. So you could eat it up and cry at the end. Now you're angry because we're not going to tell you when it is the right time to break out the tissues."

"Borya Antonovich, you're talking to me as if I were a stranger. I can understand *everything*."

"Well, then you should have understood that we're in the business of pure truth. We're only interested in *what really happened*. We're not in sales, we don't make money. We won't move a finger to make the truth more entertaining, to *bend it*, so that it jumps and turns, and keeps you ladies on the edge of your seats. Here's your truth, look!" Borya held up an empty palm. "It's gray and incoherent, it evaporates easily, it's hard to obtain, easy to appropriate — *is not interesting*. And you people think, if you paid for the tickets, then there must be an entrance somewhere and a popcorn stand! That's not our show. We're after the unnecessary. Time. And you, the Russian public…" Borya paused and shook his head bitterly. "At least you used to like your truth bloody. You tried to search…you fumbled in the dark, you were ok with that. But now you only want a cheap laugh, on the double! You can't look at another person's death, you don't want to know about your own death. Any hour of death, if it is examined attentively, swells up with terrifying, inexplicable details. Close attention to a single minute is dangerous. It's dangerous to tempt death with attention. When someone dies, that's the end, everything has already been said. And if someone keeps asking questions, if someone tries to get *too close*, then the witnesses start to *invent things*, they open their souls to what never was, the non-existent, the almost-happened, the could-have-been, and the past begins to think independently in millions of minds at once. This thinking past is dangerous, it is quicksand, it'll swallow everything. You can't look into it *for a long time*. The case is closed. We're leaving. Pack up your stuff."

Goltsman — disheveled, oblivious, fixed on the inner workings of his self — appeared in the hallway, maneuvering a new, enormous purple suitcase on wheels out of his emptied office. He pulled the handle upright with several jerks and buttoned his thick black overcoat.

"I don't feel very well," he said. "I put everything I didn't need on the desk. Will someone throw it away? I'm going. I called a taxi. Masha —" He wanted to kiss her, touch her, fall into her arms, but he was already leaving, and she was watching me. She looked intently at Goltsman, fixing him in her memory with his unevenly shaven cheeks, the heavy-lidded eyes, and sniffled into her hand. "I wish you the very, very best," Goltsman said, turned around and walked off, trundling the suitcase.

Borya belted out a snippet of an aria, jumped off the window sill, rushed to open and hold the door for Goltsman and followed him downstairs, to help him get into the taxi.

For a thousand rubles and a bottle of vodka I found out that Anastasia Vladimirovna Petrova was buried in section 14 in the

Vagankovo cemetery. As I drove there, staring at the license plate of a slow-moving truck in front of me, I realized I was as nervous as if I were going on a date; the ineffable, impalpable fabric of her life somehow did get caught on reality, a scrap remained, and I could be close to her, six feet above the only proof of her existence.

Section 14 turned out to be four enormous squares in the old part of the Vagankovo cemetery, to the left of the entrance, so packed with the dead that there was no space to put your feet between the graves. Headstones and crosses faced different directions, hid in the grass and behind one another. I skirted the edges trying to find my way in; I had thought that something would grab me right away, a name or a photo, but I spent two hours searching the graves one by one. Petrova's name was not there, but there was one unmarked headstone.

I went into the office. The watchman's room was occupied by a man in a clean blue undershirt, reclined comfortably in his chair. I asked about finding a grave. He told me to keep walking around. Was there a map of the burial sites in the archive? No, you'll have to walk around yourself. Was there a specific section where people were buried in 1984? No. Maybe the watchmen will remember the surname? Thousands of graves, both watchmen on the rounds. Enough to make you give up.

I went to the 'Registration' office next, and read the wall display from start to finish waiting for the woman at the registration desk to be alone.

"I can't find it," I said, offering her 500 rubles and a pathetic, defeated smile. "There's probably more than one Petrova there."

"*Petrova,*" she leafed through her book to December 1984, and then took out a second book. "Here we go: buried with Stepanida Ivanovna Stepanova. A rather large lot, two by two. It says here: a grave mound. Look for it by the size of the lot."

I went back to the man in the clean blue shirt. A hundred bucks, and he came out of the guard booth, following me like a balloon on a string. We divided the 14th section between us and started looking for a double lot. There were lots I couldn't reach at all; I would get back to the path and circle the edges of the graves, looking for a way in.

Then, my hired gun raised his arm and waved for me to come over. Hello, Tasya.

There were three crosses surrounded by a rusty fence; the gate was tied shut with a plastic bag. Clay mounds of the individual graves rose through the foam of fallen leaves like a woman's breasts.

But the girl Olya was not there.

I climbed over the fence, licked my finger with saliva and cleaned off the last name, lowest on the headstone, almost eaten by the ground: Petrova 2.12.84. I've caught up with you.

I was the only one left, I thought. Then I noticed that asters still fought to bloom on the graves, one bush planted on each mound. The crosses were decorated with plastic wreaths. Perhaps someone still came here. But certainly not her daughter. Not Iraida.

I wrote down the underground residents of this communal apartment: Stepanov Aleksei Nikolayevich, June 28 1937, Viktor Alexeevich *(must be the son)*, January 23 1969, Yevgeniya Alexandrovna 1953, Stepanida Ivanovna, June 7 1978 *(the wife, then?)* Yevgeniya Alekseevna *(the daughter)*, April 1 1975, I. M. Chuburkov, August 10 1978, and the most recent, Anna Ivanovna Kolotilina, February 14 2000. Who were these people in relation to Tasya Flam?

Another 500 rubles to the office, and I learned that the lot was registered to a Ms. Kolotilina. I called.

A small woman's voice answered:

"That's me. Only my mother might remember Granny Nastya. She works until 5." Then she made excuses and refused to meet until I promised to thank her appropriately. 11 o'clock on Saturday, then. I contemplated the fact that ordinary people often remember more of their lives.

I packed a gift set — chocolates, a tin of coffee, a box of tea and a bottle of vodka — and walked from Baumanskaya metro station to the German cemetery, where I got lost for a little while, after I took the wrong turn thinking I was on Soldiers' street. I found my way back to the cemetery, and suddenly was reminded of the day, years ago, in spring or summer, when I stood there with my son: my wife had gone to visit her father-in-law's grave, and I insisted on staying behind and keeping the boy with me, so there we were, waiting next to the colorful flower stands. Suddenly we heard hoof-beats: girls led up a pony. I paid them, my son climbed on the pony's back and grasped at the mane braided with ribbons, and we all happily departed away from the sadness and rode for a while, until the girls announced they were not taking us back, no riding in circles, and dropped us off at a playground with a wooden sign that said 'Little Bear'. I recognized it as I walked past it.

It took me three tries to get to the right street.

The mother, Tatyana Ivanovna, heavy, enormous, wide, with teeth sticking out in different directions, sat down opposite me. The China cabinet behind her contained several hundred Kinder Surprise toys. I silently put my offerings out on the table.

"Who are you to Petrova?"

"Aleksei Stepanov was well-off, he had an estate in Mikhnevo. He was married to Sofia's sister, Nastya's aunt. Aleksandr is his brother; Yevgeniya is the brother's daughter. Aleksei Stepanov also named his daughter Yevgeniya; and he also had a son with his housekeeper, Tatyana. He recognized the boy, Viktor, and his wife accepted it. Viktor left home at the age of 16. Stepanida Ivanovna is his wife. Granny Stesha. She's my aunt."

Fuck me, I thought. I'd have to draw a diagram. The upshot was that Tasya's aunt was not happily married, having a husband who productively screwed the housekeeper.

"They say that Petrova's granddaughter killed herself."

"Olga? She poisoned herself."

"Why?"

"Maybe she was affected after being assaulted in her building's entranceway... But she didn't talk to Granny Nastya. Olya was alone from the age of 13. That's when her mother got married and went abroad."

I listened some more and inquired:

"Why isn't Olya buried on your family plot?"

"I don't know, we'd have been happy to help. Iraida only got in touch after her mother died. We were surprised: why doesn't she bury her with Olya?"

"Do you remember Olya's surname? The year she died? How old she was?"

"I don't remember the year exactly, it was twenty or thirty years ago. She was quite young. Her surname was Voznesenskaya. Her husband grieved terribly."

"*Her husband?!*"

"Granny Stesha said he was tall, handsome. He was the first in the funeral procession and all but threw himself into the grave. He was living in a holiday home when Olya took poison. They lived well. Olya's apartment went to him. Tsurko's only granddaughter, Olga Voznesenskaya, poisoned herself while in a marriage that at least appeared happy from outside."

Recently, I've found that at around seven in the evening, my eyes always start closing of their own volition, but when I go to bed, everything's bothering me: I don't like to read — it's all made up; there's women's soccer on TV; I go out on to the balcony, sit on a folding chair and study the building opposite — as long as bums aren't drinking and singing in the courtyard and there aren't any Chinese-made fireworks shooting up from the sand-pit to the 12th floor windows.

On a night like this not too long ago, someone rang the doorbell. I held still, barely breathing. They rang again, without urgency; I thought they'd wait a little and leave, but snuck up to the peephole to look anyway. I felt myself blush — I embarrassed myself with my cockroach-like scuttling around in the dark.

It was the secretary. I opened the door.

"Good evening. Your telephone is turned off."

She came in, too shy to look around too much, tried to take off her shoes and find a coat hook. I was lost, terribly, terribly lost at the suddenness of all this, and acutely aware of my own homely, armorless appearance that she had never seen before, my disheveled, untucked, vulnerable self — and on top of everything else, my light bulbs had burnt out. I kept silent, not knowing what to do with myself and eventually just sat down on the floor to calm down, with my back to the wall, full of minor sufferings, and barefoot.

"Doesn't the light turn on?" She clicked the plastic switch. "Do you live *here*?"

"Yes."

"But there's nothing here. An empty room. What do you sleep on?" She was no longer an employee, she had the right to ask questions. "Boris Antonovich gave me your address. I stood by the entrance. I got so cold, I didn't know the door code, no one came out for a long time." She walked over to the balcony to see what I saw when I looked out, then crossed the room again and sat down, not touching me, but close.

We sat next to each other as if we had agreed to meet like this every night, to come together and talk, finding common interests. I couldn't quite pull myself together and come up with a lie, a pretense; I sat there, turning into a child, until suddenly I blurted, quite despite myself:

"Alyona's left me," and I made a tearing motion with my hands, a show of pain.

"I know," she said. "Did you love her?"

"Yes."

She waited, and then said:

"Then why did you torment her?"

She wanted me to say something, for example: Who told you that love means there's no point? Love means no death. When you're happy and in pain at the same time. It's bittersweet. Terrifying and painful. Your hand hurts, your fingers, your eyes, your memory hurts — the city hurts, the streets, the houses, the trolley bus routes hurt, time hurts: months, days. Some hours hurt more than others.

"You can't possibly be living here. You just don't want me to find out what your home is like. Pardon me for saying this, but you don't seem happy to me. What did you used to do? Boris Antonovich told me, but I suppose we can't talk about it? He said you were in the FSB, and then you helped young people get out of sects?"

"No, of course not. I made it all up."

"What for?"

"I had to start with something."

The secretary sighed and asked, a bit angrily:

"What else did you make up? Who else did you make up? Do you set up your tin soldier army in the morning and decide: you can keep living, but you, you're done? You shouldn't have said that, about making things up. Now I'm going to think about this all the time!"

"Why? We laid it all out — and there's still not a word of truth in it?"

"No, it's not that. I don't know," she turned to face me suddenly, and her hair brushed against my face. "Now, when we are alone, and I can't even see your face, can you tell me — just this once — what you really think?"

"I'm not instructed to form opinions. My job is to take a look, reconnoiter — and come back. Just as Borya told you."

"I don't believe him. I don't believe you either. Only Aleksandr Naumovich, but he didn't say anything."

"Well... the police found the bodies, right? They didn't know at the moment whose children these were. The cops — they're experienced people, they see corpses every day, and they were the ones who said, right away, the boy was a suicide. They must have seen the clear trace of the muzzle on his temple; there is always damage to the skin, the gunpowder gets in, it's very clear."

"But the police didn't find the gun."

"Who knows — they were moving the bodies, it might have slipped off the staircase."

"And the fact that Shakhurin kept his hand in his pocket?"

"It was his left hand, remember? He was highly agitated, it was probably shaking, so he put it in his pocket to hold still. If someone else were shooting at him, he would have thrown his hands up instinctively, both hands."

"Why did Vano clean his gun?"

"He was just a boy. He was afraid of his father, he didn't want to be found out. And some people have this down to a reflex — if you fire a weapon, you clean it. There's an answer to every question."

She stood up, seemingly wanting to leave, to be alone and think.

"And you personally? Do you really not care? I understand — you have your instructions — but still. Do you not care who fired the shot? Nina could have lived a long and happy life."

"It does not concern me. I've been given a mission: to make sure everyone is heard. Do you feel anything when you play computer games? It's the same thing."

"And for that, you gave seven years of your life? That's all you wanted?"

What did I want? I wanted one of them to come forward, to emerge from the fog. I wanted to see Nastya Petrova, Flam — but she did not wish to become an old woman, she left without photos of her fragile, rheumatic self, without endless complaints to nurses who come to take out the bedpan. What do I want. I would like to die, but remain alive... or the other way around: to live, but be dead.

"What else did Boris Antonovich say?" I asked.

She was silent for so long I was sure she wasn't going to answer. Then she spoke:

"That you wouldn't stop. That you'd wait for everyone to go away, to leave you alone and then you'd keep at it."

"What else?"

"That it was dangerous. Everything connected with this woman, Anastasia Petrova, is dangerous. That this is clear even from the fate of her lovers and husbands. He also said, but not about the woman, about something else: *she* will still prove stronger, and it's better for a person not to learn this, to keep hoping. He thinks you'll have no way to return. If you go. That's almost everything."

"He said something else about me, didn't he?"

"He told me not to visit you."

"And yet he gave you my address."

"He wanted to make sure I didn't go looking for you... there." A piece of paper appeared in her hand. "I went to the House of Government, I talked to the neighbors. Everyone says they remembered Olya Voznesenskaya as a very cheerful person. Whenever Petrova bought her something for school, Olya was thrilled. She studied at the foreign languages Institute. She gave up her studies when she fell in love with Vladislav R-ov. She planned to marry another man, but killed herself."

She didn't pause to wait for a thank-you or any questions, just went on: "I went to the Institute and persuaded the administration to show me Voznesenskaya's case for a minute. This is everything I wrote down."

She put the sheet of paper on the floor between us, so she wouldn't have to get any closer to me. "Anyway. Here's the point: call me if you need anything. I don't want you to have to do it alone. I'm not afraid of anything. I can do anything if you need me to. Just don't lie to me."

I waited for her steps to fade, then disappear behind the bang of the building's door. Then I pulled out my cell phone, pushed a button, and in the light of the tiny screen studied the first clear trace, the print of a narrow, running young foot: Voznesenskaya Olga Petrovna (*father Pyotr Voznesensky, who was he?*), born March 6, 1953, graduated from school #122 in the Frunzensky district. In the winter of 1973 (*she was 19 — that's when R-ov appeared*), she asked for a leave of absence for health reasons. She also transferred from full-time studies to the night classes. There was a memo of removing her name from the fourth-year students' list dated December 1975 — that's about when she died, at the age of 22, with time enough for a husband and her unhappy love. And there was the residential registration: Zholtovsky street, now Yermolaevsky Lane, building 10, apartment 27. She changed her last name when she got married, to Ovsyannikova. I read closer, and found what I missed the first time: Olga Petrovna Voznesenskaya was born *the day* after the official death of the Emperor.

Number 10 on Yermolaevsky Lane had no Ovsyannikovs listed in the phone book.

On Wednesday, I went back to the passports and registration office (open from 4 to 7), gave the clerk money, and named the address and the name:

"I am trying to locate this person. She moved out of here. Can you tell me where she went?"

A week later they told me Olga Ovsyannikova, nee Voznesenskaya, moved in 1973 to 7 Kuusinen Street."

"Alone? Don't you have her husband's name as well?"

They did not.

The address they gave me had a resident named Ms. Levina listed in my database. No Ovsyannikovs. Feeling futile, I called, and a rude voice replied, guttural and savage — they must've rented to migrants or something.

"I'm trying to locate a person," I said. "Olga Petrovna Voznesenskaya, she was once a resident at this address. Have you heard this name?"

"I'm her husband."

In his voice as we spoke: it was as if something was taking off. Something that didn't happen with anyone else was happening with him, he found his life finally needed, he wanted to talk.

"I am collecting materials about Olga Petrovna's family for a museum. I would like to meet with you. Just a few questions, it won't take long. Where's a convenient place for you?"

"Let's meet in the apartment then, you can see where Olya lived..."

I hurried. I didn't want to lose him, so I gave him my phone number, and immediately thought it a mistake to have done so. But then again, he asked for it. It was hard to do this alone. On Sunday, Ovsyanikov called:

"Sasha (*who the fuck said you could call me Sasha?*), first, (*here we go, this is bullshit, he must have talked things over with his Ms. Levina*) I've got some guests over from Kyiv, there are lots of people in the apartment. And second, I know so little..."

I protested energetically, and he agreed to let me call later. I called in ten days:

"We wanted to meet."

And now he cut me off:

"*You* wanted to meet. I have nothing to say."

"Ten minutes. Wherever you want. I'll send a car for you. You don't have to say anything. Just listen to me and say: this is true, and this is not true."

"No."

"Could you at least talk to me on the phone?" He had to find it terrifying, and interesting, to see what I'd dug up...

"We're already talking."

"Did you meet Olya's grandmother, Petrova?"

"Granny Nastya. She was a tall, stooping old lady, very imposing, like Anna Akhmatova. In her photographs and oil portraits she was quite a stunning woman. I know that she met her husband in Japan. Or was it China? Everyone says she wasn't tall? She was my height, and I'm five nine. Vasya? He wasn't hard to control, more like Forrest Gump. He had a crew cut. He was very knowledgeable, like a dictionary. He had a wonderful memory. He played chess brilliantly."

"When did you get married?"

"In 1971. We divorced six months later. I went abroad for three years, and she was supposed to join me. But something happened *to them*."

"Did you see each other after the divorce?"

As if he hit something heavy in the darkness, he said:

"Yes."

"People told me her husband walked behind her coffin at the funeral."

"There was no other husband. That was me."

"Did her father come to the funeral?"

"Yes. He went to the cemetery every week."

"Was Olya beautiful?"

"Very," lots of warmth in his voice, all of a sudden.

"Like her grandmother?"

"No! She was different."

"When did she die?"

"In December 1975?"

"Was her death connected with her illness?"

(Very curt and quickly):

"Yes. She had a concussion."

I thought: here comes the well-rehearsed lie, to end things quickly.

"An injury?"

"Yes, she fell from a window sill."

"A window sill?"

"Yes. She was washing the window. She hit her head on the hardwood floor."

"I was told about an unhappy love for some musician…"

"I don't want to remember that. I'm sorry. It's rather painful."

Why was Ovsyanikov scared? His former wife, to whom he was only married briefly, committed suicide thirty years ago. He was 60 years old. How did he live? For what? Did he want to preserve his memory of her? Does he want me to give him more information, more memories — or is he afraid of more pain that would come with that? Because, if you think about it, what kind of role did he, A. A. Ovsyanikov have in this story, where his wife fell in love with another man and could not live without him.

I stood in the middle of the room, thinking and listening, then quickly got dressed and drove to Goltsman's. He opened his apartment door without asking who was there as though he slept near the intercom buzzer. He just stood there with his face distorted by fatigue.

"Why aren't you asleep?" I stepped over two bags in the doorway: was he going away to the dacha?

"I'm checking into a hospital."

"You told me last time that everything was fine!"

"That's what they said. But they still wanted me to do more tests, remember? I went, they ran me through their Japanese equipment."

"And what did they say?"

"The doctor who examined me said I had to go to hospital immediately. He said I had a polyp. It has to be removed."

After each reply, Goltsman paused, perhaps feeling disgusted. It irritated me regardless.

"But does this need to be urgent? Can you go spend some time with your son, and do it later?"

"I asked them. I wanted to wait until autumn, to work on an essay about the Odessa underground. But he said: no, you're losing blood. You have low hemoglobin. Weakness. The pain in your stomach will get worse. He also asked if I had anyone to look after me. But he said: not for long." Goltsman waited and then added, as if placing the last pebble on the table. "They do the surgery at the cancer clinic."

"But a polyp — that's... That's not bad. The cancer clinic — it's just because that's where they have the experts. We'll visit you. Just call me and tell me where you are."

Goltsman, without looking at me, stood up and made the tea. He moved heavily, deliberately, as if he were walking uphill with a heavy backpack.

"What are you going to do?" He didn't ask "what are you doing?"

"When?" I took the hot cup and smiled intently.

"In general."

"I'm going to get old. If I can make any money, I'll start spending it on prostitutes. If I don't, I'll get a job selling newspapers at the Kievskaya metro station, in the tunnel from the radial line to the ring line. There's a steep staircase there and constant drafts: in the summer, the gusts of air lift up girls' dresses, and if you sit on a reclining soft chair behind the stall and look up..."

I was at Vagankovo cemetery again. It was Easter once more, and everyone had bouquets of flowers, the spring sun was shining, a trumpet player lifted the instrument to his lips whenever he saw visitors who looked well-to-do. People, lively and indifferent, studied the statues of bandits and nobility as if only those who were unlucky had to end up in a cemetery. I saw the secretary standing by the crematorium, among the black headscarves of those waiting for the burial service. She acted reserved, until the very last moment, when I extended my hand for a handshake and her face slipped, as if a sudden gust of wind rippled a still puddle.

"Are you happy?" I asked.

She shook her head no, and her face slipped again, the set crust cracked, revealing something alive, the surface of the soul:

"Everything's turned out well. Only a few things didn't work out."

"Love and an interesting job," I prompted.

"You guessed it."

"Just like for everyone."

People carried bouquets in shining and rustling packets, and large scooters drove past with decaying wreaths. "What's your name?" I asked.

"Are you mental? You know my name."

"I just can't sleep. I have nowhere to live. A lot of people invite me to stay with them, but not for free." She was still looking at me. "Do you think I'm looking a bit worse for wear? I've got no one to wash my clothes. No money to buy new ones. Never mind, I like old clothes! Torn clothes. I only miss hot water." We walked between the graves. "I talked with you so much during these years... We've been through so many stories together. And even worse. I got everything from you, I shouldn't want anything more. I notice all the signs of being in love in myself: I'm timid, I can't bring myself to look you in the face. I stutter whenever I talk to you; you don't laugh at my jokes. Look at me: I walk and shake, I can't imagine how to take your hand. I never thought that I would feel this way. Like a schoolboy. In the mornings I think: I'll see her. And that's the reason I get up. And life has meaning, a joyful meaning."

"You avoided me."

"I thought... I imagined a lot of things. But I thought you would definitely push me away, and then you'd feel bad about it. And I can't give you anything. Not even money. I don't know how be a husband, or a lover, or even a friend."

"You keep saying, pain. But there are other feelings too," she replied weakly and dully, not taking her eyes off me. "What's up with Alexander Naumovich?"

"He's going to have surgery, they'll cut a polyp out of his colon. I told you about Goltsman to get you to come out. But actually... Do you have your phone with you? Here's the number. Aleksei Alexeevich Ovsyanikov. Tell him I asked you to look for Olya Voznesenskaya's grave, to take a picture of it. Say you're at the cemetery right now, you're by the crematorium, where do you go next? Don't let him think, just keep talking, you're walking, let him hear you breathe..."

I knew he needed a woman's voice, he'd be glad to hear from this girl, who had heard about his love. It'd been a month since I talked to him, enough time for all the memories it stirred up to swallow him, to consume him — he wouldn't refuse this new and strange girl. "But you don't need the grave," I said. "You need to ask the question: who were Olya's friends? At least *one* living person, and not just a name, but what they do, where they live. Talk quickly, and remember — your voice must be full of blind force, you can't see him, but you are certain that he can't help but reply to you. Go on!"

Maria walked away, placed the phone to her head, as if she were warming her ear with her hand, and I watched and snarled like a wolf at the graves — I hated them, there was no way to prepare for this. Even for old age. Even for the contempt of the young. Nervously, I looked around: she was listening and writing something down!

"Got something?"

"She was friendly with a Kholmyansky. They went on holiday together. His name is Alexander. A playwright. He didn't name anyone else."

"He chose the most harmless person. The one who would remember things in his favor."

"Olga is buried next to her father and grandmother. Her father's second wife looks after the grave. I couldn't hear the name clearly: Elina or Evelina. But she's the only one who has the key to the iron gate around the grave plot. She doesn't give it to anyone. Olya's grave is marked by a bronze rose. It's been sawn off twice already," She was trying to draw me into the search, make me walk with her and tell me the rest on the go.

"Don't be offended," I said. "But I have to go alone from here."

I followed the directions Maria gave me, thinking about what kind of people would come to the cemetery in the middle of the night to steal a bronze rose off a grave. There's an amazing amount of energy in our populace.

Finally, I saw them: the three gravestones together: MARGARITA MIKHAILOVNA VOZNESENSKAYA, 1907 — 1984, PYOTR PETROVICH VOZNESENSKY, 1927-1995, OLGA VOZNESENSKAYA,1953-1975. Apparently, when they buried Pyotr Petrovich, they also touched up his daughter's gravestone, because both now had Orthodox crosses engraved on them. There were carnations, willows and fir branches, all arranged on top of the graves in precise patterns, and small blue flowers on Olga's grave, also in neat order. I would like to find the hands that created these patterns, faithful hands with a good memory.

In the cemetery's registry office, the clerk told me:

"Natella Trofimovna Voznesenskaya. The grave is registered in her name."

Must have been an officer's daughter. Officers after the war gave their daughters fanciful names: trophy films, trophy cigarette lighters, the lust for happiness — they wanted to escape their fate.

"I won't give you her phone number," the clerk said, refusing to take the 500 ruble note I offered. She recognized me and thought about the fatal troubles caused by harmless-looking people who ask such questions. I gave her a thousand and told her to dial the number herself, she could listen to me speak to Ms. Voznesenskaya.

She did dial, but Natella was not at home. The clerk gave the person who answered my number, but I knew they wouldn't call — I wouldn't.

Outside the office, Maria was waiting for me — so unexpected, it gave me a start when she touched my sleeve.

"Here," she held out two keys on a wire ring and an address written down. "If you want, you can stay with me, as long as you like. Just like that."

She stayed next to me, thinking we might walk back to the metro together.

"I'm sorry," I said. "But after looking at all these graves I have to be alone. To think things over."

I turned into the bushes, unzipped my pants and with pleasure, finally peed onto a concrete fence with the slogan "United Russia is a strong Russia." Mr. Alexander Kholmyansky, you're next.

KHOLMYANSKY

I FOUND MENTIONS OF KHOLMYANSKY IN A FEW PREMATURELY-written memoirs, whose authors did not have the assurance of publication provided by a golden supply of laureate medals in boxes with velvety, seemingly dusty insides; Kholmyansky was remembered as "the new hope of Russian drama," that was not to be fulfilled. He left for the States and disappeared there. On the Internet I found the email *holm@vogue.ru* and a photo of a hung-over fellow in a knitted cap standing in front of an advertisement for laundry detergent. I wrote to the address and two minutes later received an auto-reply: the account does not exist. I spent the next two weeks sending out feelers, phone calls, sniffing the air — and suddenly Kholmyansky turned up in Moscow. He was panning for gold at television mines, and he agreed to meet at Café Délifrance.

I caught myself expecting a young man — because Olga died young.

Kholmyansky came in, tall, six-five at least, spoke slowly, lazily, and looked all droopy as if somehow made out of an empty pillow case, a narrow-shouldered boy in a sweater and light pants, with tired eyes behind glasses, and the serenity of a an absent-minded, unfussy, melancholic — I would like to be like that well into my old age. He had a feeble handshake, like a person with a heart defect. We sat down at a tiny table, Kholmyansky filled his pipe; the waiter in a long apron assessed my appearance and gloomily said:

"Pay straight away, please." I ordered a Coke with ice and three pastries. Kholmyansky looked away, as if he had nothing to say. I was prepared for this: he had lived in America, where people like him learn to boil the past down to simple, easily digestible anti-Soviet mush, plus he was also a writer, all the more likely to mix the truth with marketable fiction without distinguishing what was what.

"I knew Olya from when we were in the eighth grade, she lived nearby," he said. "Her home became a club — we met every day, Olya was the soul of our company, and when she died the group fell apart. That was the best time of my life. They were three pretty friends — Olya Biryukova, Maria Kotova who was the prettiest, with red hair, and Olya. Then me, a boy called Rashid, another boy called Alik, who was chubby," he smiled: being chubby now seemed comical.

"Describe Ms. Voznesenskaya."

"She wasn't conventionally beautiful, you had to look closely to appreciate her. She had this little upturned nose; she was tall, slim, dirty-blonde hair... She looked like Cate Blanchet a little. Like an English lady. Her English was very strong — back then, knowing a foreign language meant a lot more than now. No one could have imagined she was capable of taking her own life. I remember her nickname, Rodina."

"How did you spend your time?"

"We read foreign literature, we listened to rock music records, Seva Novgorodtsev — you know him? — on a Japanese record player. We knew that we lived behind the iron curtain, that there was a world outside and we were deprived of it. And we mainly talked about how to survive in *this* country, to remain a decent human being and not perish."

"You mean this was a problem? Were people perishing all around you?"

The client gave a hostile shrug.

"Well, it really started when we all became students: this you could write about, but *that* you couldn't. We couldn't accept it! And we didn't wear our Komsomol badges outside the institute! The girls became foreign languages majors, so they could graduate and leave the country.

Rashid got a job at the Foreign Affairs Ministry. We wanted spiritual freedom, not material... Everything cost just pennies back then! We'd decide to go travel, like the characters in our favorite novels, and we'd run to the train station, give a porter on the train twenty-five rubles and have the car all to ourselves. We'd be in Kyiv by the next morning! We explored the Baltics — I remember it was such a shock when I saw the slogan 'Glory to the Communist Party' written not in white on red, but in white on blue!"

"What can you say about the Voznesensky family?"

"Her father was an official somewhere with the Moscow City Council. Maybe that explains Olya's reserve, it always seemed like there was something she wasn't saying. Her mother was a striking society woman: theater premieres, the latest books, and so on... I never met either of her grandmothers. She had an uncle? That's the first I've heard of it."

"How did Olga's marriage come about?"

"It was completely unexpected. She was the first of the girls to get married. She kept all her emotions and thinking deep inside her; we didn't really understand what happened. A teacher of Arabic started coming to our gatherings. He was an intellectual, with short-cropped hair, in a sweater... Ovsyanikov. Then this humorist appeared — he wrote a parody that was published in the back pages of *Literaturnaya Gazeta,* you know, where they used to put the semi-risqué stuff. He was an alcoholic and an intellectual, although the humor in his stories is quite vulgar. The humorist was the one who introduced her to R-ov... That was a turning point — Olya plunged into a completely different sort of life, we were all left behind with our childish pursuits. She grew up very quickly. I remember one time she took us to some basement to see Savely Pogonshikov — lots of icons, paintings, mysticism, vodka... And she became a stranger to us because of *what* she did. R-ov would go on tours and leave her his enormous orange dog in the apartment she moved into, on Kuusinen street, where she planned to live with Ovsyanikov. And it wasn't like they bought this dog together or raised it — it was *his* dog, and it was monstrous, it would bark at everyone and Olya would sit there with this dog, like its personal slave and listen to R-ov tell her on the phone about all the places he got to see. And who was with him."

"You described Voznesenskaya as a rational, rather dry person — these aren't the sort of people who commit suicide."

"She went mad. R-ov — he was living large, he had his father's fame, and huge American car he raced around Moscow, he had success as a conductor…" Then, with undying resentment: "but he wasn't a genius!"

He listened to my requests for the telephone numbers of Olya Biryukova and Masha Kotova, then shook my hand, turning me off like a table lamp. I remembered the name of that humorist — Shchukin — a long-haired fellow, regular contributor to the humor magazine *Crocodile*.

"Can I stay here for the night?"

Maria nodded, shocked and silent. She wore a horrible dressing gown that revealed her bare knees covered in bruises. She needed a different life, in which she could wear different dresses. I followed her down the gorge-like hallway with dangerous outcrops of bicycles, baskets of potatoes and various carts, stepped over the flotilla of shoes — this was a communal apartment. A dumpy woman with a fat nose and wrinkled ankles moved towards us.

"Good evening!" I said politely. "Looks like the summer's over then!"

"She can't hear you."

In the locked toilet and bathroom the lights were on. Maria's own room accommodated a fold-down couch, a chest of drawers, a chair, a bedside table with a computer on it, and numerous textbooks. Maria made sure she snatched someone's photo in a cheerful frame with hearts on it out of my sight.

"You can take the cushions off the couch. I'll make a bed for you on the floor."

"I won't fall asleep anyway. I'll just sit."

We waited for the children's running to die down and for the toilet to stop flushing.

"Let's go to the kitchen. I'll make you something to eat," she offered, then frowned, considering the seething crater of saucepans that was probably left by the neighbors, and changed her mind: "Better you stay here. I'll bring you a plate. You can turn on the television, quietly."

I wondered if she were thinking of what would happen during the night. When she turned off the light? What should she wear to bed? I grabbed a dried apple from a potpourri plate and shook it, listening to the seeds rattle in the emptiness inside with a dry, bony crack.

In the darkness, I lay down on the cushions that were slipping apart under me, pulled up a fragrant blanket and prepared for the evening's conversation — payment for the accommodations. Someone very old shuffled to the toilet as if on skis; I bet they would fall asleep sitting on the john.

"Are you asleep?" Maria wanted to drown out the gurgling and splashing. "Did you find the humorist who introduced Olya and R-ov?"

"No. I found a mention of him that said he left for Germany back in 2003. Good night."

I waited for her to start breathing evenly, asleep, then got up, found the kitchen, dragged a stool close to the window sill, and found room for my elbows in between potted violets. Down below, an occasional car sped by. Across the street, TV screens flickered in the empty rooms of alcoholics.

"Why didn't you wake me up?" Maria asked, coming into the kitchen behind me, but hiding her bare knees behind the door. "If you're uncomfortable on the floor, you can come sleep on the couch. It's wide, we won't get in each other's way. You should sleep," she worried. "You won't last long this way. You won't able to work!"

"I'll be coming soon. I'll sit here for a while and then I'll come."

It was night time — and at night it always felt to me like death paused and ceased chewing on me. It just lay there quietly, next to me, teeth on my throat — but it wouldn't sink them any deeper until morning, one could be left alone in bed. It's funny: when you're asleep, everyone leaves you alone, like you're already dead a little, and you can rest in the darkness, feeling the cold of the resting teeth on your throat.

I waited for Olga Biryukova at the Chocolateur Café. She walked straight towards me, utterly confident: a gray suit, steely, hard hair, an iron gaze, she was confident and short; she gave a firm handshake. I saw her nose was uneven, seemingly broken.

"Do you smoke?" I asked.

"Yes, unfortunately." We went up to the second floor and sat by the entrance; she brushed the menu away, lit a cigarette and ordered: "You talk first."

I delivered my lies, studying a golden bangle on her wrist, three rings, her earrings — enormous like chocolates — the gold chain on her neck and her pearl necklace.

"She came to our school in Leontiev lane in the fourth grade," she said about Olya. "It's a centrally located, aristocratic school — children of artists, musicians, directors, secretaries of regional committees. We made friends. We had something in common. She treated me like a sister. She lived in number six on Tverskaya, and Masha Kotova was in number five, across the street. We all hung out at Masha's place, don't let Kholmyansky tell you otherwise."

"Do you remember Voznesenskaya's parents? Or her grandmother, Anastasia Petrova?"

"I never heard anything about Grandma Petrova. There was Grandma Mutsa, she was the nicest person. I was also aware of a retarded uncle, a distant relative who needed to be looked after. Iraida brought back books in English from her endless trips abroad. I think she was a simultaneous interpreter."

"Olya's father was the head of the legal department of the Moscow City Council. He was very tall, with a turned-up nose, painstakingly groomed. He turned gray early. He did some things that were uncommon for a Soviet official, he did not dress like a Party member: he liked plaid sport coats, especially with mustard and earth tones, yellow ties. I only sat at the same table with him at the wake. At the wake, Petrovich got very drunk and said: if I'd known there were mentally ill people in Olya's family, I would have kept her locked up... It was Mezentsov who started to call him Petrovich."

"Mezentsov?"

She spoke with relief, as if shaking a pebble out of her shoe, coughed, and got rid of the invisible awkwardness that had hindered her from the first moment:

"Olya was married to Mezentsov. Then for nineteen years I was his wife."

I chewed intently on the chocolate pancake and carefully wiped my mouth with a napkin, trying to fit into the twenty-three years of Olya's life her husband Ovsyanikov, another husband Mr. Mezentsov and R-ov's son, the owner of an orange dog.

"The way Kholmyansky described your group..."

"Nothing of the kind! No samizdat! We only listened to the Beatles on the BBC. What discussions could we have had? We talked about men and books!"

"And that Olya was dry and rational?"

"She wasn't rational at all! She didn't think about the future at all. When a woman is *as beautiful as she was,* things tend to take care of themselves. She wasn't meant for studying or working. She couldn't work, she had no discipline, it was genetic... She didn't do anything around the house. She couldn't get up in time to go to the institute. People bought her alarm clocks, but she couldn't get up on time and didn't want to. She was terribly unfit for everyday life. But she was incredibly kind and generous. Compared to her I'm just a bitch."

"Kholmyansky said Olya wasn't conventionally beautiful or striking." Ms. Biryukova, smirking with disdain, leaned forward and spelled it out for me:

"Olya was so beautiful, so striking that she could have any man she wanted. Men fell for her at first sight. All of them. Anywhere. My future husband, Mezentsov, met her when he gave her a ride in the rain. He immediately asked for her phone number, and of course, she didn't give to him, she was a modest girl. So he lurked at the place where he picked her up and every day gave her rides. When R-ov's red Mustang appeared at that spot instead of Mezentsov Zhiguli, Olya told Mezentsov to go away, and that she didn't love him, and it hurt his feelings. The two men fought in public!"

"Why did she marry Ovsyanikov?"

"Olya's father, Petrovich, fell in love with a nurse from the local clinic. Natella was her name. It was a very difficult time for everyone — scandals at home, terrible scenes. Olya had to choose whether to stay with her mother or go live with her father, and she decided that instead she would get married and move out. She knew that it wasn't for long, she didn't love that Ovsyanikov, Lyosha, at all, and he knew it, but he loved her passionately. He was a kind person. Olya decided that at that difficult moment, Lyosha would comfort her."

"Did Olya love Vladislav R-ov?"

The woman considered the question and answered simply:

"Yes. Very much. Vladislav was very handsome, very touching. He was gallant, dressed her from head to foot. I didn't fit in with his people; it was clear that Olya suddenly found herself among men — and women — who were really decadent, even depraved. One day, she got a call from another woman who said, I heard that you used to look after Vladislav's dog. Now it's my turn. What should I feed it? How many times a day do you take it for a walk? The bastard! Why give her the telephone number? He doesn't remember anything? *He remembers everything!*"

"Olya died."

"It was their break-up that killed her. Olya was a person of great sincerity, and it clashed with a man who lived exclusively for his own pleasure. After R-ov, Olya was taken to the clinic and put on tranquilizers, in a terrible state. She didn't sleep, even when she took sleeping pills, she said she heard voices. I saw that she was in a bad way, really bad, she had no control of herself. She didn't look after the apartment on Kuusinen well, it was furnished with the shards from the divorce, bits and pieces from former owners, there were cockroaches in the kitchen."

"Did she write anything before she died?"

"A personal note. Without Mezentsov's permission I can't tell you what it said."

"Did Olya ever tell you anything about Nina Umanskaya?"

"No."

No. And that was it. No.

I left, went to flag down a car, and received a text message: "Are you coming for supper?" I remembered being asked that question before in my life, back then I always said no.

Maria did some work: she had cleared away two shelves for me in the dresser, and filled them with t-shirts and boxer-shorts she bought for me, guessing the size. I had to eat slowly; I praised the cutlets and chose a desert. Cleaned-up neighbors came into the kitchen one after another to meet me, pushing their children out from behind their backs.

I excused myself to take a breather on the staircase, found a crumpled cardboard box behind the rubbish chute, put it down on a step and sat on it — it was warm, I could sit there for a long time.

"What's wrong with you? Is everything really OK?" Maria squeezed in next to me. Of course, the woman felt like she had to share everything, she'd been taught to dissolve herself in her man, to live by his interests and desires. "How was your meeting with Biryukova? Is there anyone else to look for now? Are you sure nothing's bothering you?"

Something did bother me: Biryukova was feeling guilty about something. In her personal truth I had glimpsed a passing, pale shadow of rivalry: one doesn't just destroy photographs of one's best friend who took her own life. Maybe it was the terror of things repeating themselves, of Olya's life resembling that of her grandmother's: the girl's beauty, the multiplying husbands and lovers, the ghosts... and I began to sense that there was more than one person to blame.

"I need: Karina Proskurina — the bridesmaid at Olya's wedding. Natella — the second wife of Pyotr Voznesensky, a medical worker, presumably from the clinic that served the employees of the Moscow City Council. And above all, Stepan Mezentsov, husband of Olga Voznesenskaya, later husband of Olga Biryukova."

In the kitchen I turned out the light and sat closer to the window sill. I counted the trucks, excluding the Gazel vans. Cool air came in from the window; I took off my t-shirt. Maria spent a long time making noise in the bathroom, then looked into the kitchen, asked:

"Let's go to bed."

"I still won't fall asleep."

"Just try. You look terrible."

"I'll sit here. And then I'll come."

"I'll wait for you. When you sit like that, it's as if you're going somewhere."

Tomorrow night, I thought to myself, she would try to cry at this point.

The second husband of the suicide Voznesenskaya, Stepan Mezentsov, received me at the Rossiya Hotel. A stout secretary informed me I was at 'Mr. Mezentsov's office.' He was a youthful-looking, 70-year-old man, was incredibly slow in his movements and very surprised to encounter a character with my questions.

"She was a sincere person. She was not a cynic. She was ironic. She liked narrow trousers made of thin material, to fit her figure. She was incredibly beautiful. Olya's parents did not object to our marriage."

"We went to the Baltics for our honeymoon, found a house on an island, five kilometers to the nearest dwelling. And we lived alone on our own land. There was a bath house. At night Olya went to swim in just a night gown," he sat very still as he said all this, his eyes fixed on those nights, a long time ago. "Only sometimes in the evening we drove the car to a restaurant to have supper. I was utterly happy."

"You weren't concerned about the age difference between you?"

"Sixteen years is not that much. My affair with Olya was the first true passion of my life. I left a respectable family for her, a luxury apartment with six rooms on Tverskaya Street opposite the Minsk hotel, with a maid... I never regretted it."

"Did Olya introduce you to her Grandma? Anastasia Vladimirovna Petrova."

"No. I only knew Mutsa."

"Do the surnames Umansky or Shakhurin mean anything to you?"

"No."

"How did you meet Voznesenskaya?"

"In 1974. I drove her home, in the rain. And then I found her *(he added in a whisper)*, using the experience of a professional Moscow rake. I gave her rides. She couldn't make herself go to classes, she said she would just sit there and cry and she didn't know why."

"Did you understand that she was ill?"

"Yes, but I didn't realize the full extent of it. Basically, we were married for only six months, and she spent three of them in the psychiatric hospital in Kuntsevo, at the psychiatric hospital. There I realized just how ill she was. One day I went to visit her not during the usual hours, but in the morning, and she looked at me with this *absolutely glassy stare.* She said: unless you take me with you, I'll kill myself. I took her out of there. Olya put on a beautiful dress, and we went to a restaurant. She seemed completely happy. But three days later she killed herself."

"How did she die?"

"Olya killed herself on my birthday. I went to work in the morning. I always tried to call her during the day, and that day she didn't answer. My father found her and called the ambulance. I couldn't handle the funeral — I just wasn't fit to do it. I went to Sverdlovsk to work on a movie and stayed there for two months."

"Did Olya leave a note?"

"Yes."

"If it's not a secret... Could you share?"

"Volodya, I love you. But I can't bear to suffer anymore."

I wondered if he made it up on the spot.

"Could I look at it?"

"I didn't keep it for some stupid reason."

"Do you go to the cemetery?"

"I used to go. But then I went there once and I couldn't find the grave."

"I heard that after a while you married Olya's friend?"

"I couldn't forget Olya. I married Biryukova and for a long time

I found her to be a great consolation. She is a very kind woman, but eventually she grew irritated with my constantly looking back, at the grave."

On the bus I held out what had been said in my mind, stretched the fabric of the words, noticing the threadbare patches and knots, and thought: you become part of the fabric yourself, without noticing, and then one day — this is your life. I read the ads — "Animals put down. Removal, castration, sterilization. Evenings and weekends." A billboard tried to fight AIDS with a slogan "Life is worth more than a moment of dubious pleasure," and I chuckled: who'd come up with the *dubious* part? Suddenly, briefly and not painfully, but still with fear, I thought about my own past: I had to learn, while there was still time ahead of me, to make the past inhabitable, to measure it with my steps, to plan what to put where. I should test it out, break it in, like a pair of shoes, so that it'd be warm when I needed it, so that it'd be cozy and I'd know how to use it: where to turn when I needed to feel happy and which corners I should avoid even if someone called my name from there.

I stayed out late walking around a supermarket, looking at chocolate for weight loss and the seven-stack pyramid of condoms under an enormous poster that said, "Family Planning." Among thrashing fish, an enormous lobster lay on an ice pedestal, its claws tied shut, just in case, with neat white strips of paper. There were mute drops of moisture, like tears, hanging on his antennae.

THE OTHER WIFE

I don't like august. it's short. weak. pointless, enslaved by autumn and unstable. It's covered in withered birch leaves, filled with thoughts of school, illnesses and work. The grass smells as if it's saying farewell. I touched Maria's hand while we sat on a park bench, to see if she were cold. She sighed and drew closer as if trying to hear something inside me.

"Tell me about your day."

I felt that Mezentsov did not live with Olga immediately before her death, and at best just dropped by to spend the night occasionally. I also thought he hadn't just lost her note without any reason.

I was a little frightened: every person I met told me the story of a beautiful girl taking her life, but the story kept changing with the light falling on a new trigger, a new reason every time. They were playing with me; I had to guess which hand the call was in, but I knew: in these games all the hands turn out to be empty. R-ov knows *everything* I need, I simply need to find a way to unclench his fingers.

"In a bad mood again?" Maria stroked my shoulder. "Then let me tell you about my day. I found Shchukin's email in Germany and sent him a message. I've tracked down Karina Proskurina, the bridesmaid at the wedding, but only on the internet so far, I'm still looking for her phone number. I found a woman who worked at the Mayor's administration who remembers Natella Voznesenskaya, but this lady is retired and lives at her dacha. Finally, tonight, I got ahold of her and she gave me three numbers for Natella: the home number, the dacha at Serebryany Bor (if it hasn't been taken away) and her sister's apartment."

I heard a rasp in Maria's voice — as always when a person is preparing to say something important:

"I am worried about you. Everything connected with Petrova, and now with Olya — it's like we're being lured into a trap. You've already done a lot. You can't get them all back. All of this," — she drew a big circle with her arm to encompass the world, — "this…it isn't just your life, you're not the only one alive. There are other lives too. Quite different from yours, and in fact completely unaware of your existence. Do you understand? *This* is a completely different life! And if you can't get this girl back, this other girl, that doesn't mean, there is no reason for you to exist anymore. You can also stay," she shook me lightly by the shoulders. "You can stay with me, if you want, or with others. I really need you. You'll always be here," she closed her eyes, kissed me very lightly and laughed.

"Why are you laughing?"

Maria whispered:

"Why not?" and she kissed me again.

I wasn't thinking anything; I don't have deep thoughts.

I have nothing to say to anyone. And I can't do anything. I've never won anything in my entire life. When all the other boys dreamed of being pilots, I wanted to be the plane's first engineer. I wanted to be the base player behind the long-haired front-man in a band on the stage of the Railroad Workers' Culture Center. I wanted to be the ball boy. The radio operator for a heroic reconnaissance group. I avoid lottery tickets. I am weak, and I try to warn people about it in advance. "Will you leave Voznesenskaya alone?" Maria asked.

"No. I represent the interests of the dead. I do have a choice. But what choice does she have? For her, it's me or nothing."

Natella Voznesenskaya agreed to meet me on a Saturday, at 10 in the morning provided we would finish by 11. At 9:40 I sat down on a bench next to the drained Patriarch's Ponds, where years ago

I waited for Shakhurin's brother. I read *Sport Express*, raising my eyes occasionally at the new all-girl police patrols. The sparrows whizzed above my head like bullets and stuffed themselves with what looked like cheerful pleasure into a bush, trimmed to look like a ball.

At five minutes to ten, I got up and went to the building, punched in two door codes, and found the apartment to the left of the elevator. A smiling, gray-haired, youthful and bright woman raised her hand up high for me to shake it.

We went to the kitchen, and she threw off her sandals; she wore a lot of eye make-up, black trousers — she was ready for this, she was in full combat readiness for another strike against Iraida Tsurko.

"Did Pyotr Petrovich have any contact with his mother-in-law, Anastasia Vladimirovna Petrova?" I asked.

"He met the Tsurkos rarely, we visited them twice a year. He was very proud, he didn't want to depend on them, didn't want privileges. He talked a lot about Anastasia though. He appreciated her as an erudite conversationalist, a well-read person, with an interesting life. Like Iraida, she gave herself entirely to her work. Women like this should not have a family."

"Petrova had a son."

"They were very thorough in concealing Vasily's schizophrenia. They said it was the consequences of childhood encephalopathy, but there was also heredity down Tsurko's line."

So she was informed that Petrova's brother killed himself.

"They say that Anastasia Vladimirovna and Iraida were rather dry, distant people," I ventured.

"Anyone who abandons their children is not a woman!"

"Abandons?"

"When Olya turned two, Iraida said: Petya, I've been offered a job abroad, you won't object, will you? Of course, he couldn't object. But deep down he hoped that she wouldn't leave. Iraida left. And she stayed abroad until her daughter died, only coming back twice a year. She spent her summer vacation in Sochi, in a sanatorium named after the Tsurkos, and also came at New Year. She had lovers at her job.

Petya knew about it. He wasn't a monk himself. But whenever Iraida came back, they put on lavish evenings, receptions, and invited all kinds of guests to show what a wonderful family they had. Olya was brought up by Mutsa and the housemaid."

"And then Pyotr Petrovich left for you…"

"They agreed to divorce when their daughter graduated from high school. But he couldn't wait. On the 30th of December 1971," this was her sacred date and she pronounced it triumphantly, "I opened the door to find him on my doorstep with a small suitcase. Iraida caused a terrible scandal, she roused everyone she could. For half a year we were terrorized with phone calls."

"As a medical professional, can you give an objective assessment of Olga's mental health?"

"I noticed immediately that Olya seemed troubled and spent some time just observing her. At the age of 20, a girl like her should be lively, cheerful, but Olya couldn't stand bright light. Her favorite writer was Dostoyevsky. She simply adored him, and Wagner was her favorite composer. She didn't like loud voices, loud music playing, she didn't like clothes with garish colors. She hardly slept for almost a year. She herself believed it was the consequence of a light concussion she got when she fell ice-skating and the medication she had to take afterwards. I worked at the Kremlin hospital at the time, and I convinced Petya to show Olya to the head psychiatrist of the country, Dr. Snezhnevsky. I remember I waited outside his office, while he talked to Olya — it took so long, three hours! Finally Snezhnevsky called me in and told me Olya had to be hospitalized immediately, she was seriously ill. We lied to her — told her she had a neurological problem and had her admitted into the psychiatric ward at the Central Kremlin Hospital. She was there for half a year (*Mezentsov said three months*) and made angry phone calls: what are you doing? Have you put me in a loony bin? Later we found out she tried to slit her wrists while in the hospital. After that, the doctors told Iraida: if Olya loves you *that* much, you must spend at least half a year with her. And what did Iraida do? She talked to Olya: you know, I really must work. And went away! And Olya went to live alone at Kuusinen. (*Alone — where was Mezentsov? Why couldn't the girl move in with you? Did she not want to?*) Of course, we kept an eye on her, but I could see she wasn't getting better. The doctors were in shock when they found out that Iraida had gone away."

"Why did she worship her mother so much?"

"She was a girl, after all," Natella answered — she clearly didn't like the question.

In passing, I thought: Olya didn't marry Mezentsov officially. Even though he called himself her "husband," now people would call him a "boyfriend," someone who came and went; I didn't doubt his story of abandoning the six-room apartment with a maid on Tverskaya, but I could see little evidence of him staying in Olya's life for very long.

"What do you think, why was Olya attractive to Mezentsov? He was well-off, with a good life."

"Olya was the complete opposite of his wife. Mezentsov's wife was a business lady in a pant-suit, you know the type. And Olya was quiet, serene, feminine, romantic. When Olya was taken to hospital, we said to Styopa, I mean, Mezentsov: you have to decide what you will do now. She is seriously ill. He said he loved her and would stay with her forever. He promised to help her recover."

"What about Ovsyanikov?"

Natella visibly lost her train of thought and got up to turn on the kettle. The question blew a hole in her carefully rehearsed little play: she'd built up a fable about a bad mother of a sick girl and the cruelty of fate that separated two lovers just as they were beginning to walk together down a happy path edged by rosebushes. She enjoyed the way I nodded, the way my eyes grew warmer and kinder as she spread the seeds of what she wanted me to hear, the way I was her ally, her convert, her recruit — when I asked the awkward question and toppled all her cardboard decorations, the path and the bushes, and the evil mother too. Her homely, vulnerable truth suddenly looked pathetic and laughable, because that's what always happens when someone tries to arrange several personal truths into a shared Truth — the path turns muddy and rocky and no one wants to follow it.

"Ovsyanikov? I think he graduated from the institute of military interpreters. Olya's illness really showed in her relationship with him. Everything about him annoyed her: the way he *ate;* the way he washed; the way he talked. I remember her whispering, he makes so much noise when he drags his feet..."

"Did Olya take her break up with R-ov hard?"

"The legend that Olya killed herself because of her unhappy love for R-ov was made up by Iraida's friends. It's nonsense! Olya and Vladislav were merely friends. It was impossible to fall in love with him, he was not that kind of guy."

"Then why did she decide to kill herself? She was young and beautiful..."

"Schizophrenics are suicidal. It's a sudden decision: they hear a voice, for example, that tells them, *it's time to leave.* They're all very smart. There aren't any fools among schizophrenics."

"How did she die?"

"She died on Styopa's birthday, on the 29th of November *(Mezentsov told me she took poison on his birthday, but died later, in December).* For a while, every year on this day he came to her grave with a large bouquet of roses.

"On that day, Styopa went away on a trip *(Mezentsov said he went away to work).* Olya came to see us, I made pies, and invited her to stay. That was on Sunday. On Monday evening *(the 29th of November 1975 was a Saturday, I checked),* I had office hours, when Pyotr Petrovich called: something's happened to Olya. He was at home watching football *(at the end of November?)* and instead of calling me he had dialed Olya's number by mistake. She picked up and answered, slurring her words, and then the connection broke off. Pyotr Petrovich dialed again. Olya screamed: *leave me alone!* This was at seven or eight in the evening *(Mezentsov said they called during the day and got worried when Olya didn't reply).* We took the car and rushed to her place. The door was open *(as if someone had just left or the girl wanted to be found);* Olya was lying there in her best suit, made up beautifully, and perfumed."

"Was she conscious?"

"When I bent over her, Olya only whispered, Natellochka, forgive me... And then she passed out. On the floor I found a bottle of the psychotropic pills Mutabon. She had a prescription for it. I had given her the bottle myself just two days earlier, 100 pills. We tried to pump her stomach, but it was pointless. We tried to call the ambulance, but neither Petya nor I could remember the address. For two weeks Olya was treated at Sklifosovsky hospital, and then died."

"What was in the note?"

"Papa, Styopa, forgive me. She wrote after she had already taken the pills. The letters were shaky."

"Were you in charge of the funeral?"

"Yes. The hardest thing was to tell Grandma Mutsa (*Petrova, evidently, took any news calmly*). Mutsa was in the hospital at the time, we were afraid the news would kill her. Styopa and Petya were in a terrible state. They tried to throw themselves off the balcony *(I looked at the window: the third floor)*, I didn't leave them alone. Before the funeral, Petya was given pills, and an injection, but nothing worked."

"And Iraida?"

"As I was about to leave for the cemetery, a common acquaintance called me and passed on a message from Iraida: if she, meaning me, comes to the funeral, I'll make a scene right by the coffin. But she certainly was not at the funeral."

This, of course, would have to be checked.

Natella brought photographs of Olya and unexpectedly said I could take them, so for politeness' sake I looked at each one, as she talked:

"Everything could have worked out well. People with these illnesses can live long lives, and hold important positions, and have long remissions... If only the girl had had a normal mother..."

In the taxi, I once more looked through the photographs indifferently: headscarves, plaits, clips, holding the hair of this stub-nosed girl, an unsmiling bride without a veil, the still-smiling thickbrowed Ovsyanikov in shining black shoes, ironic kisses, a short black dress with a white belt, knees in thick tights — *everything collapsed*, the entire story of Olya Voznesenskaya collapsed under the weight of people's testimonies; it was dragging me down, too. But I still had something, my net had fish in it, I had people to talk to before I went to help R-ov remember everything.

THE OTHER HUSBAND

"I BOUGHT YOU A NEWSPAPER. VLADISLAV R-OV HAS RETURNED TO Russia," Maria said at dinner.

I glanced at the picture of a bearded gentleman in a vest and at his answers to the interviewer's questions: Do you drink vodka? no; Smoke? yes; I try to live in St. Petersburg, I have founded a charitable school at St. Catherine's Church... All the profits from my concert went to the needs of ill children... My children should be truly Russian; I must instill spiritual values and patriotism in them. Do you intend to be buried at Novodevichy? Of course, it's a holy place... I've come to realize that one must live with his people.

Maria held each photograph of Olya Voznesenskaya carefully.

"If you are just going to throw these away, give them to me instead."

"No, we'll sell them. We'll tell Ovsyanikov we have Olya's photos. He'll think, what if these are different from the ones he has? And he wants to possess her — have her all to himself. So he'll take the bait and crawl out of his shell a bit. That's when we'll get him."

"I feel sorry for the poor man, actually. I think all of this pains him more than others — and that's why he doesn't want to talk to you."

Ovsyanikov... Yes, he is ecstatic, intoxicated now. The light inside him has been turned on — he talks with the clouds, he raves, and time retreats before him, letting him go back and forth freely. When I called, his half-erased life became LIFE again, his holy icon was renewed; he is wandering now with his Olya in the reborn city, showing her what has been built, and what was remained. He shows her the future, he forgives her, every day he forgives her, and he finds tears on his face in the mornings and doesn't want to let go of his dreams — he has been summoned, called for, he is wanted. This man spent thirty years in the torture chamber of their apartment, on the bed her father gave them as a present, finding her hair in the corners mixed with the hair of the big orange dog — thirty years as a discard, as a footnote, a worm smashed into the mud in her footprint. He sat there, and he couldn't understand it: they did get married, didn't they? There was a real wedding — he didn't dream that up? He couldn't betray her, this girl with her monstrous, warped, mad power — he could not accept the fact that she could be forgotten, erased, decomposed just as he could not accept the fact that she had treated him the way she had. He bet on love. He believed love would conquer everything, *his* love would conquer everything, his love would not deceive, he only needed to wait — years, decades perhaps. He would wait thirty years, so that when she did return, he could rise at once and greet her with a peaceful smile, not even surprised to see her again. He would cry for the first time in thirty years (and he has often imagined *how* he would cry — with dignity — and every time the hot proof of tears filled his eyes).

When I called, Ovsyanikov understood: *This was it,* everything had come true, he had waited out everyone, and now Olya would be given back to him — he could change everything, correct the past, *he* would become her author. He was waiting for my call in his apartment at Kuusinen, eager to have my surgical lamp turned on to him, because he thought we would explain his life to him, give it back, deliver Olya to him, and then clear out.

Karina Proskurina, the classmate and bridesmaid at the wedding of Olga Voznesenskaya and Ovsyanikov, giggled when I called, and asked me to repeat the year of my birth three times:

"Did you know Olya yourself? We all loved her... Do you have a hobby? We can meet at McDonalds on Tverskaya. What do you look like?"

I told her as plainly as I could. She asked:

"And what color are your eyes?"

Karina Proskurina came in a black rain-coat slick with rain; she was short, with curly hair, freshly applied lipstick, and glitter on her eyelids, cheeks and chest.

"We met in the first year at the Institute, we were both English teaching majors. Olya didn't really come to lectures in the second year. She was very fashionable. Everyone back then tried to look like Twiggy, the model and Olya looked exactly like her — tall and skinny. She smoked three packs a day, she lit one cigarette from another. She had pretty legs, she had sex appeal. And she was very popular. Olya couldn't stand vulgarity, she was very well brought up. Whenever there was even the slightest hint of vulgarity in conversation, she felt physically unwell, she literally felt sick."

"Did Olya take the divorce of her parents hard?"

"Olga loved her mother *terribly*. If you said anything against her, she'd scratch your eyes out. Iraida had this air of superiority about her — she was the lioness. But no, she didn't bring Olya anything, all this talk about presents from abroad is a myth. But she took out her resentment towards Petrovich on Olya. I think Iraida's divorce really pushed Olya over the edge. Everyone thought that they had this wonderful life, and then all of a sudden, after another magnificent party, Petrovich announced: I'm leaving. It was terrible! Iraida cried for nights on end, she took Olya into her bed and tormented her with her outbursts, her hysterics, she didn't let her sleep, Olya ate less and less..."

"What's Vladislav R-ov's role in all of this?"

"She couldn't cope with this pain alone, but she didn't want to call R-ov or see him. She said if a woman waits for a man by his door in the rain, the most she'll get out of it is he'll bed her a couple times. So she thought he was a waste of her time."

"She was introduced to R-ov by Yevgeny Shchukin, a humorist. Have you heard of him?"

"Oh, of course. Olya fell head over heels for this Shchukin. He was all she could talk about for a while. He was married and an alcoholic."

"Do you remember Stepan Mezentsov?"

"Yes. Biryukova married him eventually. I ran into them at the Central House of Writers — Biryukova and Stepan — and I waved to them. I remember I asked why they didn't bring Olya with them, and Biryukova shushed me: quiet! Olya's dead."

"You mean that Biryukova and Mezentsov knew each other and were friends, while Olya was still alive?"

"Of course! I think Olya may have even found out that Biryukova was pregnant from Stepan, they have a son, you know. I spoke to Olya about Mezentsov, and she said she knew he was also having an affair with Biryukova, but she said, 'it's not time to change the stage-props now.'"

"Do you know anything about the circumstances of her death?"

"I know that when Olya had her stomach pumped out, and regained consciousness she said, You shouldn't have bothered, I don't want to live."

"When was the last time you saw Voznesenskaya?"

"Not long before she died. Olya, who used to get drunk from a drop of champagne, met me in an incredibly wild state, with half a bottle of white wine in her hand *(but Natella Voznesenskaya said Olya didn't drink)*. She wanted us to go and buy some more wine, and get drunk! You know, these days, I wouldn't think twice about it, but back then I ran away in horror, with only one wish: never to see Olya again."

"What do you think was happening in Olya's life? I keep getting stories about all the men she loved — there's a long list..."

"You know, everyone somehow has a sense of how much time they have allotted on this earth. And every woman is given three or four great romances in her life, even the ugliest, most undesirable nerd. Three or four romances. I think Olya knew that she had little time, and she just lived her life quickly and beautifully. If you're worried about corrupt morals, that's not the story here. It's just that life does not run smoothly, there are twists and turns that can be very painful — she had more twists than others. I don't know... if she had had children, perhaps she would've forgotten some of the pain."

SILENCE

I TRIED TO STAND IN THE MIDDLE OF PUSHKIN SQUARE, BUT COULD not find a spot where I wouldn't have been in anyone's way. I didn't want to go into the sweaty guts of the metro to stare at my own reflection in black glass. I just stood and looked at people — *millions* of them — and felt like a passenger, squeezed in the crowd, while the world moved on.

Maria threw open the door as soon as she heard the steel gnawing of the key on the lock, and hugged me like a long-awaited arrival, with sudden tenderness. I realized I was poised on the verge of some celebration, of which I had been completely unaware — had I forgotten something?

"Is it your birthday today?" I asked.

"No, don't be silly. Today we're alone. The neighbors have gone away!"

Maria herded me inside, touched me with happy impatience, ran off to adjust something. Her new dress flashed by. I wouldn't get away from her today — her eyelids flashed with glitter.

"I cleaned the bathroom all day. I've made a bubble bath for you — *deep relaxation,* now you'll fall asleep," she kissed me and ordered, "Now take your clothes off. Here's a towel for you — the orange one." A bubbling jet of water whisked up a foamy white beard in the bath, a shaggy hump that started to spill over the edge. Maria turned down the water, switched the flow to the shower head, and smoothed down the foam. It was quiet.

"Lie in it for 20 minutes. Close your eyes. And don't think about anything."

I locked the door and touched the towel: it was new and woven. A piece of a material world that was unfamiliar to me. Terrycloth. Calico. Quilts. Suspenders. Papier-mâché. Corned beef. Meringue pie.

Through the cool foam and the hot water I put my foot on the slippery bottom and sank down into the bath. The foam rustled around my chest and trembled at the smallest breath, like a living, carnivorous mass. Somewhere on another floor a child was crying, someone shouted, "Yes, my dear!" and the water squeaked like a mouse as it flowed into the drainage hole. I looked at other people's things: the dirty bathroom mitt, stuck into the towel dryer, the tubes of toothpaste with squashed backs, and a plastic turtle with flexible flippers. My forehead felt hot and scratchy, and I bent my knees in the foamy whirlpools, brushed the foam aside and freed up a patch of almost black, murky water. I stretched out my hand and took the nearest bottle which was conveniently shaped so as to fit into my grip. I read on the label: "Stress Relief — relieves stress and anxiety with rosemary." I sat for a few minutes more, then stood up, legs encased in white foam, and got out.

When I came into Maria's room, it was lit with a low red glow; I saw a cord stretching around the corner from a socket in the wall.

"Don't turn on the light! Don't touch anything!" Maria shouted from the kitchen. "Go into my room. Sit on the bed and wait. Don't look!" Out in the hallway, I heard her fussing with something metal-sounding. I waited on the bed, naked, wrapped in a damp, cooling towel. I was sure I knew what would happen next, and I was right: she turned on the music — rustling Arab tambourines and wailing — and ran in with her hair down, a bare stomach, her hips wrapped in a cloth with small coins, scales. She shook herself, and danced rather monotonously, putting one bare foot out and then another, sometimes whirling. I thought about how happy I would be if she were going away for a week and I could spend the holidays alone. I looked at her, pretended I was looking, pretending I was impressed, I smiled blissfully, but inside I sighed because of the clumsiness and awkwardness of her body, the lamp with a red cloth hung over it, from the wretchedness of what was to come, from her wretchedness, from mine — was that how she saw me?

"Now have you looked at me?" she breathed into my face. I smelled chewing gum.

We stroked each other and lay together meaninglessly for a long time. Eventually, she fell asleep, without taking her arms off me with their small child-like hands, and she slept trustingly, like children sleep. I didn't dare to get up for a long time, scared of waking her up.

From: Evgenij Shchukin <e_shchukin@mail.ru>
Dear Alexander,

I knew Olga for a very short time, and witnessed a fragment of the drama whose origins and conclusion unfolded out of my sight.

There are sacred things that need to be protected. Otherwise it is easy to fall prey to one's own emotions, as Mezentsov does, for example. No one has the right to another person's life. Memory of the dead is also a kind of life. To break into it, looking for scapegoats, is something that no one has the right to do, including people who have for some reason laid claim to this right.

Vladislav R-ov invited me and my wife to Olya's home on Kuusinen street as the *de facto* master of the house and a person who was close to Olya. There we met. I think this was in the spring of 1973. Later, all of us — Olya, Vladislav, myself and my wife and I — spent a month's holiday in the south.

There, in the south, I noticed a certain shift, a breakdown in Olya's relationship with Vladislav. Neither of them gave me any cause to interfere; they only allowed me to be their mute witness, and this was not easy for me.

Later, back in Moscow, by a twist of circumstances my wife and I stayed with Olya at Kuusinen street for two months. Vladislav also turned up there from time to time. These two months were the time when I could have found out or asked in more detail what was on her mind. But I had enough problems of my own to take on other people's. I also assumed that everything connected with Vladislav was painful for Olya.

With Olya, my relations were purely friendly, based on gratitude. She took us in when we were homeless, quite selflessly, and in Moscow this means a lot. Any 'love' between myself and Olya is out of the question, and not just because I was married and would not leave my wife.

She lived as careless as a bird; I basically took over the running of the household and I never ceased being amazed by her ineptitude. I couldn't tell you how she ever managed by herself, what she ate, who did the cooking or the cleaning. Her parents gave her clothes, books and money which she spent on cigarettes. I had to feed three adults and entertain guests.

Now, about Vladislav. Vladislav attracted people because of his position, his pedigree, money, charm, ease and generally being gifted, which meant he was often the prey of vain women. How Olya joined their number is a mystery to me. Perhaps she saw him differently? Or was a spoiled girl at the bottom of her heart, and could not live without being spoiled by someone?

Outwardly she was friendly with me, smiling and solicitous — alone she was rather miserable, and I think she enjoyed having company. She didn't sleep much. We used to stay up talking past midnight, and then I remember, the light in her room would not go off much longer. I think she suffered from insomnia. Or rather, she was half-asleep all the time.

We soon moved out to an apartment I rented, and our contact with Olya became very infrequent: birthdays and phone calls. Vladislav also vanished or almost. I don't know if they saw each other at that time.

Once he called me and said: Olya is at the Kremlin hospital, at the nervous disorders section. He said she wouldn't mind if I visited her. I interpreted this to be a request from Vlad himself, who did care about Olya in his way. When I went to visit her, Olya was genuinely happy to see me, but we didn't have a frank conversation. I can't imagine how we could have, given the circumstances and the setting.

A woman's soul is a subtle thing. Especially when the woman, as I later found out from her friends, *(Why? What happened after her death? What were you accused of?)* attempts suicide a number of times and ends up in hospital.

To blame Vladislav for anything would be the same as blaming a pothole for injuring a person with a sight defect who was wandering along this road.

Everything you wrote about other alleged husbands Olya had is a complete mystery to me. I didn't see a single living husband once. I never heard of any. Perhaps Mezentsov was her husband?

Olya called me after a long break.

She asked to meet *(I doubt we'll find any witnesses to confirm this).* I found it strange, but I remembered her kindness to me and couldn't refuse her. We met in the city, took a walk along the boulevards, reached my apartment, went inside and shared a bottle of wine. She only sipped, I understand these things, I'm a drinker myself — she didn't need it. She looked fresh and rosy, not at all the look of a degraded, drinking woman.

I remember she was really dressed up. She was beaming, but once again, there was something of a broken doll's look to her. I rather wanted to drink a little, the better to endure the awkwardness and falseness of the meeting *(She didn't drink, that's important)*: again, she didn't talk about anything serious, I couldn't even imagine what was going on in her mind. She laughed and joked. Now, of course, I blame myself — had I known what she was planning to do, I would have grabbed her, held her, locked her up. That's the whole trick: How do you know? We didn't really keep in touch, each of us had their own life. The people who were near her, why didn't they see it?

Mezentsov called that night and said that she had taken a large dose of sleeping pills. He knew Olya met with me that day. How? Did he see her? Did he call? These are questions without answers.

I didn't go to the funeral because I knew that I would be seen in this very context *(And too many people thought you were to blame)*. I'm a living person who cared about Olya. I regret that I didn't become a true friend to her. A lot of things interfered. I won't explain. If she had been in love with me, I would have known it, I'm not stupid. But that did not happen. I am no one's rival.

Did she call someone else that evening? A few hours went by *(how many?)* after she left my place; she must have spent them somewhere.

She did not leave anything but bewilderment, pain and questions after herself. Olya only touched my life tangentially. Ask your questions of those who participated directly, if they will share anything.

May the memory of Olya be bright and good.

All the best. *Yevgeny Shchukin.*

I informed Ovsyanikov we had photographs of Olga. Ovsyanikov prevaricated for a week (he had exam boards), and then told me to meet him at 4 o'clock at Vagankovo. He was shorter than me, frail, large-headed, with expressive eye-brows. His hair was still black, and slicked back.

"Have you been waiting long? I went into the church."

"Shall we go to the grave?" I suggested.

"I'm afraid. Iraida forbid me to meet with you."

I gave him the photographs, he looked at them. He had them already, but he took them, mumbling:

"I'll give them to Iraida."

We walked back and forth by the cemetery fence, along the river and the swamp, and he began to explain:

"Iraida has always been like that. Once she decides something, it must be carried out. We called her Iron Felix."

"Why did Olya treat you the way she did?"

"I was just so pushy myself... I liked her so much, I tried to see her every day. Iraida warned me: I'm leaving in a month, so if you want to get married, do it now. Olya and I looked at each other: let'o! There were two receptions: Pyotr Petrovich hosted one for his guests at Prague — and not at Peking, as you were told — and Iraida celebrated at home. Olya knew herself that this was not going to last. She wrote to me in Africa. Such cheerful letters! 'Yesterday, I sat down to play cards with a three-year-old kid, and he's already cheating!'"

"When did she become friends with R-ov?"

He chuckled at the word "friends":

"When I left for Africa, it all started."

"And yet you remember her warmly." I couldn't bring myself to say, 'you love her.' "And you forgave her."

Ovsyanikov thought about the question.

"I forgave her when things turned out the way they did... When she died."

"Did Olya have any contact with her grandmother — Anastasia Vladimirovna?"

"Probably. Petrova, I remember, had some fans and dresses from Japan."

"From China."

"There were oil portraits of her. I also remember Olya dancing, and Petrova watching her. She was a grand old lady. Like Gogoleva or Pashennaya."

"Did you hear that Petrova loved a man by the name of Umansky?"

"No."

"And there was also one incident: on the Great Stone Bridge a boy shot a girl and then shot himself."

"I never heard of that."

So there was no hope here either.

"Would you like a ride?"

"No, I'll go to the metro. I need to take a walk. To think." Shaking his hand, at the last possible moment, I tried to shake him out of his stupor. I asked:

"But later... did things work out for you? Did you have a family?"

"Yes. Yes," he gave a happy, wry smile. "My daughter looks more like Olya than she looks like me."

At home, Maria's neighbors were moving around, I had to wait in her room before going into the kitchen. I asked her to turn down the light and we found seats each in their own corner.

"I found out that R-ov is coming to Moscow for two days," Maria said. "On the 5th of February he has a concert at the Great Hall of the Philharmonic."

She moved closer.

"I called Alexander Naumovich," she pressed up against me and suddenly started to cry quietly. Shocked, I stroked her hair — was he dead? — without actually feeling anything. Well, old people are the first in line.

"No, what are you saying!" she sobbed. "He's getting ready for the surgery. He was so happy I called, I think he even cried. He is very scared. They won't tell him exactly when the surgery will be."

"I'll go and pay them. That's what they are after, that's why they're dragging their feet. Bastards. He's an old man, he doesn't understand what they want from him. I'll take care of it, don't cry."

"I just thought... I couldn't stand the thought of something happening to him."

"It's a minor surgery, really — they just make a little hole these days. You can get up the next day and go home for the weekend." I felt I was living through a dream now, in a floating room, and looked around me with eyes that were newly kind, intoxicated, vulnerable to taking in new places. I saw her as if I just gained sight after having been blinded: before that I had only heard her voice — she was sitting at my feet, she had such eyes, and beautiful, delicate bones. She was a living being, she could feel pain — and so she should not be deceived, she should not waste her life on me. I saw her as a nurse, an unfamiliar but very dear person who comes and heals you when you have a cold, and a sore throat and a fever. I bent down and grazed my lips across her hair, across the top of her head, and listened to hear what else she would say.

"And I thought, what if something happened to you!" She looked at our fingers, as if sensing but not seeing the web that connected them. "I love you."

"You mean: I should take you and do what I please? Haven't you had anyone before me? Am I the only one? Until death do us part?"

She didn't like this.

"No. Just..."

"It would be better if we didn't see each other again."

"What do you mean?" She seized my hand, she caught my gaze and did not let it go. "Are you angry?" she caught her breath, gaining courage. "You don't need me?"

"That's right. I'm going to check my email."

(In fact, I need you once a month. A month or so and I can get over the disgust from the last time. Your month has only just begun, and I will hurry to tell you: you have small and droopy breasts with dead, chewed-up nipples. A pale, flabby stomach. A horrible birthmark, ginger, and your smell, I didn't like it. I didn't like the way you stuck out your lips when you pressed against me, how you threw your head back. You have a sort of one-off attractiveness, of course. And you may get to take your clothes off a few more times, but after that...)

Swaying with insomnia, I finally crept to the kitchen across the squeaking floor. Soon, I would leave this place. I listened — no one was crying. R-ov was coming to Moscow. I was anxious about this meeting — it would be the last. There would be nothing to think about after it, I would stretch and say: *that's it.* I'd be free, I'd fall asleep, and see the morning again with joy many more times. I'd save up some money, go to the European Soccer championship and visit the new flea market on Shkolnaya street to find a tin Budyonny cavalry soldier from the 1920s. I could start an Internet shop. I could begin to find joy in snow. Or take up fishing, study bird species, and the names of grass. I could tell all these things to my children. This could be the future Me. They don't know it yet, and I don't feel it, but it could be Me.

I had a new alert in my inbox: a radio Liberty story with some old lady who served under the emperor at VOKS — Union of

Soviet Societies for Friendship and Cultural Relations with Foreign Countries. Yawning myself blind, I scrolled through the mockery of all things Soviet in the Q&A format. Ambassador Umansky had a lover at VOKS — right, who do they quote for that? One Zoya Lodeinikova, veteran of VOKS, author of a memoir. She was still alive, and retained a passion for "everything Mexican."

I checked the memoirs. "Konstantin Alexandrovich *took an urn with the ashes of his daughter and his grieving wife* with him to Mexico." The usual nonsense. "In Moscow he left his beloved woman — she worked at VOKS as a secretary and stenographer." Except Petrova was an assistant to the deputy People's Commissar and was employed at the People's Commissariat for Foreign Affairs.

I found this Lodeinikova quickly and called her.

"Yes. I remember. The woman's name was Lida Ivanova. It was such a tragedy... They planned to reunite after his return. But the government did not approve of divorces and this kind of love. And Ehrenburg even wrote about how Umansky suffered when he left — because of Lida. I'll be happy to give you her telephone number. Although she is very sick. No, she doesn't have any children. She's quite alone. She didn't have anyone apart from Konstantin Alexandrovich."

I fought to maintain my balance, and to catch my breath. I couldn't believe it — it wasn't Petrova? She was really telling me Petrova wasn't *the* woman? We had built the case on her, but *it wasn't Petrova* — not Petrova, otherwise known as Flam, also Topolskaya, also wife of Mr. Tsurko whose name she didn't take. It wasn't her whom Ambassador Umansky had loved and wanted to marry in '41. Instead it was Lida the stenographer, and he hid this woman, this cunning Jew, so well that for sixty years everyone pointed their fingers at Tasya without prompting or prodding. It was funny how he had tricked us — so cynically! That's exactly what happens to investigations — you dig for seven years in the wrong spot, and then the truth — almost unnecessary at this point — drops into your lap from where you least expect it. I won't be going anywhere tomorrow, I didn't need R-ov, I had dragged a whole battalion of new skeletons into this story, stirred up an army of shadows. I collapsed on the table, scared to take a breath, clutching at the piece of paper with *Lida Ivanovna's phone number.*

"What's wrong with you?" Maria felt for my pulse and rubbed some smelly substance on my temple. "Can you hear me? I'll open the window." A rubber clamp contracted on my arm — a blood pressure cuff — what for? She bent over me, her hair tickling me.

"Is that better? What happened? Can you tell me what you felt? Does your head hurt now? Your heart? Can you see OK? Is your arm numb?"

I couldn't talk, I stretched out, bent over, as if my body was trying to yawn, and straighten itself.

"If you don't get better, I'll call the doctor."

I lay in a dark warmth, looking at the shabby corner of the room. Maria went away to make a phone call and ask for advice.

"Drink this. And take this pill."

The hours went by, and I opened my eyes: she was next to me the whole time, she bent over me right away.

"They say: it's not Petrova," I said.

"What? God, the main thing is that you're alive, do you understand that? Now you need to sleep. Rest. We'll talk in the morning."

"I'm not going to fall asleep. You see what happened? If it's not Petrova, we failed. The other guys — the tough guys who are covered from all sides, who bury everyone — they took us on and tricked us. There, on the bridge, there is nothing, everything has gone away, and so we can't do anything, it's all gone, everything goes away! I don't want to!" I sat up and would have leaped to my feet, but she stopped me.

"Listen," she said seriously. "I promise you. It's Petrova. Ehrenburg wrote about her. We weren't wrong, you have many witnesses, and it all fits. Who wrote about this Lida? Just one old lady! Why did you believe her? So what if there was a stenographer, and some people gossiped about her and Umansky — they remembered the rumors, they read Ehrenburg and they put it all together. She didn't know that it was Petrova, go to sleep!" And she held me, firmly. "But even if it wasn't, what's important is — you're not alone!"

"I'm going. I can't lie down."

"Wait," she kissed me. "Give me a bit of time, lie there and listen to me — then you can go." She lay next to me, not touching me, and spoke in a soft but discernible voice. "Imagine it's summer, the end of June. Where the city comes to an end, we're standing with you on a hill, the grass is tall, the sun's hot. I love it when it's warm, when there's a warm wind. You're wearing a white shirt and light pants, sandals on your bare feet, and I'm in a light red dress. We have a son. And later we'll have a daughter too. And then maybe another child. But so far just a son. He looks like you when you were young. Especially when he smiles. He can't keep still, he has to keep running. To catch butterflies. But he's scared of bees. Our son runs downhill, into the forest, you shout to him not to run too fast down the hill. We follow him, the path is overgrown, the grass tickles our legs, you help me avoid the nettles. Where the trees begin — the birches and oaks, and the thorns — we stop and kiss. We'll always like to kiss. Even when we're old and our grandchildren are growing up. I'll still be beautiful. I'll always be young for you. And we'll stand there, where the shade is, holding each other, and our son will come running up and take us both by the hand, and we'll stand still, listening to the birds sing, to something chirping and rustling in the grass, and we'll be so happy. He will lead us further, across a small gully, where there are dry leaves and it's damp. Past black stumps. You hold my hand. You always hold my hand. Our boy climbs up faster than us, he is the first, and he shouts with joy. He calls us to come quickly — he's seen a river there. Children always get excited when there's a lot of water. When the opposite bank can't be seen and it's summertime. He will see so much more! There's so much that lies ahead for him. You tear off a willow leaf. It's narrow, like a boat... And you talk to me... We talk all the time, even when we're silent, between us... there is never... silence..."

ALL THE GRAVES

I DIDN'T THINK I SLEPT, BUT WHEN I WOKE UP, THE DAYLIGHT WAS reliable and unhurried. I lay in bed for a long time.

Lidia Ivanovna Ivanova, in a broken, feeble voice, did not refuse to meet, but she asked me to see her in two weeks, when she would have recovered from an illness. I waited six weeks, confident that the old lady wouldn't die before I saw her.

Number ten in Simferopol alley, fourth floor, a door covered in fake leather. It took her a long time to reach the door, to walk inaudibly from far inside her apartment, but she did, and she opened the door.

A white shirt and a woolen vest. She was small and upright. She had a short, neat haircut. Lips touched with lipstick. She had gotten ready. When old people get ready, they dress in the way they would like to lie in their coffins.

Lida Ivanova was positioned inside an iron frame on wheels — she had broken her hip, and this was the only way she could get around. The apartment smelt insistently of old age.

She had thought of everything: she gave me slippers and seated me at the table close to a photo of herself as a young willowy beauty next to the hero Valery Chkalov, drunk with the success of a trans-Arctic flight to America. She had me read the inscription, which, she made it clear, discomfited Chkalov's wife quite a bit: "Dear girl, my compatriot Lidushka. I give you this photo as a memory of myself. And I will say some words to you that are the dearest to me: there is nothing better in life than to live in the Soviet Union. Remember this all your life, this is where happiness lies."

Parents? Ordinary white-collar workers. She graduated from school and took courses in foreign languages at the People's Commissariat for Foreign Affairs. And then went to America, to manage the Embassy's offices. *(At the age of 20, the daughter of ordinary workers and not a Komsomol member? Unimaginative lying, lucky for you that it doesn't matter now).* There was a crisis there. She wanted to go home.

Lida Ivanova replied cautiously, drily and succinctly. Through the skin on her arms I could see her bones.

The first time? She met Umansky in Washington at the train station. They were friends. Where did they see each other in Moscow? At the Troyanovskys'. They went to see Ehrenburg. Umansky didn't dance, was forever unhappy about his lot, spoke foreign languages well.

How did you say goodbye? He came to VOKS. He brought some souvenirs and a cake. What's wrong with that? He didn't say goodbye to everyone! Just the Chairman and me. But why didn't he stay for his daughter's funeral? He thought he'd come back soon and bury her.

How did she find out about his death? She was on her way to work and saw a newspaper displayed in a mourning frame. She came to work and told everyone. She wasn't at the funeral. No, she knew about it. She just didn't go to it.

"Ehrenburg wrote that before his departure for Mexico, Umansky suffered because he was leaving the woman he loved behind..." I said, and trailed off suggestively.

"That's about me. Did his wife know? I don't know. Raisa once said as a joke: I'll only give my husband to Lida."

"Do you have a photograph of the two of you together?"

"No."

"Did he think about taking you to Mexico?"

"We didn't talk about this."

"Did he promise he'd get divorced."

"No."

"Do you regret what you did?"

"No."

"Did he love you?" I was tired already.

Lida Ivanova replied more slowly, articulating the outcome of long reflection:

"I think so, yes. There was love involved."

"And really: what did he tell you when he said goodbye?"

"I don't remember." I kept up a ponderous silence, and after an eternal pause she told the truth:

"That we were not parting forever."

"Do you know this name — Anastasia Vladimirovna Petrova?"

"No."

"Do you know who killed Nina Umanskaya?"

"Shakhurin's son. He didn't want to part with her."

I closed the notebook, and she perked up, looking at my hands:

"I hope you won't tell anyone about this?"

"Of course not." *(Why would anyone want to know?)*

"Then wait!"

How I hate these cheap confessions at the door.

"Before he left, Umansky went to see some acquaintances, very high-ranking people. And he said: I want to change my life. And he said: I mean Lida."

Downstairs, out in the yard, wandering between bright-colored metal contraptions built for kids, I realized I forgot to ask: why didn't she get married in her long life after Umansky? Perhaps she thought, or something convinced her, that true love only happened once. And that one not only had to wait for the living, but stay faithful to the dead, and *the glow of it* would be enough for her forever, and she still loved the way she had loved. Or she was unlucky, men didn't stay with her, the war devoured her best years and the men of her own age. Did she seize then on her memories, did she go to see Ehrenburg year after year? What did they talk about? About one thing: Kostya, Kostya, ah, Kostya. And it worked: the man who had been blown to fiery pieces in Mexico was still alive. In her constantly rehearsed memories, and in Ehrenburg's obliging collection of the last crumbs of her life with Kostya, life went on and she could think about what Kostya would have become with her beside him in this life. That's why the former stenographer went to the writer.

To stop this torture, out of pity, Ehrenburg may have resorted to cunning and written a *lie* — he raised her and put her on an island, and after that she kept going without him, alone in her fairytale land, touching the wild flowers and lifting her face up to the rainbow, and when darkness fell, she opened the book, looked at those three incomplete words and fell asleep peacefully: she was there, *they* were there, nothing would destroy their love, they were already in heaven.

Yes, I thought, days later, our investigation followed a false trail from the very beginning. The *femme fatale*, Tasya, a woman who could be different with different men, deceived us.

As I thought this, the phone range, and I looked at it as it rang: Ivanova, had she forgotten something?

"I've spent days worrying about how badly I spoke to you. I just can't leave it like that. I should have told you everything I know. But it's so painful..."

So I brought coffee, and cookies with when I went to see her again, and put them out on the table for her. Ms. Ivanova wore the same blouse as last time, but appeared somehow softer; I discovered a plant stand with a flower in the room — I couldn't remember seeing it there before. She was in a hurry, Lida Ivanova, and understood that I, whoever I was, whoever had sent me, was the last person, and no one else would listen to her.

The simple parents she'd described last time were phantoms: she grew up in the family of her uncle, N.I. Pakhomov, the People's Commissar for Water Transport. She lived in the House of Government, her uncle was a friend of Kalinin, and she saw the Emperor three times. The first time he came to Kalinin's dacha for lunch and sat down at the table, Kalinin introduced the diners in a circle, all rather jokingly, and she waited with horror to hear what would be said about her: "This is

Lidka. She's only just started working, and is already complaining that she has a low salary!"

The second time was also at Kalinin's dacha, but the one in the Caucasus, when the Emperor passed her a plate, saying, "Try this. You'll like it." She chewed on the stuff, embarrassed to spit it out, waiting for the inevitable question, "Do you know what that was? Sheep's balls!" The third time was also in the Caucasus, at the Emperor's dacha, where they went bowling. She bent over to throw the ball, and suddenly she heard the Emperor's voice behind her: "Catch!" The pretty girl quickly turned around: the Emperor threw a pomegranate at her — she managed to catch it right next to her chest with the dexterity of a monkey, and he was delighted: "She gets everything right!" She didn't remember anything else. What they talked about, what they ate, how the emperor was dressed — she didn't remember.

After she finished her studies, she was given a position at the Foreign Trade section and approved for an assignment in the U.S. Her parents cried, but Kalinin approved it, she was just over twenty. She liked it in America, the Ambassador's son took her riding in the limousine, the stores dazzled her, she was afraid to come back. Then her uncle was executed, and her passport disappeared from the apartment. Umansky was appointed Ambassador to the States. He didn't dance, didn't drink, and wasn't mean. Close relations between them only began in Moscow.

Lida Ivanova came back, her passport was missing, and she received a referral to VOKS; Chairman Smirnov received her in a gloomy, dark office and inquired if she had any relatives arrested. She shut her eyes in horror: "My aunt's husband." Suddenly, out of a dark, completely empty corner behind her a swarthy man appeared whose profession it was to know everything, and quietly explained, "That is not a direct relative."

While Umansky's family was still away, she went to see him at the Moscow hotel, and the waiter brought food from the restaurant, and once spilled boiling water on her legs. Then they also met in her room, she lived in a communal apartment, a large room in an Arbat lane, with two windows that looked out on to the garden of the American ambassador — at night the people of truth stood watch on the staircase, it was frightening to walk up in the darkness after work, knowing that there was someone invisible there, who would also whisper, "Come up, don't be afraid." They boiled water in the kitchen, and the rooms were heated with firewood. Umansky helped her get enough firewood and carried the logs to her room himself. He took her everywhere: to the Bolshoi Theater, to the conservatory to hear R-ov's 7th Symphony. He wasn't embarrassed or afraid, he introduced her to everyone. *As if she were his future wife.* They would come home by tram or on foot, he knew Moscow well. He showed her the addresses of the great people.

"I don't think he was happy to be leaving *(Ehrenburg describes him jumping for joy)*, he came to see me soon after the death of his daughter. He cried, I don't remember what he said. The next day he came to the office to say goodbye, and in the evening he came to my home, not for long *(So in the time between Nina's death and Umansky's departure, he saw her three times? Perhaps he really did fall in love with her, this middle-aged man...).*

"He flew away. In two years *(one and a half, in fact, but it seemed longer to her)* there was just one telegram, on New Year's Day, and the last line was "All my thoughts are of Moscow."

And then he died. And there was nothing she could ask him.

"Did he give you any presents?"

"A Swiss watch. He said: you can sell it if times are tough. I forgot all about it, and then many years later I found the watch. I took it in my hand — and it started working," A watch from his hand suddenly started working, still alive with the start his hand gave it. "And I *cried so hard*. Kostya had now certainly touched me for the last time, and it felt so painful: what if it was all in vain that we... the country killed so many for their old faith."

There was no snow or ice like last year; my face turned into cardboard and ached with cold. I trudged along the purple asphalt, shoulders hunched, turning my short collar against to the wind, and then I ran. I squeezed by the sign reading "Patients without shoe covers will not be admitted," gave the watchman 50 rubles in reply to his "Pass?" and went upstairs. Coming towards me along the glassed-in walkway, bathed in milky light, was a man with a bandaged neck on bowed legs. He breathed loudly through a short blue tube stuck into his throat. Along the sides, well-settled relatives of long-term hospital patients pushed wheelchairs with bald, gammy-legged people of about the same age.

In the main building, the sixth floor was full of strolling people with puffy crimson cheeks, bandaged noses, and with sheets wrapped around their waists like skirts. I walked to the receptionist past a hunched group of patients waiting to have their bandages changed. Doors into wards were open; the rooms resembled the waiting rooms of a railway station, and I looked in at random. At an empty receptionist's desk in the middle of the floor, a phone rang and a table lamp burnt hotly. I bent across the counter, looked for a sheet of paper with the appointments for the wards, and found the one I needed.

I walked between the beds in the ward, trying not to look at the rows of ancient Adam's apples with gray fluff on them, the livid faces, the devices for extracting shit, the slurping jars, the fat relatives' backs, the sleeping, gaping mouths. But I didn't see who I was looking for.

A voice said, "That's the one."

I looked with polite hostility, knowing beforehand that it wasn't him.

"No," I said, but then hesitated on the threshold, turned around and went back. I bent down to the last bed and held my breath to avoid the smell. Goltsman. I couldn't recognize him, there was nothing left of him — a wingless bird's skeleton stretched out under a blanket.

Goltsman had withered at an almost magical speed, he seemed naked, peeled, with the color of his bones and tissues revealed; bumps and bruises had appeared on his skull, his teeth had turned yellow, his head lay on the pillow like a lead weight in a halo of tangled hair. He was not surprised to see me, was not cheered up, did not try to sit. He had sunken down somewhere where he could no longer do anything.

I shook his warm stick-like hand. A cooling bowl of porridge was waiting on the bedside table, and a piece of bread was placed on top of a tea cup. A pitying lady from among the locals pushed forward a chair for me with a gesture that communicated both her ferocious disapproval and preparedness to forgive me if I would straighten up and visit.

"Why didn't you call me?" I whispered angrily, suppressing my disgust. "Are you being prepared for surgery? What on Earth is happening? Alexander Naumovich!"

As if he didn't hear me, as if he had moved somewhere, and I was still talking in the direction of the place where he was before, his eyes blinked at me out of a motionless expanse of his face, as if set in a pile of sand. He had new features: his eyelashes, eyebrows, cheeks, the color of his eyes. I had never seen him like this before; his hands, his crooked fingers and his wide, grubby fingernails. He lay there silently, and spoke barely audibly, as if he were starting in the middle of a story.

"They say, it's cancer."

"The doctor says that?"

"The doctor doesn't say anything."

The doctor didn't come often. First he came and said they were going to do surgery. Now he said to wait. Other patients, who were admitted later, had already had surgery.

"We just need to give him some money," I whispered. "I'll sort everything out."

"But they say it's cancer."

"Who told you that? Didn't they say at the check-up that it was a polyp?"

"A polyp," he confirmed — this seemed to be a fact he remembered every minute. "But here, whoever I talk to says it's cancer. Were your feces black? Yes. They say: oh, that's not a polyp. Everyone here has cancer."

"*Don't! Listen! To anyone!* What else can they say? They have cancer, and so everyone has cancer. You should have gone to be treated in normal conditions, for money. Not to this dump. How do you feel now?"

"OK... Not bad. I suppose the illness has affected my appearance?" he looked closely at me, with hope.

"Never mind. What do you expect? I would have croaked long ago in conditions like this! Can you sleep, at least?"

He showed me with his eyes: no. And even more quietly said:

"There are some... very ill patients. They scream. They throw up all the time. One of them is fed through a tube."

I went into the toilet and counted the cash I had on me, 10,000 rubles. Someone stuffed rags around the rusty pipe that went through a hole in the wall — to prevent the rats from climbing through. The toilet bowl was red with rust.

Goltsman was sitting up when I came back.

"I called Masha. Her telephone's turned off."

"You need to eat properly," I said cheerfully, blocking the view for the rest of the ward and stuffing the money into his hand. Goltsman smoothly maneuvered it under the blanket. "Buy food and eat it. Try to go for walks — at least a little. Watch the news on TV. And don't listen to anyone! I'll talk to the doctor. Alexander Naumovich! I don't recognize you. Nothing bad has happened yet. Never mind what anyone's told you. You have to live. Every day. And be happy." I held the remains of his hand and pressed it hard to emphasize separate words. "No one knows how much each of us has left. But as long as we're alive, we can do everything! I have to work. Write me what books you would like me to bring you."

"Are you going to talk to the doctor *now*?"

"I'll talk to him. But you must remember — you're not alone. We need you very much. We have so much ahead of us. In our work," I stammered, and stopped talking; while I was on my way here, I had wanted to talk. I realized I wanted him to find out that we were wrong... He always found correct, unfamiliar words, somehow he made everything seem positive. There was no Goltsman anymore, but even to this, different, confused shade, I still wanted to complain about *everything*: that it wasn't *her*, after all, but the stenographer Lida, that Voznesenskaya was a dead end, that we lost. Who else could I tell? No one. I waited, letting his mind move onto something other than black feces, waiting for him to ask, what about you? How's the bridge? Tell me, perhaps I can help somehow.

He glanced around me at the others and asked:

"You should go. The doctor might leave soon."

"Everything. Will. Be. Fine," I said in a wanton, sneaky and unrecognizable voice, and smiled so hard that my cheekbones hurt.

"You'll come back later?"

"Of course."

"I'll wait," he began to move and sat up more comfortably, dragging his dry, long extremities, as if they were paralyzed.

By the door I turned around, and red with shame, I winked at him cheerfully, and waved, as if to a friend, like a bastard. At the office of the Chief of the section — 'Doctor of Science' on the plaque — supplicants with bulky briefcases stood and sat in an informal line. A tall old woman with a regal posture, in a black dress, slipped 1,000 rubles into her lacy sleeve.

I just had time to think that I couldn't stand to wait one more second, when the Chief walked out of his office lazily, summoned by a phone call or perhaps the needs of his bladder. Taller than me, newly tanned and with very white teeth, a pleasant, dreamy Komsomol face with his hair parted, boyishly, on the side, it was amazing how he could stand there and not notice any of the people. No one even dared to make a sound or touch him on the arm. I snorted a friendly rebuke — at last! — and nodded to the chief, to show that I was a cheerful and healthy person who had brought money with him. Without quite waking up, he looked at me and said:

"Oh, it's you," with a thin, insipid voice.

"Of course!" I replied and went into his office, which was lined with vases, boxes of brandy and gilded objects. There was a bearskin on the wall. I sat down; the Chief shut the door and hovered above me quizzically, with the tips of his fingers nestled in the pockets of his white coat that appeared to be still sewn shut.

"I'd like to sort out the matter of Mr. Goltsman having a separate room," I said, and put a 500-euro note under the pile of hospital papers on the table. "He can't sleep."

"Goltsman?" the doctor asked, as if trying to remember something he had promised. He searched about the desk and leafed through papers. "A private room can be a real challenge... but we'll have a double tomorrow afternoon."

"That sounds perfect. What about his surgery? Can't it be sped up? I'll be very grateful to you."

"Of course it can. Has he been here for long? I just don't remember him visually," he hadn't looked at me once, keeping his eyes on case histories on his desk. "And you are his...?"

"We work together. I'm personally interested." I finally saw the doctor's name and patronymic on the plaque on his desk. "Vyacheslav Alexeevich, I would very much like you to operate. Everyone sings your praises."

"I'd be happy to... But there's his case physician, there's a certain procedure. I'm a researcher, you see, a hundred and sixty two publications — I'm booked six weeks ahead, and that's with only the most critical cases. And I also get phone calls every day. From people who are very hard to deal with. Ah, there he is, Goltsman, Alexander Naumovich. Yes, he's been here for a long time. We really have put it off for quite a while..."

"You must be so overworked," I sighed with admiration, and added a second 500-euro note to the first one, lifting the papers on the table a little, to catch his shifting gaze for a moment.

"It's not even a question of resources," he said, and made a vague gesture in the direction of my investments. "Time, there just isn't time."

"Perhaps you could find the possibility somehow... He's a war veteran."

"He fought in the war?" the chief of department replied respectfully.

"Yes. He's a Major General of State Security."

The chief of department nodded with rapidly increasing respect.

"Now then, that's it! Well, maybe...Is it Tuesday today? What have I got on Friday?" he dialed a number. "Hello? What have I got on Friday? Ah, yes. And what's that? Aha. Yes. I remember. And then the second one after that, right? He hasn't called? I'll call him," he carefully hung up. "You know," he winked at me conspiratorially, "what if we do it on Thursday?" he even frowned at his own audacity. He whispered, with relish, as if it were a forbidden swear word, "At *nine* on the dot."

"I'll be so grateful to you."

"Right, and he's got..," the Chief read the file, shook his head with understanding and dragged out the words with incomprehensible satisfaction. "He has a tumor of the colon. Quite a large one. There are suspicions of metastases into the liver." He said "metastases" in passing, and I felt cold, as if the window had been opened, and I shivered, and rubbed my forehead, but it was nothing: I wasn't leaving the office, I came to pay and go away cheerfully, I'd look into ward 16 and say goodbye. I'd lie if I had to.

"Is the surgery difficult?"

The chief of the department looked at me rather strangely for the first time and started doodling:

"We have to do something. At least remove the primary tumor. We'll make an anastomosis — a bypass. Another connection."

"Will it take long?"

"Three hours."

"After that will he be able to work?"

The doctor suddenly noticed that I was tired, that I had missed the point and didn't understand him. He spoke even more slowly and clearly:

"Our task is to remove the tumor. And if possible *to extend his life.* You can forget about work."

"All right. What else is required apart from surgery? Drugs? We'll buy everything."

"His temperature has started to rise. You can buy Tienam. Ti-e-nam, write it down. But it's expensive, it comes from Switzerland. Three to four vials a day. There should be someone to take care of him after the surgery: to help him to turn over and make his bed. In fact," now it was the doctor who was trying to catch my gaze. "The most important thing happens after the surgery. Does he have relatives?"

"A son. In America."

"He must be told to come here urgently."

"You mean he'll die?"

"The risk is significant. Very significant. There's his age, and vascular diseases. There may be serious complications after the surgery. Pneumonia, a heart attack. That's the way they usually go. Call his son."

"What if you don't perform the surgery?"

He shrugged: "You can take him if you sign a letter."

"And then? How much time does he have?"

"No one can tell you. Maybe a few weeks. Days. Serious pains may begin. Or he may just go easily, and not feel anything, maybe tomorrow." He couldn't understand why I wasn't saying anything. "Shall we go ahead with the surgery?"

The people outside the door squeezed tighter to make space for me when they saw I wanted to sit down. I was the same as all of them — everyone came out of that office with the same face and began their waiting.

"Right! Which one of you came to see Goltsman in the 16th ward?"

I humbly rose, and a fat-faced guy who looked like a butcher led me through two doors and down the stairs.

"Do you smoke? Mind if I do? Your granddad is insane, he's deaf! I explained to him, so he'd understand that he'd have surgery. He stared at me: *yes*. I said: *I'm — your anesthetist.* Understand? *I'm — going — to — breath — for you.* This Red Army granddad of yours, didn't understand: *what do you mean?* Is he nuts? I explained again: you'll lose consciousness, *and I'll breath for you.* Your breathing depends on me. If I do everything properly, if the drugs are right and good..."

I gave him 200 dollars, then pushed open the door in front of me. I went out and looked around. I was in an internal courtyard, a path led diagonally to the entrance. I stood for a while, pretending that I had just gone out for some fresh air, then quickly pulled off the torn shoe covers, threw them into the trash can and with calm, broad steps moved to the exit, hunched over, looking at the ground, as if I was cold or had something on my mind, while most of all I was afraid to hear the begging, frantic tapping of dry fingers on the glass, on the window. Outside the gates I straightened up and walked faster, and only slowed down in the lane that led away from the metro. No one would guess where I had turned. I waited as long as I could, then I grabbed my phone with the intention of turning it off, but couldn't resist checking messages. One of our paid informants had called. I dialed back.

"Yes."

"Your target has a concert tomorrow. He is staying at the guest house of the Georgian Embassy. This evening he's likely to be alone in his room."

I arrived in Skatertny Lane at half past five, stretched a black knit skullcap I had bought in the metro tight over my head, and walked back and forth on the ice past the Mercedeses with blue lights on the roof and the bodyguards standing like posts. Would I be let into the Guest House: with dirty boots, shabby jeans and an army jacket? At the check-in, I torturously wiped the soles of my boots on the doormat and was surprised to discover a path of dirt leading to the counter; I was not alone. Two women with dyed blond hair were speaking to each other with strong accents. They were not interested in me.

"Room 413, they're expecting me."

"There's the elevator."

The elevator was flanked by two squashed Soviet couches with threadbare red upholstery. The hallway on the fourth floor looked like a dormitory, with cheap doors on each side. I thought I wouldn't be surprised to find a shared bathroom at the end of the hallway — and there it was. What was the brilliant and perilous Vladislav R-ov doing in such a dump?

His door was in the corner, and I could hear music playing loudly inside — of course. I knocked. There was a noise in the room, and the door opened.

The man was 66 years old. I saw that a lot had changed. The once irresistible seducer met me in a cheap sweatshirt. His shoulders were still broad. He was wearing jeans. His beard was graying. His wrinkles had already started to devour his eyes. He had a well-shaped nose and stubbornly long, artistic hair. I tried to see *that* face through the rubbish. Or at least hear *that* voice.

In the narrow, cold room there were two narrow beds.

I sat down on one of the beds and spread out photographs of the young Olga Voznesenskaya in a fan, out of his reach, but so he could see them well. R-ov briefly glanced at them and turned his face at me, obediently. I was just something he had to endure. He had been waiting for us every day since the minute our telephone call found him in America. He must have recalled a lot of things and perhaps regretted something, he imagined *what* we were like, and we were like *this* — at first glance, nothing to be afraid of.

"Yes. Yes. Yes. Such a tragedy!" he sighed like an old man, overcoming his fear, he had nothing to be afraid of, he was the first to talk.

I said nothing. He leaned closer to me with hope:

"Was she depressed?"

"Yes."

"She loved my dog so much! It was a wonderful dog, a St. Bernard... I lost it tragically."

"People remembered an orange dog. I thought it was an Airedale..."

"No, no, we didn't have many of those back then."

And fell silent.

This really had no point. Petrova wasn't the woman. I was going to leave, then sat down:

"You had some sort of an unusual car?"

"Yes, a Javelin. Olya's girlfriends? I never saw any. Friends? No, I didn't know any. At home? I never visited her. Her father and mother? I never saw them. Her grandmother? I didn't see her. But she loved her grandmother very much. I don't remember anyone. Mezentsov? Yes, I think so..."

"Do you at least remember Shchukin?"

"He's been my friend since I was 14 years old."

"Why did you ask Shchukin to visit Olya in the hospital?"

"Was she in the hospital? I don't remember…"

"Why did Shchukin meet Olya on the day when she tried to kill herself?"

"Did he meet her? He never told me anything about it."

I got up and asked him by the door:

"What happened with that dog of yours?"

"Ah, Bonya died in a terrible car accident. I was driving from Petersburg to Moscow. There was a terrible frost. It was minus forty degrees. The ice was awful. But you can never foresee… something like that. I did a good deed: I saw a dog freezing in the middle of the road. And I picked it up. I warmed it in the car. I took it to a village. And the dog was so happy, it ran to the houses. And I remember, I thought: now we'll drive well. And then somewhere near Kalinin I crashed the car, just totalled it. My whole face was cut. My head was dislocated from the vertebrae. I still suffer from headaches. Even today. And Bonya… Bonya flew through the windshield and hit a tree so hard that he broke it. And he lay in our home until spring, we couldn't even bury him — the frosts were so severe that you couldn't dig a grave, especially as he was so big."

"Goodbye."

Suddenly R-ov said in a different, unrestrained voice:

"Can you leave the pictures for me?" He tried to ask casually, without holding me up, like he didn't care, but he was still asking, afraid to point at the pieces of paper, the rough copies made on a printer, from which his love in a black dress looked out, lost and devoted.

I went to Novodevichy cemetery on Palm Sunday. It was empty, only a few people had come to visit the Communist graves. And then the snow started.

From the main gates I went straight ahead and turned right, randomly, cautiously, raising my legs high so as not to step on anyone. An upturned fishbowl protected the flowers on the grave of a Red

Army soldier. I walked past the inscriptions: Beloved Son, Dear Baby Innochka, something about an artillery captain. The nameless and insignificant could afford to put on their graves words they wanted, but the marshals and People's Commissars, the Iron Men, stood silently, like idols, back to back: Furmanov and Ostrovsky, next to Molotova-Zhemchuzhina and the mother of Marshal Zhukov. Next to the Kalinins and the stone boy, Mitya Dimitrov, eternally aged seven, there they were — the Shakhurins: a granite bench, massive as a sarcophagus. In the corners of the grave plot — a stump from a felled tree, a stump from a rotten tree and a stump from a tree that was broken by a terrible storm that swept through Moscow in August, when the crosses were lifted off the Novodevichy monastery.

Three people, a family, three black cubes: raised on a gray column, the father's cube is the largest and tallest, to accommodate his titles and regalia; the mother's, narrower, is next to it, and Volodya Shakhurin's marker, a single black obelisk, is attached to his mother's. Each marker was slightly turned to the other one — there were three larches behind them. The opening in the foundation that was meant for a flower-bed was filled with the whiskers of nettles, dandelion and rib grass. The smooth black granite reflected my face.

I turned and walked towards the tower with the walled-in ashes of the willing and unwilling members of the society of cremation supporters. In the wide part of the tower, Dmitry Ulyanov's grave spread, fundamental and luxurious. A bit to the side — I recognized them from a distance — were the Umanskys. I turned to make sure: indeed, nothing blocked the line of sight between the beautiful Nina Umanskaya and the gifted boy from the Fourth Empire. Raisa Mikhailovna was born on the 9th of March, her slab was in the top right; Nina's father was born on the 14th of May, the slab with his official position was to the left and more expensive, made of stone; and Nina was born on the 16th of August. Her slab was directly under her father's. Under Nina Umanskaya's slab, the facing of the tower had cracked, and there was green moss on the bricks around a dark crack. Still, this was better than the modern glass portholes that let you look at the metal cubes or the plastic boxes with ashes. The mother and daughter had poor, standard-issue slabs, with a couple of holes drilled through them as if they were photos torn carelessly out of an album. There was no place to leave flowers; no one had placed a jar with asters at the foot of the tower, only a rowan berry bush was trying to grow nearby. Still, someone had stuck a carnation behind a corner of Nina's slab. Someone had brought it, perhaps on her birthday at the end of August, someone had been unpleasantly present here besides us, someone had remained, whom we hadn't found.

A woman digging at the earth under the nearby slabs stood up straight and looked at me. She thought she owned the place, but it was I who wanted to be in charge.

"Who are you?" I asked.

She sensed something and immediately introduced herself:

"I'm one of the Orlovs. My father was sent to Uruguay and died there in 1944. Of cancer. At the age of 42! He was a foreign intelligence officer. And over there is Dekanozov, a worthless person!"

Dekanozov was the only person in the Soviet Union to whom the war was declared formally: the Germans called him to the foreign ministry in the morning and announced it. But Dekanozov on that terrible day of the 22nd of June quickly gained his composure, declared in an unwavering voice something along the lines of *we'll still be victorious*, and strode toward the exit, while Ribbentrop rushed after him and whispered, "It's all Hitler's doing. Nothing to do with me. It's all Hitler's doing." Or so the story goes.

"And those are the Umanskys," she said, and pointed.

"I know everything about them. Their daughter was killed. The father and mother died in a plane crash, the flight was delayed..."

"The flight was delayed because of Nina Umanskaya's mother."

I didn't say anything to that. Then asked out of politeness:

"Why do you think that?"

"They said that at the funeral, and my mother remembered it. Raisa Mikhailovna took the watch from Nina's wrist to remember her by, a gold watch. The watch didn't break on the bridge, and Raisa

Mikhailovna wore it. And on the day of the flight — where were they going? Costa Rica? — she left it at home or lost it in the car. She noticed on the way to the plane that she didn't have the watch. She looked under her feet, in her bag. Someone helped her."

"The military attaché Vdovin."

"That's right. The plane engines had already started. Raisa Mikhailovna asked him to run to the car to see if the watch was there. The flight was delayed, he ran off and looked for it with the driver, and from a distance Vdovin waved to her: no, I can't find it. Raisa Mikhailovna said: that means there will be no good travel for us today. And she sat in the front rows, where it's not so shaky."

"What about the flowers?" I found it hard to talk, catching my breath, it was as if I was falling into the woman's homely face, everything was coming to an end, it was so painful. "Maybe you know who brings Nina flowers?"

"I do. They don't have anyone left. My mother is also here," she said. With a warm, caressing look she glanced at something black under her feet. "And my son," she bent down to the loose earth and whispered: "My son... So value life. Value love. Value each other!" she said, as if she were talking not only to me, as if she had seen someone else next to me. Suddenly, blindingly, with a relieving force I saw that everything had come together, was linked, the middle of the bridge, the riverbanks had disappeared, and I was looking down into the wrinkled water.

Everyone was still sleeping, and I moved inaudibly, standing by each window. The taxi had already come, I could see the light and the white of the unfolded newspaper inside the car. Now I wanted to sleep, my jaws ached for a yawn. I got dressed, hitting the familiar corners, not getting my arms into the sleeves and getting angry at the stubborn buttons — mine were the superfluous, irritated movements of a person who hasn't slept. In each room I heard the sea coming nearer, the wind howled and the waves lapped; the sea erases small things, it erases everything — and I stopped above another person's breathing — a bunch of black hair stuck out from under the blanket. This was my wife, and in the darkness I said, "Wife." I called her, knowing that no one would reply, but for some reason I got scared: perhaps, she was dead? I bent over her and asked her three times, right in her ear: are you alive? The fourth time my hand barely detected some movement (I was stroking her hair), which did not depend on my desires, on me — she was alive.

We drove quietly through the courtyard, and I thought about things, looking at the side of the road: nothing precise, nothing separate, but rather everything at once, or perhaps it was the buildings and the streets that were fixing me in their memory, unraveling me, like a bandage, to the end, and the faster and further we drove away, the less that of me there was to fix, and then nothing remained at all, and I didn't have to look out the window anymore. I made myself more comfortable to catch a nap, untying my left sneaker — I had chafed my foot, above the heel, painfully.

We arrived early, and trembling, I walked up and down, to keep from freezing, until it got warmer, and I could wait on the bench, watching the boys on the field playing football — the last time outside, tomorrow the snow would fall, and they wouldn't be let out again, no matter how much they asked. I supported the ones that were losing, one to four, and dreamed of passing the ball — *just once* — but the ball didn't fly my way. On the neighboring bench, a serious boy set out his plastic armies of animal-like monsters, half-lizards with jagged swords and laser cannons and spider men. He adjusted the claws of robots armed with machine-guns, whispering military commands, pleased to see that I was watching his preparations for battle. I looked at him: he had a narrow forehead, little Tatar eyes, rough fur on his head; if I had known he'd be here I'd have brought him my cavalry soldiers, sailors of October, red Cossacks, motorcyclists and machine-gunners, border guards, nurses, banner-holders of the 50s, the tin productions of Tula, Bryansk and Melitopol, soldiers of Victory, commanders on parade in baggy coats, division musicians and skiers of the Finnish war. I waited for him to look at me and when he did I nodded. I was leaving, and for some reason I didn't want to leave unnoticed.

On the platform, high above the river, the stalls were waiting for buses with tourists, and I limped along, looking for iron and tin. Among the busts of Lenin, Stalin and Dzerzhinsky, there was only one stall with a set of six Soldiers on the March of the Leningrad Carburetor Factory, but without a commander. You could buy them all for 200 rubles, but the sporty-looking, warmly-dressed man standing behind them announced: *three hundred* dollars; I laughed and walked to the stairs, looking around again at the boy — he stayed by the stall, but also looked around at me: why didn't I stay to look? And I started to imagine having a son: I'd have a son, I thought, and then I would start dying. Who would be brave enough to sit beside me? The medical staff would run off to take tea breaks and smoke breaks, and my son would be far away, off doing work and looking for fun, he'd have grown up and grown out of my life by that time. I would call for my small boy before I left, the one from the past, and he would come running, the door would slam and he would jump onto the bed and throw himself onto me, onto my last breath, with his light heaviness, his bruises and scratches, giving everything that a child can give — warmth, the touch of purity, calm, and what is the hardest of all for them a kind of living motionlessness. He would hold out to me, as he always used to, a stubborn pistachio that wouldn't crack open, and I would take it and fix the gray, bone-like nut in my teeth, and the shell would crack. And I would place the wrinkled nut with my fingers right in his mouth, and die. The boy would not leave me, he would come right away, as soon as I called he would hear...

The sun appeared unexpectedly, I had not hoped to see it until spring. I went down, entering the damp shade, where the icy and wet grass was, under the bridge. I walked further under the bent, kind willows where one could glimpse fir trees with bent tops that looked like Scythian hats. Grown-up children were playing like knights with wooden swords, learning simple fighting moves under the eyes of admiring and unattractive girls who wanted to be their girlfriends, and tried to share in all their pursuits. On a tree close to the path a piece of white and red barricade tape had been braided by someone's nimble hands.

It was time: I left the road, and putting out my arms for balance, I slid on my heels down the short path which dropped sharply, and then ran on up the far side of the ravine between the oaks. Here, the roots were sticking out of the ground like steps, the dead leaves had already formed a thick rug. I felt tired and close to a rest I had earned.

I couldn't resist and turned around — was there anyone there? No. And there couldn't be, I knew. But I waited anyway. A person, a vertebrate being, finds it hard to believe that no one can see him, that no one is watching over him like a mother every moment, that no one needs him and no one feels sorry for him. I saw a river in front of me, the lights were bent there, turning away from the water; closer to the water were dry linden trees with branches broken at the elbows, only hanging on by strips of bark.

I couldn't stop looking to the corner, to the place where the path came out of the forest and led to me by a short route. I still couldn't believe that no one had come, and when I actually could believe it, it still seemed that there would be someone, they were simply late, or they would come when it was too late, they'd regret it and blame themselves.

The water was even and smooth, opaque like the sky, only to the left and right, a couple of leaves rocked up and down, a feather and a white packet of cigarettes angrily crushed into a ball.

On the far side of the river cars rolled by. A dry leaf bobbing in the surface scratched at the stone slabs, and the grass growing between them.

I could see a barge behind the supports of the bridge. A woman walked along the river, carrying something attached to her chest — I thought she was coming to sell stuff at the market, but when she came closer, it turned out she was carrying a child in a sling around her neck, and the hairless head of the sleeping baby stuck out high out of the cloth.

I shuddered — I saw the boat so unexpectedly. It was now in the middle of the river, its approach concealed by the noises of cars on the bridge. The boat approached, seeming to be headed past the jetty; an indistinguishable faded flag waved on the stern, feebly, like a flame that had not yet decided whether it was worth spreading.

The boat sailed evenly, not breaking the breathing of the river, becoming a part of it. In the empty portholes and windows, I couldn't see any people — the boat seemed to be sailing by itself. As it passed the jetty, it suddenly made a sharp turn, stopped, and rolling heavily, it began to back up. On the stern a human figure appeared with a looped rope in his hand. Its presence was so undeniable that I wondered if it had been there before and I simply hadn't seen it.

1997 — 2007

GLOSSARY

By Carol Ermakova

22nd June (1941) — Nazi Germany broke the Molotov–Ribbentrop Pact by invading the Soviet Union.

Abakumov — Viktor Semyonovich Abakumov (1908-1954), prominent Soviet official in NKVD, brutal head of MGB, later executed under Stalin.

Aleksandr Orlov — Alexander Mikhailovich Orlov (1895-1973), general in the Soviet secret police and NKVD with several foreign assignments who turned spy and fled the Soviet Union to the U.S.

Alexandra Kollontai — Alexandra Mikhailovna Kollontai (1872-1952), Ambassador to Norway, famous for her strongly-held idea on free love, the role of marriage etc.

Boris Sheremetiev — Count Boris Sheremetiev (1652-1719), an admirer of West European ways and a diplomat, later an important military commander.

Bukharin — Nikolai Ivanovich Bukharin (1888-1938), Marxist, Bolshevik revolutionary and prominent Soviet politician later tried and executed under Stalin in the Moscow show trails.

Bulganin — Nikolai Alexandrovich Bulganin (1895-1975), important Soviet politician who served as Minister of Defence then Premier of the Soviet Union.

Bunin — Ivan Alekseyevich Bunin (1870-1953), renowned writer revered as the heir to Tolstoy's Russian realism.

Cambridge Five — ring of spies who passed information to the Soviet Union during World War II.

Cathedral of Christ the Savior — an important church in central Moscow, destroyed on Stalin's orders in 1931 and replaced by an open air swimming pool in the Khrushchev era. The church was rebuilt in the 1990's and reopened in 2000.

CheKa — literally 'Emergency Commission', the first of many Soviet secret police organizations.

Comintern — The Communist International, an international communist organization led from Moscow.

Comrade Poskrebyshev — Alexandr Nikolayevich Poskrebyshev (1891-1965), Soviet official and secretary to Stalin.

Daziaro — Joseph Daziaro (1870-1885), artist in Russia.

Gromyko — Andrei Andreyevich Gromyko (1909-1989) prominent Soviet statesman who held posts including Minister for Foreign Affairs and Permanent Representative to the United Nations.

GRU — Main Intelligence Directorate of the General Staff of the Armed Forces of the Russian Federation, i.e. Russia's main foreign intelligence agency, established 1918.

Gzhel — a famous style of Russian ceramics with a distinctive blue and white design.

Itzik Feffer — (1900-1952) Yiddish poet and vice-chairman of the Soviet Jewish Anti-Fascist Committee executed during Stalin's purges.

Kondraty Bulavin — a folk hero who led the Don Cossack uprising known as The Bulavin Rebellion (Astrakhan Revolt) in 1707-08.

Levitan — Yuri Borisovich Levitan, (1914-1983), famous stentorian radio newsreader in post-war Soviet Union.

Lev Karakhan — (or Karakhanov) Lev Mikhailovich Karakhan (1889-1937), Soviet diplomat.

Little Octobrists — Communist youth organization for primary school children prior to joining the Young Pioneers and the Komsomol.

Lyubyanka — (or Lubyanka) former headquarters of KGB and formidable prison located on Lubyanka Square in central Moscow.

Mark Gallai — (1914-1998) Soviet test pilot and engineer.

Marshal Konev — Ivan Stepanovich Konev (1897-1973), Soviet military commander in World War II who retook much of Eastern Europe including Berlin.

Maxim Litvinov — Maxim Maximovich Litvinov (1876-1951), prominent diplomat under both Lenin and Stalin. Later dismissed and replaced by Molotov.
Daughter: Tatyana Litvinova; wife Englishwoman Ivy (Valterovna) Lowe.

Mercader — Jaime Ramón Mercader del Río (1913-1978), Spanish communist who murdered Leon Trotsky in 1940.

Merkulov — Vsevolod Nikolayevich (Boris) Merkulov (1895-1953) worked for MGB and NKVD under Beria, executed with Beria under Stalin.

MGB — Ministry for State Security, i.e. Soviet secret police, formed in the late 1940's, one of many organizations in Stalin's Empire.

Mikhail Koltsov — Mikhail Efimovich Koltsov (1989-1940), prominent figure in Soviet intellectual elite, renowned journalist for *Pravda*.

Mikoyan — Anastas Ivanovich Mikoyan (1895-1978),prominent Soviet official who managed to outlive Lenin, and Stalin, becoming the First Chairman of the Presidium of the Supreme Soviet under Brezhnev.

Molotok — a Russian equivalent to e-bay.

NKVD — The People's Commissariat for Internal Affairs, vast law enforcement agency of the Soviet Union which oversaw Stalin's political repressions.

Old Believers — separated from the rest of the Russian Orthodox Church after 1666 when reforms were introduced to the liturgy, dogmas and rituals. They subsequently faced persecution, causing many to flee to Siberia.

Orzhonikidze — Grigol Ordzhonikidze (1886-1937), Georgian Bolshevik and close associate of Stalin.

Pieter Picart — a Dutch artist supported by Peter the Great who oversaw the development of new printmaking techniques in Russia.

Prince (Vasily) Golitsyn — (1643-1714) an important Russian statesman, advisor to Tsarina Sofia, led the charges into the Crimea in the late 1680's and 1690's.

Pugachev — Yemelyan Pugachev (1742-1775) led a great Cossack rebellion during the reign of Catherine II.

Rudzutak — Jānis Rudzutaks(1887-1938), Soviet politician born in Latvia, persecuted by Stalin.

Samizdat — from the Russian meaning 'self-published'. Forbidden texts, often copied by hand or reproduced in secret, and passed illegally from friend to friend, initially among the dissidents of the Russian intelligentsia.

Sberbank — the largest bank in Russia and Eastern Europe, and the third largest in Europe.

Shashlyk — or shashlik, a type of shish kebab very popular in Russia, especially in the former Republics of Central Asia, Georgia etc.

SMERSH — literally Special Methods of Spy Detection, Soviet counter intelligence agency in World War II.

Solomon Mikhoels — (1890-1948) Soviet Jewish actor and director of the Moscow State Jewish Theater, Chairman of the Soviet Jewish Anti-Fascist Committee executed during Stalin's purges.

Sorge's group — a reference to Richard Sorge's spy ring (Germany/Japan).

Stalin's Falcons — the famous Soviet pilots of the 1930's.

Stanislavsky — Konstanin Sergeevich Stanislavsky (1863-1938) famous for his innovative acting method.

Stepan Razin — a folk hero who led a Cossack uprising in southern Russian in the late 1660's.

Strelets rebellion — 1698 uprising of *strel'tsy* musketeers against Peter the Great's modernizing reforms.

The Emperor — a nickname for Joseph Stalin.

The Empire — a nickname for the Soviet Union under Stalin.

The Great Patriotic War — period of World War II from June 1941-May 1945 when the Soviets were fighting Nazi Germany and its allies on the eastern front.

Trial of the Twenty-One — (March 1938) last of the Moscow show trials, where prominent Bolsheviks accused of belonging to the Trotskyite block and conspiring to overthrow the Soviet Union were tried and found guilty.

Umansky — Konstanin Alexandrovich Umansky (aka Kostya) (1902 - 1945), of Jewish descent, Soviet diplomat, editor and journalist. Daughter Nina, wife Raisa Mikhailovna.

Vasya Stalin — VasilyIosifovich Stalin, Stalin's son by his second wife, Nadezhda Allilueva.

Vladimir Shchuko — Vladimir Alekseyevich Shchuko (1878-1939), a Soviet stage designer and architect, particularly renowned for his impressive, high profile projects in the neoclassical style during the pre-war Stalinist era.
Son Boris; daughters Marina and Tatyana.

Volodya Shakhurin — son of the People's Commissar for the Aviation Industry

Vyacheslav Molotov — Vyacheslav Mikhailovich Molotov (1890-1986), a prominent Soviet politician and diplomat, a protégé of Stalin, who held many important positions in the Soviet Union.

Vysotsky — Vladimir Semyonovich Vysotsky (1938-1980), extremely influential Russian singer-songwriter still acclaimed today.

Yakov Stalin — Yakov Iosifovich Dzhugashvili, Stalin's son by his first wife, died in a German concentration camp.

Glagoslav Publications Catalogue

- *The Time of Women* by Elena Chizhova
- *Sin* by Zakhar Prilepin
- *Hardly Ever Otherwise* by Maria Matios
- *The Lost Button* by Irene Rozdobudko
- *Khatyn* by Ales Adamovich
- *Christened with Crosses* by Eduard Kochergin
- *The Vital Needs of the Dead* by Igor Sakhnovsky
- *METRO 2033* (Dutch Edition) by Dmitry Glukhovsky
- *METRO 2034* (Dutch Edition) by Dmitry Glukhovsky
- *A Poet and Bin Laden* by Hamid Ismailov
- *Asystole* by Oleg Pavlov
- *Kobzar* by Taras Shevchenko
- *White Shanghai* by Elvira Baryakina
- *Myths about Russia* by Vladimir Medynsky
- *King Stakh's Wild Hunt* by Uladzimir Karatkevich
- *Depeche Mode* by Serhii Zhadan
- *Saraband Sarah's Band* by Larysa Denysenko
- *Herstories*, An Anthology of New Ukrainian Women Prose Writers
- *Watching The Russians* (Dutch Edition) by Maria Konyukova
- *The Hawks of Peace* by Dmitry Rogozin
- *The Grand Slam and Other Stories* (Dutch Edition) by Leonid Andreev
- *The Battle of the Sexes Russian Style* by Nadezhda Ptushkina
- *A Book Without Photographs* by Sergei Shargunov

More coming soon...